One day I just knew I'd find a romantic hero of my very own who'd be captivated by my (ginger) beauty and tamed by his love for me. He'd rescue me from my crazy family and sweep me away to a world of glamour and passion, and we'd live happily every after. Mills and Boon had promised; didn't this happen to every heroine, from humble chambermaids to feisty slave girls? All I had to do was sit tight and wait my turn. Sooner or later my hero would come along and sweep me off my feet.

Except he didn't.

In fact all my handsome princes had the very unfortunate habit of turning into frogs almost as soon as I kissed them. It was all very disappointing.

Ruth Saberton was born in London in 1972. A chance meeting with a stranger whilst holidaying in Cornwall resulted in Ruth marrying a fisherman and moving to beautiful Polperro, near Plymouth. In between writing novels and short stories, Ruth also teaches Media Studies and English at a secondary school in Cornwall.

KATY CARTER WANTS A HERO

Ruth Saberton

An Orion paperback

First published in Great Britain in 2010
by Orion Books Ltd,
Orion House, 5 Upper St Martin's Lane,
London WC2H 9EA

An Hachette UK company

7 9 10 8 6

A CIP catalogue record for this book
is available from the British Library.

ISBN 978-1-4091-0318-9

Typeset at The Spartan Press Ltd,
Lymington, Hants

Printed and bound in the UK by
CPI Mackays, Chatham ME5 8TD

The Orion Publishing Group's policy is to use papers that
are natural, renewable and recyclable products and
made from wood grown in sustainable forests. The logging
and manufacturing processes are expected to conform to
the environmental regulations of the country of origin.

To my wonderful Nanny Southall, who always encouraged me to write and had to suffer reading all my endless pony stories. You are much missed but never forgotten. This book is for you.

Chapter One

As the carriage came abruptly to a halt, Millandra's heart began to pound. She placed her small hand above the gentle swell of her breast and held her breath. Could it be that their carriage was being held up by the infamous highwayman Jake Delaware? Jake Delaware, famous for always claiming a kiss . . .

I write the name Jake, underline it and doodle a question mark in the margin. I'm not sure if they had the name Jake in the eighteenth century, but it's such a masculine name, isn't it? It's kind of edgy and a little bit dangerous with just the right amount of rough thrown in for good measure. A Jake is tall, with strong, muscular forearms, thick, dark hair and fine chiselled features. Somebody called Jake would wear tight white breeches and a billowing crimson shirt and look totally manly, whereas some one called Nigel wouldn't.

I chew my biro.

Jake it is.

'Stand and deliver!' The voice contained a potent masculinity that made the small golden hairs on Millandra's slim arms ripple deliciously.

Millandra sounds just right for a romantic heroine; it's kind of fluffy and girlie and blonde. I'm going to make my heroine willowy and graceful with flowing golden tresses.

And totally unlike my good self, who is somewhat short and ginger.

Millandra wouldn't be seen dead in DM boots and a tatty old hoodie. Nor does she get plastered after a crappy day at work, because Millandra doesn't have to work. She just wafts around all day in flowery frocks looking beautiful and fighting off her suitors.

I bet if *she* had a flat tyre Jake wouldn't expect her to change it and get covered in dirt. He'd leap off his horse, kiss her hand and then get to work straight away. No man on earth would tell the Lady Millandra to fetch the jack and do it herself because a modern woman really should know how. No, Millandra never has to struggle with a jack and wheel nuts that were fastened by Geoff Capes while her fiancé shouts encouragement down the mobile.

Lucky cow.

Wish I'd lived in the eighteenth century.

Germaine Greer has a lot to answer for.

Anyway, do carriages have tyres?

I make a mental note to find out. Not that we have many carriages about in west London, but they've got to operate on the same principles as cars, surely?

The carriage door swung open.

'*Good evening, ladies and gentlemen, I apologise for the inconvenience but I must relieve you of a small road tax before you continue on your way.*'

Millandra found herself trembling like a willow tree in the breeze. Would he shoot her? Or would he pull her into his arms and ravish her?

Isn't ravish a great word? I've never been ravished in my life but it sounds like great fun. James, my fiancé, isn't the ravishing type. He'd be too worried that his boss might find out and his chances of promotion would be

2

scuppered, which is fair enough I suppose; one of us has to be sensible. But wouldn't it be fantastic to be so irresistible that your man can't control himself?

Oh well. Don't suppose that happens in the real world. Not in the world of Katy Carter anyhow. Back to Millandra . . .

'My lady,' said the highwayman, taking her small gloved hand in his. Millandra felt the heat of his flesh through the fabric and her heart beat even faster. 'Allow me to help you from the carriage.'

Abruptly his hands were around her slender waist and she was clasped against his strong chest.

The last time James lifted me was when I was too pissed to climb the stairs. He put his back out for a week. Luckily for my hero, Millandra's a size zero. It would ruin this novel if Jake pulled a muscle. I have serious plans for Jake's *muscle* in the next few pages.

As he held her tightly, Millandra found herself drawn to the jade eyes that gazed most powerfully down at her. Although the lower part of the highwayman's face was obscured by the dark triangle of his mask, she could feel that his sensual mouth was curved into a smile. Beneath the tight lacings of her corset, Millandra's heart was fluttering like a trapped bird. As his hand moved higher she felt—

'Katy? Will you second the proposal?'

Proposal? What proposal?

I look up from my writing and it's a shock to find myself back in the middle of an English Department meeting. Jake vanishes and nine pairs of eyes are trained expectantly on me.

I shove the novel under my teacher's planner while Cyril Franklin, the head of English, looks at me with the usual mixture of impatience and frustration. He taps a pencil against his mossy teeth. 'Well, Katy? Do you agree?'

Agree with what? That Marmite's fantastic? That Brad is sexier than George? I'm in danger of looking like a total plonker, which isn't unusual, but I promised James I'm going to turn over a new leaf and focus on developing my career. No more drifting around with my nose in a book. No more wearing gypsy skirts and platform boots. And – James is especially adamant on this one – no more dreaming about being a bestselling romantic novelist. And I'm trying really hard! But it's like giving up cigarettes (thank God James doesn't know that I still have a sneaky one in the boiler room; he absolutely *hates* me smoking). I just *have* to write. Hence the fact that *Heart of the Highwayman* is being secretly scrawled in Wayne Lobb's English book.

All the other teachers are waiting for an answer, which wouldn't be a problem if I only knew what the question was.

'Um,' I begin, 'obviously it's a very important issue.' Everybody nods, so I must be on the right track. If I just agree with Cyril, he'll leave me alone and hopefully we can all go home early, right? I take a deep breath, fix him with my best *I'm totally fascinated by all matters educational* expression and add, 'But in my opinion it's an excellent idea.'

'Really?' Cyril looks amazed. 'You agree with me?'

'Absolutely!' I enthuse. 'Totally!'

My colleagues are deadly quiet and I feel a prickle of unease. What can be such a big deal? Changing the GCSE course? Inviting Jamie Oliver in to overhaul our pitiful canteen?

On second thoughts, that really isn't such a good idea.

The kids at the Sir Bob Geldof Community School would eat poor Jamie alive. They'd ram his wraps up his bum quicker than you could say 'turkey twizzler'. Gordon Ramsay would fit in much better.

'It's official then!' Cyril taps something into his laptop. 'Seconded by Katy and unanimously agreed to by everybody else in the department, I presume?'

There's deafening silence. Ollie, my colleague and friend, looks daggers at me and then draws his finger across his throat, while the elderly Miss Lewis pops a Murray Mint into her mouth and crunches loudly.

'Agreed?' hisses Cyril, as menacingly as somebody who dresses in polyester possibly can. The others see crappy timetables swiftly coming their way and shoot their hands up in the air. I can practically hear the bleating.

'Wonderful,' smiles Cyril. 'The Sir Bob's summer school is officially up and running. It will start on the first day of the holidays.'

'Summer school?' I mouth at Ollie.

He nods. 'Traitor!'

Summer school? No way! I *need* those six weeks. I'm looking forward to them already and it's only April. James will be delighted. He's always going on about what easy lives teachers have with all their endless holidays. A comment from somebody who has never attempted to teach bottom-set Year 11 last thing on a Friday afternoon or tried to scale a mountain of coursework that makes K2 look like a small grassy knoll.

'Katy can't possibly do summer school,' says Miss Lewis sharply, spraying Ollie with shards of Murray Mint. 'After all,' she continues, reaching across the table to pat my ink-stained hand, 'she's getting married in August. Planning a summer school will be far too much for her.'

'Oh dear,' I say, trying really hard to look devastated at missing out on this career-enhancing opportunity. 'What a shame. I was so excited I wasn't thinking straight. I'd never be able to do the summer school justice with all the wedding preparations.'

Saved!

And meanwhile, back in my bodice-ripper . . .

'Unhand me, sir!' gasped Millandra. 'I insist you release me this instant!'

Jake threw back his head and laughed. Millandra couldn't help but be thrilled by the deep rippling sound.

'To pass through this forest,' he told her, 'you must pay a toll.'

'I have no money upon my person,' she said.

'Then,' Jake told her firmly, 'I shall have to find another way for you to pay.'

His hand rose to cup her breast. Millandra felt her nipple—

'Go on!' Ollie hisses. 'Don't stop now!'

I glare at him. Ollie knows I can't bear people reading what I write. Bit of a drawback if I want to be the next Jackie Collins, but I'll cross that bridge when I come to it.

He wiggles his eyebrows suggestively and fans his face.

I bet Jane Austen never had to put up with such disrespect.

Just wait until I'm number one on the *Sunday Times* Bestseller List. If he's not careful, I'll write him in as Millandra's ugly fiancé. Then he'll wish he'd never laughed. And when Spielberg buys the film rights, he'll be *really* sorry. I'll go on TV and tell the nation that the inspiration for my pustule-ridden, hunchbacked arch-villain is actually Oliver Burrows, an English teacher from Ealing. He'll never be able to hold his head up in school again.

Yes, that'll show him!

I've known Ol for years. We go back so far that dinosaurs were roaming Ealing when we first met. OK, so that's a *slight* exaggeration. I met him during my teacher-training year and we bonded in that way that only prisoners of war or those traumatised by teenage thugs can bond. No one can understand the terror of trying to entertain a class of chewing teens with PhDs in boredom unless they've been there. Ollie and I have shared tales of woe and countless boozy evenings for nearly eight years and he's one of my closest friends, probably because I've never muddied the waters of our friendship by fancying him. Not that he isn't attractive; in fact, if you like clever-looking guys who spend all their spare time climbing and canoeing and doing lots of other exciting things that require beanie hats and Quiksilver, then he'd be right up your street. It's just that I have a picture in my mind of the perfect romantic hero, and he doesn't wear combats or wire-rimmed glasses and he certainly doesn't drink milk straight from the carton! Nor does he spend hours hunched over an Xbox making poor Lara Croft contort herself in all kinds of mind-boggling ways. No, lovely as he is, Ol simply isn't my type, unlike my fiancé James, with his floppy fringe, smart suits and promising career with merchant bank Millward Saville. James, who reads the *Financial Times* for fun, rather than *Viz* like Ollie does. James, who wants promotion and pensions and . . .

Oh bugger.

And a dinner party tomorrow night for his managing director to show just how suitable James is to be made a partner. Our flat will need to be perfect, as will the meal, which will be home-cooked to show off my wifely skills. Millwards is practically medieval in attitude, and although

7

I'm supposed to be a career woman, I'm also meant to be a fantastic cook and hostess, the type of woman who will support my husband as he rises to the top, hold down a high-flying career of my own and make a soufflé.

It doesn't help that Ed Grenville, James's arch-rival, has a wife who's such a genius in the kitchen that in contrast Nigella appears amateurish. Sophie, with her perfect blonde bob and immaculate house and immaculate children, would make a Stepford Wife appear sloppy. I've got my work cut out if I'm going to compete with her.

I'm exhausted just thinking about it.

I'm starting to wonder if I'm suited for this corporate wife stuff. I bet Jake doesn't expect Millandra to cook supper for his fellow highwaymen. He's far more likely to gallop off into the forest with her to a shady dell where there's wine cooling in a babbling brook and a picnic laid out on a blanket. He'll feed her strawberries and then lie her back on the blanket and start to kiss her throat. She won't have to spend her Saturday trying to disguise Marks and Spencer food. Oh for the good old days when women faked orgasms rather than our cooking!

Not that Millandra will fake her orgasms.

If I ever get the time to write one for her, that is.

Catching my eye, Ollie mouths, 'Pub?'

I nod. Now I've remembered the dinner party, I could do with a drink or six.

Forget making Ollie the villain of my novel. I'll buy him a pint and soften him up for the brilliant idea that has just occurred to me.

Pub here I come.

Chapter Two

'One glass of white wine and a packet of pork scratchings!'

Ollie deposits the spoils of his trip to the bar on to the table. 'Did I ever tell you about when I worked in a slaughterhouse?'

I grimace. Ollie's famous for his disgusting collection of student jobs. From plucking turkeys to a gutting line in a chicken factory, you name it, he's done it. I really don't want to hear about the revolting skin diseases of all the pigs he's looked after. Suddenly I don't fancy my pork scratchings any more.

Ollie peers at me over his Guinness. 'Tell me all about the latest work of literature. Is it rude? I'm sure I could see steam coming off that exercise book.'

'You'll have to wait until it's published like everybody else,' I tell him, picking unenthusiastically at my scratchings. Is it my imagination or can I see a pustule?

'But if I don't find out what happens to Millandra, I'll explode,' he wails. 'It's the only thing that kept me going through the rest of the meeting. Besides,' he fixes me with a beady look from behind his trendy glasses, 'it's the least you can do after volunteering us all for summer school.'

'Sorry about that. I wasn't listening.'

'Too busy thinking about Millandra's nipples? Can't say I blame you. I could hardly think of anything else myself.'

I chuck a scratching at him.

Ollie catches it. 'Don't waste them.'

'You don't eat pork scratchings!'

'*I* don't,' his eyes sparkle through his glasses, 'but Sasha does!' and on cue his red setter appears, drooling messily on to the sawdust floor and looking as though she hasn't been fed for months. 'Here you go, girl!'

Time to take the plunge. 'Ol, I need a favour.'

'Not my body again?' He grins.

My face does an impression of a tomato ketchup bottle. Bloody Ollie always knows exactly how to embarrass me.

Although personally I don't fancy Ollie, about four years ago, at an end-of-term party, I got trolleyed on a potent cocktail of cheap white wine and the overwhelming relief that six weeks of teenager-free time was stretching ahead. On the way back from the party with my beer goggles firmly in place, I suddenly decided he was teaching's answer to Brad Pitt and surprised us both by snogging his face off. All I can say in my defence is that I was totally pissed and it was one of the rare times Ol was single. Luckily he went to the Andes on a hiking holiday the very next day and by the time he returned I'd got together with James, so things soon went back to normal.

Ollie often likes to make me squirm by alluding to this drunken escapade.

'You want me,' he insists. 'You might deny it but you do.'

'I bloody don't. Your body's totally safe from me. I'm not asking you for carnal favours.'

'Boring,' sighs Ollie. 'So what *do* you want?'

'It's more a question of who. Have you seen Vile Nina lately?'

Ol wags a finger at me. 'I thought we'd agreed not to call her that. Nina's all right when you get to know her.'

I think I can be forgiven for being sceptical here. Out of all Ollie's girlfriends, Nina with her Sabatier tongue has to be one of the worst. They've all been totally vile but she's the top of the vile pile. Still, it won't help my cause if I antagonise him.

'Sorry, of course she is. Anyway, are you seeing her at the moment?'

Ollie looks shifty. 'Sort of.'

He's shagging her then.

Men.

Nina with her blonde hair and Jordanesque cleavage probably is attractive if you like that kind of thing, which unfortunately most men seem to. Ol was smitten for months. At first they'd been like Siamese twins joined at the tongue, but when Ollie tried to pick up his social life, Nina tightened her grasp. I have strong suspicions that he wasn't even allowed to go to the loo alone, that's how possessive and paranoid she is, and poor old Ollie could do so much better. Still, I've kept my feelings to myself. It never does to diss your friend's partner, does it?

Ol's honeycomb-hued eyes narrow suspiciously. 'What's all this sudden interest in Nina for, anyway? You can't stand her.'

OK. So maybe I haven't done such a great job of pretending to like her. That doesn't mean I can't appreciate her talents. Like cooking, for example.

'Doesn't she run a catering company?'

'Yep. Domestic Divas.'

'Are they expensive to hire?'

He shrugs. 'About four hundred quid or so for a night. Why? Are you interested?'

Bollocks. It may as well be four trillion billion quid, that's how skint I am right now. James has just borrowed what meagre funds were left in my account to ease another of his cash-flow problems, and my Flexible Friend has fallen out with me, so it looks like hiring a caterer is out.

I'm stuffed.

'What is it?' Ol asks.

With a heavy sigh I tell him all about the dinner party, about how James's promotion totally depends on impressing his boss and about how terrified I am of cocking up. Again.

'You know I'm useless in the kitchen,' I wail. 'I'm going to ruin everything. James is desperate for promotion. He says we really need the money and I can't let him down. Not after the last time.'

'Ah yes,' says Ollie. 'The famous getting plastered at Henley Regatta and passing out in the strawberries.'

'Yes, yes! OK!' Why is it that my friends always remember my least glorious moments? Why can't they hold on to all the fabulous things I do, like . . . like . . .

Well, I'm sure there *are* lots. There's far too many to recall, that's the problem. But getting bladdered in front of James's boss at Henley didn't exactly put me in the good books.

'Hasn't Nina taught you to cook?' I say slowly, as though the thought has just occurred. 'I'm sure I remember something about you being trained up to help.'

'She had me marinating, sautéing and basting until I was on my knees.' He takes a swig of Guinness. 'It was nothing like *9½ Weeks* and I really missed Fray Bentos.'

Then he looks at me and groans. 'Oh no you don't, Miss Carter! I can see where you're going with this.'

I fix him with my most desperate and hopefully winning gaze. 'Ollie, you could save my life here if you helped me cook for this flipping dinner party. I'll never manage it alone. You know how useless I am.'

'Yep,' says Ollie. 'You'd burn water.'

'James's boss will be expecting something amazing. Come on, Ol, I'll be your best friend for ever. I'll do all your marking. Walk Sasha. Take your cover lessons. What do you think?'

'I think I need another drink.' Ollie looks longingly towards the bar. 'You're asking me to give up precious Saturday drinking time to cook for a bunch of bankers.'

'Please! I'm a desperate woman.'

Ollie drains his pint. 'Why do you have to impress these idiots? If they don't like you as yourself then sod 'em.'

'I can't be myself,' I say miserably. 'I'll be a total embarrassment to James.'

Ollie plucks a note out of his wallet. 'In that case, Katy, why does he want to marry you?'

And leaving me to ponder this very valid point, he weaves his way through the Friday-night crowd. I stare sadly into my wine glass. How can James love me as I am? I'm not all elegance and grace like Millandra or blonde and skinny like Nina. I'm short and ginger and frequently say the wrong thing. I can't cook, I wear the wrong clothes and I'm a total disappointment to his mother. I've tried really hard to support his career and improve my image, but I never seem to get it right.

I've known James even longer than I've known Ollie, because he used to live next door to my godmother, Auntie Jewell, in Hampstead. In fact we practically grew up together, because my sister Holly and I used to spend our school holidays with Auntie Jewell while our parents trekked to Marrakesh or Morocco or basically anywhere else where they could smoke dope all day and forget about their children.

Not that I'm bitter or anything. It just *might* have been nice to have had normal parents who cared about my homework and who actually fed me on a regular basis. Reading tarot cards before breakfast is all very well, and of course I'm glad I know how to cleanse my chakras, but when you're seven, a bowl of Frosties and a packed lunch is slightly more useful, isn't it?

Anyway, I'm digressing.

Auntie Jewell isn't really my auntie at all; I think we only have the most tenuous of family ties, something really vague like cousins eight times removed. I do know that she was great friends with my grandmother and our families have remained close ever since. The story goes that Auntie's parents, in total despair at ever getting their wayward daughter off their hands, paid for a London season and launched her on the unsuspecting cream of polite society. I've seen the debutante pictures and she was stunningly beautiful, if unrecognisable without her long silver hair and obligatory mini zoo of pets. She pissed off her peers, hardly surprisingly, by receiving a proposal from the extremely eligible Rupert Reynard, Duke of Westchester. Their wedding was the social event of the year, attended by royalty, and after honeymooning in Cannes they settled down to married life in Rupert's ancestral home. At this point the story varies depending upon who you talk to. Our version is that Jewell finally had enough of her husband's womanising and ran away with the under-gardener. No doubt Rupert Reynard saw things very differently. Jewell has never breathed a word about her reasons for leaving her husband, but relations between the two families have been strained ever since, not least because Rupert left her penniless.

'You can't take it with you when you go,' Jewell always shrugs whenever anyone points out the unfairness of her situation. 'Besides,' she'll add cheerfully, 'I did all right in the end.'

Which is true. She became a model and spent the early Sixties as the muse of famous pervy artist Gustav Greer. His blobby pink pictures of a naked Jewell grace galleries from the Tate Modern to the Saatchi. 'Dreadful things,' Jewell likes to shudder. 'The poor man couldn't afford to pay me so I used to take sketches and pictures instead of cash.'

Just as well she did. For some inexplicable reason the art world decided that Greer's nausea-inducing pictures of Jewell's boobs were actually fantastic works of art and worth a fortune. Gustav fuelled the frenzy for his work by conveniently suffocating on fumes when he tried to paint his own body. Suddenly Jewell found herself possessed of a very desirable collection of modern art, which she promptly swapped with a friend for a Hampstead house. And there she's stayed ever since, tending her herb garden and growing ever more eccentric.

The times I spent living with Jewell were among the happiest of my childhood, and I was always devastated when my parents reclaimed me. It was so reassuringly normal to go to the local school and bring back A3 sheets dripping with poster paint for Jewell to stick up in the kitchen, rather than being praised in a rather random fashion by whichever of my mad parents was least stoned. It was nice to go for tea with girls called Camilla and

Emily and not have to worry about inviting them back to my parents' chaotic house. How could I ever have invited friends home? *They* all lived in neat and tidy semis with colour televisions and fitted carpets. We had a crumbling barn conversion swarming with cats and dogs, where there was no television of any kind and where carpets were an unknown quantity. At my friends' houses we ate fish fingers and chips; at mine we took pot luck with whatever my mother wanted to conjure up on the erratic Aga. And how could I explain to other children that my parents were hippies and still lived life as though it was the Seventies? At home it was easier not to have friends at all, but at Jewell's I could totally reinvent myself, and I loved being an anonymous schoolgirl rather than Katy Carter from that strange family at Tillers' Barn.

James St Ellis lived next door to Jewell and his life was a thing of amazement to me. Every day he came home from prep school for an hour of homework followed by an hour of music practice before he escaped into the garden. We spent summers building dens and climbing trees, or at least what summer he did have before his parents dragged him off to the South of France or to summer school. We made up stories, dared each other to eat insects and once we even ran away to the end of the road. James loved to come into Jewell's kitchen and eat sausages and chips at the old pine table and, if we were really lucky, Fab lollies from the freezer. But Holly and I were never invited back to his house, and if his mother ever caught us playing in his garden she'd shoo us home with a curled top lip and wrinkled nose. Not that James cared. He'd rather have been at Jewell's anyway. He spent hours making a hole in the fence so that he could squeeze into our garden, and didn't seem to care that he had splinters in his hands for a whole summer.

Then, one Christmas holiday, James didn't want to play any more. He'd started at Winchester that autumn and had more exciting friends to hang out with. Our dens fell down, the gardener mended the hole in the fence and it was as though James had never existed. Sometimes we'd glimpse him, taller and more aloof, getting out of his parents' car or sitting on the terrace with a friend, but he didn't deign to speak. And that was fine, because at this point my parents decided to move and James was the least of our problems. Holly and I were dragged to Totnes, and for the next few years were shunted between Devon and London like two sulky parcels. James's parents split up, the house next to Jewell was sold and our playmate was forgotten. Holly buried herself in textbooks and I discovered Mills and Boon novels, hoarding them and reading each tattered copy over and over again until my world was full of mysterious sheikhs, strong brooding tycoons and granite-jawed millionaires. One day I just knew I'd find a romantic hero of my very own who'd be captivated by my (ginger) beauty and tamed by his love for me. He'd rescue me from my crazy family and sweep me away to a world of glamour and passion, and we'd live happily every after. Mills and Boon had promised; didn't this happen to every heroine, from humble chambermaids to feisty slave girls? All I had to do was sit tight and wait my turn. Sooner or later my hero would come along and sweep me off my feet.

Except he didn't.

In fact all my handsome princes had the very unfortunate habit of turning into frogs almost as soon as I kissed them. It was all very disappointing.

Just as I was considering suing Mills and Boon under the Trade Descriptions Act and my sexual organs had forgotten what they were for, Fate decided it was time to put me out of my misery. Rewind to four years ago: I was getting dressed up for Auntie Jewell's birthday party without a clue that my life was about to change in the most unexpected way.

Jewell's birthday parties are legendary. Every year she posts a notice in *The Times* and sends out invitations to her eclectic collection of friends and relatives, who drop everything in order to attend what's always a fantastic bash. That year the theme was *A Midsummer Night's Dream*, and I'd spent weeks starving myself to get into a green shimmery fairy costume.

OK, I'd spent ten quid on control knickers, but my intentions had been good.

Anyway, just minutes before I was due to leave, my then boyfriend decided to dump me by text message, leaving me with a dilemma: did I howl until I looked like a goblin or did I head out to the party alone? Usually I dragged Ollie along for moral support because Jewell adored him, but that summer he'd pushed off to the Andes. Deciding to leave my broken heart for later, I set out for Jewell's party in Ollie's temperamental VW Beetle, complete with fairy costume, wings and wand. What could possibly go wrong?

Quite a lot as it turned out, because Fate has a nasty habit of flicking V signs at me. Unless you've broken down on the A5 dressed in a fairy costume, you can't possibly have any concept of what it means to be embarrassed. Tooting lorry drivers and whistles abounded as I desperately tried to look under the bonnet before eventually remembering the engine lived in the boot. Not that I had a flipping clue what to do once I *did* locate it. It just made me feel better to be doing something, *anything* rather than throwing myself under the next juggernaut. Even the AA didn't want to know, because Ollie hadn't paid his membership.

Ollie was *very* lucky he was in the Andes . . .

I'd collapsed on to the ground and buried my head in my hands. I was well and truly up that famous creek without a boat, never mind the paddle. What on earth was I going to do?

And then it happened. The moment I'd been dreaming about since I was about twelve. A beautiful sleek Mercedes pulled up, the door swung open and a tall, lean body slowly uncoiled itself.

'Can I help?'

I looked up and was instantly lost for words, which for me is pretty darn unusual. I opened my mouth to speak but it was as though he'd pressed my mute button, because I couldn't make a sound. This tall, dark stranger was simply too beautiful to be true. He had eyes of the most amazing ice blue, cheekbones so chiselled the royals should ski off them rather than trekking to Klosters and long, black gypsy curls that blew in the wind. The sun shone behind him like a halo. Well either that or he really was an angel.

'Has the car broken down?'

I'd forgotten all about the car, but my voice box was well and truly buggered, that was for sure. He could have stepped straight from the pages of my latest Mills and Boon.

Just my luck to be dressed like Tinkerbell.

The man stepped forward, his eyes crinkling as he looked (most powerfully) down at me. Then he said, 'Bloody hell! Katy? Is that you?'

I screwed my eyes against the sun and tried to figure out who he was, but no, he still looked like he'd materialised from a romantic novel.

'It's me, James,' the stranger said, taking my hand and pulling me to my feet. 'I used to live next door to your Auntie Jewell? Don't you remember? We used to play together all the time.'

My chin was practically in the London sewer. This divine-looking man was snotty little James? This alpha male who smelt of expensive aftershave was the same annoying creature who used to rip the wings off flies and pull my ponytail?

No. Way.

'It really is me,' James laughed, dropping a kiss on to the corner of my mouth. 'But I promise I won't throw worms at you any more! You look amazing, Katy. Who'd ever have thought you'd grow up to be so beautiful?'

Luckily for James the cliché police were off duty, not that I cared. Being five foot three and ginger, I know I'm not beautiful, but hey! A girl's allowed to get swept off her feet once in a while, isn't she?

And sweep me off my feet is exactly what James did. He insisted on chauffeuring me to the party, where he was greeted with rapture by Jewell, but he never left my side or let go of my hand. That night he whisked me away to a beautiful hotel where . . . well, you can probably work that out for yourselves! Anyway, the rest is history and by the time Ollie came home I'd practically moved into James's smart flat and was head over heels in love with my perfect romantic hero. And if Ollie was a bit narky and made snide comments, then it served him right for not paying the AA.

So there you have it. James St Ellis is perfect. And I still can't believe that somebody so perfect would be interested in dumpy little old me. OK, so at times he can be a bit bossy, but he's only doing it for my own good. It's because he loves me and wants the best for me that James sometimes comes across as a little bit insensitive. When I think about it, lots of the things he says make perfect sense: I do need to dress more smartly, lose a stone and think about the future if I'm to make the most of myself. And he's right: my disrupted education isn't as good as it could be – and is certainly no match for his Oxbridge one – so I do need to listen to him when it comes to finances, politics and career stuff. If he's bossy it's only because he cares, unlike my parents, who never gave a monkey's what I did. My life with James is a million times removed from the haphazard one I had with them. I really have been rescued by a handsome prince and my own fairy tale has come true! So what if I've had to change a little and improve myself so that I'm good enough? James is worth it because he's everything I ever dreamed about when I was growing up.

He's *my* romantic hero, and if I'm not exactly the perfect romantic heroine then I'm working on it, because I do love James. I'm sure I do. When he's bossy or grumpy I remind myself how stressful it is working in the City, especially with all this credit-crunch stuff going on, and that he doesn't mean the things he sometimes says to me. He's on edge; who wouldn't be seeing their colleagues and friends losing their jobs on a daily basis? I'm the one he comes home to, the one who listens and the one on whom he vents his bad temper. I can't say I like it much, but nobody ever said relationships are easy; you have to work at them, don't you?

Although placating James's bad moods has started to feel more like hard labour lately . . .

But that's what adult relationships are all about, working things through I mean, and loving the other person even when they're not behaving in a particularly lovable manner. Real love deals with issues rather than quitting, which has always been my parents' preferred method. They'd row, Dad would vanish off in his VW van and Mum would hook up with someone called Rain or Baggy for a few months until Dad came back full of tall tales and with his pockets packed with hash. Not quite the example I want to live my life by! My preferred method of rebellion has been becoming a total square, working as a slave to the system and subjugating myself to the patriarchy – my mother's words, not mine – rather than exploring my inner goddess or trekking off to Marrakesh.

I prefer to think I'm made of sterner stuff than my parents. This is just a bumpy patch. The economy will pick up, James will get his promotion and everything will go back to how it used to be. I just have to be patient and not rise when he's narky, which is easier said than done. I'm biting my tongue so much lately I'm starting to worry the Ed Psych will add me to the school's list of self-harmers . . .

So I can't let James down with this dinner party. He's been so stressed about money lately, what with the wedding to pay for, his mother always on the scrounge and his share portfolio worthless. Apparently Iceland isn't just somewhere Kerry Katona goes shopping; it's also where James put his last bonus, which even I know isn't good news. Since I scrape by on a teacher's wage and make church mice look rich, I'm not much help to our joint finances, so James *has* to get this promotion. He's adamant that everything depends on it.

I *have* to get this dinner party right.

No pressure there, then.

Just as well I'm in the pub. I seriously need a drink just thinking about tomorrow.

Ollie returns, this time with a bottle of wine, and fixes me with a steely glare.

'OK. I'll do it. But,' he adds swiftly before I can fling myself at his feet in an ecstasy of relief and gratitude, 'on one condition.'

'Anything!'

'I'm allowed to come too with a guest. If I'm spending all sodding day cooking, I'm bloody well going to get to eat something.'

I pause for a minute. What will James think about this? He's not Ollie's greatest fan, but on the other hand Ollie *is* clever and would be a brilliant conversationalist. What he doesn't know about eighteenth-century literature isn't worth knowing. I must make a mental note not to get him started on *Fanny Hill*, though. That really would go down like cold sick with a stuffy gathering of merchant bankers.

'Who's the guest?' I ask suspiciously. 'Not Nina?'

'Chill out. She's working. I'll get my thinking cap on. We need somebody entertaining and fun to get the evening up and running.'

Although, as I think I might have mentioned, I don't find Ollie attractive, it seems that the rest of the female population does, and he's never short of dates. Most of them, although stunning, have slightly lower IQs than a lettuce and aren't going to pose much of a threat to James's dinner guests. Julius Millward is an old goat, and adding a pretty girl to the equation can only improve things.

This dinner party is so going to be a success!

I beam at Ollie. 'Bring whoever you want!'

'Cool,' Ollie says. 'Now, get that wine down your neck and listen up. We've got a menu to plan.'

Chapter Three

The silken blindfold whispered deliciously against Millandra's eyelids. Although she couldn't see anything, she could smell the heady scent of honeysuckle, and the springy moss beneath her small feet hinted that she was outside. A breeze kissed her cheeks and lifted tendrils of hair from her face. Jake's hand, pressed into the small of her back, guided her through the maze of trees.

'Now, my lady,' he said, as they came to a halt. 'Do you trust me?'

There were a thousand and one reasons why she shouldn't trust him, Millandra knew. Jake Delaware was the most wanted felon in England, a notorious highwayman who terrorised the King's Highway and who was quicker than lightning with rapier and blunderbuss. A gentlewoman should know better than to venture into the forest alone with such a character. But his gentle kisses and the knowing touch of his hands had overcome all other sensibilities.

'I trust you,' she breathed.

With a swift motion the blindfold was pulled from her eyes to drift down to the mossy floor.

'Oh!' gasped Millandra in amazement.

Spread before her astonished gaze was a feast fit for a princess. Laid out upon a sumptuous velvet cloak strewn with wildflowers was a fare of delicate pastries, strawberries and *summer fruits, quails' eggs and champagne. Deep in a shady forest glade, dappled with dancing sunbeams, it was the most romantic sight she had ever encountered.*

'I promised that I would wine and dine you as well as Lord Ellington could,' said Jake, 'if not even better.'

And as Millandra smiled up at him, at the strong tanned throat, dancing emerald eyes and rippling beechnut hair, she felt certain that Jake Delaware could outdo her other suitors in every other way . . .

OK, so I don't suppose that Jake had to do battle in Sainsbury's on a Friday night with every Nigella and Jamie wannabe in west London, nor did he have to lug eight groaning bags home on the 207 bus, but you get the picture. And even though he's only a fantasy romantic hero, I'm pretty impressed with him so far. Lucky old Millandra. Bet she's the kind of girl who just nibbles daintily on a crust of bread before declaring herself full, unlike those of us who'd shovel the lot in until we feel like a sausage about to burst its skin, and who sips champagne daintily rather than swigging it like there's going to be a world shortage. Still, she is a romantic heroine and I guess that's all in the job description.

I put my notebook away and turn my attention back to the task in hand, namely figuring out how to get off this bus with my shopping avoiding a) doing serious damage to someone's shins and b) severing my fingers with the twisting plastic bag handles. I'm not sure why Ollie needed to buy so much stuff. The amount I've just spent could have fed me for a month, and now I'm the proud owner of countless fillet steaks, cream, peppercorns, foie gras and numerous other bits and pieces that I haven't got a clue what to do with. Ollie piled the trolley so high I practically had vertigo just looking at it.

Still, at least I'm on my way to Wembley as regards this dinner party. Ollie's going to cook an amazing meal and I'm going to dazzle and impress James's senior colleagues.

What can possibly go wrong? His promotion's as good as in the bag. Our troubles are over.

The bus crawls through the rush-hour traffic towards Ealing Common. The rain is falling steadily and the bus windows start to fog up. On the grey pavements people scurry along, bowed beneath umbrellas and dodging puddles. I don't need to be psychic to predict that by the time I get home I'll be sodden. I expect Millandra looks fantastic when it rains, all ringlets and flushed cheeks, unlike me, who with ginger frizz and a red nose looks more like Chris Evans with a head cold. Sometimes life really sucks.

As anticipated, by the time I reach number 12b Allington Crescent, I'm soaked through to my knickers and feeling very fed up. My fingers are a nasty greeny-white shade from lack of circulation and my Doc Martens have sprung a leak. I also have a horrible suspicion that I've left Year 10's coursework on the bus, which although it has the short-term advantage of saving me hours of marking, will eventually mean yet another visit to the Lost Property office. I'm practically on first-name terms with the lady who works there now, which gives you an idea of how forgetful I can be. I must have forgotten the pin number for our joint account too, because the card was declined so I had to use mine.

Maybe I am a bit scatty.

Or, as James puts it, disorganised.

I can't help it, though. When I'm deep in my notebook and thinking about sexy highwaymen, there's not a lot of room for the twenty-first century. And to be honest, when it's a choice between a forest glade with Jake or hauling my shopping up the street, I know which I prefer.

I heave the carriers up the steps to our front door and then stand panting on the doorstep for a minute. I'm trying really hard to lose weight for the wedding, but it doesn't seem to be happening. I partly blame the thoughtless bastard who installed a vending machine in the staff room. Honestly! After two lessons I'd kill my granny for a Kit Kat, so any hope of resisting temptation is futile.

Our flat's on the top floor of what used to be a rather large Victorian townhouse. We've got lovely views over towards Ealing Common, which almost makes up for the fact that you need to climb three steep sets of stairs to get to the front door. Still, as James likes to point out to anyone who'll listen, this flat is an investment and holds a lot of equity. James knows *loads* more than I do about finance, not hard really since you could put all I know about money on a postage stamp and still have room for *War and Peace*, and I'm sure that he's right, just as he's right about all the blond wood flooring and minimalist furniture. I'm sure it *does* look better than my clutter, but it's not exactly comfortable. I once threw myself on to the futon and put my back out for two weeks, not to mention that I cracked two of the slats, which really upset James. As I lay groaning amid the wreckage, he was racing to the phone to call the Conran shop to check he'd taken out insurance. I suppose it's nice to have a man who cares about domestic stuff, but sometimes, to be honest, it really pees me off. All this white makes me nervous; a herd of polar bears could move in and go unnoticed. I'd really like a few squidgy cushions and an Indian throw just to add a spot of colour to the place. But like James says, I'm not a student any more and it is time I developed some adult tastes.

Guess I hang out with teenagers too much.

'I'm home!' I call, as I drag my shopping into the hall and take my coat off in record time. If I drip on the floor it ruins the wood, apparently, so I hastily kick off my shoes and put them in the rack.

I can't hear any noise from the lounge, which suggests that James is probably working away somewhere plugged into his headphones. With a sigh I lug the shopping into the kitchen, where I switch on the shiny chrome kettle and reach for the biscuit tin. I could murder a HobNob! Bugger the wedding-dress diet! I have thought about dieting. I have!

And it's the thought that counts, isn't it?

Munching contentedly, trailing crumbs all over the floor, I start to unpack the shopping, marvelling at the amount Ollie's managed to persuade me to buy. There are ingredients here I haven't even heard of. What on earth is a vanilla pod used for? I rattle the packet just in case the answer flies out, but instead end up tipping the whole lot everywhere. Great. I've only been back ten minutes and already I'm wrecking the joint. There's something about this kitchen and me that means that whenever I enter it I end up creating the kind of mess that's more in keeping with a big-budget disaster movie. My sticky little paws make prints all over the chrome cooker, the funky steel bin vomits forth all the detritus from my culinary attempts and my feet virtually suction themselves to the floor.

The sad truth is this kitchen is too good for me, and I have a horrible feeling it could be a metaphor for my life with James, the hero who's too good for the heroine. Mills and Boon never mentioned that bit, did they?

But it's Friday night, the end of another busy teenager-riddled week, and I'm not going to let myself start to dwell on the uncomfortable thoughts that sometimes beat like dark moths around the edges of my mind. I brush them away. It's the wedding stress that sometimes gets to me, that's all. And I know a great cure for stress! It lives in the door of our Smeg and goes by the name of . . . alcohol!

I grab a glass and uncork the bottle. The cool pale gold liquid glugs cheerfully into the glass and even more cheerfully down my throat; just what I needed after Sainsbury's on a Friday night. I never knew people could get so frantic about their food shopping. Somebody should tell all those women rushing around like demented Formula One wannabes that Domino's do a mean takeout!

At the thought of a Meat Feast with extra cheese, my stomach does an impression of Vesuvius erupting. Perhaps I'll order one. I know I'm not meant to be eating crap, but surely one pizza won't hurt? And maybe some garlic bread as well. I'll do some extra sit-ups to make up.

Extra sit-ups? Who am I kidding? I'll do *some* sit-ups.

En route to retrieve the number, I happen to pass the biscuit tin, which I take as a sign from God to help myself to a couple more. Once I've ordered us a pizza, I'll get on with unpacking the shopping, and I'll even sweep the floor. That's got to be a workout in itself.

Perhaps I'll even have *cheesy* garlic bread.

But you know what they say about the best-laid plans and all that. Just as my eager little fingers are poised over the phone, ready to dial, the kitchen door flies open and in sweeps my future mother-in-law.

Picture Cruella De Vil's meaner older sister and you've got a pretty good picture of Cordelia St Ellis. Groomed and plucked and waxed and suctioned to within an inch of her life, she looks pretty much like a desiccated skeleton, albeit one dressed in Joseph and with Chanel-tipped talons. It costs a lot of money, apparently, to look this well preserved, so Mrs St Ellis is lucky her son still has a well-paid job. Cordelia doesn't work. Blimey! There's no way she could fit in earning a decent crust. Keeping her ageing body embalmed is a full-time occupation.

Either that or she has a pact with Satan.

As I guiltily try and swallow my biscuit, Cordelia pauses elegantly in the doorway and regards me in the same way you might regard a lump of gum that's stuck to your foot. Her eyes are flinty grey and her mouth is pursed like a cat's bum. I'm in the bad books.

Again.

She didn't like me when I was seven, and time hasn't altered her opinion.

'What do you think you're doing?' she hisses, sounding as horrified as if she'd caught me torturing babies. In fact I'm pretty sure she'd rather I *was* torturing babies, instead of stuffing my face with calories. It would be a minor crime in comparison.

'I'm just having a snack,' I try to say, but sound instead like I'm speaking Klingon and spray the pristine marble work surfaces with regurgitated HobNob. 'Just the one biscuit.'

'Are you deliberately trying to sabotage my son's wedding?' she demands, hands on hips so bony they could grate rock. 'Do you want to be even fatter than you are already? Well? Do you?'

It's a tough question, because I really want those biscuits. Funny how I never used to think I was overweight till I met James. A little cuddly in places, and I have boobs for sure, but fat? Still, Mrs St Ellis, professional body fascist, has seriously disabused me of any misconception that I might be acceptable.

'But I'm starving!'

'You are not.' Cordelia tips the contents of the biscuit tin into the bin. 'Children in Africa are starving. You are merely greedy. If you want to eat between meals then have an apple.'

Is she mad? Who eats apples rather than chocolate biscuits?

'If you carry on eating at this rate, we'll never get you into that size eight Vera Wang.'

Quite frankly I have more chance of flying to Mars than I have of fitting into a size eight wedding dress. I'm size twelve on a good day, breathing in and wearing granny knickers.

'Er, Cordelia,' I venture, 'I'm not entirely sure about that dress. I've seen one in Debenhams I really like—'

'Debenhams!' echoes Cordelia, as horrified as though I'd said I wanted to get married stark naked and with tassels on my nipples. 'Debenhams! Are you insane? A high-street store?'

To be honest, until I met Cordelia St Ellis, I was under the impression that high-street stores were *exactly* where most people bought their clothes. She's never had to eke out a teacher's salary, though, and if it's not Harvey Nicks or Harrods then she won't give it house room.

She must be gutted to be gaining a daughter-in-law whose idea of heaven is a trolley dash in Top Shop. If she wasn't such an old boot I'd almost feel sorry for her.

'Yes,' I say bravely. 'It's a lovely dress and only six hundred pounds.'

And it is my perfect dress. Not the elegant cream tube Cordelia's selected and which might just about go round one of my thighs, but an off-the-shoulder romantic dream of a dress. The type of thing Millandra would wear to a ball or that Jake would lift gently from her soft skin . . .

Am I getting obsessed here? That's what happens when I can't write stuff down. In any case, I tried the dress on and it was *perfect*, skimming over any less-than-toned bits and making my boobs look like soft high peaches. The creamy satin was just the right shade for my pale skin and made my flesh look warm and tanned. In fact it's the only dress I've ever worn that's made me look good!

I tell you, I could practically have fancied myself.

I simply have to have it!

But Cordelia's looking at me as though I've sprouted another head.

'Debenhams!' she whispers, one bony claw held the-atrically to where her heart would be if she had one. 'I take you to Vera Wang, *where Jennifer Aniston shops*, and you want to go to Debenhams?'

I'm tempted to say that if she throws in Brad Pitt I'll go to Vera Wang with joy, but since Cordelia truly believes that James is Brad Pitt, Einstein and baby Jesus all rolled into one, I keep my mouth shut.

'What's wrong with you?' asks Cordelia, slumped now against our electric Aga. 'Are you trying to ruin the wedding?'

'Of course not!' I say, although actually wanting to take her Vera Wang brochure and shove it up her backside. 'It's just that I tried on this other dress yesterday and it looked much better. My friend said I looked lovely.'

Probably best not to tell her that the friend in question was Ollie and that the expression he used wasn't 'lovely' but 'totally shagadelic'. Which, thinking about it, is prob-ably one of the nicest things anyone's ever said to me.

Cordelia looks extremely doubtful. But then she hasn't seen me trying to squeeze into the size eight sample of the designer silk sheath she's set her heart on. I looked like a snake shedding its skin in reverse.

'And,' I continue, 'I can have it practically off the peg! All they need to do is shorten it a little.'

'Off the peg?' shudders Cordelia. 'I think not. There's not going to be anything cheap and tacky about this wedding. If James insists on . . .' she pauses and the words *marrying you* hang almost visibly in the air like something out of *Harry Potter*, 'having this wedding, then I shall do my utmost to make it perfect for him. And if that means a designer gown for his fiancée then so be it.'

It's lucky for Cordelia that I've been doing anger management strategies with my tutor group this week, because otherwise she'd be wearing the frying pan. And since it's a Le Creuset and requires two men to lift it, I don't think she'd have been a pretty sight. But as she's going to be my mother-in-law I take a deep breath and count to ten while she continues to huff and puff about my (many) flaws, the main one apparently my being related to my eccentric parents, which seems a tad unfair since I'm hardly wild about this myself. When she finally stops recalling the episode in 1989 when Dad passed out on her doorstep – he'd been a bit confused about where Jewell lived – I seize my chance to speak. After all, who knows when she'll next let me get a word in?

'I really like that dress,' I say, through gritted teeth. 'My dad says he'll buy it for me too, so you needn't worry about paying. I was going to go back and put a deposit down.'

'There's no need for that,' Cordelia says hastily, no doubt picturing me in some hippy number drifting up the aisle in a cloud of cannabis smoke. 'I'm more than happy to buy my son's fiancée a wedding dress. Now tell me, how did today's fitting go?'

Have you ever had that horrible feeling when your blood goes all icy cold and seems to drain out of your body, leaving your legs all rubbery and your fingers numb with terror? Well that's how I feel right now.

The fitting.

Oh shit.

I forgot the fitting.

My mouth opens but for once I can't find any words. What can I say? That while I was supposed to be being pinned and prodded and peered at in one of London's most exclusive boutiques, I was actually out on the piss with my friend? That while I was meant to be choosing colours and silk slippers I was hooning around Sainsbury's having trolley races with Ollie?

'Um,' I squeak, HobNobs and wine curdling nastily in my stomach, 'I didn't make it to the fitting. Sorry.'

'Didn't make it to the fitting!' shrieks Cordelia, sounding just like Lady Bracknell discussing handbags. 'What do you mean?'

'That I didn't get there?'

At this you'd have thought I'd shot her. Cordelia's cheeks drain of colour and she practically staggers to the door.

'Have you any idea what you've done? I've had to pull strings to get them to fit you. I've had to use my own good name and pay over the odds. That dress was going to be for a supermodel!'

Well, no wonder it didn't fit me then. The only thing that I have in common with Kate Moss is that we both breathe.

'I'm really sorry,' I say.

'Sorry! I don't care about sorry, you stupid, ungrateful girl!' Cordelia's shrieking is now on a par with the noise a 747 makes on take-off. I hear a door open and footsteps echoing on the wooden floor. Fan-bloody-tastic. Here comes James, who'll be less than delighted that his preparation for the partnership interview has been interrupted. Once he appears, Cordelia will be all sweetness and light and I couldn't look more like the villain of the piece if I was wearing a black cape and twirling my moustache. How she manages to pull this off I'll never know; it must be some kind of twisted talent.

'I can't believe you've done this to me! I've never been so hurt in all my life!' Cordelia's voice rises by several decibels and her eyes flicker in the direction of the hallway. She can hear James drawing closer and is gearing up for an Oscar-winning performance. Her flinty eyes are working overtime to squeeze out tears and her hand flutters to her throat. Even I'm pretty impressed, and I'm a woman who sees kids turn on the tap on a daily basis.

'What on earth's going on?' James demands. He's wearing his glasses and his dark ringlets are tousled from where he's been running his hands through them while he works. His eyes are red-rimmed and ringed by deep purple shadows and my heart goes out to him. He's under so much pressure, and now I've gone and made things worse.

'If you want to know why I'm so upset, ask Katy!' wails Cordelia, a Niagara Fall of tears gushing down her face. 'Ask her to tell you how she deliberately sets out to hurt me and rejects me at every turn. All I've ever done is try to befriend her, but she hates me!'

My mouth hangs open on its hinges at the unfairness of this. 'I don't hate you! Of course I don't!'

She takes a big shuddering breath and her eyes brim anew. Wow. I'm amazed the RSC don't burst in and sign her on the spot. ' I wish I could believe that, Katy, but whenever I try to do something nice, you fling it back at me.'

I rack my brains to think of a time when Cordelia has ever done something nice for me, and by nice I mean genuinely nice and without a spiteful subtext, but no. Nada. I cannot think of such an occasion.

'Like the time I paid for you to have a week at that spa,' she continues, mopping her eyes with the hankie that James hands her, 'and you refused to go.'

I'm struck dumb by her utter nerve. It wasn't a spa, it was a week at an army-style boot camp designed, and I quote my future mother-in-law, 'to burn off that spare tyre, because nobody wants to look at a fat bride'. Not of course that she'd dared say this until I'd returned; Cordelia's far too cunning for that. She revealed my 'treat' in front of James and off I set to Hampshire, in my naivety all excited about mud wraps and hot tubs, only to discover I was signed up for dawn runs, assault courses and a sadistic trainer who barked orders at me. I'd lasted thirty minutes before sprinting down the drive, scaling the wall and begging Ollie to come and rescue me.

Looking on the bright side, that was probably the most exercise I'd had in ages, so it wasn't a total waste . . .

'That *was* rather out of order, Chubs,' sighs James, taking off his glasses and pinching the bridge of his nose. 'It cost Ma a fortune.'

'It just wasn't really my thing,' I try to explain but am drowned out as Cordelia wails even more loudly about my lack of gratitude before burying her face in James's shoulder and blubbing all over his Paul Smith shirt. James pats her back soothingly and shoots me a black look over the top of her head.

Great. In the dog house again. Just give me a bone and call me Rover.

'I'm trying to work on the Amos and Amos report, which as you well know is vital for my promotion,' he says to me, and the note of irritation I'm starting to become familiar with creeps into his voice. 'So what's happened now?'

'I missed a dress fitting,' I tell him. 'It's no big deal.'

'No big deal?' whimpers Cordelia. 'That fitting was at Pilkington Greens! They asked Vera Wang especially if we could have that dress. I had to . . .' she pauses for effect and her voice quavers dramatically, 'really grovel.'

'You missed the fitting for your own wedding dress?' James is incredulous.

'Not on purpose! Anyway, I've already found a dress.'

'See,' wails Cordelia. 'She's rejecting me in every way. I've never been so hurt in all my life!'

'I had to go to Sainsbury's,' I explain swiftly, 'to buy food for your dinner party, James. I forgot I was supposed to be in Kensington.'

'So it's my son's fault?' Cordelia gasps, her hand flying to her throat. 'You're blaming poor James?'

'I didn't say that, but he wants me to cook this dinner. It's really important, isn't it, James?'

'Not as important as my mother,' he snaps.

'I can't listen to Katy blaming you for a minute longer.' Cordelia reaches across the cooking island to grab her Louis Vuitton bag. 'Call me later, darling, I'm too *wounded* to even look at her. You know how sensitive I am.'

Sensitive? Bulls in china shops take more care, but of

course I can't argue, I'll just look even more of a bitch. I shake my head sadly and wonder how she always manages to make me look like the bad guy. James will take her side, he always does, and I'll have to grovel. Again.

'I feel one of my migraines coming on. Oh!' Cordelia clutches her forehead and all but falls to the floor. 'You'll have to drive me home, baby angel, I can hardly see straight.'

'Don't worry, Mother,' says the baby angel soothingly. 'Of course I'll take you home.' But over the top of her head he shoots me another very ugly glare. He will have to drive all the way to Richmond now and sort out returning Cordelia's car tomorrow, all of which means time away from sucking up to his bosses at the golf course and yet more black marks for me.

'I can call you a cab, Cordelia,' I say helpfully.

'You will not!' snaps James. 'My mother is far too upset, thanks to your insensitivity. I'll take her home myself. '

They shuffle along the hallway and out down the stairs, Cordelia groaning and James soothing her gently, while I try very hard to think about nice things. Like I said, I've been doing anger management at school, which is just as well right now. When I hear the front door slam I scream with all my might, just like the Ed Psych taught me. Thinking of nice things is hard because there's a total dearth of them in my life at the minute, so I smash three dinner plates instead. A silly move really, as James loves his Crown Derby and will now be even more pissed off with me than he is already.

Surely being in love isn't meant to be this stressful?

Still, at least I now have at least an hour and a half of glorious uninterrupted time to myself. There's no way Cordelia will allow James to come back home without feeding him one of her gourmet dinners first. She's under the impression that he's totally incapable of locating the oven and bunging in a meal and that I'm some bra-burning feminist who makes the poor boy fend for himself.

As if I'd burn my bra!

That would be downright silly for somebody with a D cup.

I pour another enormous glass of wine and retrieve the Domino's number from the bin. I seriously need some comfort food and I order the biggest, most fattening concoction that I can think of. I'm buggered if I'm going to fit into that dress of Cordelia's now. And as for sit-ups . . . well sod 'em!

As I perch on the stool by the kitchen island, smoking a sneaky fag and counting the minutes until the delivery boy arrives, I catch sight of Wayne Lobb's exercise book, dog-eared and rained on, sticking out of my rucksack. Instantly my pulse starts to calm a little and my anger begins to lessen. I pull the book out, open it at a fresh page and rummage in the debris at the bottom of my bag for a pen. After uncovering several Tampax, a fluff-coated sweet and some confiscated jewellery, I strike lucky and find a leaky biro. For a moment I chew the end thoughtfully, crunching the plastic the way I'd like to crunch up my prospective mother-in-law.

I take a big gulp of wine and then begin to write . . .

Millandra's evil stepmother Countess Cordelia was one of the most loathsome women in London . . .

Didn't someone say the pen is mightier than the sword?

Chapter Four

I normally love Saturday mornings. James tends to race off to the golf course at some ungodly hour, which leaves me free to loll around in bed until lunchtime eating toast, drinking tea and reading trashy novels.

Heaven!

Then I usually potter round the flat and think about doing some housework before venturing into town and letting my credit cards come out to play. I love drifting round Camden Market, rummaging through the second-hand clothes, delving into treasure chests of bric-a-brac and trying on pairs of enormous chunky boots that make me so tall that I practically require oxygen. Then I'll buy a hummus pita in the covered market and take a wander down to the canal, looking at all the interesting couples in their ethnic sweaters and funky hats, holding hands and looking so happy. Sometimes I wonder what it would be like to have my own stall. I'd sell second-hand clothes, I think, rich burgundy silks and dark purple velvets, frothing cream lace and busy paisley prints. I'd have long hair and piercings. I've always hankered after some piercings. I'd *really* like a navel ring but James thinks they're common. He's also pointed out, rather bluntly I feel, that there's no point since I don't have a flat stomach. I know he's only trying to spur me on to get fit, but I do wish he'd be a bit less blunt sometimes.

Still, I like the Camden dream. It's nearly as good as the one when I'm a bestselling writer living in a remote clifftop cottage. In this dream I'm very *French Lieutenant's Woman*, all long swirling skirts and windswept locks as I stare moodily out to sea before striding away into the mist.

The trouble is, James doesn't really feature in either of my dreams. Not because I don't want him to, but because he'd absolutely hate either of those lifestyles. He can't bear Camden because he thinks it's full of 'hippy scroungers', and as for the country, well, he'll only venture there to shoot hapless pheasants with his work colleagues or to network at country-house parties. If he's not within two feet of tarmac, he gets twitchy. So I guess that means that we'll always be city folk, which is such a shame, because I always wanted to live in the country.

But marriage is all about having to make compromises, right? And James is my romantic hero, my soulmate, so I guess I'd better get used to it.

Anyway, today is a Saturday unlike normal Saturdays. James didn't get back from Cordelia's until midnight and then spent an hour on his laptop, pointedly ignoring me. So I sat in the kitchen with Jake and Millandra, drinking my way through an entire bottle of wine, while James tapped away into the small hours, the set of his shoulders speaking volumes about his disapproval.

I was seriously in the bad books.

By the time I'd reached the bottom of the bottle and written a particularly vicious scene where Millandra's raddled old stepmother is rejected by Jake, I was starting to feel brave and more than a little wronged. I had every right to choose my own wedding dress! If I wanted to eat the entire contents of the McVitie's factory it was up to me, not her! As I drained my eighth glass, I was fired up with righteous indignation.

It was time Cordelia butted out of my wedding, and I was going to tell James so!

You probably won't be surprised to hear that James didn't take this very well. In fact we had the most massive row and I ended up sleeping on the sofa.

I'm not really sure how that came about, to be honest. I'm still pretty certain I was in the right. It didn't help though when James unearthed Wayne Lobb's ex-exercise book and read the latest chapter.

'What's this shit?' he'd roared, shaking the exercise book in my face. ' "Lady Cordelia's thin lips drew back to reveal her stained teeth. Jake felt himself recoil as a rabbit from a serpent. Those mean dark eyes seemed to devour him as her bony hands took an iron grasp upon his manhood." Are you fucking insane?'

'That's mine!' I'd cried, snatching it back from him. 'That's my novel!'

'It's fucking slanderous, that's what it is!'

'Any similarity to any person living is entirely co-incidental,' I said, which was a mistake. Nobody likes a smart-arse, least of all James.

'It's pathetic drivel!' He'd slam-dunked the book into the bin. 'Wake up to yourself, Katy! You are not a writer. You're a mediocre teacher in a shitty sink school and you ought to be on your knees thanking God my mother's actually taking the time to bother with you. I don't see either of your parents rushing over to help out.'

For a moment I was speechless, stung by his invective. 'She's horrible to me,' I said at last. 'She tells me what to eat and won't even let me choose my own wedding dress.'

43

'She's doing it for your own good,' James said patiently, as though talking to the village idiot, a job for which he clearly thinks I'm overqualified. 'Come on, Chubs, admit it, you don't exactly have the best taste in the world.'

I hate it when James calls me Chubs. I know it's a pet name and everything but it's hardly one that makes me feel sexy and desirable. I tried to tell him this but he just laughed and said it suited me; after all, I was chubby, wasn't I, so he could hardly call me Skinny. I suppose he's right, if size twelve is chubby, and like he says, if I really don't like my nickname I can always diet.

Ollie says he knows an easy way I could lose twelve stone of useless male . . .

'Admit it,' pressed James, feeling that he had the advantage, 'you still dress like a student, and if it wasn't for me this place would be jam-packed with ethnic shit. To be honest, I was immensely relieved when my mother offered to lend a hand with the wedding. I was dreading that you'd arrange karaoke and turn up looking like a milkmaid, all heaving bosom and flowing ribbons.' At this he shuddered delicately and I saw my dream dress turn to ashes. 'So, Chubs, tomorrow you'll apologise to my mother, and if we're really lucky she might just agree to help you salvage this wedding, if you still love me and want to get married, that is,' he added, expertly playing the guilt card. He knows me well enough to be aware that I do a mean line in guilt and could probably keep the Catholic Church going for years. 'Or did you not make the wedding dress fitting on purpose?'

'Of course not!'

'Maybe this is your way of telling me you want to finish it? Even though I still love you in spite of everything, maybe you don't love me any more?' His eyes looked dangerously bright and he bit his lip bravely. 'I've tried so hard to help you, Katy. I've tried to help you lose weight, I've made allowances for all your social cock-ups and I still want to marry you in spite of your family, but maybe that isn't enough any more?'

And at this point James proceeded to remind me of all the myriad ways that I'd embarrassed/humiliated/disappointed him. I must admit that they made a pretty scary list. And I'd forgotten at least half, like the time I threw up at Anthea Turner's Charity Ball (Anthea was lovely about it, in case you're wondering) or the time I drove his beloved Audi TT through a deep puddle (OK, it was more like a small lake, but how was I to know when it was so dark?) and totally wrote it off. By the time he reached the end of this very long and very depressing list, I was amazed he still wanted to marry me and was crying so hard I looked like a frog.

'I'm sorry,' I choked. 'I'll try harder with your mother.'

'And with everything else,' he told me while I sniffed and blubbed. 'I'm only saying this for your own good, Chubs, but you really need to sort yourself out. Not everyone's as tolerant as me, you know.'

'I know,' I sniffed. 'Sorry.'

'You're always sorry, Chubs, aren't you? Just as well I know you can't help messing up.' He ruffled my hair and yawned. 'You can make it up to me by cooking the most fantastic dinner tomorrow and wowing the boss. You know what Julius Millward is like – if he's stuffing his fat face he's happy and hopefully more inclined to promote me. And let's face it, we need that promotion to pay for the wedding.'

'We don't have to have a big flash wedding,' I said

quickly. 'I'm happy to get married quietly somewhere. We could go abroad even.'

'Don't be silly, my mother would never forgive me,' said James. 'Now, I need to sort out the Amos and Amos contract before Julius Millward comes over and then get a decent night's sleep, which I won't get with you sniffing next to me until the small hours. I suggest you kip in here tonight and think about how you can make things up to my mother.'

And off he went to our bedroom, leaving me to spend a restless night on a sofa that makes a bed of nails look snuggly. As I lay back on the hard suede and watched the orange sweep of car headlights march relentlessly across the ceiling, I thought how much I missed the cats and dogs that roam Auntie Jewell's house like a friendly furry sea. It would have been really lovely to bury my face in warm fur and sob into something living and breathing rather than into the scratchy sofa. I'd have loved a cat, but James doesn't like animals; he thinks they smell and shed too much hair. So I spent the night alone, listening to the swish of traffic through rain and the distant rumble of late tubes. Sleep was never going to come, so eventually I gave up even trying. I fished my exercise book out of the bin, sat back at the kitchen table and wrote until my hand started to cramp and the hands on the clock told me that it was eight thirty-five. After making a cup of coffee so strong that the spoon practically stood up and saluted me, I picked up the phone and took a deep breath.

It was humble pie for breakfast, and knowing Cordelia, it would be a bloody huge slice.

Two hours on I still have indigestion. After twenty minutes of grovelling, Cordelia graciously deigned to rearrange my dress fitting and generously forgave me.

Forgave *me*? As I sit in the kitchen and try to ignore the biscuit tin, I feel like I'm living in some weird parallel universe. Between them my fiancé and his mother have me on the emotional rack and I'm sure I don't deserve it. Surely choosing my own wedding dress isn't too much to ask? All my friends think it's high time I stood up to Cordelia, but it's OK for them to give advice they'll never have to act on.

As I sip my coffee I ponder why I'm such a sap when it comes to standing up to James and his mother. I'm not like this anywhere else, honestly. At work Ollie says I'm like a cross between Robocop and a sergeant major, and it's true to say that I never have discipline issues. Six-foot Year 11 lads tremble when I roar at them, and that's saying something. So what goes wrong when I get home? I guess I'm just too exhausted from being tough all day long to continue after three thirty. Once that bell has shrilled and Sir Bob's kids have been let loose to terrorise the good people of West London, all I want to do is collapse with a big glass of wine, close my eyes and recover from the trauma of my day. Teaching sucks the life out of me, and after a day doing battle with teenagers I just want an easy life.

The only problem is that I don't seem to be getting one. Far from it.

Has my relationship with James always been so out of balance? When I told him I'd phoned Cordelia and apologised, he nodded, poured himself an espresso and then asked me what I was going to cook for dinner. There was no hug and no apology for making me sleep on the sofa, and I felt like a naughty girl being given the stern treatment by her head teacher. I was almost expecting a report card and a stint in detention.

I sigh and wrap my hands round the coffee mug. Last night I was so sure I was in the right, but I'm starting to doubt myself now and, as the kids at school would say, it's doing my head in.

'I'm going to play a round of golf with Julius Millward,' James announces as he reaches for the keys to his BMW. 'Shouldn't you be preparing for tonight?'

I drag my thoughts back to the present. No doubt I should be marinating, flambéing and basting by now. And I would be if I knew what all that meant. I blame Nigella Lawson. That domestic goddess stuff has totally stitched up an entire generation.

'It's all taken care of,' I say airily. At least I bloody hope it is.

James fixes me with a steely gaze. 'You know how important this evening is, don't you, Katy?'

How can I not? He's been going on about it for weeks.

'I know we really need to show them that we're partnership material,' I parrot dutifully.

James is still eyeing me suspiciously. 'So I can count on you not to balls anything up?'

'Totally!' I tell him. 'That promotion is in the bag.'

'I hope so,' James replies, pulling his golf clubs out from the cupboard. 'This wedding has cleaned us out and that new BMW wasn't cheap. And Chubs,' he adds over his shoulder, 'make sure you wear something suitable. Try to dress a bit more like Sophie. She always looks the part.'

I'm practically gnashing my teeth in rage. Sophie looks like someone's rammed a broom up her arse and put a tax on senses of humour. Sod that for a packet of biscuits.

Talking of biscuits, I'm feeling a little peckish. I wish that misery made me want to starve and fade away, but unfortunately it has the opposite effect. Come to think of it, so does happiness, and doubt and annoyance and just about any other emotion you can name. Just my luck. I bet Millandra would starve into a delicate decline, whereas I'll end up making Jabba the Hut look undernourished.

Just as I'm polishing off the last of the HobNobs, and flicking a mental V at Cordelia, the doorbell rings. Peering down into the street, I see Ollie clutching a vast box and waving frantically at me, so I buzz him up and wait to be amazed.

'Christ,' says Ollie when I open the door, 'you look like shit.'

'And good morning to you too,' I reply.

Ollie heaves a big polystyrene box on to the worktop.

'Seriously, you look awful. What happened?'

'Tough night.' I flap my hands dismissively. I'm not prepared to analyse my relationship with Ollie. He thinks James is a wanker at the best of times and I can't risk him refusing to help me with this dinner party on principle because he doesn't want to help my fiancé out. The only row I've ever had with Ollie happened when James refused to insure me on his new BMW. James's reasoning was that I could use the tube or the bus easily and didn't need a car. 'Besides, Chubs, you're hardly the best driver, are you?' he added, going on to list all the scrapes and dents I'd added to the outgoing Audi TT. I made the mistake of telling Ollie this, and he was totally outraged on my behalf.

'He's such a bully!' Ol exploded. 'Grow a bloody backbone, Katy, and tell him to insure you on the car. You're his fiancée, for God's sake!'

Of course I stuck up for James, who was only thinking of the car, and Ollie went on to say some very harsh things and I was so hurt that we didn't talk for a week. Eventually, over a sneaky fag in the school boiler room, we made our peace and agreed that in the future we wouldn't discuss our respective partners. So far it seems to have worked.

Ollie looks at me thoughtfully through narrowed toffee-coloured eyes but doesn't pry any further. 'Well, stick a pan of water on to boil and let's get this show on the road.'

I grab one of our Le Creusets and practically put my back out.

'Too small,' says Ollie, peeling back the tape on his polystyrene box. 'It needs to be really large to fit,' he pulls back the lid proudly, 'this fine fellow!'

Oh. My. God. I stare at him aghast. From within the box a large claw is waving jauntily at me, a claw that is practically the size of a man's fist.

'What the hell is that?'

'It's our starter,' Ollie says proudly. 'Isn't he a beauty? I got him for an absolute song.' Somehow he manages to pluck the creature out of the box without having any limbs severed. I stare across my kitchen at the world's most enormous lobster ever, who regards me with beady black eyes.

'It's alive!'

'Course it's alive, you muppet.' Ollie wiggles it at me. 'Grr!'

I step back hastily. Those claws look mean.

'Doesn't that mean we'll have to kill it?'

'Yep,' says the murderous Ollie. 'Which is why I asked you to put the water on to boil.'

'We're going to boil it alive?'

'That's the usual way. Although you can put a knife through his brain, I suppose. I can't say I've ever really fancied that, though.'

I look at the lobster and the lobster looks at me. Am I imagining it or is there a pleading look in his dark eyes?

'So a pan of boiling water is best,' Ollie continues cheerfully, lobster under one arm as he fills the biggest pan I own. 'Don't look so worried. It'll be quick.'

The lobster is waving its claws frantically. Ollie puts the pan on the hob and bungs the lid on. I feel faint. I know I'm being a hypocrite here because I eat meat, but I'm not used to being faced with the realities of where my yummy burger actually comes from. In Sainsbury's, steaks come in nice little packages; they don't line up and moo at me. I look again at the lobster and I swear to God it's starting to tremble. It knows what horrible fate is about to befall it. I can practically hear it begging.

Having a vivid imagination is such a curse!

Steam is rising from the pan and the water boils like the pits of hell. Ollie whacks in some sea salt and lifts up the unfortunate crustacean.

'No!' I scream, hurling myself across the kitchen with a speed that would have done Kelly Holmes proud. 'You can't!'

I'm face to face with the lobster. Its antennae wiggle desperately and I can almost hear it sobbing. Behind me the pot boils merrily.

'Katy,' says Ollie patiently. 'Please step aside from the pan.'

'It's barbaric!' I shriek. 'We can't murder it!'

'It's the starter for your dinner party and I don't imagine that they'll want to eat it alive.'

'Can't we have melon or something? Anything we don't have to kill?'

I'm sure the lobster nods.

'Not quite as impressive as my Thermidor served in the

claws,' says Ollie, dangling the lobster above the hissing water. 'And I thought impressing these tossers was the name of the game? A fresh lobster will definitely do that.'

He's right, but at this moment I don't care. I just know I can't drop this hapless creature into a vat of boiling water. I can't!

'Ollie, look at him,' I say desperately. 'He's terrified.'

'Don't anthropomorphise him,' says Ollie sternly. 'You've taught *Animal Farm* too many times. He's dinner, not a pet.'

'Ollie! Please!' I'm nearly in tears. 'I can't boil something alive that's looking at me. Please don't!'

'Oh God.' Ollie lowers the lobster wearily. 'Rick Stein would be spinning in his grave if he was dead.'

'Bugger Rick Stein.' My heart beat starts to slow as I'm sure the lobster's does. 'I'd have nightmares for years. I'd probably turn vegetarian.'

'Melon balls it is then,' sighs Ollie. 'This leaves us with a slight problem.'

'Does it?' All I feel is total utter giddy relief.

'What do you suggest we do with a nine-pound lobster?'

'Can't he go back to the sea?'

Ollie starts to laugh. 'I didn't get him from the sea! I got him from the market. And since it's now,' he checks his funky surf dude's watch, 'one thirty, I can't exactly take him back.'

'Well,' I say, having a bit of a *Free Willy* moment, 'you're not going back to the market, are you, Pinchy? I'm going to take you back to the sea.'

'Pinchy?' snorts Ollie. 'Are you mental?'

I give him an arch look. 'I'm not the one boiling animals alive.'

Ol shrugs. 'Point taken. But what do we do now? There isn't a lot of sea in Ealing.'

I'm thinking swiftly. 'We'll have to keep him here until we can take him to the coast. And we'll have to make sure James doesn't notice.'

'What's all this *we* stuff?'

'You brought him here. So you're totally involved.'

'I was going to cook him,' grumbles Ollie as he lowers the relieved Pinchy into the sink, 'not play Animal bloody Magic. And anyway, where do you think you can hide a brute this big?'

And then I have my brilliant idea. Minutes later the bath is full, I've lobbed in about a ton of sea salt and Pinchy is looking very much at home. I pull the shower curtain round the bath and *voilà*! One secret lobster, saved from a hideous death by me.

Brigitte Bardot, eat your heart out!

And James will never know, right?

★

While my new pet makes himself at home, I'm dispatched to Sainsbury's to buy melon and Parma ham. I dash round like Speedy Gonzales on a really fast day, but even so, negotiating the harassed-looking families in the narrow aisles takes a while, and by the time I return, Ollie is surrounded by bubbling pans and gorgeous smells.

'You're seriously talented,' I tell him, dipping my finger into a creamy brandy-scented sauce. 'This is gorgeous.'

'Fingers out!' Ollie raps my knuckles with a wooden spoon. 'I reckon this'll take me another hour. Then I can push off and you can pretend that you've been slaving all afternoon. '

'I owe you one,' I say fervently. Bless him, he's even laid

the table and made it look like something out of an interiors magazine.

'Don't worry.' Ollie throws finely sliced fillet steaks into a pan, where they sizzle and spit. 'I'll call the favour in sometime. In fact, I've a stack of GCSE coursework that needs grading . . .'

'Anything!' I promise. 'You've totally saved my life.'

'I have,' Ol agrees, chucking in a handful of pepper-corns. 'But never mind that now. Stop it!' He slaps my hand away from the pan. 'You're distracting me. Why don't you go into town and buy something to wear? Then when you come back I'll be out of here and you can pre-tend that you've done all the hard work *and* managed to make yourself look gorgeous.'

It's worth any amount of GCSE marking if I can make tonight a success, and blowing him a kiss, I'm only too glad to leave the cooking behind.

I spend a happy couple of hours in Ealing Broadway, where I shove a Big Mac down my neck and spend ages in Waterstone's perusing the romantic fiction and convincing myself there must be a market for Jake and Millandra. Then I embark on the serious task of finding a suitable outfit for tonight. What I ought to do is buy something in Laura Ashley, all flowery print and velvet trimming, but I just can't face it. Eventually I choose a pair of green velvet flares and a soft grey off-the-shoulder sweater, which I feel is sophisticated but sexy. I then buy about half the bangles and necklaces in Accessorize and treat myself to a sham-poo and blow-dry in Toni & Guy. I'm all for saving Pinchy but I don't really fancy getting in the bath with him. There's something about the way he looks at people's limbs that makes me a little nervous. Thank goodness James showers at the golf club. Somehow I think he'd prefer Pinchy in a cheesy sauce rather than floating in the jacuzzi bath.

When I finally get home at just before six o'clock I'm feeling pretty darn good about myself. My hair is all curly and bouncy, my new clothes are deliciously heavy in their carriers and for once the make-up girl at the Clinique counter has done a good job. I pause and examine my reflection in the hall mirror. Perhaps the eyes are a little Lily Savage? I lick my finger and scrub some of the greeny-gold eye shadow away. I may well be putting on a show for Julius Millward and Co. but it doesn't do to look too theatrical. Besides, I don't need another lecture from James about how Sophie always looks so natural and fresh. If I had an au pair, a clothing allowance and worked part time in an art gallery, I'd look fresh too. But my classroom is more like Beirut than Bayswater, so I feel I can be forgiven for looking more than a little frayed around the edges. When I try telling this to James, though, I just get sarcastic comments about all my holidays and finishing at three thirty every day. Well, I tell myself, as I hang up my coat and saunter into the kitchen, if bloody Sophie had to battle with apathy and raging hormones on a daily basis, I bet she'd look as knackered as I do. And besides, I'm the fastest texter in west London and know all the latest slang. At least *I* am in touch with my generation.

OK then. The one beneath it.

The kitchen smells divine, and what's even better, Ollie has cleared up and every surface sparkles. On the breakfast bar is an A4 piece of paper on which he has scrawled a long list of instructions. I skim-read it quickly and check the pans to make sure I know exactly what I'm dealing with. Sure enough I find fillet steak chasseur, baby corn, mangetout and carrots sitting on the hob and a pan of fragrant rice all drained and ready to be heated. Inside the fridge, the melon and Parma ham is ready plated and a large chocolate mousse shimmers and wobbles in a silver dish. It looks so good it's all I can do not to dig in straight away.

I pour myself a celebration glass of white burgundy and set to following Ollie's instructions. Soon pans are bubbling merrily, Norah Jones is crooning softly and the fat white pillar candles in the fireplace are flickering romantically. I give myself a mental pat on the back, knock the wine back and take my new clothes into the bathroom. I feel like I'm wrapped in a warm, cosy bubble. Everything is going to be perfect, I just know it.

'Now,' I tell Pinchy, as I heap my jeans and sweater on the floor, 'make sure you keep really quiet tonight.'

Pinchy regards me beadily. He's not particularly vocal, which although it doesn't make for a very rewarding conversation, leaves me pretty confident that he'll go unnoticed. Instead he wiggles his antennae and does a leisurely lap of the bath.

'There!' I smooth down my new trousers and spray some Coco down my cleavage. 'What do you think? Pretty sexy, huh?'

But Pinchy's busy swimming and doesn't so much as even glance my way. Typical, even lobsters ignore me. Still, I decide as I fluff up my hair and pout at myself in the mirror, I look respectable. The hippy chick has been banished and in her place stands a demure-looking merchant banker's fiancée. Feeling pleased at this transformation, I pull the shower curtain around the bath and leave Pinchy to carry on his aqua-aerobics.

Another glass of wine later and I'm feeling a lovely alcohol-induced warmth and confidence. This is a bit of a balancing act, though. I want to stay at the stage where I feel like the most gorgeous creature on the planet, but I know that too much more will turn me into a burbling wreck. Tonight really isn't the night to get trolleyed.

'This smells wonderful.' James has crept up behind me and wraps his arms around my waist. His lips brush against my ear lobe, sending ripples of goose bumps down my arms. I melt against him and feel almost faint with relief. The cold war between us seems to be over, because he's been disarmed by the mouth-watering aromas of Ollie's cooking. 'You are clever, Chubs.'

Actually, I *am* clever. I can read *Beowulf* in the original and know all about trochaic feet, but James doesn't give a toss about that kind of stuff. What matters to him is having a wife who can cook and keep house.

He should have stuck to the *Beowulf*, because I'm seriously crap at the other things.

Still, I smile brightly and feel relieved I'm forgiven for upsetting Cordelia. 'It's nothing,' I say. 'It took me no time at all.' And I'm not exactly lying, am I?

'I'm sorry that I was so grumpy earlier,' James says, cupping my breasts in his hands and kissing my neck. I wait to feel a Mexican wave of desire, but it doesn't come, not even the teeniest tremor. It seems that even if my mind doesn't want to hold grudges, my body does.

'It's just I'm so stressed at the moment,' he continues, dropping feathery kisses on to my bare shoulder. 'This wedding is costing a fortune, and if I'm going to go places at Millwards and make serious money, then I really need this evening to go well.'

'But,' I venture, because this seems like a valid point to me, 'shouldn't they promote you because you're good at your job rather than because your fiancée can cook a nice meal?'

'It's all about image,' says James, giving up on trying to turn me on and helping himself to wine instead. 'The partners do an awful lot of networking and their wives have to play a part in that. If Julius is going to promote me, and,' James has a smug smile on his face, 'I rather think he will, he'll need to make sure that he has the entire package. We'll have to buy a bigger house, obviously, if we're entertaining, and make sure that you get the hang of what cutlery to use and what wines to serve. Corporate entertaining is a vital part of a wife's role. And this smells divine. I'm sure you'll be up to it.'

You know that bit in *Titanic* when the Kate Winslet character sees her life all mapped out for her and tries to fling herself off the back of the ship? Well, that's how I feel as I tend to the dinner and paste a rigor mortis smile on to my face. Can I really spend the rest of my life pretending to be somebody I'm not? I can't imagine that Ollie will be on hand to help me for the next forty years.

In spite of all my good intentions I pour another glass of wine. I'm going to have to tell James the truth about tonight or our marriage is going to be totally based on a lie.

'Darling—' I begin, but am rudely interrupted by the buzzer.

'I'll get it!' cries James. 'It's bound to be Julius; he was just behind me in the clubhouse.'

I give up and let him rush to the door. If he was a dog he'd be barking excitedly and wagging his tail. It looks like I'm going to have to lie through my teeth this evening and fess up later.

Oh what a tangled web . . .

'Katy!' cries James, bursting back into the kitchen. 'Julius and Helena are here!'

'How marvellous,' I trill, like a character from a Noël Coward play. 'How super to see you both!' and I air-kiss the twig-like Helena and try to do the same to Julius. Unfortunately Julius Millward is an old lech of the first order and manages to plant his wet rubbery lips on mine and give my bottom a squeeze. It's all I can do not to puke into the carrots.

'Something smells divine,' booms Julius as James pours him a glass of wine.

Helena is peeking into the pans.

'What's in this?' she demands, sniffing suspiciously. 'Is there cream in it? I can't eat dairy.'

'Um,' I say helplessly. I haven't a flipping clue what's in it.

Helena glares at the sauce. 'It looks like cream to me. And brandy? I can't drink alcohol, you know. I'm detoxing.'

I want to grab her head and ram it in the saucepan. Why on earth go to a dinner party if she's on a detox diet?

'Stick your detox diet up your arse, you raddled old bag,' I say.

Actually I don't say that but I'd like to. What I really say is a very apologetic mutter about how there's only a bit of cream in it, which could be true for all I know. Fortunately Julius saves the moment by booming that it's about time she had a 'bloody good feed' and whisking his wife away from the kitchen and into the sitting room. Then the doorbell shrills again and moments later I hear the haw-haw tones of Ed and Sophie Grenville.

Gritting my teeth so hard that I'm amazed they don't

shatter, I pick up the wine and glasses and force myself to be sociable.

'Katy!' Sophie brays, and we do the air-kissing thing. 'What a sweet little outfit! Where's it from, Agnès B?'

Something in Sophie, possibly the way she acts as though she's still head girl and about to banish me on to the lacrosse pitch, brings out the worst in me.

'Trousers from Topshop, jumper from House of Oxfam,' I tell her breezily and have the satisfaction of her hand recoiling from my shoulder. 'They have some real bargains. I'll have to show you.'

'Oh! Lovely,' says Sophie, as enthusiastically as though I'd asked her to eat worms for dinner.

James shoots me a look that I choose to ignore. Three glasses of wine have made me bold. Sod him.

'I'll get it!' I say brightly as the doorbell sounds again. 'That'll be Ollie and his dinner date.'

'No doubt some random tart,' I hear James say nastily. Sometimes I really don't like my fiancé very much, and I have a distinct feeling that now is one of those times.

I open the door and in bounds Sasha, all lolling pink tongue, drooling mouth and long ears. Definitely not the dinner date I had in mind.

'Are you mad?' I hiss. 'James hates dogs! He's allergic.'

Ollie fixes me with a steely gaze. 'I'm not leaving her on her own all evening, not when I've spent all day over here saving your neck. Especially not because of,' he practically spits the name, 'James.'

'Point taken.' I glance nervously at the sitting room door. 'Let's pop her into the office and she can sleep there.'

Ollie looks a bit put out but shoves Sasha into our tiny box-room-cum-office, where James's Mac beeps and whirs to itself on the desk surrounded by stacks of neat papers and his briefcase stands guard by the door. Apart from this, the room is pretty much bare. Surely a red setter can't do too much damage in here?

Ollie takes his coat off and puts it under the desk. 'Sasha! Lie down!'

Sasha obediently folds herself up like David Blaine in his glass box and pants hopefully up at us. I heave a sigh of relief.

'Good girl.' Ollie strokes her silky head and then gently shuts the door. For a few moments we stand in the hallway like nervous parents waiting to hear their baby cry. Then the doorbell sounds again and I practically shoot into orbit.

'Chill out!' Ollie's long legs stride to the door. 'That'll be my dinner date.'

I lean weakly against the wall. The strain of giving this dinner party must have added years to me, and we haven't even started eating yet. There's no way I can do this for the next forty years. I'd rather disembowel myself.

'Come in,' I hear Ollie cry. 'Thank God you could make it.'

In spite of myself, I crane my neck in order to see who has had the misfortune to fall for Ollie this time. Not that I care, obviously! But because I'm madly curious to see who could put up with Ollie's smelly socks, terrible taste in music and dribbly dog. Normally it's a willowy surf chick type with big boobs and a vacant gaze. I'd bet my month's salary that tonight is no different.

It's just as well I'm not a betting woman.

The creature that explodes into my narrow flat is certainly no surf chick. In fact it's no chick at all. It's a man.

Or at least I think it is.

'Darling,' trills a vision in flowing purple. 'I simply *adore* the trousers! Velvet flares! So retro! So Seventies!'

I goggle at him. I'm afraid I simply can't help it. I've never seen a man wearing lilac eye shadow and pink lipstick. Well, not since about 1985 anyway. And I've certainly never seen one wearing what looks like a purple cloak. Think Doctor and the Medics meets Michael Praed in his *Robin of Sherwood* days and you kind of get a picture of the vision standing before me looking more like a wacky entrant to the Big Brother house than a guest at a dinner party for stuffy merchant bankers.

It's Frankie. Ollie's cousin, lead singer of the Screaming Queens, camper than a Cath Kidston tent and on a mission to shock.

Shit.

'Hello, darling,' says my guest cheerfully. 'I've brought you a present.' Reaching beneath his cloak, he pulls out a giant cactus in a blue china pot. I eye it nervously. It looks lethal. New York street gangs' knives are blunter than the spikes on this two-foot monstrosity.

Frankie shoves the cactus into my arms, nearly turning me into a kebab. 'We got this especially for you.'

'It's a fiancé replacement for all the times yours is off playing golf,' explains Ollie, carefully turning the plant pot around to reveal my beloved's name daubed in fluorescent green paint. 'I think it's a vast improvement on the other giant prick called James.'

'Very funny,' I hiss. 'Bring a bottle of wine next time.'

'I adore giant pricks,' wheezes Frankie, whose mascara is starting to run. 'Can't wait to meet the real James.'

'Now's your chance,' grins Ollie, and sure enough James is emerging from the sitting room looking to refill glasses.

Before he spots James the Cactus and all hell breaks loose, I reverse swiftly into our bedroom and kick the door shut.

I am going to bloody kill Ollie. I might have known he'd pull a stunt like this. Talk about shaking up the evening.

As I hide the cactus beneath the pile of coats on the bed, I think murderous thoughts about what I'll do to Ollie when I can get my hands on him.

En route back to the sitting room I take a detour via the kitchen and help myself to another glass of wine. Something tells me that nothing except getting plastered will get me through this evening.

'So,' Frankie is saying, gesticulating wildly with purple-tipped fingers and looking in the midst of my soberly dressed guests like a parrot who's swooped in to have a chat with the local sparrows, 'I quit my job to set up my own rock band.'

'Really?' says Ed, who appears quite curious.

'I've got my demo disc with me.' Frankie delves into his robes and pulls out a CD. 'Shall we put it on?'

James, looking murderous, takes the disc, and seconds later Norah Jones is replaced by a din that sounds like hyenas playing the saucepans. Ears are practically bleeding.

'Isn't it awesome!' says Ollie, and the worrying thing is he's being sincere. 'The Queens are going to be huge.'

'Suck on it, baby!' shrieks Frankie, eyes closed and lost in rhythm. 'Give it to me hard!'

James presses the stop button and abruptly there's an awkward silence.

'Shall we eat?' I say brightly. 'James, would you help me with the starters, darling?'

'What the fuck is going on?' spits James as he bundles

me into the kitchen. 'Are you deliberately trying to ruin my chances?'

'Don't blame me!' I protest, delving into our fridge and passing the starters to him. If he's got his hands full I figure he can't punch Ollie. 'I didn't know he was going to invite Frankie.'

'You invited bloody Ollie,' James growls, 'so I hold you totally responsible. Just make sure you keep him under control.'

The words 'or else' hang heavy in the air and I gulp nervously. I have a lobster in the bath, a loony red setter in the office and the lead singer of the Screaming Queens in my sitting room. These things do not bode well.

I lay out the starters and everyone makes polite conversation. James and I try to join in, but our 'darlings' and 'sweethearts' are positively glacial and you couldn't cut the atmosphere with a chainsaw, never mind a knife. Frankie is telling an outrageous story about one of his band members, Sophie and Helena are planning a trip to the Sanctuary and James is trying to talk business with Julius, easier said than done over Frankie's excited cries and actions. I stab at my starter and wish it was a voodoo melon. Ollie would be rolling around clutching his guts. God knows, it feels like the entire cast of *Riverdance* is warming up in mine.

We move on to the main course, and I have to admit Ollie has done an excellent job. Frankie is too busy eating to make outrageous comments and Julius compliments me on my culinary skills. Helena pointedly restricts herself to vegetables. Well, it's her loss. Ollie might behave like a fiend but he cooks like an angel. The steak melts on my tongue and the sauce explodes across my taste buds. Julius hoovers up seconds and even James looks mollified. Perhaps I'm going to get away with it.

But in my past life I must have been totally evil, because karma is about to come back with a double whammy. Nipping to the loo, bladder overflowing with wine, I peek round the curtains to check on Pinchy.

Who isn't there.

Fuck.

I sink on to the loo seat feeling cold all over at the thought of a nine-pound lobster on the loose in my flat. Where on earth has it gone, the ungrateful creature? I'm starting to wish I'd let Ollie boil it alive. Lobster Thermidor has never seemed so appealing.

OK, I tell myself as I try to breathe slowly and get my heart rate down to a less cardiac-arrest-inducing rhythm. This is a small flat and that's one big mama of a lobster. There are only so many places it can be. It's pretty hard to lose a lobster.

Or at least I bloody hope it is.

With any luck it's crawled into a corner somewhere and died. Or hibernated. Or whatever lobsters do in their spare time.

Escaping from the loo, I sneak into the kitchen and neck Chardonnay from the bottle. There's no time for wine glasses when Pinchy's on the loose. All my resolutions about not getting pissed have gone down the toilet, where I sincerely hope Pinchy has also gone. Then I attack the cheeseboard. Sod the calories; at this rate I'm not even likely to live long enough to worry. Selecting a lovely runny Brie, I whack a load on to a cracker, cram it into my mouth and chomp gratefully.

Chubster? Moi?

'There you are!' wheezes Julius Millard, standing in the

doorway and leering at me. As he speaks he wags a finger. 'Eating all the Brie, you naughty little minx!'

Christ! I'm not the only one who's pissed. Julius advances like the Severn Bore and pins me against the Aga, obviously convinced that I'm totally up for it. Never in the history of the planet has anyone been more mistaken. But I'm in a tricky position, and not just because the Aga is burning a hole in my velvet flares. Do I tell Julius to piss off and risk him giving Ed the promotion out of spite, or do I bite my lip and think of England?

Actually, isn't that called prostitution?

While I'm deliberating and Julius is all but licking his lips, there's a sudden roar from down the corridor. At least I think it's a roar, although perhaps it's a scream. In any case I'm saved because Julius jumps backwards like Skippy.

'What the hell?' I hear James yell, and then more ominously, 'Katy!'

'Excuse me!' I say brightly, ducking under Julius's arm. 'I think James needs me.'

My fiancé is standing in the office doorway, his face absolutely puce with rage because our minimalist box room has been transformed Laurence Llewelyn-Bowen style into Narnia. And I don't mean lampposts and wardrobes. James's office is white with paper. Scraps flutter in the stirred air and drift down like home-made ticker tape. The laminate floor is hidden beneath sheets and sheets of paper, James's Apple Mac is upside down beeping feebly and the Italian leather briefcase looks as though it's been attacked by Godzilla.

Right in the middle of all this chaos sits Sasha, chocolate eyes wide and innocent and plumy tail thumping with the joy of having her exile interrupted by so many visitors. I'm not going to point out that maybe she's been

66

bored and lonely because, quite frankly, I don't think James will give a damn.

Hanging from Sasha's drooling mouth are the remains of a blue file; the blue file that contained the report James has slaved over for weeks. The report that he was going to present to Julius tonight to prove just what an amazing partner he'd make. When I think of the hours that have gone into that report *I* feel sick, so goodness only knows how James must feel.

'I can explain!' I say quickly, putting my hand on his arm, but James shakes me off like I'm plague-ridden.

'Don't bother,' he hisses.

'But Ollie really helped me and—'

'I said don't bother!' James spins on his heel and stalks down the hallway, self-righteous anger dripping from every pore. The bedroom door slams.

'Oh dear!' says Sophie, so loudly that lost tribes in the Amazon rainforest reach for ear plugs. 'Was that the Amos and Amos report? Fancy leaving it in such a vulnerable position when it's so important. My Edward would never have done that.'

'Absolutely not,' agrees Helena. 'And I'm sure you would have made certain your dog was well trained, unlike that brute.'

'She's not a brute,' snaps Ollie. 'She was bored.'

'Know how she feels,' drawls Frankie. 'Shall I skin up?'

I want to disappear, wish myself on the moon, anywhere but here.

Julius Millward peers into the office in confusion.

'Darling,' gasps Helena gleefully. 'You'll never guess what James has done!'

'James didn't do it,' I point out. 'This is my fault.'

Helena fixes me with a steely glare. 'The wife of a

67

Millwards executive should support her husband, Katy. Her role is to be his helpmeet.'

Just as I'm about to tell her to stick the 1950s wife act up her arse, there's another howl from James. Only this time it's pain rather than rage.

'My God!' splutters Julius, as my fiancé ricochets out of the bedroom. 'Whatever's going on?'

It's a fair question, because James is leaping up and down and clutching his backside. Julius, Helena and Sophie stare at him, mouths opening and shutting like goldfish. Closer inspection reveals that hundreds of tiny spines are firmly embedded in the seat of his suit.

I glance across at Ollie, who meets my eyes guiltily. James the Human has just had a close encounter with James the Cactus, and I am holding my friend totally and utterly responsible.

'Chubs!' James is shouting. 'Why is there a giant cactus in our bed?'

I open my mouth to explain but for once am lost for words. Unlike Frankie, who is howling with laughter.

Julius drains of colour.

'I think we should leave,' he says. 'This is a lunatic asylum.'

'There's no need,' I say hastily. 'It's all a misunderstanding. I can explain.'

'You don't need to,' snaps Julius. 'I can see exactly what's going on. You're a disgrace.'

'*I'm* a disgrace? What have I done?'

'Inviting these . . . these . . .' Julius gestures at Frankie and Ollie. 'These faggots! Drinking yourself into a stupor and trying to make a pass at me in the kitchen.'

'I'm not gay!' squeaks Ollie.

I stare at Julius Millward in amazement. 'Why would I make a pass at you?'

'For the promotion, I presume,' he says.

'That's bollocks! You trapped me in the kitchen! He did!' I try to catch James's eye but he looks away.

'Your behaviour's shocking,' snaps Julius. 'How could I possibly trust James to entertain Millward Saville's clients after tonight? You're not the sort of wife I'd expect one of my partners to choose.'

'James is marrying me because he loves me! Not because he needs someone to entertain his clients,' I tell Julius. 'Right, James?'

James remains silent, studying the hall floor intently.

Oh. Maybe not, then.

'Fetch your coat, Helena,' barks Julius.

'I'll get it,' creeps Sophie.

'And you,' adds Julius, glaring at James, yellowy moustache bristling in indignation, 'had better think carefully about the type of people you associate with if you want to get anywhere at Millwards.'

'Julius, please,' pleads James, dragging his attention away from the parquet floor. 'It's all a misunderstanding.'

Is it? Abruptly the room starts to spin and roll and I realise that I am in fact very drunk indeed.

'Actually, it's not.' I tell him, suddenly feeling very brave. With the exception of Ollie and even Frankie, I can't bear these people. They are a bunch of . . . tossers! Why am I so worried about what they think of me? Why can't they just laugh and enjoy themselves? Sasha didn't deliberately sabotage the report; I didn't make James sit on a cactus. I sneak a look at him trying to subtly pluck spikes out of his trousers and bite back a giggle. This is *really* funny! What's the matter with them all?

I try hard not to laugh, but when Sophie hands Helena her Louis Vuitton tote and a crimson claw pokes out, practically giving her the V, I can't contain myself any more. Laughter bubbles up like a geyser.

'We're leaving,' barks Julius. 'I can't spend another minute in this madhouse. Young man,' he adds to James, 'if you want promotion and to move in the right circles, I suggest you find yourself a more suitable fiancée!'

The room is rocking now, dipping and rolling like crazy. I feel liberated, rebellious and strong.

And maybe just a little bit pissed . . .

My legs buckle and I slither to the floor, tears rolling down my cheeks as I watch the claw waving jauntily at me.

'Bag,' I gasp, pointing. 'Your bag!'

'How dare you call me a bag? I've never been so insulted in all my life!' shrieks Helena.

'Really?' mutters Ollie.

'Your bag!' I wheeze again, clutching the stitch in my side. 'Not *you're* a bag, *your* bag!'

But I'm drowned out by the strains of Helena screaming blue bloody murder as she discovers the stowaway. Julius Millward turns purple with rage, James is prostrate with horror and Frankie's laughing so hard that his mascara drips on to the floor. The hall starts to shift and buck like a fairground ride and I close my eyes giddily. Abruptly everything goes black.

Which is probably just as well.

Chapter Five

I'm dying.

Seriously, I'm pretty sure I'm on my way to meet my maker. Or, knowing my luck lately, I'm off to the other place.

Anyway, I hope the end comes soon because it feels like somebody is driving a JCB around my skull and scooping out huge slushy wodges of brain. And just for good measure they've got a pneumatic drill going too, somewhere just above my left eye, in a relentless beating rhythm. So much for all that being half in love with easeful death Keats bollocks, this feels like the Terminator has come round to practise on me.

'Oh God,' I moan, grinding my knuckles into my eyes. 'Take me now.'

'I'm not sure that anyone would want to take you now, darling,' drawls an amused voice. 'You look a fright.'

I'm not alone?

Cautiously I stretch out my arm and sure enough my fingers encounter warm flesh. Warm, breathing *male* flesh.

What have I done?

'Oooh!' squeaks the random male lying next to me. 'Hands off, you naughty girl!'

The penny doesn't so much drop as plummet to earth and blast my death fantasy into a million pieces. Scenes from last night's dinner party replay themselves through my mind like a horrible trailer for a disaster movie – the disaster movie that tells the story of me wrecking my relationship, James's promotion and, let's be honest, my entire world in general.

Oh God. I'd *rather* be dying. Please, let the earth swallow me right now. Let my bed go up in flames, anything rather than waking up and facing the fact that I've ruined my life.

I screw my eyes up tightly and wait for a thunderbolt to strike me, but sadly there's bugger all response to my desperate prayers. Peeling back concrete-heavy eyelids, I prepare myself to face a day that's surely number one in the top ten of Katy Carter's crappiest days.

'Morning!' chirrups Frankie. 'You look fucking awful.'

I'm not surprised because, quite honestly, fucking awful is *exactly* how I feel. I can't reply either because somebody's superglued my tongue to the roof of my mouth. But Frankie looks great. His skin was cleansed, toned and moisturised before sleeping and his eyes are puppy bright. Even if I lived in a vat of Crème de la Mer for a year I could never look that good, especially not after drinking as much as he did.

It's official. God is a gay bloke.

I close my eyes and groan. I pray that this is all a hideous dream and in a minute I'll wake up with James nagging me about going to the gym rather than cooking a lardy bacon sandwich.

I open my eyes again, but life is not that kind. I am indeed in Ollie's spare room and sharing a bed with a gay singing sensation. Last night really did happen then.

Shit.

Katy Carter hits rock bottom and is starting to dig.

'Morning!' The bedroom door bursts open and in bounds Ollie with Sasha bouncing at his heels. The smell of bacon wafts in too, and in spite of my monster headache my mouth starts to water. Ollie knows just how much I love my bacon sandwiches and many a drinking session has ended with us making an Everest-sized pile of them. He'll make some girl a great husband, even though the fact that he too is all shiny and lively after a night of constant drinking makes me want to throttle him. Nobody deserves to be that effervescent after practically swimming in alcohol.

'How are you feeling?' asks Ollie.

'Duh!' says Frankie, sitting up and clutching the duvet to his (waxed) chest. 'Just look at the poor girl. I've seen healthier corpses.'

'Oh dear, that bad?' commiserates Ollie, depositing the sandwiches on the windowsill and cruelly ripping the curtains open. Even the British weather decides to flick a V at me and the room is instantly flooded with beams of golden sunshine. Dracula confronted with daytime couldn't be in more haste to hide from the light than me burrowing under the duvet, my brain swivelling most unpleasantly inside my skull in perfect time with my churning stomach. If my Year 11s could see me now, they'd be put off drinking for life. I am a whole new course in Personal and Social Education.

Ollie plucks the duvet from the bed and waves a bacon sandwich under my nose. 'No use hiding away in here. It's time to get up and face the music.'

'Leave me alone, you bastard.'

'Eat me! Eat me!' squeaks Ollie as the sandwich is shoved under my nose again. I wish I could resist it. Bet Millandra would. But sadly I'm not a delicate romantic heroine but a chunky flesh-and-blood Katy Carter with a raging hangover and a ruined life to boot. In spite of my broken heart and churning stomach, I start to laugh.

'Can't I even die in peace?' I complain. 'Oh, go on then. Give me a sandwich. Or two.'

'Not for me,' shudders Frankie as though confronted with boiled brains rather than Denmark's finest. 'No carbs.'

'All the more for us then,' says Ollie cheerfully, tossing some bacon at Sasha, and we chomp contentedly for a while. 'Better?' he asks eventually.

I nod, and thankfully my brain stays in one place. Ollie always knows how to cure my hangovers. No one looks after me like Ol, although he's not quite off the hook yet for last night's debacle.

Once the sandwiches are finished and I've drained several mugs of tea, I start to feel vaguely human. I'll be mainlining Alka-Seltzer all day but at least I'm recovering my speech and vision. All I have to do now is trundle over to Ealing, grovel to James and everything will be fine. He'll be pissed off for a bit but eventually he'll come round. Everyone makes mistakes, right?

'Er, nice idea,' says Ollie doubtfully when I reveal this cunning plan. 'But maybe you should give him some time. He was a bit angry last night.'

'A bit angry?' cries Frankie. 'He was breathing fire. Thank goodness I managed to save the lobster.'

'That lobster was to eat,' Ollie points out, 'and wouldn't life have been easier if we'd cooked it? The bloody thing's in my bath now; it must have had more long soaks than Cleopatra.'

'That ghastly woman practically fainted when she found it in her bag. I honestly thought her husband was going to

74

hit James,' recalls Frankie. 'But we can't blame Pinchy. He was only exploring.'

'It's not *Pinchy* I blame,' I say darkly.

'So it's my fault James is a knob?' Ollie runs his hands through his hair until it stands on end. 'How do you figure that out?'

'You know exactly what I mean.' I haul myself out of bed and catch a glimpse of my grim reflection in the mirror. My velvet flares are creased and my make-up wouldn't look out of place on Alice Cooper. Although my legs feel like boiled string and I will possibly scare small children, I'm determined to go back home and pour an enormous tankerload of oil on to the troubled waters of my relationship. James loves me, right? We'll probably laugh about this when we're old and grey. If I can eat humble pie for Cordelia, then I'm more than capable of having seconds and thirds for the man I love.

'You're mad.' Ollie shakes his head. 'Absolutely bloody bonkers. You're lucky you passed out last night, that's all I can say. James was ready to kill you.'

OK. So James wants to taste blood, preferably me-flavoured. I know how much last night meant to him so I can understand he's a bit annoyed.

'A bit annoyed?' echoes Ollie when I repeat this train of thought aloud. 'He threw you out! Why do you think you're here? We wouldn't have wrestled a mad drunken woman into a cab and watched her spew all the way here out of choice.'

Actually the thought of why I wasn't at the flat hadn't even occurred. Whenever I'm in trouble I end up with Ollie. I cock up and he looks after me. That's how it's always been. Waking up in Ollie's house is par for the course after a drunken night out.

'Was James very mad?' I ask, a question that is on a level with wondering if the earth is round. Katy messes up and James gets angry. It's practically one of the laws of physics.

'Mad? He was fucking furious! Especially when you puked all over the seagrass matting in the bathroom,' recalls Frankie.

My blood runs cold. James *loves* the seagrass matting. It took him months to choose the exact shade and texture that he required. Personally I find it rather scratchy, but hey! Like he says, it's just as well I have him to guide me, because what do I know about style?

'All that fuss over a carpet.' Ollie looks bemused. Carpets to him are there to collect crumbs and random bits of fluff. Sometimes they might get hoovered if a transitory girlfriend can bear it no longer, but otherwise they just cover the floor to be walked over, not cried over.

Frankie raises an eyebrow. 'Darling, are you sure he's not gay?'

I ignore them. Of course James isn't gay. Just because he doesn't want sex very often and likes interior design doesn't mean he's gay. Probably if I was thinner we'd have shedloads of red-hot shagging. And if interior design is only for gay men, then who on earth goes to IKEA at the weekend?

Actually, who *does* choose to go to IKEA at the weekend?

'I'm going home to apologise,' I say with great dignity, or at least as much dignity as somebody who looks like a missing member of Kiss can muster. 'I let James down and it was a disaster. And you,' I give Ollie a steely gaze, 'did not help.'

Ollie opens his mouth, presumably to repeat his point about James being a twat/wanker/dickhead, but catches the expression on my face and shuts it quickly. Not for nothing can I teach bottom sets and terrify kids twice as tall as me.

'Maybe Sasha wasn't such a great guest,' he admits, following me as I clomp down the stairs. 'And perhaps I was trying to stir things up a bit by inviting Frankie.'

'I heard that!' carols Frankie.

My coat is hooked over the banister. Studiously ignoring Ollie, I shrug myself into it. I am so out of here. I am on a mission. I will grovel like no one has ever grovelled and I will save my relationship.

Because, says a nasty little voice inside my head, what else have you got without it?

'You deliberately set out to make trouble because you know how stuffy Julius Millward is. How could you, Ollie? I told you how important that dinner party was and you went out of your way to wreck it. You're meant to be my *friend*.'

'Katy!' Ollie grabs my arm and pulls me around to face him. His hands clasp my upper arms tightly and he draws me close until my face is just inches from his. Any closer and that dark stubble would graze my cheeks.

Millandra found herself most powerfully drawn towards Jake. As he clasped her in his manly arms her heart beat so fast within her tender breast—

I give myself a mental shake. Ollie is no Jake. Ollie is about as far removed from a romantic hero as it's possible to get. He burps, he leaves the loo seat up, he thinks *Dad's Army* is funny, he wears glasses for reading . . . I could go on and on and on.

Still, I often forget just how strong he is. Surfing and skiing build muscles that marking books never touch.

'James treats you like crap,' says Ollie bluntly. 'You're

77

an utter doormat and it's about time you realised it. He's a snob, he's shallow, he's egotistical, he's vain and I know I've said it before but what the fuck? He's an utter, utter wanker.'

'You don't like him then?' I try to joke, but Ol isn't in the mood to laugh.

'He's spent so long telling you how crap you are that you actually believe the shit he's fed you,' he continues. 'I've seen you losing what shreds of confidence you do have and I can't watch it for a minute longer. He's not some storybook hero, Katy, he's just a knob, so for Christ's sake, dump the tosser.'

I gape at him.

'And he's only interested in you for the money,' adds Ollie. 'All James cares about is cash.'

Ah yes. The money.

Obviously *I* have no money. Have *you* ever met a rich teacher? I make church mice look like the Beckhams. What Ollie means is that Auntie Jewell is seriously loaded and has always loved to make extravagant comments about her will. But no one ever takes her seriously.

At least I don't think they do . . .

'You're being ridiculous,' I say.

'Am I? Didn't Jewell lend James ten grand shortly before you got engaged?'

'There was a perfectly good reason. James's share portfolio hadn't performed well enough to buy my ring.'

'He's a merchant bloody banker!' hollers Ollie. 'He earns more cash in a week than we do in six months. Why would he need to borrow more?'

I can't answer, but put it this way, my credit-card bills aren't the only ones stashed under the kitchen sink.

'James sees you as the perfect opportunity,' ploughs on

Ollie with all the tact of a charging rhinoceros with extra-thick skin. 'It's bloody obvious. He thinks you're going to inherit her estate. He can't wait to get his greasy mitts on that house in Hampstead.'

'That's bollocks! Besides, it's a bit of a long-term game plan.'

'Is it?' Ollie shrugs. 'It seems to me that his cash-flow problems would be solved a bit too easily by good old Auntie Jewell.'

I glare at him, wishing I'd had my tongue removed at birth. Why did I ever tell Ollie about James's cash-flow problems? Ol's an English teacher – what does he know about futures and options and gilt-edged stocks?

Well, about the same as me probably, but that's not the point, is it? Like James says, financial markets are uncertain and at times he has to take risks. Jewell's always been happy to help out. She even buys shares from him sometimes.

'Sorry if it's harsh,' says Ollie, mistaking my silence for agreement, 'but it's time you woke up and smelled the coffee. They call this tough love.'

Bloody Ollie and his addiction to 'let it all hang out' talk shows. When Jerry Springer came to the UK I was in a state of terror for weeks. I wouldn't put it past Ollie to drag me on to some show entitled 'Hey, girlfriend! You're in love with a wanker!' just for the sheer and bloody hell of it.

'James thinks he's engaged to his own personal cash-point. He must have been jumping for joy that day he met you again and you took him to Jewell's party. No wonder he proposed.'

'Thanks a lot,' I say.

'It had to be said.'

'No it didn't!' To my dismay, hot tears are prickling against my eyelids and I've got a nasty golf ball of a lump in my throat. 'You didn't have to tell me a man would only want me because I've got a generous godmother and might inherit some money one day.'

I swallow back the tears and concentrate instead on pulling on my boots. The laces writhe in my fingers so I give up and just tuck them in. Hopefully I'll trip as I walk out and break my neck. Then he'll be sorry.

'That wasn't what I said!'

'Yes it was.' I'm making a break for the door, sprinting away so quickly that I must surely be a likely contender for the 2012 athletics squad. 'That's *exactly* what you said. I'm so crap and useless and ugly and fat that no man would ever want me. I'd have to bribe them with an inheritance, that's exactly what you said.'

'I didn't say that.' Ollie looks confused. 'I never said you're fat or ugly or crap. I think you're confusing me with your charming fiancé.'

'Shut up, Ollie!' Bugger, I'm crying now. How very annoying. I wish I was one of those feisty types who do a mean line in cold and dignified anger, culminating in some dastardly revenge. It's just my luck that when I get mad I end up looking like a tree frog. 'At least now I know exactly what you think of me.'

The door swings open and then I'm running down the path, shoving open the rotten gate and hotfooting it along the pavement. It's not easy to run in my unlaced boots but I'm giving it my best shot.

Ollie makes to follow but is minutes behind because he's desperately trying to locate any shoes Sasha hasn't destroyed and ensure that his flapping dressing gown is secured. Mrs Sandhu next door is peeking out from behind her net curtain at this high drama and is more than ready to be outraged. In any case, I've got precious minutes on him, which I need because, let's face it, I'm about as athletic as an arthritic slug. If I have to run much further I'll probably have a severe heart attack, but it'll be a happy release. My breath comes in short, painful gasps and there's not so much a stitch as an entire seam in my left side.

Next new year I really will honour that resolution to get fit and join the gym. I'll go with James and faithfully compare myself to the Caramac-tanned clones pounding the machines like well-toned zombies. I'll soon be one myself.

Then let's watch Ollie eat his words.

And, obviously, James will be pleased too.

Coming towards me is the 207 bus, my ticket out of here, and I fling myself towards it with a speed and energy that would really impress the PE staff at Sir Bob's. The only time I normally move this fast is to beat the kids to the canteen. Many a Year 11 has been taken aback to see a fogey teacher run so fast in platform boots.

'Katy!' Ollie whips around the corner of Milford Road like the Road Runner. 'Wait! I didn't mean it the way you think. What I meant was—'

But his words are lost in the rumble of the bus's wheels and the chug of its engine. For a split second I'm torn between hurling myself on board and listening to what he has to say. Ol isn't known for being cruel, although Pinchy might beg to differ, and rowing with him feels wrong. On the other hand, the ease with which he's assumed James can't find any other reason to be with me apart from the vague notion that I might inherit some money is really hurtful.

Besides, I'm in the right here. Time to occupy the moral high ground.

I leap on board and the doors hiss shut behind me. I pant and puff for a second or two, take a blast on an inhaler offered by an old lady, hurl myself on to a seat and wait for the bus to whisk me away to Ealing.

Ollie reaches it just as it pulls away from the kerb.

His mouth is opening and shutting like a telly on mute and I just about decipher my name. His chestnut hair is blowing in the wind, his feet are bare and he's even forgotten to put his glasses on. God only knows how he's made it this far.

'Go away!' I mouth and my breath steams up the glass.

But Ollie is jogging alongside the bus now, his dressing gown flapping dangerously.

'Oh my!' gasps the old lady next to me, eyes like saucers firmly fixed on his lower regions, and takes a series of puffs on the inhaler. I daren't look.

'I don't think you're crap!' yells Ollie, dropping back as the bus gathers pace down the Uxbridge Road. 'I've never thought that! I think you're—'

But now we're too far ahead and all I can see as I crane my neck to keep a glimpse of him, tanned and strong and quite frankly ridiculous in his blue and white striped dressing gown, is a rapidly diminishing figure whose mouth is still shouting words that fall heavy like stones in the crisp morning air.

I sink into the seat and close my eyes. The headache starts to beat at my left temple and I am ridiculously close to tears again. My fiancé hates me and my friend thinks I'm a loser.

The moral high ground feels like a very lonely place.

Chapter Six

'And take that with you too!'

Thud! A black dustbin sack lands by my feet and joins the other twelve that I've already discovered sitting by the steps to my flat. James has had a very busy and cathartic evening chucking out everything I own.

'I'm sorry!' I shout up to the kitchen window where every now and again James's head bobs past, en route to find more of my belongings. 'Just let me in so that we can talk about it.'

'What's to talk about?' James appears at the window and glowers down at me. 'Julius has given Ed the promotion. I'll be lucky if I even have a fucking job after your marvellous little performance last night, so no, Katy, we have nothing to talk about. I'm even more in the shit now, thanks to you.'

Whoosh! Another bag takes flight and whizzes past my ear. As it lands there's a horrible crunching sound. I jump back hastily. James is still very pissed off with me then.

'But I didn't mean it!' I wail. 'I'd never do anything to hurt you on purpose. Last night was an accident.'

'Accident?' James laughs; a horrible, mirthless sound. 'That's a first. Your idiot friend's dog ruins my report, you have a lobster roaming the flat, you invite some random queer, you make a pass at Julius, you puke on the seagrass . . .'

I knew the sodding seagrass was going to come into it somewhere.

'. . . you tell Helena she's an old bag—'

'I didn't! I was trying to tell her Pinchy was in her bag.'

'Don't discuss semantics with me!' shrieks James. 'You're a teacher in a shitty sink school, remember? Not a barrister. I heard what you said. And then there's this!'

He vanishes for a second before lobbing another object at me. I step back hastily and thank God I do because I practically have my eye put out by James the Cactus. As I recover from nearly becoming a kebab, I feel relieved that Ollie and Frankie had the foresight to rescue Pinchy. I don't fancy the thought of the Arnold Schwarzenegger of the lobster world being hurled at me.

'That nearly hit me!'

'Shame it didn't,' spits James, chucking my platform boots over the window ledge. 'Let's see if my aim is getting better.'

Ten bums in a row, I think as I duck behind our green wheelie bin; he really means it. There's no way I'm going to be able to grovel and beg forgiveness while he's set on using me for target practice. My second cunning plan was to offer him a placatory blow job, but since this is now physically impossible, things are looking pretty grim. As I cower in the kerb with all my worldly goods raining down around me, it suddenly occurs to me that I am well and truly in trouble.

Maybe Ollie had a point. Perhaps this isn't such a good idea.

I started to have my doubts as the bus wound its way along the Uxbridge Road and away from Ollie. By

Hanwell I'd started to chew my nails; by West Ealing I was longing for a cigarette; and once the bus stopped at Allington Crescent I was trembling. Already traumatised because I had no change for the fare and had to resort to delving into the lining of my jacket to scrape out the few coins that had made their way inside, and still smarting from Ollie's pearls of wisdom, I'd begun to lose my conviction that James would welcome me back with open arms. I was the veteran of many sad and snively nights on the sofa and fully prepared for being yelled at/cold-shouldered/made to grovel, but being pelted by my own belongings?

This never happens in Mills and Boon. I know exactly how it *should* go. I knock on the door, cry prettily, James melts and takes me into his manly hero's arms. Right?

Er, no. Wrong, apparently.

'Forgive me, Jake,' gasped Millandra, tears like perfect diamonds slipping down her peachy cheeks. 'Forgive me for giving away your hiding place to the evil Sir Oliver. I swear that I am no spy.'

Jake folded his arms against his strong chest.

'How can I ever trust you again?' he grated. 'Because of you a good man had his neck stretched at Tyburn today. How do I know you haven't been sent to lead me to my doom?'

'Because I love you!' she sobbed, sinking in grief to the tips of his riding boots.

Above her tightly laced corset, Millandra's pert breasts heaved with passion. In spite of his anger, Jake felt his desire stir. Reaching down, he took her small hand and pulled her against him,

'Oh God,' he groaned into her soft hair. 'You drive me wild.'

That's what's supposed to happen between a romantic

hero and heroine after their major falling-out. I should know because I've read just about every bloody romantic novel there is, from the Brontës right through to Jilly Cooper, and I think I can be forgiven for feeling cheated. I don't remember the bit where Mr Darcy threw a cactus at Elizabeth Bennet, and I've never taught the scene where Romeo chucks Juliet out of the Montagues' pad.

This isn't supposed to happen! James is supposed to be *my* romantic hero.

James is slowing down, presumably running out of things to launch into orbit, so I peek out from behind the wheelie bin. An impressive collection of my belongings clutters up the pavement and my handbag has burst open, the contents spewing out like tatty entrails. Thank goodness my phone's survived its fall from grace. The pink casing is cracked but the screen's still working and tells me I have six missed calls. I can never resist my phone, and even though I'm in the middle of a relationship meltdown, I simply *have* to check. Ollie has called me five times and left five messages, which I delete without listening, and Maddy, my best friend from uni, has called me once. I feel a twinge of guilt. I haven't called her for weeks. Not because I haven't wanted to, but I've just been so busy. I love Mads. Totally and utterly adore her. She's zany and impulsive and a law unto herself, and from the moment we both arrived as terrified freshers to settle into our small rooms in a truly gruesome 1960s' tower block, I knew that I'd found a kindred spirit.

I won't call her right now because Maddy can talk for England and I'll need a lovely gossipy rant a bit later on. Failing that, I may have to hotfoot it over to Lewisham and plead for a bed for the night, because it doesn't look like James is about to change his mind.

There's only one problem with this option, though. I get the feeling Maddy's husband, Richard, isn't desperately keen on me.

OK. I'll be honest. I don't get Richard and Richard certainly doesn't get me. We trust each other about as much as Tom and Jerry. Richard thinks I'm a bad influence on Mads and I just don't know how to deal with him. At uni Maddy was wild. She snogged our lecturers, stayed up all night to produce a term's worth of essays and even kidnapped the Dean for rag week. She drank like a fish, baked exquisite space cakes and dated a string of totally unsuitable but wildly exciting men. For three years life was a crazy whirl of parties, snogging, sobbing over useless men and attending the occasional lecture when we managed to tear ourselves away from *This Morning*. Whereas I just scuttled in her wake, Mads was the original party animal, always up for a laugh and always thinking of crazy things to do.

Which is why I was gobsmacked when she married a vicar.

Don't get me wrong. I don't have a problem with religion or church particularly. Mads loves Richard to bits so I don't have a problem with that either. It's just that the vicar's wife thing was never what I thought she'd do. Richard is ten years older than us and really committed to his job, which means Mads has to be too. She has to cook dinners, teach Sunday school and be nice to the bizarre parishioners who knock on the rectory door at all hours. Richard doesn't party, doesn't drink, doesn't smoke, doesn't swear and has the unfortunate habit of asking me how I stand with God, a question that's pretty hard to answer for a girl who doesn't even know how she stands with her bank manager. Although Mads has never said much, I get the feeling that the Reverend Richard Lomax doesn't approve of me, so if I turn up with my umpteen plastic bin bags, pet lobster and tales of dinner-party woe, I strongly suspect his sympathy will be with James. Maddy, bless her, hasn't changed at all (apart from the bonking of random men, I hope!) and is still lovely, fun and totally scatty. Maybe Richard has taken that exhausting manic edge off her and perhaps she's loosened him up a bit? It seems to work for them anyway.

So their rectory in Lewisham is my last resort. Not only is it so brimming with visiting troubled souls that it makes the M25 look a peaceful option, but I don't really want to discuss my failings in front of Richard. He already thinks I don't tell the truth to James. 'You're not big on honesty in relationships, are you, Katy?' he once commented when I was frantically trying to get James's Audi fixed so that he had no idea I'd a) borrowed it and b) pranged it, and raised a cool eyebrow when I pointed out that I wasn't lying, just not telling James the *whole* truth.

Hmm. Something tells me that if I step over the threshold of the rectory today I'm in serious danger of spontaneously combusting.

I'll just give James one more try. He can't seriously want to throw away all those years just because of one rubbish dinner party. I know he loves me really. Why else would he have stayed with me so long?

Going forward more boldly than Captain Kirk, I make my way towards the front door and press the buzzer hard.

'What?' snaps James from three storeys above.

'Let me in,' I plead. 'I'm really sorry. Let me explain.'

'There's nothing to explain,' James replies in a tone so icy that my lips are all but frozen to the speakerphone.

'Julius Millward made it perfectly clear. It's you or my position at the bank.'

What?

WHAT?

I can hardly believe my ears. 'You've chosen that lechy old bastard over the woman you love?'

'Sorry, Chubs,' shrugs my (ex)-fiancé. 'But I didn't really have much choice, did I? I can't afford to lose my job.'

'But you can afford to lose me?'

The following silence speaks volumes and my eyes fill with tears. He's made his choice then.

'Fine,' I say, my throat tight with tears. 'I understand.' But I don't. How could he switch from loving me to throwing me out? Even the wind changes less rapidly than that. Jake would *never* abandon Millandra so carelessly. He'd tell Julius to shove his job up his backside or challenge him to a duel.

'By the way,' adds James, 'could you post the ring through the door? Since you've screwed up my promotion, I'll have to settle some of our bills another way.'

I glance down at my engagement finger. Sure enough there is my whopper of a ring, a mass of glittery diamonds that all but screams 'Mug me!' when I stroll along Ealing Broadway. I can't say that I ever really liked it, but James insisted that we went to Asprey's and he loved the ring, so to tell him that I really wanted the little emerald one I'd seen in the antique shop seemed a bit ungrateful. And he loved showing it off and boasting that he'd spent more than two months' salary on it, so at least he was happy. To be honest, I've just lived in terror of losing the bloody thing.

I pull it off and weigh it in the palm of my hand. Then a thought occurs.

'Where's my notebook?' I ask.

James snorts. 'You mean your great novel with all your choice comments about my mother?'

Note to self: never, ever write when pissed.

'Er, yeah,' I say. 'Sorry about that.'

There's a sound of rummaging from within.

'Ring first,' demands James.

It's a bit insulting that he thinks I'm going to run away with it. For a minute I consider flogging the damn thing and vanishing off to Greece for half-term, but then I think about my novel. OK, so at the moment it's only a few scribblings in Wayne Lobb's exercise book (don't worry, I've given him a replacement, which is now covered in graffiti and gum, in case you're wondering), but I couldn't bear to lose it. It may well be pathetic drivel like James says, but it's *my* pathetic drivel and I can't wait to be lost in my fantasy world of dashing heroes and masquerade balls.

I push the letter box open and the ring plops on to the mat below. 'Can I have my notebook now?'

There's a click from James's end of the speakerphone so I move away from the door and peer up to the kitchen window. Far be it from me to call my fiancé – sorry, ex-fiancé – predictable, but I don't have to be psychic to know that Jake and Millandra will come flying down in the next few moments.

But I didn't anticipate that they'd come floating down like inky confetti.

For a second I'm too taken aback to understand what is happening. A snowstorm drifts down around me, little pieces dancing in the wind and scattering across Allington Crescent. Some dust the bin liners, others land like mutant leaves on the cars parked below and the rest float along in the gutter, lilac ink feathering in the muddy water. I'm frozen with disbelief. He couldn't be so spiteful? No matter how pissed off he is, surely he wouldn't be cruel enough to destroy weeks and weeks of my writing? To wilfully rip up my dreams and hopes as though they mean nothing?

I crouch down and scoop up a handful of mush from the kerb. The name Jake is barely distinguishable from the smudges of ink. At least, I think it's the ink that blurs the writing, but it could be that the tears trickling down my cheeks are to blame.

All those hours, all my beautiful romantic dreams, which, although probably pathetic, have helped me to escape from a life that was getting more miserable by the day, are totally gone. Jake and Millandra are so real to me that I can practically see them. I know what they're going to say, what they like to eat; I even know what their favourite colours are, for God's sake! They're my friends.

And it feels like James has just murdered them.

'Oh dear,' shouts James, through the letter box, where he's been retrieving the ring. 'It's not very nice when something that you've slaved over is deliberately destroyed, is it? Still, why don't you sit on a cactus? That'll cheer you up.'

I dash the tears away with the back of my hand. I'm not going to sink to his level. I won't even dignify him with a reply. Instead I crumple the few pieces that I have retrieved into a sad soggy ball and drop it back into the puddle. There's no point in scrabbling around like a creature demented. *Heart of the Highwayman*, along with my home and my relationship, has gone for ever.

I'd better call a cab and load up my bin bags. Not that I'm sure where I'm taking them, since I seem to have lost my best friend as well as my fiancé.

I scroll through my mobile's phone book, looking for people I can call on in a crisis. People who won't mind if a red-eyed, snotty-nosed Katy turns up with her life in tatters and snivels on them for a few days, people who'll call James a bastard, make me endless mugs of tea and dish out sympathy.

Ollie. No way. I scroll past him. If this morning's version of sympathy is anything to go by, I'll be suicidal by teatime.

My sister Holly? My finger hovers over the call button. Can I really face that dark flat in Cambridge, the endless fascination with maths and the long psychoanalytical conversations that Holly and her intellectual friends love to have? Since my mental gymnastics are on a par with my physical fitness, I'm not convinced I'm up for it.

Maddy? Can I bear to explain all this in front of Saint Richard? I think I'd rather stick pins in my eyes, to be honest.

Auntie Jewell. She'll take me in without any questions asked, but is it fair at her age? How about if I only stay a few days? We can drink pink gin and talk about the war and watch UK Gold all day. That's exactly what I need to do.

My finger dives down and dials. Heart pounding, I listen to the phone ring and imagine it shrilling in the cool black and white tiled hall in the Hampstead house. I wait and wait but there's no answer. She could be anywhere. St-Tropez, Mum and Dad's, or just meditating naked in the drawing room (don't even ask).

Bugger. A cardboard box under Waterloo Bridge it is then.

And knowing my luck, all of those will be taken.

The early sunshine is starting to turn a sickly hue and the sky is swollen with lemony-yellow clouds. A cool wind whisks up the remains of Jake and Millandra and spots of rain patter softly on the bin bags. Experience tells me that fairly soon there'll be a downpour of the type only found in London, where the rain leaves the skin gritty, cars hiss through shallow puddles and people scuttle by with their heads bowed against the spray. Not really ideal conditions to be sitting on the pavement with all my worldly goods. With a heavy sigh, I decide that I'd better move my bags away from the gutter and come up with some kind of a plan pdq, because it doesn't look as though James is going to take pity on me. In fact he's put the blinds down and turned his stereo up.

Cheers then.

Thanks for the past four years, Katy!

And all the blow jobs.

Bastard.

It's a sad thing to be almost thirty years old, homeless and sitting in the gutter with the last four years of your life crammed into bin bags. I heave the bags along the pavement, almost sobbing in frustration when they tear and spew my belongings all over the tarmac. Bugger Richard, I decide grimly, I'm going to have to call Maddy.

I'm just rooting around in my bag for my mobile when there's a hideous screech of brakes and a blast of a car horn. An ancient, bright yellow Capri complete with *Dukes of Hazzard*-style musical horn skims me by inches and comes to an abrupt halt. The acrid scent of burning rubber drifts on the wind and the road now has an impressive set of tyre marks. I don't so much jump as orbit the moon several times. Thank God I got the bin bags out of the way when I did, I think, and myself too, otherwise I'd be nothing more than a splat of Katy jam. And wouldn't that make James's day?

I flick a V at the reckless driver who has narrowly avoided putting me out of my misery. Then the car pulls up just feet in front of me. Fantastic. Dumped, homeless and now embroiled in a road-rage attack. Whatever I did in a past life to deserve all this crappy karma just doesn't bear thinking about.

'Well, there's gratitude for you!' The door creaks open and Frankie unfurls his long limbs from within. Loud fart sounds follow as his leather trousers peel away from the nasty plastic seats. 'Shall we go back?'

This question is addressed to Ollie, who's leapt out of the passenger door and is surveying my bag-lady look in amazement. Fortunately the stripy bathrobe has been re-placed by a faded pair of Levis and a baggy sweater, so the good citizens of Allington Crescent won't have to blush. Unlike me, as I remember our heated row of earlier on.

'That's never your car?' I ask Frankie.

'I borrowed it.' Frankie pulls off his Raybans. 'It belongs to Ricky from the Queens. I won't begin to tell you the favours I now owe him, darling. Suffice it to say that Ollie owes *me* big time.'

'He does?' I'm a bit stunned. Frankie is twirling his feather boa and Ollie is glaring up at the kitchen window. Perhaps it's shock but I feel like I'm in a very surreal dream.

'What's going on?' asks Ollie, taking in the bin bags and assorted flotsam and jetsam of my life.

'I'm moving house,' I tell him. 'James has been very busy literally throwing my belongings out.'

Ollie shakes his head. 'He really is a wanker, Katy. I know you're upset but believe me, you're well out of it.'

Actually, I feel numb rather than heartbroken. I'm more devastated by the loss of my notebook than I am about the loss of my fiancé. I expect my broken heart will come later. There's bound to be lots of weeping into my pillow in the dark depths of the night and desperate plotting to win James back, along with the obligatory crash diet, disastrous life-changing haircut and listening to mournful Enya CDs. But right now I'm too stunned to feel anything apart from a growing sense of relief that I won't have to be shoehorned into Vera Wang after all. Jeez. That would have been like trying to squeeze toothpaste back into the tube.

'I'm going up to sort this.' Ollie's striding towards the door. 'He can't just throw you out like that. You've got rights, you know, Katy. It's your home too.'

'No!' I grab his sleeve and tug him back. The last thing I want is a scene. 'Leave it.'

'Leave it? You've paid into that place. You can't just let him chuck you out. I'm going to go and speak to him.' Ollie hammers on the door. 'Open up! I want a word with you!'

By 'a word' he means that he wants to thump him. I bet James is cowering behind the Chubb locks, chains and peephole. He's so security-conscious that our flat makes Fort Knox look sloppy in terms of security. Ollie's got more hope of flying to the moon this afternoon than he has of getting in there.

'Ollie, please stop,' I plead. 'It's James's flat, not mine. It always has been.' And as I say this I realise it's true:

everything in there has been chosen by James, has his taste stamped on it and reeks of understated expense. It's a bummer losing my security, but there's nothing about the Allington Crescent flat that will break my heart to leave behind.

'Let's get this lot into the car then.' Ollie gathers up the heavy bags as though they're made of tissue paper. 'It's going to pour down any minute.'

'What are you doing?'

He fixes me with a look normally reserved for his thicker students. 'I'm putting your things in the car. We'll drive them back to Southall and sort you out.'

'I'm fine,' I insist. 'I was just about to call Maddy. I thought I'd see if I could go there.'

'Well, that's one idea,' Ollie says. 'But you need to get this lot moved and make some plans. And run it by the Rev, I would have thought. So let's take you back to mine first.'

'I'm not sure that's a good idea. Not after what you said earlier.'

'Oh come on,' Ollie sighs. 'I didn't mean any of it the way you took it. I was just so bloody annoyed. I wish I'd kept my mouth shut. I will in future, honest, so just put your sodding things in the car, will you? Or would you rather stand out in the rain?'

'I'll come back for a bit,' I say grudgingly. 'Just until I'm sorted.'

'Fine.' Ol makes light work of scooping up a bin bag. 'It's entirely up to you.'

I squeeze into the Capri. Catching a glimpse of myself in the rear-view mirror is a hideous experience. I need a gallon of Optrex and ten tons of Clarins Beauty Flash Balm to even look halfway to human. No wonder Ollie thinks James needed Jewell's money to persuade him to be with me. I'm almost inclined to agree.

'What's all this?' Frankie leans across, holding handfuls of what looks like handwriting-covered confetti. 'Is it yours?'

Ollie inclines his head to look. Of course he recognises my writing. And I know that he understands exactly what James has done.

'Bastard,' he breathes.

'It's rubbish,' I say. 'James was right.'

'He bloody wasn't.' Ollie shakes his head. 'It was great. I loved reading about Millandra's nipples.'

I give him a watery smile. 'Millandra's nipples are no more so you'll just have to find another fantasy.'

'Oh well,' he shrugs. 'Jordan on a trampoline it is then.' Meeting my eye he gives me a wink, and despite the fact that this is a seriously shit day, right up there with the time that my pet hamster died, my spirits lift a little. If I've still got my friends, I think I'll just about get through it.

As the car pulls away I crane my neck and look back at my old flat and my old life as both vanish into the past. Is it my imagination, or does the blind twitch at the kitchen window? I can't tell.

Then the car turns the corner and we're away.

How weird that nothing is left of yesterday's life except a car full of black plastic. I'm nearly thirty years old and this is all the last four years amounts to. My life is easily crammed into bin liners. It's like I was never there.

Apart a few pieces of torn-up paper whirling in the breeze, lost, aimless and useless.

I close my eyes.

I know exactly how that feels.

★

Late that evening I'm in Ollie's spare room again, minus Frankie thank God, munching on a doorstep of Dairy Milk that Ol has thoughtfully provided. I'm snuggled beneath my duvet and swigging a bottle of Blossom Hill that I've discovered in the barren depths of Ollie's fridge. Frankie and Ollie have gone out to a Screaming Queens gig, which means I've got the house to myself for the evening, apart from Sasha, who's opted to stay on suicide watch. She's pretty crap at it because all she's done is launch herself on to the bed and fall into a sound sleep, paws and nose twitching and tail wagging as she dreams exciting red setter dreams that probably involve ripping up contracts and smashing Apple Macs.

'I haven't forgiven you,' I tell her sternly. 'This is all your fault. And yours!' I call out to Pinchy, who's floating in the bath and feasting on some very expensive fish food. 'Both of you are to blame.'

So this is what my life has come to. Talking to lobsters and drinking wine from the bottle.

'No way,' I say to Sasha. 'It's time to sort out my life. Things can only get better, right?'

Sasha opens one bleary eye and then closes it again.

'Well, I bloody hope so,' I mutter. 'Think I'll top myself now otherwise.'

Ollie has installed me in his spare room while I 'sort my shit out'. This might take a few millennia, as there's a sewage farm's worth of shit to sort.

I haven't unpacked yet, so all my junk is still strewn around the room. It looks as though I'm about to have a jumble sale. My bags are on the floor, my clothes thrown across the bed and I'm wearing Ollie's tracksuit bottoms and thick walking socks; just as well really because this place is freezing. It might be early spring but the temperature is unseasonably low, and in Ollie's house central heating is a fanciful concept rather than a reality. I pull the duvet up to my chin and sigh.

James might be a pain sometimes, but there's a lot to be said for under-floor heating.

On my lap is a spiral notepad. I'm going to make a list and sort my life out. Lists are cool! I'm really good at them. I make hundreds of them at work, detailing all the books that I have to mark, kids I need to see and things I need to buy from Sainsbury's.

Yes! I'm fab at making lists of things to do.

Sadly, though, I'm not so fab at crossing off the things I've done or, if I'm honest, actually doing them.

But today I must knuckle down and take things seriously. I'm nearly thirty and it's time I took control of my life. No more James, no more Cordelia and no more waiting for things to happen. I'm going to be proactive.

Now, just how shall I go about this? I chew the pen thoughtfully. It's all very exciting really. If I don't think about the gap on my ring finger and the sad sense that all my dreams have evaporated, of course.

My new life starts today. This could be my chance to be the new improved Katy Carter Independent! Single! Slim!

Once I've polished off this Dairy Milk, obviously.

I click my pen, put Jake and Millandra to the back of my mind, and start to write.

1. *Find somewhere to live*
2. *Find fabulous new boyfriend*
3. *Lose two stone*
4. *Write bestseller*

There! I have a life plan. Number one is easy. Ollie has said I can crash here for a while, and now that we've put the strange events of this morning behind us, things are pretty much back to normal.

It's a bit weird living in a boy house – you know, all stereo gubbins and vast telly and DVDs but bugger all in the way of cushions and lamps and homely stuff. Not that this matters because I'm not going to stay for long. Once I've finished this list I'm calling Mads and inviting myself over to Lewisham. Richard can hardly turn away a soul in need, can he? That's got to be against his vicarly duty.

Number two is a bit harder; maybe that would be more logical after step number three. And two stone? I frown and put a line through that. Ol practically lives on Indian takeaways and it would be rude not to join him. Maybe I'll make that one stone. I'll cut out the lunchtime chips or something.

Don't be ridiculous, Katy! I cross out one and write half. I need my strength at lunchtime. Who could battle Year 11 on an empty stomach? Just you try, Jamie Oliver. Salads, my bum! Only a massive plate of stodge gets me through until three thirty. I'll just run up the stairs a bit more often. That should do it.

Number four. I pause. Slightly more tricky. What I really need is some time out and some inspiration. I can just picture myself striding across the moors like Emily Brontë, and writing purple prose. Or maybe I'll just write a book all about James's evil mother.

On second thoughts nobody would believe it. Cordelia makes Lady Macbeth look like Little Bo Peep. Perhaps I'll ask Ollie if I can borrow the English Department laptop and resurrect Jake and Millandra. I know that the laptop is *supposed* to work the funky interactive whiteboard, but nobody at Sir Bob's has managed to suss that out yet. Ollie just shows videos ('Media studies!' he protests when questioned) while the laptop collects dust or plays endless games of *Tomb Raider*. I'll be doing Lara Croft a favour. The poor girl must be getting RSI from all those suggestive poses that Ollie loves to put her in.

Besides, I can't keep pinching kiddies' exercise books.

I'm just contemplating hauling myself out of bed in search of the laptop when the tinny tone of my mobile pipes up. It must be James, I think as I delve under the detritus on the bed, ringing to say that he's sorry and please come home. It wouldn't be the first time. He'll apologise for tearing up my notebook. Will I forgive him? Of course I will. I love him, after all. We'll be laughing about this by breakfast time. It won't take long to scoop all my bin bags into the BMW. He'll kiss me, put the ring back on my finger and life will be back to normal. I'll say sorry for ruining the dinner party. I'll apologise to Julius. I'll sleep in my own bed. I'll no longer be nearly thirty and homeless.

What a relief!

After a few frantic seconds trying to locate the phone, I eventually find it buried beneath my chocolate. I glance at the glowing fluorescent screen and am crushed to see the word 'Mads' flashing. I was so certain that it was James. He's never gone this long without calling me before.

Bollocks.

I think he really means it this time.

'Hi, Mads,' I say despondently.

'And hello to you too!' chirrups Mads. 'You needn't sound so thrilled to hear from me. Why haven't you called?'

I smile in spite of my disappointment. I can just picture

Mads in her crazy cluttered kitchen, perched on the work-top, a pencil pinning up her wild tar-coloured curls and a big glass of wine in her hand. Richard will be closeted in his study with some earnest soul, which means she's free for a good gossip.

'Sorry.' I curl back up under the duvet. 'Bit of a crappy time.'

'James again?' she sighs. We've spent many hours analysing James lately. I'm actually starting to bore myself, so goodness only knows how my friends must feel. 'What's he done now?'

'He's dumped me,' I tell her, and proceed to spew forth all the gory details. As I talk, I get the distinct impression that although she's totally outraged on my behalf, Mads isn't really surprised.

'So here I am,' I conclude, nudging Sasha with my toe because my leg is going dead thanks to having several stone of dog snoozing across it. 'I'm nearly thirty, single and homeless.'

'Bugger,' says Mads, queen of the understatement. 'You must be gutted. Glad it's not me.'

Let me just explain that much as I adore Mads, tact and sympathy aren't quite her forte. In fact I seem to recall that she got sacked from the university nightline for once telling a suicidal student to stop wittering on about it and just make his mind up. Mads is a great one for getting on with life. She doesn't sit about and brood, which is why it will be so good for me to move in with her right now. She's exactly what I need to turn my life around.

'There's one major problem with that idea.' Mads sounds a little worried when I tell her that me and my bin bags will soon be arriving at the rectory. 'There's one huge reason why it isn't going to work, unless you want to change your life in a big way.'

I hope this isn't leading up to one of those do-you-know-Jesus conversations, because right now I don't make a very convincing sunbeam, more of a rain cloud really. Maddy isn't usually given to such discussions, but four years of marriage to a vicar is bound to have some effect on a girl.

'Richard?' I ask.

'Of course not,' Maddy laughs. 'He adores you.'

'And I adore him,' I fib. I adore Richard like I adore Brussels sprouts.

'No,' continues Mads, 'the problem is that we don't live in Lewisham any more. We moved to Cornwall last week, remember?'

'Duh!' I slap my hand against my forehead. Of course! I knew the big move was on the cards. What sort of crap friend am I that a major event in my best friend's life gets forgotten? 'Sorry. How is the new church?'

'Katy, you'd love it. It's amazing.'

An amazing church? I try to picture it. What are the criteria? Opposite Pizza Hut? On-site shoe shop?

'It's beautiful,' gushes Maddy. 'Really ancient, twelfth century at least, Richard says, and it's got the most stunning view over the sea. I can hardly get anything done because I'm just gaping out the window all day long. You wouldn't believe the sea, Katy! It's never the same from one second to the next. And guess what? We've got an Aga. An ancient cream Aga. I can warm up baby lambs.'

'Baby lambs?' I echo. 'Have you gone totally mad? Since when have you used an oven for anything other than heating up a takeaway?'

'I could if I wanted. I think I could do anything!'

Maddy's excitement fizzes down the phone. 'Tregowan's fantastic!'

'It's miles away,' I wail. 'I can't move in with you now you live in Cornwall!'

'It would make commuting to Sir Bob's a bit tricky,' she agrees. 'But come and stay by all means. In fact why don't you move down? You'd love it here. You could stride along the cliffs and write that novel you're always talking about. All that wind and surf is very inspirational.'

'James tore the novel up,' I say sadly.

'Bastard! Well, sod him, babes, you're well shot. Move here and chill out for a bit.'

I sigh. 'I wish. I've got my job to think about it.'

'Quit,' says Mads, for whom life really is that simple. 'You need a change; now's your chance to escape from teaching.'

Escape from teaching? People have escaped more easily from Alcatraz.

'Besides,' she adds slyly, 'you should see the men down here. They are bloody amazing. Real men, if you know what I mean. Action men!'

For a split second I have the weirdest mental picture of a little fishing village populated by plastic dolls with grippy rubber hands and swively eyes. I don't think Action Man had a willy either . . .

'Surfers! Farmers! Hunky fishermen,' carries on Maddy. 'Muscles! Tans! Fit bodies, none of these city wimps. Oh Katy! You lucky, lucky cow being single. Get your arse down here now. You're always on about finding the perfect romantic hero.'

'I thought that was James,' I say, and my throat tightens with grief.

Mads snorts. 'Hardly. Babes, he's spent so long

grinding you down that you don't think you deserve better, but believe me, you really do. I bet I can find you a dozen guys who are a million times better than him. Come on, get your arse down to Cornwall, you'll love it.'

'It sounds amazing,' I laugh, through my tears. 'But I don't think I can right now.'

'Why not? Because you're moving in with Ollie?'

'I am not moving in with Ollie.' I'm nipping this rumour in the bud. 'Well, not like that anyway.'

'More fool you,' says Mads. 'Ollie's lush.'

'He's just a good mate.'

'Yeah, right!' scoffs Maddy. 'Men always have a motive. You mark my words.'

'Not Ollie,' I say firmly.

There's a glugging sound in the background as Mads tops up her drink. 'If you don't want to jump his bones you're blind, girlfriend! But it's up to you. Anyway, at least think about coming down to us for a bit. Life isn't a dress rehearsal, you know.'

I take another sip of my wine and think about this. 'Where did our twenties go, Mads? Whatever happened to all that time? Why is it that I don't recognise anyone on MTV any more? How did I manage get to thirty and still be agonising over everything?'

'We spent our twenties agonising,' Maddy reminds me. 'Hours analysing and dissecting every word and gesture. Remember? Will he call? Does he like me? Does he really mean what he says? Does my bum look big? Blimey. What a waste of energy!'

I sigh. 'I hope I don't have this same hideous sense of déjà vu when I'm forty.'

'Well, you know what to do about it,' Mads says sternly.

'Quit that miserable job, get your butt down here and write that flipping book. It'll be such a laugh.'

'And I'll find my own Mr Rochester, right?'

'Course you will,' she says. 'Easy peasy.'

If only life were that simple. I swirl my wine thoughtfully. Is it really as easy as sticking two fingers up to it all, packing my bags and jumping on the train? Surely not? I've got credit cards to pay for, and responsibilities. And what about the kids at school? I can't just vanish off into the sunset and leave them to it. Without me to teach them, my Year 11s are more likely to get ASBOs than GCSEs. There's no way I can just abscond.

I try to explain this to Mads, but she won't have it.

'It's as hard or as simple as you want it to be,' she says firmly. 'Just remember that. Oh! Hello, darling! Evensong over already?'

I take it she isn't talking to me. From the kitchen, which in my mind's eye has morphed into some cavernous space complete with mammoth Aga and frolicking baby lambs, comes the low murmur of conversation.

'Oh, just the one,' I hear Mads say. 'I've only just opened it. Yes! It's Katy! She sends her best love.'

I do?

I mean, I do!

'Better go,' she says. 'Rich has brought a whole load of waifs and strays back with him.' She lowers her voice. 'Don't forget what I said, will you? About all the gorgeous men here?'

'I'll think about nothing else,' I assure her. 'And I'll definitely come and check it out soon.'

'Well make sure that you do,' Mads whispers. 'I've got loads more to tell you but I can't talk right now. Call me soon, OK?'

'OK,' I promise. 'Love you.'

'Love you too!' she carols and then the phone goes dead. I'm left alone in the bedroom and it seems almost rudely quiet. For a moment I'm disorientated. In my mind's eye I'm in a Cornish kitchen, listening to Mads chat and hearing the endless roar of the sea. But in reality the roaring I hear is traffic on the Uxbridge Road, not the waves churning against snaggle-tooth rocks, and the only voices are those of the Sandhus next door, who are having a row right next to the party wall.

'Could I really do it?' I ask Sasha. 'Could I just give it all up and start again? Could I really pick up that dream of just writing for a while? And is there a Mr Right just waiting for me?'

Sasha doesn't know, but she gives a positive thump of her tail.

I sigh. 'It's a nice idea, but life isn't really like that, is it?'

Still, talking to Mads has perked me up a lot, and even though my life is still empty and lonely and generally pretty pants, right this minute I at least have a little spark of hope.

Leaving the phone switched on, just in case James should decide in the next five minutes that actually he can't live without me after all, I heave myself out of bed and pad downstairs.

Where did Ollie leave that sodding laptop?

If I can't get to Cornwall and bag one of Maddy's romantic heroes, then the least I can do is create my own . . .

Chapter Seven

I spend the best part of the following two weeks surgically attached to my duvet and existing on a diet of Dairy Milk and Blossom Hill, neither of which do much for my complexion or my master plan of losing shedloads of weight in order to win James back. Ollie rings in sick for me and delivers cups of tea and sympathy in regular doses, and while he battles with the teenage hordes I cry myself sick, develop a worrying addiction to Jeremy Kyle and bash away on the laptop. But it's hard to imagine being the fragrant Millandra when I feel so grotty and I end up deleting great chunks of my writing, which makes me even more fed up.

As for Cordelia, it's almost indecent just how keen she is to unravel the wedding arrangements. I have one short phone call in which her relief is palpable, and ironically it's the most civilised conversation we've ever had. But from James I hear absolutely nothing, and that hurts. A lot. I know that things weren't always perfect but I thought he loved me and that it was stress at work that was making him so grumpy. I never thought for a moment I was the problem. So I'm a bit spontaneous (read disorganised in James's book) and I suppose I do have a tendency to have my head in the clouds, but those are hardly hanging offences. And James did choose me, so it stands to reason that there are many things about me that he does like.

All these thoughts are inconsiderate enough to go whizzing round in my mind at about four a.m. Night after night I pummel my pillow, snivel a bit and have to literally sit on my hands to stop myself sending desperate little text messages into the ether. Ollie and Mads are fantastic and I bang on at them non-stop but I'm going to have to change the record soon. Ollie's eyes are starting to glaze over and yesterday Maddy asked whether I had Tourette's.

In the two weeks since James literally threw me out of his life, Ollie's been working very hard on his tough-love theory. In the kitchen we have a 'James' box into which I have to put a pound every time I mention his name, while the dartboard in the hall has James's photo Pritt-Sticked to it and as a regular part of my therapy I hurl darts at my beloved's face. I'm too darn busy to slip into a decline because I'm being dragged all over west London to parties and pubs, and Maddy is constantly on the phone telling me about all the gorgeous men she's lining up for me in Cornwall. Everybody is so busy trying to cheer me up and chivvy me along that I feel totally exhausted. All I want to do is curl up and howl for a bit in peace. Surely that's par for the course when an engagement breaks up?

Apparently not. In fact it's rather insulting that my friends think I should be celebrating rather than snivelling.

I keep trying to explain that I can't give up on James without a fight. Ollie makes puking noises to such comments, but he's hardly one to talk, is he, seeing as he still has Vile Nina phoning and turning up at all hours? And obviously Nina is really thrilled that I've moved in. Not.

Ol says he's told her that it's over between them, but

Nina's having none of it. She's going to cling to him and Ollie, as usual, is too soft to tell her to get lost. Maybe he should take lessons from James? He didn't take long to boot me out. Perhaps I should have put up more of a fight.

The problem is I'm not much of a fighter. As much as I'd love to be one of those feisty types who command admiration wherever they go, the sad truth of the matter is that I'm more inclined to keep quiet and live in hope that I go unnoticed. I spent years at school trying to keep my head down, hoping the teachers didn't spot me, ditto university, and even now I'm still doing it, which is probably why instead of driving a JCB into James's car and planting cress in the seagrass, I've been snivelling into a pillow and pickling my liver for the last two weeks.

I'm even starting to bore myself.

Well, I decide on the third Monday that I bunk work (thank God any doctor I see clocks 'teacher' on my notes and instantly signs me off with stress), no more Mrs Sappy Person. It's time to take matters into my own hands and stop being so dependent on Ollie and Maddy. Millandra would fight for Jake. So it's about time I did the same for James. You have to work at relationships, right?

Once Ollie has left for Sir Bob's, muttering darkly about covering skivers' lessons, I tear into the bathroom, lob Pinchy into a bucket and scrub, pluck and exfoliate as though my life depends upon it. Not an inch of me is left untended. I even put a scarlet colour through my hair. So what if the bathroom looks like Dracula has paid a flying visit and my fake tan has dyed the edges of Ollie's bath robe nicotine yellow? The end result is totally worth it. I twirl in front of the hall mirror and admire the glowing reflection. My skirt hangs looser on my waist and even my face looks slimmer. The wine and misery diet has worked wonders.

I could practically fancy myself.

My master plan can't fail.

It's a lovely sunny morning. The sky above the London rooftops is taking a break from its usual leaden hue and is all duck-egg blue streaked with pink-edged clouds. I take this to be a good omen – you don't teach English for this long without learning something about pathetic fallacy – and as a celebration I buy myself a latte and a blueberry muffin from the little Italian café by the station. I even treat myself to *Heat*. Once on the tube, I sweep a sheaf of *Metro* pages on to the floor and settle down on my seat. The fabric prickles against my bare legs and for a moment I wonder if I should have stuck to jeans. But then James wouldn't have the benefit of my newly thinner and fake-tanned legs. I catch a glimpse of myself in the tube window and give my reflection the thumbs-up. When James sees how fab I look, I know he'll want me back. He's surely missing me by now?

The journey passes pleasantly and I wonder why people moan about the tube. Soon leafy Ealing is replaced by rows and rows of terraced houses, their narrow gardens stretching down to the railway lines, lawns dotted with assortments of plastic toys, washing dancing in the breeze and bare earth just waiting for planting. When the train plunges beneath London, I amuse myself by reading about the latest celebrity break-up, which cheers me up a lot. I mean, if Jennifer Aniston and Kylie can't hang on to a man, then *of course* it's harder for us mere mortals. I just need to put some more effort in, that's all, which is *exactly* what I'm doing now. By the time I reach my stop and emerge into the sunshine, I feel much more positive. Everything's going to be OK. I just know it.

All I have to do is find James's office and I'll be sorted, but this might be easier said than done. Now where was Millward Saville again?

Dredging up the directions from my Swiss-cheese memory, I cross the square and head towards the imposing glass and marble building opposite. It glitters in the sunlight and practically blocks out the dome of St Paul's that cowers behind. Kind of fitting really, since Millwards is probably one of the biggest cathedrals to Mammon that you will find anywhere. Judging from the lack of people entering, it appears that most are already hard at worship.

I square my shoulders and inhale. Exhale stress out. Inhale calmness in. See! I knew that yoga video wasn't a waste of money. So what if Ollie was right and I never got to any of the actual workout? I think I've pretty much sussed the basics.

Up the marble steps I tip-tap in my heels like one of the Billy Goats Gruff. Come on, Katy! Don't be intimidated! In my little power suit (bought for school but only worn once because the kids pissed themselves laughing and asked if I was on interview), I'm as good as any of these city types. I'm just like Ally McBeal.

But a bit fatter.

'Katy!'

I turn round, but sadly it isn't James running in slow motion towards me with his arms outstretched but Ed Grenville, chins wobbling and glasses slipping down his nose, lumbering up the steps behind me. He doesn't look overjoyed to see me, which, given our last meeting, is understandable.

'Good Lord, Katy,' Ed pants, shaking his head and

pushing his glasses up his nose with a stumpy forefinger. 'I didn't expect to see you, old girl. Kind of takes a chap by surprise.'

'Don't panic, Ed,' I say airily. 'I haven't got a lobster with me, or a cactus. I've just come to chat to James.'

From the look of abject horror on Ed's face, you'd think I'd said I was about to do a naked tap dance, complete with nipple tassels, on the trading floor.

'James isn't in yet.'

I'm taken aback. James is late? I couldn't be more surprised if he'd told me the earth was flat. James is *always* at work by seven a.m. Greenwich could set their clocks by him.

'He's really taken this break-up hard then,' I breathe. No wonder he isn't answering my texts or picking up the telephone. He's too upset to face me, too riddled with guilt to speak without breaking down.

'Well, um,' Ed says.

'Don't worry. I won't let him know you've told me. I know he'd hate to be embarrassed at work.'

He smiles weakly. 'I'll tell James you popped by. Why don't you go home? I'll get him to call you.'

I can take a hint. 'What time will he be here? Shall I pop back for lunch? Or is lunch still for wimps?'

I laugh at this, but Ed certainly doesn't. His gaze is fixed on a bright red Mercedes convertible pulling up with a flamboyant screech at the bottom of the steps. The driver, who has a windswept mane of blonde hair and the most enormous pair of sunglasses, is busily kissing the passenger, who responds with such enthusiasm that they are practically having sex on the dashboard.

The passenger, who is unmistakably James.

All the blood in my body curdles.

'Sorry, old bean,' Ed says.

My stomach lurches and for a hideous moment I think the muffin and latte are going to make my reacquaintance. I swallow bile quickly.

'Who the hell is that?'

'Alice Saville.' Ed can't look me in the eye. 'She's doing some work experience here. She's, um . . . she's been working under James.'

'I bet she has.' In the car James and Alice, who must be eighteen at the most, are still kissing.

'If your dad's the chairman of the bank you can pretty much keep your own hours,' explains Ed. 'She's always late. Especially now she's with James.'

No wonder all my texts have gone unanswered.

'How long has this been going on?' I can't stop looking; it's like they're eye magnets or something. 'And don't bloody lie to me, Ed.'

Poor Ed mutters to his feet, 'A month?'

Maths isn't my strong subject, but that seems to pretty much pre-date our dinner party from hell. I look again at Alice Saville, all honey skin and platinum hair, and I know why James has really dumped me. It wasn't anything to do with lobsters or dogs or cacti. It wasn't even because I'm not a perfect size ten. He simply got a better offer.

'I'm sure it won't last,' bleats Ed. 'But you know how obsessed James is with money, old girl.'

Don't I just. It seems to be all he thinks about recently. I've lost count of the times I've heard him yelling down the phone about extending his terms or exploring other options.

'Rumour has it,' Ed's voice drops to a whisper, 'that he's made a few errors of judgement when speculating. Maybe he needs Alice to help him out of a tight spot.'

'Ed, stop trying to make me feel better. It's sweet of you but it's not working.' I dash tears from my eyes with the back of my hand. 'She's gorgeous and he's mad about her. It's over.'

Trying desperately to muster my dignity, I shake off Ed's hand before running into the street. Then I'm crying in earnest, with tears dripping down my cheeks and splashing on to the pavement. I can hear Ed calling but I'm beyond caring. All I want to do is get away. I don't think I have ever felt this stupid or humiliated in my entire life.

Which is really saying something.

Chapter Eight

Splosh! Ollie zooms past me at a furious front crawl, creating his own mini tsunami, which shoots right up my nose. Spluttering, I doggy-paddle to the side of the pool and gulp lungfuls of air. I'm not suicidal just yet so drowning isn't top of my list of things to do, although drowning Ollie might be fairly soon if he carries on this exhausting means of distracting me from my woes.

'Come on!' Ollie powers past, on his back this time. 'Put some effort into it, Katy. You know it makes sense.'

'No it bloody doesn't,' I mutter resentfully. Tell me what exactly makes sense about starting the day all cold and soggy? I know life with James was tricky sometimes, but at least I got to stay in bed until half seven and eat my breakfast while glued to GMTV. No one woke me up at six and made me swim at such an ungodly hour.

I set off again, bobbing in Ollie's wash, and grit my teeth. The sooner I move in with Auntie Jewell the better. Ollie may think he's doing me a favour by taking my mind off my broken heart with all this physical exercise, but to be honest I think I'd be happier being miserable. I'd really like some time to wallow in my bedroom, sobbing into my pillow and generally doing the entire broken-hearted thing. If it's good enough for Jane Austen's characters then I'm pretty sure it's good enough for me.

As I swim, I try to take my mind off the fact that I'm a) knackered and b) puffing like Thomas the Tank Engine, by continuing *Heart of the Highwayman* in my head. Not the best place to write it, but since I'm surrounded by gallons of water I haven't much choice. Besides, I'd rather think about Jake and Millandra than contemplate the plaster that has just bobbed past my nose. I'll probably contract cholera and die before I get to finish my book. Literary critics will find the torn remnants and weep over my lost genius, A-level students will be forced to discuss what I actually meant, and Richard and Judy will run a writing competition in my honour.

Eat your heart out, J. K. Rowling!

Millandra buried her face in her pillow and wept bitterly. It had been three long weeks since Jake had ridden away and not a word since. Every morning she would walk in the gardens, her velvet cloak drawn tightly about her slender body, and climb to the brow of the hill. There she would wait in the billowing mist for his ebony steed to come galloping into view.

Surely he loved her still?

But why didn't he come?

Treading water at the deep end, I realise that I haven't a clue why Jake is avoiding Millandra, and I'm probably the last person on the planet to be able to offer an insight. While Millandra weeps into her lacy pillow, Jake's probably out on the piss somewhere, chatting up tavern wenches and test-driving the latest turbo-charged horse. Who knows how the male mind works?

Not me. That's for sure.

'Out you get.' Ollie holds a towel while I heave myself in beached-whale fashion out of the pool. 'That was better today. Do you feel good?'

'Fantastic,' I mutter, wrapping myself in the towel. I'm wet, exhausted and teaching Year 11 in approximately thirty minutes. Oh yes. My cup runneth over.

'Great!' he beams. 'Same again tomorrow?'

'Can't wait,' I mutter darkly, collecting my bag from the seating area and swiftly checking my mobile just on the off chance James might have called while I was in the pool. The screen remains stubbornly blank. No surprise really. He's probably shagging Alice somewhere.

'Stop sighing,' orders Ollie from the locker area. 'And you'd better not be checking that bloody phone.'

'Of course not.' I hastily tuck the mobile down into my bag.

'Better get a move on,' he says. 'Coming for a coffee?'

'I want to grab a shower first,' I say. I might as well make the most of having a wash that doesn't necessitate moving a beady-eyed Pinchy. Is it my imagination or does he look a bit too closely when I take my kit off?

'A Pinchy-free shower,' Ollie nods. 'Good idea. Actually, we ought to think about taking him down to the coast fairly soon. I can't afford to keep him in sea salt and fish food for much longer.'

'We ought to buy a pump really. The water needs bubbles. That's what they have at the lobster hatchery in Padstow.'

'Bubbles?' Ollie fishes his keys out of his Quiksilver rucksack. 'It's a lobster, not Joan Collins in her *Dynasty* years. The sooner we get it into the sea the better.'

'I'll visit Maddy soon,' I promise. 'I'll take Pinchy with me. And then I'll get sorted, Ollie, find somewhere to live. Jewell says I'm welcome to stay at hers.'

Ollie ducks his head round the lockers. 'Don't be daft. It'd take ages to travel from Hampstead to Ealing every day. Stay at mine as long as you like. There's no hurry, Katy.'

But he's wrong; there is a hurry because Maddy has a point. This isn't a dress rehearsal, which is just as well really, because I don't think my main performance would be up to much. Besides, I don't think I can take much more of Nina's thinly veiled irritation. Two's company and all that.

As I run the shower, I think about how weird things are at the moment. I'm in a no-man's-land. No home of my own, no partner, no plans for the future. I feel like a tiny boat adrift on the sea when the tide is high and the night is dark. Even Jake and Millandra have deserted me. They don't seem to like the laptop.

Whoever thought laptops were a good idea never had to lug one from one end of Sir Bob's to the other. Wayne Lobb's exercise book was much more practical. It didn't weigh about ten stone, nor did it bash against my legs when I ran for the bus. But hey! This is the twenty-first century, and if I'm going to be a bestselling author it seems that I've got no choice but to get to grips with one. Like the rest of my colleagues I now shuffle around Sir Bob's with my laptop slung over my back like some kind of hi-tech tortoise. And like the rest of them I'll be suing the education authority in ten years' time when my poor old back gives out.

'Something has to change,' I say to myself. 'Something has to happen, something that will change my life.'

And then it does.

But not exactly in the way I expected.

When I said that something had to happen to change my life, what I actually meant was something good, like a major lottery win or going downstairs to find Brad Pitt naked in the kitchen, or some publisher paying me millions for *Heart of the Highwayman*. That was what I meant.

Something good for once.

What I hadn't expected was that I would find a lump in my breast.

My hand skims over the slippery flesh, soap suds oozing between my fingers, and despite the warm water I feel horribly cold. I'm imagining it, I tell myself sternly, I'm being dramatic. Everyone's breasts can be a bit bumpy, right? And that's all I can feel: a little knobbly bump. If I take my hand off and then try to find it again, the chances are I won't be able to.

So I move my hand away and count to five, then to ten just for good measure. Actually, let's make that twenty. Slowly I move my fingers back, just to the underside of my right breast and, eyes screwed up tightly, give the soft flesh a prod. Sure enough I feel it again. A hard little lump, maybe no bigger than an elongated marble, but definitely there, lurking beneath my skin where it has absolutely no right to be.

'Ugh!' I cry, whipping back my fingers. The lump feels slithery, as though it is ducking and diving beneath the flesh. Still unable to believe it, I prod and poke a bit more, feeling sick when the mass moves of its own accord, until I can no longer pass this off as imagination.

I really do have a lump in my right breast.

With shaking hands I turn the shower off and stand dripping for at least five minutes. It doesn't matter that my skin now resembles a plucked turkey or that I can hear the bell ringing for morning registration. Normally when that bell goes I give Pavlov's dogs a run for their money.

But not today.

If this is just my imagination I will never, ever moan about anything again. I'll never whinge about Ollie leaving his socks by the sofa, or bitch about Nina, or moan because my stomach isn't flat. I'll do all my marking, give money to charity, be nicer to my parents, go to church, not be mean about Richard . . .

Anything, basically.

It seems like a good bargain, a fair trade.

I prod again.

Apparently not.

The lump swims beneath my touch. It's nebulous and elusive but very definitely there. I may have a fertile imagination, but it's not this good. Highwaymen and corseted heroines are more my style, rather than medical dramas. I'm so not into those. Just ask Ollie. He can only watch *Casualty* when I'm out of the room.

So I'm not exaggerating or being hysterical. There really is something lurking *Alien*-style beneath my skin, a strange little lump nestling inside the flesh, quietly waiting to see how I react.

Well, guess what? I don't know how to react, because this just doesn't feel like it's happening to me. Stuff like this happens to other people. Women with bald heads and pink ribbons. Brave people. Old people. Other people.

Somehow I get myself dressed and then realise that I haven't bothered drying first. My tights glue themselves to my legs and my feet slither around in my shoes. My hair drips icily down my neck. Without quite knowing how I've got there, I find myself outside the leisure centre clutching my bag to my chest and standing still while crowds of hooded teenagers dart past like shoals of fish. I ought to be shouting at them to get a move on to lesson one, to take off their trainers and spit gum out; you know, all the really useful things that teachers have to do in between lessons, but something inside me has broken. I'm like one of those dolls that speak when you pull a string in its back, only my string has snapped.

The world has shifted.

It looks the same but it feels different.

I have to talk to someone. I *need* to talk to someone, someone who loves me, someone who cares.

If only Maddy was still in Lewisham to make me gallons of tea and stuff me full of biscuits. Mads wouldn't panic. She'd go into vicar's wife mode and sort this out for me. She's bound to know somebody who's been in the same position and who's been OK, because Mads is an optimist. While I'm seeing visions of chemo and pink ribbons, she'll be quoting practical statistics and buoying me up. I could go and find Ollie, but I don't really want to discuss my boobs with him.

I want to talk to James.

It has to be James. James knows my body inside out. He'll know if there was a lump there before. Even if we've split up we can still be friends, can't we?

I scroll to his number and press the green button. The phone rings and rings and somewhere in the City the tinny tones of Bach are becoming ever more insistent.

'Come on,' I mutter. 'Answer it!'

'Welcome to the Orange Answerphone . . .'

Blast. I've left so many messages lately with this polite voicemail woman that I'm surprised we're not on first-name terms. I'm probably on her Christmas list. Maybe James is at home? Sometimes he does like to work from home. Maybe he's there now in the remains of the office that Sasha didn't destroy. I can just picture him, hunched before the computer, tapping away furiously and tutting in annoyance at any interruptions (usually me) that distract him. Knowing James, he'll have his headphones on too and won't even answer.

I'll give it a try anyway. I scroll to 'home' and feel a pang. I guess I'll have to change that, now that I don't officially have a home.

'Hello!'

I'm taken aback by a breathy female voice. Then I feel a huge surge of relief. I've called Millwards by mistake! I recognise that breathless squeak. James's PA Tilly, a Sloaney blonde with a brain like Aero, always gasps into the phone.

'Sorry, Tilly,' I say brightly. 'I was looking for James. It's Katy. I must have the office by mistake.'

'Oh!' squeaks the voice and then goes very quiet. In the background I hear the unmistakable and grumpy tones of James demanding to know who's calling him at home.

At home? Not Tilly then. Alice sodding Saville.

'Listen, Alice,' I say briskly, jamming the phone under my chin and rummaging in my bag for my emergency cigarette supply. 'Put James on, will you?'

'He's pretty busy,' squeaks Alice.

'Can you tell him it's really important?' I drop the lighter because my hands are shaking. I delve into my emergency cigarette pack only to find that it's empty. Bloody Ollie! I'm going to *kill* him. Lobsters and cacti I can just about forgive, but nicking my cigarettes? That is punishable by death.

Down the phone line there's the echoey sound of footsteps on the wooden floor.

'For Christ's sake, who is it?'

'Nobody,' Alice says quickly. 'Wrong number, darling.' And then she hangs up on me. Bloody cheek of it!

A tear runs down my cheek and plops on to the concrete floor. My feelings are swinging from wild dangerous rage to bleak despair. Much as the angry and hurt part of me wants to cut James's nuts off with blunt scissors, the bigger part is reeling with disbelief at being replaced so quickly. This is what I get for washing his socks for four years, is it? This is the thanks I get for being a loyal girlfriend.

And, says a quiet voice, for being a total doormat.

Well, bollocks to him.

I stomp across the playground towards school and head straight for the girls' toilets. It's ten past nine and all is still. Inside the loos there's the faintest smell of smoke, and I throw out two stroppy Year 9 girls trying to hide in the furthest cubicle. Once they're safely gone, I climb up on to the toilet seat and, with an almighty stretch that's worthy of a yoga guru, push hard against the ceiling tile. Bingo! Cigarettes, papers and lighters rain down around me in a tobacco-scented shower.

Don't you just love teenagers? They are so predictable.

Scooping my loot into my bag, I scuttle past my classroom and hotfoot it to the boiler room, the last known gathering place of the secret smokers at Sir Bob's. One emergency cigarette, one last weep about James and some serious worrying about the lump is the order of the morning.

Safely ensconced in the boiler room, I take a huge drag on the cigarette, but even the lovely nicotine rush fails to lift me. There's just too much to deal with for one morning. Too many thoughts and far too many questions that I'll need to find answers for. And there's one question that is looming far larger than any other.

I flick ash on to the floor and square my shoulders. What on earth is this lump all about? Should I ignore it?

Or do I do the sensible thing and get it checked out? That's what all the women's magazines would advise. Nine out of ten breast lumps are benign. I know all that stuff.

But what if mine's that one out of ten? The way things are going for me lately, it would hardly be a surprise.

Is not knowing it's cancer worse than finding out something awful? Would I rather know that James has installed a new, slimmer, more beautiful girlfriend in the flat than just bibble about in ignorance? Is it better to know I really do have a lump than to pretend that I never found it, wander into the staff room and as usual fritter away my free lesson drinking coffee and surfing the internet? Should I ring the doctor and do the sensible thing?

The trouble is, I've always been crap at being sensible.

Maybe now is the time to start.

★

The doctor's surgery is overflowing with patients, all of whom are spluttering and snuffling, and the phone rings endlessly. We're all crammed into a small room lined with very narrow chairs, and some patients even have to lean against the walls or wait over by the reception area. It's like there's an attempt to beat the world record for the highest number of sick people shoved into one small space; all we need is Roy Castle to appear and we'll probably do it. Somebody is sniffing meatily. Someone else has a hacking cough and I can practically see the germs multiplying and squabbling over who they get to land on next. This little surgery in West Ealing could be a very successful weapon should Britain ever decide to use germ warfare. I've only been sitting here for half an hour and already my throat's sore.

'Katy Carter,' says the receptionist. 'Dr Allen, room five.'

I put down my dog-eared copy of *Hello!* and pick my way over various stretched-out limbs towards the consulting room. A dozen pairs of eyes swivel resentfully in my direction. I ignore them; after all, I've waited for over an hour, time during which I have diagnosed myself with every conceivable ailment from terminal cancer to scabies.

'Watch it!' whines a ten-year-old, over whose foot I go flying. 'You tread on me and I'll do you for GBH, you stupid bitch.'

Don't you just love kids? Given the mood I'm in, the H would be so G that he wouldn't live to tell the tale, and I'm just about to tell him so when I catch the eye of his mother.

Maybe not. She looks like she eats small ginger people for lunch and picks their bones clean for supper. The average Sir Bob's parent then.

The doctor looks up and smiles as I open the door. 'Please come in. What can I do for you today?'

I open my mouth to tell him but no words come out. I am so not getting my tits out for someone who looks like my grandad. No way! I'm just about to tell him I've made a mistake, but it's too late. He's shutting the door and guiding me towards a seat.

'Please, sit down.' He gestures to the yellow plastic chair next to him and glances at my notes. 'A teacher? What is it? Stress?'

Stress doesn't even start to describe it, matey.

'It's my breast,' I say at last, and my mouth feels like it's got half the Gobi tipped into it. 'I've found a lump.'

'There's no need to jump to the worst-case scenario,' Dr Allen tells me. 'It's very unlikely that it's anything unpleasant in a woman of your age. We'll just do an examination, though, to make sure. Hop on to the couch and slip your jumper off.'

Hop? That couch is almost as high as me. I bounce feebly for a few moments before finally heaving myself on. And by the way, when did I become a woman? I'm a girl, aren't I? I like funky shoes and pink stuff. Women wear sensible shoes and pay their bills on time. Women are old. I'm not old. I'm nearly thirty.

Oh God.

Nearly thirty? Whatever happened to twenty-five?

I *am* old.

'Just lie back,' says the doctor, rather worryingly rolling up his sleeves. 'Raise your right arm above your head.' I adopt a Kate Winslet in *Titanic* pose for him and try to pretend a total stranger isn't prodding at my boob. What shall we talk about? The weather? And why did I choose today to wear my grottiest bra? Greying lace and fraying strap are so not a good look.

'I've probably imagined it,' I say, as after a few seconds he's still poking silently at my flesh. 'Sorry to waste your time. Shall I go now?'

I'm all for leaping down from the couch and running as fast as my short little legs can carry me. He's a nice doctor but he's older than my dad and here I am with my boobs out. I take my hat off to Jordan; it's some crazy way to make a living. Maybe there's something to be said for teaching after all? Year 11 may be shits, but at least I don't have to get my tits out to keep them entertained.

Although it's probably only a matter of time.

'In fact I'm sure I imagined it.' I'm light-headed with relief. The stress of the last few weeks has got to me. I've probably pulled a muscle in my boob from lugging that sodding laptop around all day long. Or maybe this is a bizarre side effect of all that physical activity that Ollie has subjected me to. I always knew exercise was bad for you. From now on I will be the ultimate couch potato. I will make the Royle Family look energetic. I will—

'Ah yes. There it is,' says the doctor.

I feel the blood drain from my head and whoosh right down my body to the tips of my toes. For a hideous moment I think I'm going to pass out.

'It's a fairly small, smooth lump,' he continues, his fingers probing in time with each word. 'I'm going to refer you to the Daffodil Unit for tests.'

'The Daffodil Unit?' I squeak. I've seen women standing in the mall rattling collecting tins with the daffodil symbol on them. I've put a pound or two in, then rushed on with my shopping, never imagining that I might have to go there myself. 'But that's the . . .' My words dry up. I can't – I daren't – say it aloud.

'The oncology unit.' The doctor returns to his computer and taps in some notes while I remain frozen in my *Titanic* pose. 'They'll do a biopsy,' he continues. 'Then we'll know more.'

There's more to know? Whatever happened to 'It's nothing, go home'? I stare at him aghast.

'Do you think it's cancer?' I whisper.

'It's probably nothing to worry about, but we certainly can't rule out any possibilities at this stage.' He smiles kindly at me. 'We need to be sure. It could be a cyst. That's the most likely cause in a woman of your age. It could even be a fibroadenoma.'

A what? How can I have something that I can't even spell?

The doctor roots around in his desk for a wad of leaflets,

which he hands me with a flourish. I take them in my clammy little paws and am struck by how pretty they are – all pinks and girlie pastels. What is this? Make Cancer Cute?

'Read this literature through,' he says. 'It explains it all. And try not to worry too much.'

Try not to worry? Is he mental? How would he feel if he'd found a lump on his willy and I told *him* not to worry? Of course I'm going to worry! I'm one of the world's champion worriers. I'm practically Olympic standard. I even worry if I have nothing to worry about!

I pull my sweater back on. I seem to have done nothing else but get dressed today.

'You should hear from the hospital within fourteen days. I'll write the referral up this afternoon.'

'Fourteen days!' I gasp. 'That's two weeks!'

I sound like Tony Hancock in 'The Blood Donor'. It may only be fourteen days to you, mate, but that's a whole fortnight to me! I'll go insane. I've only known about this lump for a morning and already it's driving me demented. I can't wait two weeks. I'll be a burbling wreck. I'm the world's most impatient person. I'm a crap gardener because I can't resist digging up the seeds to see if they've started growing. And as for unwrapping my Christmas presents early . . . I'm a master at that. I will *never* manage to wait two weeks to see a specialist. I'll explode. I'll be so wound up I'll start to tick.

Basically, I'll go nuts.

And God help Ollie, who'll have to live with me.

'If you have private health insurance I can refer you to the Nuffield,' Dr. Allen offers, fingers poised over the keyboard. 'They should see you within three days.'

Oh yes! Thank you, baby Jesus! Or maybe I should

thank James, who's got an all-singing, all-dancing Bupa package? No NHS for James. When he had his wisdom teeth done last year, it was all hot and cold running nurses, plasma-screen TV and fresh coffee and papers delivered to his bedside. I was practically ready to move in myself. Yea, the Nuffield! Bring it on! I'm just about to say yes, my fiancé has health insurance and please refer me at once, when I remember that now I'm single this no longer applies. James is not about to race in and save the day.

This is turning out to be a seriously bad morning.

Clutching my wad of literature, I stumble out of the surgery and wander on to the high street. Outside it's a glorious sunny spring day. The sky is duck-egg blue trimmed with scudding white clouds so pure and fluffy they could have been borrowed from a Philadelphia advert. The park across the road teems with office workers taking an early lunch; they lounge on the grass enjoying the unexpected warmth or sit on benches munching their sandwiches. The shrill shrieks of children split the air as they race around the play area, tearing down slides and spinning giddily on the roundabout. Over by the pond, a mother and toddler are busy feeding the ducks, which are so stuffed with bread it's amazing they still float. I watch as the child laughs and is scooped up by his mother, fat little cheek pressed against hers and chubby arms wrapped tightly around her neck. Everything is so beautiful.

My eyes fill with tears, which I dash away angrily with the back of my hand.

What is the matter with me?

I don't particularly want children.

I don't even particularly like children – I'm a teacher, for God's sake – but I've always thought that maybe one day . . .

With the right man, obviously.

And without cancer.

Stop it! I tell myself angrily. Get a grip! It could be nothing.

Or it could be something, whispers an insidious little voice.

I shove the leaflets into my pocket. I'll read them over lunch and then I'll tell Ollie. He'll know how to cheer me up. It'll probably involve getting hideously drunk in some skanky pub, but right now oblivion seems like a pretty good space to occupy.

With a sigh, I head back up the high street. It's a bad sign that I feel no desire whatsoever to go into any of the shops and burn plastic. The window displays are crammed full of beachwear, flowery flip-flops and pretty sarongs all calling out, 'Buy me! Buy me!' and usually I'd be straight inside playing with my credit card. But today I feel like somebody has placed me inside a bubble. I'm looking at it all but it seems miles away, as though I'm wading through treacle rather than sauntering through the shopping centre on an unexpected bunk off school. Even the golden arches of McDonald's fail to tempt me in, which is a very bad sign indeed.

Fourteen days of this?

I'm going to starve to death.

I don't want to shop and I don't want to eat. I'm getting less sex than Mother Teresa, and she's got the excuse of being dead. My fiancé has replaced me. My novel's been torn into ribbons and there's a lobster living in my shower.

What sort of a life is that?

But at least it's *my* life.

I just hope I keep it that way.

Chapter Nine

You know how they say that a watched pot never boils? Well, I'm discovering the same is true of watched telephones. Not that I'm expecting Ollie's phone to boil. I'm waiting for it to ring. And I've been waiting since lunchtime, pretending to watch the telly and trying to grade a stack of coursework, but the phone's so silent it makes Trappist monks seem noisy. It always rings when I'm in the bath or watching *EastEnders* but never when I need it to.

Sod's law strikes again.

'Why don't they ring?' I ask Sasha, who's lying next to me on the sofa. Between us we've demolished a packet of HobNobs and a bag of Bonios. All this waiting is hungry work. Now the biscuits are gone, I've set to work on my nails. There's no need to grow them for my wedding, so I figure I may as well indulge in a good old chew. After all, it's not every day that a girl waits for the phone call that will tell her whether or not she has breast cancer.

'Are they telling the people with bad news first?' I wonder. 'Or are they saving that until last?'

Sasha knows as much as I do about this. She thumps her tail in sympathy and I attack my right hand. If the consultant doesn't call soon, I am likely to be down to my elbows.

'Just bloody ring,' I tell the phone. But it remains stubbornly silent. If phones could flick V signs at people, then that's what it would be doing. I turn my attention back to my thumb and gnaw away.

★

The time that's passed since I found my lump have been the weirdest of my life. It's as though all the things I worried about before have faded away into insignificance. Not that they weren't meaningful once, but in comparison to knowing that inside me there could be something malevolent, growing by the second and stretching out deadly tentacles, their power to move me has totally dissipated. The break-up with James is like a distant memory. I still miss him, I'm still hurt he's replaced me so easily, but it no longer matters like it did.

Mads was right. This really isn't a dress rehearsal. I just hadn't counted on the fact that my performance could be a short one. I mean, we take it all for granted, don't we? All the things we put off for later, all the places we'll visit one day and all the things we mean to do. I'm always in such a hurry. I race to work, I scurry around school like the Tasmanian Devil on speed, bells chivvying me from one place to another, and I eat my lunch on the hoof before racing off to my next lesson. Then I run for the bus, whiz round Sainsbury's, scurry home, mark books and fall into bed. The next day I wake up and do it all again.

Stop the merry-go-round. I want to get off.

Why exactly am I working so hard and tearing around at a million miles an hour?

'What's it all about?' I wonder aloud. What have I got to show for the past thirty years apart from an addiction to glossy magazines and a serious credit-card debt? What exactly have I done with my life?

Frittered it away, that's what. I sigh and fondle Sasha's soft ears. I've never really taken the time to think about what I actually want. I've fallen into a career that I never really wanted, I've wasted years on a man who never loved me the way I deserve to be loved, and I've been too cowardly to take a chance with my writing. Like everybody, I spin myself little dreams about what I might do one day, which makes the present a little bit more bearable, but what do I actually do about it? Absolutely nothing.

Twenty-nine years old and I've nothing to show for it.

It's a sobering thought.

I don't mean to be depressing. I'm not really depressed. I'm more in a contemplative state of mind. Finding this lump has really made me think about everything. Reassess and re-evaluate things I've taken for granted. If it wasn't for this sneaky mass of cells lurking under my flesh, I'd no doubt be merrily carrying on as usual, worrying about how many calories I've eaten and whether or not my love life is a failure. Not that I need to ponder that one any longer when the answer's so glaringly obvious.

'Tell you what, though,' I say to Sasha, 'whatever I find out today, things are going to change around here. I'll buy your master a beer for a start, because he's been brilliant.'

You certainly know who your friends are when the chips are down.

★

'No way,' Ollie breathed in disbelief when I told him about my horrific morning. I went back to school in the end because sitting in the house was a fast-track approach to suicidal thoughts. At school I don't have time to pee, never mind brood about things.

At three thirty, Year 11 thundered out of my room and I was left to restore order to a scene that equalled Beirut on a bad day. Posters flapped sadly from the wall, at least two chairs had a drunken list and copies of *Macbeth* were scattered across the tables. Ollie, who'd come in to tempt me out for a quick smoke, soon found himself fetching tissues and chocolate.

'You went through all that on your own?' he asked, breaking off a chunk of Galaxy and shoving it into my mouth. 'Didn't you think to call somebody?'

I refrained from mentioning James and Alice. Ollie was likely to go round and smack him.

'Nobody else to take.'

'What about me? I'd have come with you. Anyway, what did the doctor say?'

'He says it's probably fine,' I said. 'I've got all these leaflets saying lumps are really common. Nine out of ten are benign, apparently. But what if I'm unlucky? What if—'

'Don't even go there!' Ollie said, folding me into a big bear hug right there and then in the middle of my class-room. Two passing Year 11 students whistled and one called, 'Sir fancies you, miss!'

'There goes your street cred.' I pulled away and wiped my eyes on the back of my hand. 'And Miss White in the Drama Department will be heartbroken.'

Poor Ellie White has fancied Ollie since the start of term. She always tries to sit next to him at staff meetings and has even taken up early-morning swimming in the hope that he'll notice her. She really must have it bad. Unusually for Ol, though, he hasn't bothered to return the smouldering looks and invitations to accompany her on school trips. It's most out of character. He must be really into Nina.

'I can handle it,' said Ollie. 'Anyway, Ellie really isn't my type.'

'Why not?' I asked in mock amazement. 'She breathes!'

He took my hand and squeezed it. 'Quit the jokes and be serious for a minute. What happens now?'

I told him about the Daffodil Unit and the fourteen-day wait. I didn't need to tell him how I felt about that, because Ollie knows me well enough to realise that I'll be practically in orbit by then.

'I can't go private,' I said when he suggested this. 'It costs a fortune. I looked on the internet and believe me, I'd need to either rob a bank or go on the game to afford it. Private care costs serious money, Ollie. At least a hundred quid just to see the consultant, and the tests would be really expensive. It's over two hundred pounds for a blood test.'

'But for your peace of mind it would be worth every penny.'

I think about all the bank statements sitting unopened under the sink in James's flat. If it wasn't for the annoying minus sign, my account would have been doing well, 'It's a lovely idea,' I agreed. 'But it's not an option. There's no point even thinking about it. I'll just have to wait two weeks. Everyone else does.'

'It's disgraceful!' Ollie raged, really angry on my behalf. 'How can you possibly get on with your life if that's hanging over you for two weeks? It's insane.'

Auntie Jewell had thought the same when I'd phoned her. I'd tried to get hold of my mum, hoping she could swing a few crystals or beam some white light in my direction or something, but she'd gone on a spiritual retreat to get in touch with her guardian angel.

I just hoped she bumps into mine.

I'd called Jewell while I walked from the doctor's back to school and blurted out my news.

'Darling,' Jewell had gasped, and I could picture her, long grey hair drawn back from her lined face, one bony hand pressed against her chest. 'That's the most ghastly news. My poor girl! How ever will you bear the not knowing? It would drive me simply wild.'

I love Jewell to bits, but when God gave out empathy she was right at the back of the queue. One better than Mads, I suppose, who didn't bother turning up at all.

'My darling, I simply can't bear it for you. It's too awful. I could cry. I really could.'

I haven't told many people about my lump, but the way they react tells you loads about *them*. Ollie, for example, has been amazing. He's listened, made me fantastic meals, mopped me up when I've cried, rented chick flicks and not moaned, allowed me to drive the Sky TV . . . the list just goes on and on. Mads cried and said that she'd get Richard to put me on the prayer list, Jewell was dramatic but positive ('Who needs breasts anyway, darling? Nasty things! Get in the way of trampolining!') and Frankie refused to even talk about the C word. He was quite simply terrified.

I shift on the sofa and wince at the sharp stab of pain in my breast. I can't wear a bra, a nightmare in itself, because I have two stitches on the underside of my breast and an enormous pad of wadding covering them. Honestly, I look ridiculous, like I've borrowed one of Jordan's boobs.

Still, I'm not complaining. I never thought I'd see the day when I'd be happy to feel sore and bruised, but life is full of surprises. Like on Tuesday evening, when I took a phone call from a Mr Worthington, consultant in oncology at the Nuffield, to tell me he'd had a cancellation on Wednesday morning. When I tried to explain I was an NHS patient, he calmly told me that all my medical costs were being taken care of and that the referral had already been made.

Good old Jewell. She really is my fairy godmother. I make a mental note to call her again to say thanks, although that doesn't even start to describe how grateful I am. She's not answered her phone for the last two days and I'm bursting to thank her. It's truly the kindest thing that anyone has ever done for me. I mean, the lump is still there and it's a hideous experience, but at least it won't drag on for weeks.

Maybe I do have a guardian angel after all.

That's what I told Ollie, that Jewell must have paid for the private appointment and that I owed her the most enormous favour. Ollie said that anyone who loved me would have done it in a heartbeat, which was kind but blatantly untrue. My parents love me, but apart from being mad they are totally broke, and as for James . . . well, the less said about him the better.

The phone is still silent. I wander into the kitchen and fill the kettle, absent-mindedly munch on a fistful of peanuts and chuck some moulding veggies into the bin. Ollie's been so kind, the least I can do is muck out the kitchen for him. He even came to the hospital with me when I had my core biopsy, which is way beyond the call of friendship.

That was fun. Not. Next time I'll opt for something less painful, like root canal surgery without anaesthetic, for instance, although hopefully there won't be a next time. I pause in my tea-making, struck by the hideous thought that there might be a whole host of other unpleasant medical experiences to come if I'm really unlucky. I'm the first to admit that I'm a big coward when it comes to pain. Heaven help me if I ever give birth; I'll probably need a general anaesthetic. I passed out when I had my ears pierced!

Ollie knows all this, which is why he insisted on coming with me to the Nuffield. Just as well really, because I'd been up all night surfing the internet and growing more agitated with each website I visited, until by the time dawn arrived I was a ginger jelly. Without Ol to make me breakfast and get me there, I'd probably still be going around and around on the Circle Line, trying to pluck up the courage to go to the hospital.

I mash my tea bag and glance at the clock. It's two thirty now. Surely the lab tests are all finished and my results are through? My pulse is racing and I'm so awash with adrenalin that my hands are shaking. Well, either that or I'm suffering a caffeine overload.

'Just bloody ring,' I say to the phone.

The Nuffield's oncology suite was all sunny yellows and swirly pastel curtains, an abrupt burst of colour at the end of a pewter-grey corridor. Once through the swing doors and past reception, all standard-issue hospital furniture was banished, and instead a collection of women sat on squashy sofas, sipping coffee and flicking through glossy magazines, which their gazes slid over like ice. A coffee percolator pop-popped to itself in the corner of the waiting room, but apart from that all was still and reverential hush. It was like being in church, and I half expected Richard Lomax to glide past in a swirl of robes and incense.

Ollie and I squeezed on to a soft peach sofa and

prepared to wait. Nurses walked past clutching fat folders of notes, and occasionally doctors strolled by, identifiable only by the stethoscopes slung casually round their necks. Some people looked healthy, others were thin and wan. Partners sat there too in support, holding their loved one's hand or murmuring soothing words in a desperate attempt to ease the papable air of tension.

Ollie thumbed through a copy of *Hello!*. Pearly-toothed celebrities with smug smiles beamed out from their immaculate sitting rooms. Envy me! their expressions said, and at that precise moment I did. But then again, I envied anyone who wasn't waiting in this eerily still room.

'Katy Carter?' A wizened woman appeared at my shoulder. She had the bright, intelligent gaze of Mrs Tiggy-winkle. 'I'm Dr Morris. I'll be doing your examination today.'

What was I supposed to say to that? Oh goody? She made it sound like I was going for a facial.

'If you'd like to follow me,' she said, 'we can make a start.'

Abruptly every fibre of my being wanted to run; a novel experience for a girl whose idea of a healthy lifestyle is eating a chocolate orange.

'Your husband can come too,' Dr Morris added, turning to smile encouragingly at Ollie. 'That's perfectly fine.'

She thought Ollie and I were together! How funny was that? Ollie was on his feet and practically bounding into the consulting room. His breast obsession is getting out of control, I thought grimly.

'He's not my husband,' I said, and my voice sounded shrill as it scraped the silence. 'He's just a friend.' No way was I taking my kit off in front of him.

'I'll wait then,' said Ollie.

'Go and get a bun or something.' I tried to sound bright and cheery, but sounded instead like someone on the verge of hysteria. 'I'll be fine.'

'I'll wait here,' said Ollie, in the tone of voice he normally uses with stroppy adolescents. 'I'm not going anywhere.'

As I entered the consulting room and lay back on the bed, I felt dangerously close to tears. Actually, I'd have liked nothing more than for Ollie to come in with me, hold my hand and tell me silly stories to take my mind off it all, but that was a boyfriend's job, right? Watching me being cut open was too much to ask of him; it didn't feel right to expect it. To even want it moved our friendship into a really weird space.

Everything in my life was shifting and changing, solid ground was turning into quicksand, and I didn't like it one bit.

'Lie back on the couch,' said Dr Morris, switching on what looked like a giant television. 'Just slip off your bra and top.'

I did as I was told. Moments later, cold jelly was smeared across my breast and a nurse was dimming the lights. I half expected the Pearl and Dean music to begin.

'This is the ultrasound,' explained the doctor, running an instrument over my skin. 'It allows us to see inside the breast and get an idea of exactly what we're dealing with. There's no point doing a mammogram in women your age because the breast tissue is too dense to see much.'

I looked at the screen, which resembled a snowstorm. All it needed was Santa and his elves.

'There!' said Dr Morris, when a dark patch appeared amid the wiggly grey lines. 'That's the lump.'

She moved the ultrasound a little. A frown crinkled her brow.

'What is it?' I asked. My pulse went up a gear.

'It's not a cyst, I'm afraid. It has a blood supply.'

It did? I sat up in panic. What was in there? Dracula?

'Which means,' Dr Morris continued, 'that we'll need to take a tissue sample so we can ascertain what the nature of this tumour is.'

'Do you think it's cancer?' I whispered.

'I really can't tell you much just by looking at it.' The lights went up again and the nurse rummaged in a cupboard. Rustling green plastic packages containing what looked horribly like needles were piled up by the sink. 'Parts of it appear smooth, which could indicate a fibro-adenoma.'

I'd read those bloody leaflets so many times, I was now an expert. That was the benign fleshy tumour that grew from breast tissue. I'd stopped praying to win the lottery and was hoping I'd got one of those instead.

'So it's fifty-fifty,' I said. 'It could all be fine . . .'

'Best to be sure,' said the nurse, who was swabbing my breast. 'Try not to worry.'

Yeah, right.

'We're going to numb your breast with some local anaesthetic.' Dr Morris was busily filling a syringe. 'Then I'll make a small incision and collect the sample. You'll hear a click, a bit like a staple gun, and that will mean that I've taken some cells.'

'Are you all right with needles?' asked the nurse, presumably because she'd seen the look of horror on my face.

What kind of question is that? Who enjoys needles? The thought of injections makes me all but pass out. I haven't been to the dentist for years because I'm such a chicken. It's like Stonehenge in my mouth.

'Can't you knock me out or something?' I asked. Cold sweat started to break out between my shoulder blades. The idea of being conscious while she cut into me was hideous. I'd much rather snooze through it all.

'Are you a bit squeamish?'

That was possibly the understatement of the decade. I faint at the sight of rare steak.

'Just a bit,' I said.

'This procedure is unpleasant, but it won't take long.' Dr Morris tapped the syringe with her forefinger. 'I'll be as quick and as gentle as I can. Just lie on your left side and raise your right arm above your head.'

'Are you OK?' asked the nurse. 'Do you want to hold my hand?'

I thought about this for a moment. I knew that it was pathetic, that compared to lots of other treatments that were probably going on in this very hospital at this very moment mine was fairly minor, but I was really scared. That needle was looking more like a harpoon by the second, and the long silver instrument that would collect the tissue wouldn't have been out of place in a medieval torture chamber.

In fact, forget scared.

More like fucking terrified.

'I've changed my mind,' I squeaked. 'Would it be OK if my friend came in after all?'

Suddenly it seemed like a very good idea indeed to have Ollie by my side. Ol's pretty tough from all his outdoor pursuits, so I could dig my nails into his hand if things got really painful, whereas the nurse might object. And besides, it's not as if he hasn't seen a naked boob before, is it?

He's had more girlfriends than Hugh Hefner; surely the sight of my poor breast wouldn't shock him? We were friends after all. The fact that he'd got a willy ought to be irrelevant. What's the difference really between being friends with Ollie and being friends with Mads?

Only that I've never snogged Mads.

But I didn't really mean to snog Ollie. It was years ago anyway and just a drunken mistake.

'Here he is!' said the nurse brightly as she ushered Ollie into the room.

He stood awkwardly by the door, beanie hat in one hand and copy of *Hello!* in the other. He wasn't sure where to look.

'Sit this side,' said Dr Morris, moving the ultrasound screen so that Ollie could perch next to me. 'Now then, everything's super!'

Super? I caught Ollie's eye and couldn't help laughing. Surely this was the antithesis of super?

'Katy's a bit nervous,' continued the doctor, needle poised. 'Just hold her hand. Sharp scratch coming.'

Sharp scratch? Why lie? She should just say 'Massive needle stabbing you now.'

'Ow!' yelped Ollie, clutching his fingers. 'Jesus! Katy!'

'I have a low pain threshold.'

'You don't have a pain threshold at all,' gasped Ol, rubbing his fingers. 'Could I have some of that anaesthetic for my hand?'

But Dr Morris was too busy delving inside my skin to answer. Looking down, I felt faint.

'Don't be nosy,' said Ollie sternly. 'Look at the screen instead. You've always wanted to be on telly.'

So I looked away and concentrated on breaking Ollie's fingers.

To be fair to the doctor, she was thorough and she did her best to keep me as comfortable as possible. Ollie was probably in more pain than me and it took a good couple of hours for the marks from my nails to fade. While Dr Morris beavered away, he tried to distract me by reading snippets from *Hello!* and repeating all the latest gossip from school. Once I'd escaped from the consulting room, feeling very sore and dizzy, he marched me straight to the canteen and bought the biggest wad of carrot cake I'd ever seen. Then we went to the pub and got hammered. Ollie wouldn't let me buy any drinks or even thank him.

'What are friends for?' he said.

★

Yes, I think, carrying my tea back into the lounge, Ollie's a good friend. Whoever ends up with him will be a lucky girl. I just hope it isn't Nina. He could do so much better than her.

Hurling myself on to the sofa, I flick through *Heat* magazine and try to concentrate on a double-page interview with Gabriel Winters, the gorgeous actor who's starring in the BBC's latest modern reworking of a Brontë novel. It's quite scary to think that an entire generation of viewers now believe that Jane Eyre actually shagged Mr Rochester in a rainstorm before being called a slag by Bertha Mason, presumably out of the attic courtesy of care in the community. *EastEnders* meets literature is how the Beeb is selling the drama. Charlotte Brontë must be spinning in her grave. In any case, it's hard to escape Gabriel Winters at the moment; his dissolute, handsome chiselled face, lazy downturned blue eyes and sexy lop-sided smile stare down from billboards, grin cheekily from magazine covers and are frequently splashed across the tabloids. He gets through models/soap stars/members of girl bands like I'm currently getting through Kleenex. I read for a bit about how he's enjoying his role as Mr Rochester, why he thinks the new and notorious wet-trouser scene enhances the novel and what he looks for in a woman.

Thin and blonde. What a surprise.

Why are men so predictable? It must be biological.

I shove the magazine aside in disgust. I'll pass it on to Frankie, who has a major crush on Gabriel Winters, but personally I feel like using it as loo roll. I return to nibbling my nails.

And then the phone rings.

I spring to my feet and grab the receiver, feeling as if my heart is about to burst cartoon-style through my chest. This really is it.

'Hello?' says a calm, professional voice. 'May I speak with Katy Carter?'

'Speaking.' I sound like I've been inhaling helium. The phone trembles in my hand.

'Hi, Katy, this is Dr Morris. How are you?'

How am I? Is she insane?

'Fine,' I fib, because 'Going out of my mind' probably isn't what she wants to hear.

'Mr Worthington's team have met today to discuss your results,' she continues, and I hear her rustling through papers. My heart rate increases. It hasn't raced like this since my one and only step aerobic class. I can't tell from her tone of voice if she's about to give me the news I'm dreading.

'Oh?' I squeak.

'And I'm really pleased to tell you that the tumour is benign.'

For a moment I'm stunned. Then I think, benign and malign, which is which? I know I'm an English teacher, but my brain feels like it's turned to cream cheese.

'I'm sorry,' I say. 'Could you say that again?'

She laughs. 'It's good news, Katy. You have a fibro-adenoma, which is a benign tumour.'

'I haven't got cancer?' I need to hear this in plain English. Sod the medic speak.

'No, you haven't got cancer,' Dr Morris says patiently. 'A fibroadenoma is totally benign. We'll be in touch regarding whether or not you wish to have it removed. Have a good weekend.'

Have a good weekend? No kidding! Dr Morris rings off and I'm left standing in the middle of the lounge with the phone clamped to my ear. I'm stunned. I was so convinced it was going to be bad news that this unexpected reprieve has totally thrown me. I'm not prepared for celebrations.

'It's OK,' I say slowly to Sasha, who thumps her tail in doggy delight. 'It's OK! It's blooming well OK!'

It's like I've had ten tons of concrete sitting on my head for days and suddenly it's been lifted off. I could float away like a hot-air balloon, drifting above the rooftops of west London and rising into a sky of endless possibilities. Days, months and years spread in front of me, millions and millions of minutes that I can grab with both hands and use any way I want. No more moaning about James. No more whingeing about my job. No more thinking about writing a novel one day. I'm not going to waste a second.

'It's OK! It's OK! It's OK!' I shriek, over and over again, as I run around the house, thundering up the stairs with a joyfully barking Sasha at my heels. 'It's OK!' I tell

Pinchy, who I swear gives me a beady wink from his bath. 'It's OK!'

I would have kept this up for longer but Mrs Sandhu starts to bang on the wall and shout at me in Hindi. Her baby begins to wail.

Whoops.

I bound back downstairs again. I'm so full of energy, I could keep the National Grid going for a month. My lethargy has vanished quicker than Gabriel Winters' trousers in a love scene and I have no desire to nibble my nails. Life is back to normal.

Except that it isn't.

My life is so going to change.

Chapter Ten

By the time Ollie gets home from school, I'm halfway through a bottle of Moët and slightly hoarse from a long and intense conversation with Maddy.

'That man's an angel!' she squealed when I told her how Ollie had supported me for days. 'Snap him up now!'

'It isn't like that,' I said. 'Anyway, I don't fancy him.'

'Are you off your trolley?' asked Maddy, and in the background seagulls caw-cawed in agreement. 'He's gorgeous, and he's got a nice arse.'

'I agree, from a purely aesthetic point of view, but you've no idea what he's really like: overflowing bins, loo seats left up, a trail of dirty socks all round the house; he's not my romantic hero, if that's what you're thinking.'

'Welcome to the real world,' she said. 'It isn't all Mills and Boon, you know. They fart and snore and hog the duvet.'

'I know that. But he's . . .' I paused, 'he's just Ollie, a tall, dog-loving comfort blanket of a mate.'

'Bollocks!' snorted Mads. 'He's sex on a stick. I'd shag him. Nice fit body, cute face and sexy arms. Don't you even fancy him a little bit?'

Mads has a thing about arms.

'He is attractive if you like that kind of thing, I suppose,' I conceded.

'So you do fancy him!' shrieked Maddy, drowning out the seagulls.

I could have cut my tongue out. Why Bond villains bother with tanks of sharks and laser beams I'll never know. All they need to do is ply 007 with Moët and he'd sing like a canary.

'No! I was just agreeing that he isn't ugly. And even if I did fancy him – which I don't – it would never work. Ol goes for Twiglet girls like Nina.'

'He's not sharing a house with Nina,' said Mads. 'And it's not Nina he's spent the last two weeks with 24/7, is it?'

'Can't men and women be friends? Haven't you seen *When Harry met Sally*?'

'Yes,' said Maddy. 'They got it together.'

They did? I never did get round to seeing that movie, but I made a mental note to watch it soon. It's one of Ollie's favourites; I'm sure I can dig it out from somewhere. Just out of idle curiosity, though, not because I fancy Ollie.

I *don't*, but I can admire him in a purely platonic way, can't I? Mads was on the verge of agreeing when Richard came into the kitchen, wittering on about bring-and-share suppers. Vicars' wives aren't really supposed to discuss the merits of Oliver Burrows's bum and whether or not he's shaggable, so Mads rang off, but not before she'd advised me in a whisper to 'bonk his brains out'.

Next I called Jewell to share the good news and to thank her for the private treatment. She was still AWOL so I left her a message, albeit a rather rambling, incoherent one, and sent a text message to my sister. It's a strange thought that my good news is whizzing through the ether. I even texted Mum and Dad, which was probably a waste of time since they haven't figured out how to switch their mobile on yet, but the new improved me is going to be a lot nicer to her parents. In fact I'm going to be more positive in all areas of my life. I'm going to drink lots of water, eat five portions of vegetables a day, cut out alcohol – after my celebratory bottle of champagne, obviously – and rub skin food in the right way. I'm going to stop nagging Ollie about the state of the house, I'll make more time for my friends and I'll even be nice to Nina the next time she calls.

That's a tall order, but I've been reprieved! Positive karma and all that. Time for me to put something back into the cosmos.

Blimey. I must be pissed already. I'm starting to sound like my mother.

'Did you get my text?' I ask, dashing into the hall as Ollie slams the door and throws his rucksack on to the floor. I fight Sasha to get to him first and fling my arms round his neck. 'It's a fibrothingummy!'

Ollie's face splits into a massive crinkly grin.

'That's fantastic news,' he says, pulling me close with one arm. 'I texted you back but I ran out of credit else I'd have called. Anyway, I got you these.' His left arm has been tucked behind his back and now extends in my direction to offer the most enormous bunch of flowers I have ever seen in my life. Dozens of fat pink and cream roses nestle inside endless folds of pink tissue paper, fronds of fern and baby's breath framing them tenderly. The entire bouquet is swathed in silky pink and peach ribbons and bows.

Garage forecourt it is not.

It's the sort of bouquet that Jake would give Millandra.

'Ollie!' I gasp, stepping back to clutch the flowers in my arms. 'They're amazing. You shouldn't have. You've done too much already.' And I bury my face in the softest petals imaginable and inhale their delicate scent.

'I did it all because I wanted to,' Ollie replies.

'You've been really kind.'

'Oh, bollocks to kind,' says Ollie. His hand moves up to my face and brushes the hair back from my flushed cheeks. 'Katy, I—'

'Hey,' shrieks Frankie's high voice through the letter box, followed by hammering fists. 'Let me in!'

Ollie and I spring apart. Sasha bounces up and down, barking in time with every one of Frankie's blows on the front door.

'Open up, you meanies!' he wails, mouth pressed against the letter box. 'I can see you! Come on, I've brought alcohol.'

'In that case, come in.' Ollie opens the front door and Frankie falls in, clutching his Oddbins bag.

'Hello! Congratulations! Celebrations!' he cries, twirling madly round the hall. Today he's wearing a puke-green catsuit, huge furry boots and a long knitted scarf. 'I got your text, darling!' He loops the scarf round my neck and kisses me on the cheek. 'Fab news!'

'Put Frankie down and get your best clobber on,' Ollie says to me as he leaps up the stairs. 'We're going out to celebrate. I booked a table at Antonio's. Didn't you get my text?'

'Oooh! Lovely,' Frankie says, clapping his hands in excitement. 'I *love* Antonio's. The waiters are to die for.'

Ollie pauses halfway up. 'No offence, Frankie, but you're not invited.'

'Oh come on! Don't leave me out.'

'Frankie,' Ollie says in a warning voice. 'I said you're not invited.'

'Fine! Be like that, you meanie!' Frankie tosses his hair, dyed deep purple today. 'Fancy a game of James darts, Katy?'

I decline, so we go back into the lounge to watch television. As I sip my champagne and while Ollie showers, Frankie channel-hops, settling at last on *Richard and Judy*.

'I *love* Richard and Judy!' cries Frankie. 'When the Screaming Queens are famous, I'm going to be on their show all the time.'

I feel I can be forgiven for not holding my breath.

'And now,' says Judy, leaning forward and beaming at the camera, 'a guest I know you'll all be as excited to meet as I am.'

'He's had us all glued to our screens for weeks now,' Richard chips in. 'English Literature has never been so sexy. He is, of course, the gorgeous Gabriel Winters!'

'I love him!' squeaks Frankie, practically diving into the television as video footage of the infamous wet-trousers scene is played. 'When I'm famous, he'll be begging to be my sex slave.'

'I thought that was Robbie Williams's job,' I say.

Frankie is all but licking the screen. 'No, Gabriel's the one for me. I met him once at a record company do. He's gorge! I'm sure he was interested. He offered me a canapé.'

I roll my eyes. 'Don't read too much into the canapé. He's famous for bonking most of the starlets in Britain, Frankie.'

But Frankie ignores me. 'I just know!' he breathes. 'I felt the vibes.'

Gabriel sits on the studio sofa, one elegant ankle resting on his denim-clad knee. He's wearing a billowing

153

open-necked white shirt and his long honey-coloured hair cascades in ringlets over his wicked sapphire eyes.

'It's been a very exciting year,' Richard is saying. 'Are there equally exciting plans for the future?'

'Well,' smiles Gabriel, revealing teeth so perfect that dentists throughout Britain probably weep with joy, 'I intend to start work in the summer on my new film role as a pirate captain.'

'You're filming that in Cornwall, aren't you?' asks Richard. 'We've spent many lovely holidays there.'

I think of Mads and her wild claims that Cornwall is teeming with sexy men. Mmm. Gabriel Winters dressed like Jack Sparrow. I wonder if she's watching.

'I'm filming in Charlestown.' Gabriel's voice is smooth and rich, like Bournville chocolate. 'I've just bought a place in Cornwall actually, a little retreat where I can just relax and be myself.'

'Darling!' Frankie turns to me, his eyes bright with the zeal of the religious fanatic. 'Your friend might know him!'

'Cornwall's a big place,' I say. 'Perhaps you should just join his fan club?'

But Frankie isn't listening. He's muttering, 'One day you will be mine, oh yes, you will be mine!' at the screen, so I abandon him and wander upstairs to get changed for dinner.

It's not a date, I tell myself sternly, it's just two friends having dinner together. Still, I do wish I'd unpacked my bin bags. Ollie's spare room looks like a squat; all my worldly goods, which actually make a pretty sad collection, are strewn randomly all over the place.

I rummage through the sacks, discarding clothing like a crazy snowstorm. What does a girl wear on a date that isn't a date? Anything low-cut is out anyway; one decision less, I suppose.

Eventually I settle on a green gypsy top, black wide-legged trousers and my favourite wedge heels. I scrunch some gel through my tangled curls and pin my hair loosely on the top of my head. A few tendrils round my face, a slick of lip gloss and several coats of mascara and I'm good to go. I don't want to look like I've tried too hard, do I?

I sit on the bed and catch my breath. This has got to be one of the strangest days of my life. How can everything have changed so much in such a short time? I look around the cluttered room, at all my things displaced and out of context, but it no longer matters like it used to. I touch my padded breast and breathe out slowly.

I haven't got cancer.

Perhaps my luck has changed.

I'm just applying a third layer of mascara – it's a curse having ginger eyelashes – when the doorbell rings.

There's no reply from downstairs. Frankie is still watching the television and Ollie's in the shower, so it's down to me to answer the door. Negotiating the stairs in my four-inch wedge heels is tricky, but I make it in one piece. Just. Perhaps I'll practise walking up and down for a while. I don't want Ollie to spend tonight in A&E; he's endured enough time in hospital with me lately.

The doorbell rings again.

'Hang on!' I say, fiddling with the lock.

'Hurry up, for God's sake, I've lost my bloody key,' snaps a voice as the door swings inwards. 'Oh. It's you.'

Standing on the doorstep is Nina. She peers rudely over my shoulder.

'Where's Ollie?'

What am I, the butler?

'Hello, Nina,' I say sweetly, even though she's about as welcome a sight to me as cranberry sauce is to a turkey. I will be the new and improved Katy Carter, even if it kills me. 'He's in the shower, I'm afraid.' I place my arm on the door frame, preventing her from entering.

'That's fine,' Nina says. 'I'll wait.'

I find myself stepping aside and letting her into the hall. I even take her coat and hang it up. I'm not sure why I do all this, only that there's something about Nina that makes me feel totally useless. It's not only that she's well groomed and flat-stomached; it's also that she's frighteningly successful, which makes her the exact opposite of me. While I've been battling to teach English to bored teenagers, Nina has been ruthlessly establishing her catering company as *the* company to hire for any occasion. Being the laissez-faire type when it comes to structuring my career (which is probably why it grinds to a halt more often than the British train network), I always feel more than a little inadequate in her presence.

Nina looks me up and down, and her top lip curls.

'You're a bit dressed up, aren't you?'

'Ollie's taking me out to dinner,' I say. 'We're going to Antonio's.'

'He's taking *us*,' Nina corrects me, checking her gore-red lipstick in the hall mirror. 'He texted earlier and invited me. I won't pretend I'd rather it was just me, but I'll let you tag along this once. Ollie's felt so sorry for you with all this lump business. This must be his way of cheering you up.'

'You know about my breast lump?'

'He's told me all about it,' says Nina, peering beyond me into the smeary mirror and smoothing her hair. 'It's been a real pressure for him, Katy; I don't think it was fair of you to make him carry the burden. After all, he isn't your partner, is he? You've taken up time when he could have been doing other things with other people. It's been pretty selfish of you actually. But you know Ollie, he won't complain.'

I'm seething. How *could* Ollie discuss me with Nina, of all people? Why couldn't he just be honest and tell me to my face that I was imposing on him? When I think about how I asked for him to come and hold my hand while I had the biopsy, I feel dizzy with mortification.

'In that case you'll be pleased to know I'm fine,' I tell her. 'I got the all-clear this afternoon.'

'Good!' Nina claps her hand together. How she doesn't do herself a serious injury with her *Footballers' Wives*-style nails is one of life's great enigmas. 'Then you won't mind giving Ollie back.'

'Are you and Ollie on again?' I ask. Keeping up with their relationship makes me dizzy.

'Of course!' Nina's eyes widen. 'Why do you think I've been popping round?'

'Because you're a psycho stalker bitch from hell,' I say.

Actually, I don't say that but I'd like to.

'Where do you think Ollie goes after school?'

'To the gym? The pub?'

'He's been coming to mine, of course.' Nina leans forward. 'And I tell you something, Katy, breaking up and making up is so much fun!'

'Too much information already,' I say, but Nina isn't listening.

'I know how fond Ollie is of you,' she continues. 'That's why I'm happy for him to bring you along to Antonio's with us. I'll order us a cab while he gets ready.'

She stalks into the sitting room and I sink on to the

bottom stair. No way am I going to Antonio's now to shovel in carbs while Nina nibbles on a lettuce leaf or whatever it is that thin people nibble on. I'd rather walk barefoot over drawing pins. Besides, my appetite's vanished. I want Ollie's friendship, not his pity.

I climb the stairs wearily and once in my room pull off my going-out clothes and shrug on my ancient dressing gown. Let Ollie concentrate on Nina. I've no desire to spend all evening doing a gooseberry impression.

I almost jump out of my dressing gown when there's a sharp rap on the door. Ollie sticks his head around it. 'Still getting dressed? Get your arse in gear. I'm starving.'

'I'm not going out for dinner.'

Ollie shoves his way into the room, kicking through mounds of discarded clothes. 'Aren't you feeling well?'

'I'm fine. I just don't think it's a good idea for us to go out for dinner.'

'Why not? We eat out all the time.'

We so do not. Granted, we cook dinner together, hoover up chips in the school canteen and sometimes stuff ourselves with McDonald's on the way home from the pub, but we have never, ever been out to a smart restaurant, especially not with Nina in tow.

'Nina's downstairs. She says you texted her and invited her out for dinner. Apparently you and her are back on big time.' I fix him with a stern look. 'Are you?'

Ollie runs his hands through his hair, a sure sign that he's stressed. 'Bollocks. I must have sent the text to her by mistake.'

'But are you two back on?'

'Well, sort of.'

'That's a yes then. Honestly, how thick can you be? You can't date one girl and take another one out for dinner, even if it's just as friends. Go out with Nina tonight and have a lovely evening. I know it's not been easy having to put up with me over the last few weeks.'

'I don't know why you'd think that,' says Ollie.

Because bloody Nina told me, I want to scream.

'I'd do it all again gladly,' he adds. 'You're my friend.'

'Of course we're friends,' I say quickly, 'but things will get messy if we start going for meals and doing coupley stuff when you're with somebody. Yes they will!' I insist when he opens his mouth to protest. 'It isn't fair on Nina.'

How I say this without choking I'll never know. Just call me Saint Katy of Ealing.

'Since when have you been bothered about Nina?' Ollie says. 'You can't stand her.'

'It's not just about her,' I say quickly. 'Imagine if James heard that we'd been out for dinner. He'd be bound to get the wrong end of the stick.'

'Let's get this straight. You still care about what that wanker thinks? After everything he's done? And you seriously *want* me to go out with Nina?'

'She's your type. You've got history.'

'This is the same Nina that you said is so up her own arse that she's inside out? That Nina?'

Er . . . I may have said that.

'She's not so bad. She's mad about you.'

'But Katy, I—'

I hold up my hands. 'Please, don't say anything else. Just go out and have a good time. In fact, I'm glad you texted her. I'd rather be alone – I'm really tired.'

'Fine,' Ollie says looking wounded. 'If that's what you want.'

'It is! Come on, Ol, don't be funny about it. Your

girlfriend's downstairs. Go and be with her. We're mates, we can catch up any time.'

'I'm not sure we can, Katy. In fact . . .' Ol pauses, and there's a catch in his voice, 'things are getting a bit awkward here, aren't they? It might be a good idea if you started thinking about finding somewhere else to stay.'

'You want me to go so you can be alone with Nina?'

Ollie doesn't meet my eye and suddenly seems to find the hideous Seventies carpet fascinating. 'You said it, not me.'

I swallow. 'I understand. I'll give Jewell a call. I'm sure she'll let me stay for a bit and then you guys can have all the space you need.'

He drags his eyes up from the psychedelic swirls beneath our feet. 'And you're OK with that?'

Er, no, actually. I can't bear the thought of Nina getting her French-manicured talons into my lovely pal, but I can hardly say this to Ollie, can I? Nina has a talent for being poisonous when she's alone with me and all sweetness and light when Ollie appears. Consequently he can't understand why I have a problem with her and I daren't try and explain because it'll just look like I'm jealous. And I'm not jealous. Obviously not.

But because I can't say any of this I just nod instead. 'Of course I am. It's fine. By the time you get back from Antonio's I'll have everything sorted. Since James threw me out I've been effectively homeless so I don't suppose it matters where I live, does it? I may as well be at Jewell's as anywhere else. There's nothing to keep me here.'

Ollie stares at me for a moment. Then he shrugs and says, 'Fine, call Jewell. I think you've made your feelings more than clear. I'll get going, I won't bother you any longer.' And with this he stomps out of the room, slamming the door so hard the entire house shakes.

I stare at the closed door, confused. What the hell was all that about? Here I am being a considerate friend by giving him space to be with Nina and trying my hardest to save him from feeling guilty about kicking me out, and what thanks do I get? None. Nada. Big fat zilch.

Men. They make everything so complicated.

Feeling very wronged, I fling myself on my bed and close my eyes. All the champagne has made me woozy and the room dips and spins like a roller coaster. When I eventually peel my face from the pillow it's dark outside and the street lamps throw tangerine pools of light into the room. Apart from the telephone shrilling a couple of times and a murmur of conversation from the other side of the party wall, all is still.

I've got a raging thirst from the champagne and my head's thumping like a techno track, so I pad down to the kitchen to fetch some water. Then I meander into the lounge and press the play button on the answerphone. Call me paranoid, but I have to make certain it isn't Dr Morris calling back to tell me that they got the results wrong and that actually I have got breast cancer after all.

Nothing would surprise me today.

The first message is for Ollie. It doesn't make much sense but it's from a travel agent, who says he won't get his deposit back for cancelling his skiing holiday.

That's weird. Ollie never said anything about cancelling his holiday. He adores skiing and saves like crazy all year so that he can go at Christmas.

That message is obviously a mistake, so I skip to the next one.

'Hello! Hello! Katy?'

The strident tones of Auntie Jewell fill the room, and in spite of myself I smile. Jewell hasn't a clue about answerphones and frequently tries to hold long and convoluted conversations with them.

'Where are you, darling? I've been on a spiritual retreat. Terribly serious, lots of chanting. Your parents would simply adore it. Anyway, I'm so thrilled with your good news. I did a healing meditation for you, so it must have worked.'

I shake my head. What is it with my family and all the hippy shit?

'But darling,' Jewell continues, and she sounds puzzled, 'I can't understand why you've left me three messages thanking me for paying for the private health care. I wish I'd thought of it. I'd have paid in a trice. But I didn't, darling, so you must have a secret admirer. How thrilling! Do let me know. Much love! Lots of kisses! Talk soon!'

The answerphone clicks off, leaving me staring at it in horror. It doesn't take a brain like Stephen Hawkings's to work out what's happened.

Why didn't Ollie tell me?

And, more importantly, why did he pay?

I'm just about to trek back into the kitchen and liberate a few cans of his Fosters to help me solve this puzzle when there's a fierce hammering at the door. Feeling like the porter in *Macbeth*, I push past the mountain bike, piles of takeaway leaflets and various other assorted hallway crap, yelling, 'All right! All right!' and 'Bollocks!' when I crack my shins on a bike pedal. Why can't everyone just push off and leave me alone to feel sorry for myself in peace?

I yank open the door and scream in horror because a triffid almost gobbles me up.

'Calm down, Chubster.' James elbows past, kicking the

door shut and practically burying me in lilies. Sickly yellow pollen rains down and waxy leaves bash me on the nose. 'These are for you.'

'Who died?'

James opens his eyes wide until he looks a bit like the Andrex puppy on a particularly sad day. With his floppy hair and pink mouth, all that's needed to complete the picture is a bog roll.

'They're for you, to say I'm sorry and that I'll die unless you forgive me and take me back. I love you and I can't live without you.'

Have I slipped, banged my head and woken up in a parallel universe?

'James,' I say slowly. 'What's going on?'

Thrusting the lilies at me – what is it with men and flowers today? – he snatches my hands into his and pulls me against him. Even through the squished lilies and his Armani suit I can't help but notice that compared to Ollie's chest James's is really puny. And his hands . . . have they always been this clammy?

'Oh Chubs,' he murmurs into the top of my head, 'I've been such a fool. Can you ever forgive me? I've been so blind, so stupidly blind to have let you slip through my fingers.'

'I didn't slip through your fingers,' I point out, nearly giving myself whiplash as I try to remove my face from the lilies. 'You threw me out. Bin bags flying through the air? Torn-up novels? Is this ringing any bells?'

'I was an idiot,' he agrees, tightening his grip and nearly putting my eye out on a leaf. 'I let my pride get in the way of our love.'

'Oh crap.' Twisting under his arm I make a break for freedom and pollen-free air. 'You were shagging someone else. No, don't deny it,' I add seeing that he's about to do exactly that. 'Alice Saville, isn't it? I saw you together at Millwards and she answered the phone at the flat.'

For the briefest second I think I see a flicker of irritation in his eyes before they glisten with tears.

'That was a moment of madness. It meant nothing to me.'

'It meant something to me!' I cry. 'I saw you with her, James! I saw you kissing her outside Millwards and it didn't look like nothing from where I was standing. And she answered the phone. At our flat.'

James sighs. 'I guess I have some explaining to do.'

'I don't think you need to *explain* anything.'

'But I do.' The lilies hit the floor. 'I was angry, hurt, humiliated and Alice threw herself at me. It was a moment of madness, Chubs.'

'Don't call me Chubs!' I hiss. 'I bloody hate it. Almost as much as I hate the fact that you moved another girl into our home only days after we broke up.'

'I was angry with you!' cried James. 'You ruined my promotion! You knew how much that job meant to me, Chu— er, Katy. You forced me to do it, surely you can see that?'

Is he for real, making out that I'm to blame for his crappy behaviour?

'So it's *my* fault you shagged her?'

'That isn't what I said. Just listen, will you?' demands James, and a familiar note of annoyance creeps into his voice. 'I'm trying to say Alice was a mistake, that the whole stupid misunderstanding between us—'

'James, you took my engagement ring back and threw my things out of the window. What exactly did I misunderstand?'

'I acted out of passion!' he cries, and his face starts to go pink, always a sure sign that he's about to lose his temper. 'I love you, Katy, and I want you back. I want to hold you in my arms and never let go. I want your smile to be the first thing I see before I go to sleep. I . . . um . . . I want to kiss your ruby lips.'

I gawk at him. He's either having a breakdown or a potentially lethal attack of purple prose.

'Darling, isn't our love worth a second chance?' Building up to the grand finale, James steps towards me, presumably to sweep me into his arms in true romantic-hero style. I have to give it to him – he certainly knows me well enough to choose exactly the right buttons to press. He knows how I cry my eyes out over *Titanic*, has seen first hand my impressive Mills and Boon collection and on many occasions has been unlucky enough to hear me wailing my unique bathtime power ballad medley. In the past, a bunch of flowers and a few flowery phrases have been more than enough to persuade me to overlook any tosser-like behaviour, so with the monster lilies and rehashed song lyrics he can be forgiven for believing that I'll fall gratefully into his arms. After all, everyone knows that Katy Carter's a sucker for romance, right?

But something's changed and I think it might just be me.

For almost four years I've put up with James dripfeeding me comments that chipped away at my confidence and made me think I really was as useless and as fat and as foolish as he said I was. When somebody is constantly saying how hopeless you are, even if they say it with a smile and a ruffle of your curls, it isn't long before you start to believe them.

But what if he was wrong? And always has been? What

if I'm not quite as useless as he thinks I am? I hold down a demanding job. I pay my bills – most of the time. I can even cope with thinking I have cancer.

Maybe I'm not a useless little Chubster after all?

'James, don't!' I raise my hands to ward him off. Suddenly, after weeks of longing for him to realise he's made a huge mistake and that I'm the love of his life after all, I find this isn't what I want.

Isn't life a bitch?

'What's wrong?'

'This isn't going to work.' I'm looking at him as though for the first time, wondering how I never noticed how thin his lips are or how his eyes are just that little bit too close together, giving him a rather mean look. 'It's over, James, really over.' And as I say it, I'm amazed to find that I actually mean every word. I really and truly don't want him back.

It's like the past four years has been a bad dream.

'You don't mean that,' James says firmly, just as he used to when I would tell him that I didn't like oysters or that I hated opera. 'Stop being so ridiculous and come back home, Chubs. You've made your point.'

I shake my head. 'The point I'm making is that I don't want to come home with you. It's over, James. You were right, even though I couldn't see it at the time. We're better off apart. We'd be happier with other people.'

James's high colour leaches away from his face, apart from two bright spots that glow Ronald McDonald-like on his cheekbones. He starts to breathe heavily through his nose, a sure sign he's about to flip, and the skin around his mouth goes greeny-white.

'You're seeing someone else,' he breathes. 'Who is he?'

When I was a kid I used to *love* oxtail soup, guzzling it

down and mopping up the meaty dregs with a hunk of bread. Then, one memorable lunchtime, shortly after learning to read, I was studying the empty tin and with dawning horror realised what I'd been eating. Ox and tail. Ox tail. Ox tails! Gross. In an instant, something I'd loved so much became totally abhorrent to me. Just thinking about it made me want to puke.

I expect you get the analogy.

Standing in Ollie's hall, squashed against the banisters and with the handlebars of a mountain bike digging into my hip, I thank the Lord that James dumped me before I was stupid enough to marry him.

'There's no one,' I say firmly, while fiddling with the lock on the door. 'But it's none of your business even if there was. It's over, James.' I push the door open. 'I'd like you to leave. I would say let's be friends, but I don't think we ever really were friends to begin with. At least now I know who my friends are.'

'Friends?' hisses James. 'Oh, I get it. You think you stand a chance with Ollie, don't you? Don't insult my intelligence,' he adds when I protest. 'You've always had a pathetic schoolgirl crush on him. And it's hilarious, because let's face it, what man would want you when he could have someone like Nina?'

'You did,' I point out.

'Only because of—'

'Because of what?'

'Nothing.' James purses his mouth up like a cat's bum. 'It doesn't matter.'

'Tell me,' I demand. 'What did I have that Nina doesn't?' Apart from ginger hair and a bigger bum, of course. 'Why did *you* *w*ant me?'

He fixes me with wide blue eyes. 'Because I love you. Nobody will ever love you the way that I love you.'

They're the right words but somehow they sound all wonky, a bit like when Les Dawson used to play the piano slightly off key. Love isn't the emotion I'm seeing in the tight set of his jaw or the muscle that has started to tic under his left eye. Annoyance, anger at not getting his own way, maybe, but love? Don't think so.

I sigh. 'Maybe you did love me once. I know I certainly loved you. But it's over, James, because your way of loving me isn't enough.'

'You don't mean that. You need me.'

I shake my head. 'I don't, I really don't. It's over, and I'd like you to leave, please.'

'Don't worry, I'm going,' James says, trampling the lilies underfoot. The smell of funerals hangs heavy in the air. 'But this is the biggest mistake of your life.'

I press myself against the flock wallpaper, stomach against my spine in my effort not to touch him, and wish that I didn't feel so stupidly close to tears. I should know from experience how foul James can be when he doesn't get his own way. He pauses in the doorway, presumably to make some dramatic point, but doesn't notice that one of Ollie's skis is listing drunkenly in the way and tumbles head over heels across the doorstep and splat into the assorted weeds and mud that masquerade as Ollie's garden. Unfortunately I commit the cardinal sin of laughing. Not little giggles either but great big belly laughs, which compete with the jets that circle above.

'Laugh all you want,' shouts James, scrambling to his feet and trying to brush dirt from his rear. It looks like he's shat himself and I laugh even harder. 'You'll wish you'd taken me up on my offer. I'm the best thing that ever happened to you. You've had your chance to do this nicely.' He attempts to walk in a dignified manner to the garden gate, not easy when picking bits of garden out of his hair, and fixes me with an ugly look. 'You'll regret this.'

'I doubt it,' I say, and watch him march to his BMW, his back ramrod straight and fists clenched by his sides. I'm not sure what this bizarre episode is all about, but something tells me James won't be letting it go in a hurry. With a seesawing stomach I close the door on him and turn my attention to scooping up the lilies and scrubbing pollen stains from my fingers like a modern Lady Macbeth.

As I do so, I hope that their deathly scent isn't some kind of omen.

Chapter Eleven

'Gracious!' exclaims Jewell, eyeing my bulging suitcases – borrowed from Ollie because by now I'm heartily sick of bin bags. 'How long are you staying for? I'm all for us girls having our lovely things around us, but . . .' she pauses when she notices that the checked hall floor is disappearing fast beneath my laptop, two winter coats and of course bloody Pinchy in his bucket, 'isn't this a little *excessive* for a weekend?'

She's right. Elizabeth I probably took less with her when she went on progress round the land. But today I'm a woman with a mission and I'm leaving nothing to chance. My presence in Milford Road is going to be a hindrance to Ollie's love life so I've figured it's probably best I clear off to leave him and Vile Nina to it. And I know myself too well to have left stuff behind to collect later. That would be the emotional equivalent of picking at a scab.

I bend to stroke one of Jewell's cats. 'Actually, I was hoping to stay a bit longer than the weekend, if that's OK with you, Auntie.'

'Of course it is!' Jewell nods and the green feathers on her turban bob enthusiastically. 'I love having you youngsters to stay. We'll have such fun being girls together.

What do you call it nowadays? Sleepovers? We can paint our nails and give each other makeovers.'

Jewell wears lipstick the colour of clotted blood and draws her eyebrows on with a pencil.

'Lovely,' I say weakly.

'Why don't you pop all this lot,' she sweeps her hand in the direction of my worldly goods, 'up to your old room? And I'll make us a lovely cup of tea.'

My old room is up in the attic, and by the time I've heaved all my stuff up there I'm sweating and possibly one dress size smaller. Gasping for air, I collapse on to my old bed and reflect sadly upon the harsh truth that I'm nearly thirty years old but right back to where I was when I was seven. It's like I've been playing virtual-reality snakes and ladders and almost got to square one hundred – merchant-banker fiancé, nice flat in west London, a sort of social life – but I landed on the biggest snake and slithered right back down to square number one.

I know. I know. It's really pathetic, but wouldn't you be feeling just a teeny bit sorry for yourself too if you were me? And what am I going to do about Ollie and the fact that I owe him a small fortune for my medical treatment? Why didn't I twig? He must think I'm so ungrateful.

Since that fateful evening at Milford Road, things have been decidedly awkward between Ollie and me. I thanked him for paying my medical bills, of course I did, and offered to pay it all back, but Ollie brushed me off.

'I wanted to pay,' he insisted, muscular back to me as he delved in the sink for a fork to shovel up his Madras. 'No one forced me.'

'It's too much.'

'Jesus!' snapped Ollie to the washing-up pile. 'It's done, OK? Stop bloody harping on about it.'

'But it must have cost a fortune.' I knew this for a fact, having rummaged through the dustbins to find the gunky evidence, a disgusting job if ever there was one and enough to make me glad I'd chosen teaching over the more glamorous lure of journalism. Once I'd pulled some congealed Chinese from the bill, I discovered that I owed Ollie over fifteen hundred pounds, which may as well be fifteen million because I'm so broke. I'm utterly determined to pay him back, though God only knows how. Maybe I should ask Reverend Rich if Satan still buys souls.

'Just forget it!' Ollie yanked out a fork from underneath a pile of plates. Unfortunately this was the Milford Road equivalent of Ker-Plunk, and he had just pulled out the bottom straw. Plates and saucepans tumbled to the floor and shards of china exploded everywhere.

'Bloody hell!' roared Ollie, making me jump out of my skin. Laid-back way past horizontal, Ol never loses his temper, one of the reasons he's such an excellent teacher. The kids learn quickly that nothing stresses Mr Burrows.

Apart from me, apparently.

It was safe to assume I'd seriously pissed him off.

'Just stop going on about it,' he growled, bending down to scoop up broken plates. 'I don't think you owe me anything in kind if that's what you're worried about. I'm not expecting you to offer me your body in gratitude.'

I shut up there and then, stung by the fury in his voice. In fact I more than shut up. I scuttled upstairs to my room, slammed the door and blubbed until you could have stuck me on a Christmas card and called me Rudolph. Then I called Jewell and asked if I could come and stay. Ollie stormed out of the house – presumably to Nina's – and the rest you know.

My other headache is that James won't give up. He's

sent endless letters of apology and I'm now on first-name terms with the man from Interflora. I'm the owner of helium balloons, Thorntons chocolates and, as of this morning, tickets for the Orient Express. James's selective memory knows no bounds. I'm starting to think he's totally unbalanced. After the way he's behaved, does he really think I'll forgive him? I'm determined not to go back to him. I'm never going to settle for second best again. So I'm sending all his latest gifts back, with a polite note telling him to bugger off, and hiding at Jewell's until he gives up.

What a pity he never liked me this much when we were together.

Abandoning these gloomy thoughts, I check that Pinchy's settled in to Jewell's huge claw-foot bath and make my way back to the kitchen.

'Mind Tabitha,' trills my godmother when I nearly break my neck tripping over a cat lying in the doorway.

Tabitha gives me an evil yellow-eyed glare.

'Sorry.' I plop myself down at the big lime-washed oak table. As usual it's covered with donkey's years' worth of assorted tat, ranging from bills and yellowing piles of newspaper, to the python's tank and the odd snoozing cat. This looks chaotic but Jewell swears it's the world's most efficient filing cabinet.

She plonks a chipped brown teapot on top of *TV Quick*, obscuring Gabriel Winters' cheesy grin. 'Let's have a nice cup of tea and you can tell me exactly why you're here.'

'What kind of tea is it?' Jewell has been known to experiment with anything from nettles to cannabis. Apparently she once gave the vicar such terrible munchies he ate his entire stock of communion wafers. But that's another story.

'Only Earl Grey,' she assures me, pouring pale amber liquid into two mugs and pushing one towards me. She settles back into her chair, scoops a cat on to her lap and peers at me over her half-moon glasses. 'Now, either my eyesight is finally giving up the ghost or you have come to stay for a bit longer than the weekend.'

I stare sadly into my mug. 'It's all such a mess, Auntie. I've ruined everything.'

'Nonsense,' Jewell says briskly. 'You youngsters don't know the meaning of awful or terrible. There's very little in life that can't be fixed, darling, but sometimes it means swallowing our pride and admitting we're wrong. In my experience these things are often a question of just how far one is prepared to go to make matters right.'

I pick a cat hair out of my drink. 'I'm not afraid to admit I've messed up, but I think it might be a bit too late to make things right.' And in between sips of scalding tea I tell her everything: how it's over with James and how without meaning to I've trashed the best friendship I ever had. By the time I grind to a halt with this sorry tale I'm blubbing again and mopping my eyes with a tea towel.

'So that's it,' I sniff as I end my epic tale of woe. 'James has become a stalker, Ollie's with Vile Nina and I'm totally on my own.'

Jewell strokes the cat. From the hall the old grandfather clock tick-tocks time away and in the distance a siren wails. In a patch of sunlight dust motes and pet hair drift idly towards earth.

'Darling,' she says eventually, just when I'm starting to wonder if she's heard a single word I've said, 'what do *you* want?'

'Sorry?'

'What do you want to do?'

I'm a bit cheesed off at this. I thought I'd made it perfectly clear to her exactly what I want. 'I just want James to—'

'No, Katy!' Jewell's bony hand shoots across the table and grabs mine. The papery skin and ink-blue veins conceal a surprising strength and I wince as her diamond rings dig into my fingers. 'Listen to the question! I want to know what *you* want, Katy, you! Not James or Ollie or any of the other young men that you've devoted yourself to. What are *your* hopes and dreams? What do *you* want more than anything else?'

Her eyes bore into mine.

'What do you want from life, my darling? What makes you happy? All you've told me is what you can do to make other people happy. What do you want for yourself?'

Somebody has crept past and nicked my vocal cords, because I can't speak. To be honest, after all the years of being with James, pretending to like oysters when actually they taste of snot, having to read *The Times* when secretly hankering after *Heat!* magazine and keeping my home as a minimalistic shrine to his good taste, I'm not really sure what I like or what makes me happy. I only know that hanging out with Ollie used to bring me pretty close to what I think happiness must feel like, and . . . blimey! Jewell is right. There I go again, judging my happiness in terms of the men in my life.

'You,' continues Jewell with all the subtlety of a rhino galumphing over eggshells, 'have based your entire sense of self, happiness and personal fulfilment on making the man in your life happy. You have totally subjugated your own wants and tastes and needs. You have become a casualty of patriarchy.'

Did I mention that Jewell was a militant feminist back

in the Seventies? She claims to have taught Germaine all she knows ('Although the fuss she made in *Big Brother*, darling! Honestly, after Greenham Common you think she'd have appreciated the luxury!').

'Isn't that what you do when you're in love? Put the other person first?'

'Not to the extent of erasing your entire personality. Think about the last few years, darling. What did you ever do that was actually what you wanted? Even your own wedding was James's taste.'

I take a huge gulp of tea. Jewell's words are making half-buried fears take shape in my mind that slowly loom, like figures in the mist, closer and clearer.

I'm starting to feel embarrassed about the person I become when I'm in a relationship. It's as though the minute I'm with a man, I instinctively put him first and me second. I start to make gaps in my own social life just in case he might call with plans, afraid that if I'm unavailable for just one evening it will make me a crap girlfriend and give him justification for moving on elsewhere, somewhere taller and thinner and considerably less ginger. I put everything into his well-being while my own interests and friends recede into the background until even I can hardly remember the hopes and dreams that used to drive me. Eventually all that's left is a pathetic need to please and keep the attention of whatever man is kind enough to chuck a few crumbs of attention at me. All I need is a frilly gingham frock, because I appear to have perfected the 1950s housewife thing.

Hmm. I think I may have a few self-esteem issues.

The more I think about my distinctly sappy behaviour, the more I start to feel very disillusioned, because where exactly has all this self-sacrifice got me? Did James appreciate the laying down of my entire identity or did he think I was a total doormat, only just stopping short of scrawling 'Welcome' on my forehead and wiping his feet on me?

I think we all know the answer to that question.

'I'm so stupid,' I groan.

'Darling, you are not!' exclaims Jewell. 'You are a lovely, giving girl with a generous heart that some less scrupulous types try to take advantage of. Besides,' she continues, warming to her theme, 'I think your parents ought to shoulder a little of the blame for your emotional neediness. Super people as Quentin and Drusilla are, they've made the most appalling parents. No wonder you're looking for a relationship to provide you with emotional stability after spending your formative years with them.'

She pauses, and I know we are both thinking about that frosty December morning when my parents decided they simply had to go to Morocco and left me and Holly on Jewell's doorstep with a hastily scribbled note asking her to look after us for a bit. For the next six months I convinced myself that if I'd been a prettier daughter, better behaved, not complained that Mum's Afghan coat stank, eaten mung beans without moaning and basically done every-thing they had wanted, then they wouldn't have gone. I was convinced that somehow their desire to abandon their two daughters and bum round Asia smoking hash and aligning their chakras was my fault for not being exactly the way they wanted.

I don't need to be Freud to work out where all this is leading.

'But never mind them now,' says Jewell. 'It's not really a question of apportioning blame. It's more a question of where you go from here. Maybe look on this as an opportunity for change and to move on. You gave James some of your best years, so why don't you take some time out for yourself? You've had a really lucky escape with your health too. Maybe Fate's trying to tell you something?'

My hand strays to the small dressing on my breast. I feel drunk with relief when I think about what could have happened and guilty that I'm sitting around grizzling about my rubbish love life when I should be thanking my lucky stars.

'None of us knows how much time we have,' Jewell sighs, reaching out to pat my hand. 'We owe it to ourselves to make the most of every minute of every day.'

She looks so wistful and so sad when she says this that a jolt of fear runs through me. If this was a soap opera she'd tell me now that she only has weeks to live and make me swear to go out and party for her. But luckily this is real life. Jewell says nothing of the kind but fixes me instead with a mega-watt smile and the moment passes.

'Gracious! How maudlin!' Letting go of my hand, she struggles out of her seat and walks stiffly to one of the kitchen cupboards. Immediately a furry sea of animals flows around her ankles, followed by a loud purring when she opens four cans of Whiskas and forks it into an assortment of bowls. I help myself to a fig roll and munch thoughtfully. Am I too reliant on men? Am I incapable of existing on my own?

I sincerely hope not or I'm screwed.

What do I really want from life?

And then suddenly I know. It's so bloody obvious that I laugh out loud. I know *exactly* what I want to do. I've always known. And Auntie Jewell will approve because it has nothing to do with finding a man.

Well, indirectly maybe, but not a real one.

'I want to write!' I cry. 'I want to see if I really can do it. I'd like to go away from London and stomp across the moors and walk in the rain. I want to have the chance just to see if I could be a real writer.'

Or find out if my stories really are pathetic drivel written by a teacher in a shitty sink school, as I seem to recall James so charmingly putting it. I'd like some time out to dedicate to handsome highwaymen and passionate pirates.

Jewell claps her hands. 'That's the spirit! And that's what you shall do!'

'Yeah, in my dreams. What about the practicalities? Where would I live? How would I live? How will I pay my credit-card bills?'

This last one is an increasing worry. My bills – which I would like to point out were run up by James in my name – are starting to make Everest look like an anthill.

'Money? Pah!' Jewell lobs the empty cans in the bin. 'That shouldn't come between you and your dreams. Hand your notice in at work, move in here for a while and play it by ear. Or go and visit lovely Maddy in Cornwall. As for those bills . . .' she rummages in an enormous handbag and plucks out a Coutts chequebook, 'let me be your fairy godmother. I'll pay off all those hideous credit cards so you can concentrate on your writing, and before you protest,' she adds quickly, seeing my mouth fall open, 'I will expect every penny paid back when you have your first advance. In fact I may even demand a percentage of your sales. You can't say fairer than that, darling. Anyway, think what I'm saving on a wedding present.'

'Auntie, I can't borrow your money. And I certainly can't live off you.'

She gives me a beady look. 'You'll still need a little part-time job, darling; I'm not that wealthy. But I'd much rather give it to you than lend more to James.'

'You've lent James more money?' My chin is almost in the wine cellar.

Jewell nods. 'A thousand here and a thousand there, cash-flow problems he said, but darling, I was starting to wonder what was going on. Don't think I didn't notice him eyeing up my house too, trying to estimate the real estate. He had pound signs in his eyes. He's far too much like his mother in that respect. I'm very fond of James, darling, and I was delighted when you bumped into him again, but I do wonder about his motives sometimes.'

There's not much I can say to this because I'm starting to wonder myself. I feel really ashamed of James and even more ashamed of myself for not seeing through him. Love wasn't so much blind in my case as deaf and dumb to boot.

'But James earns tons of money,' I point out. 'Why would he need to borrow from you?'

Jewell shrugs. 'I've no idea, darling, but Cordelia always did have expensive tastes. Maybe that rubbed off on James.'

I think of the bespoke shoes and Turnbull and Asser shirts that graced his half of the wardrobe, whereas I was practically best mates with George at Asda.

Yes, I think we can safely say James likes the finer things in life. Paying for them, though, seems to be another matter entirely.

'Never mind him, anyway, he's history,' says Jewell firmly. 'It's time you moved on, darling. Fetch some Moët out of the fridge and let's toast your new start as a romantic novelist!'

Experience has taught me that once Jewell's got a bee in

her bonnet, there's no point trying to stop her. Canute probably found it easier to turn back the tide.

Jewell pops the cork, fills the glasses and then holds up her champagne flute. 'To Katy Carter, her new career and a new romantic hero!'

As we clink glasses, I try to look all independent and empowered, but actually I don't feel like that at all.

I feel really lonely.

And very, very scared.

Chapter Twelve

'We're approaching Liskeard! Liskeard is the next station stop!'

This nasal announcement takes me by surprise, and it's almost a shock to find myself in a railway carriage so crowded that it makes a tin of sardines look roomy. My pen hovers over the page of my new writing book and for a second I wonder where the castle and Millandra have gone.

I've never known time to pass as slowly as it has on this train journey from Paddington down to Cornwall. I used to think that double maths dragged when I was at school but it's nothing compared to being crammed on to this train. I'm sitting next to someone who has a major body-odour problem so have been forced to breathe through my mouth since Reading. I sound like Darth bloody Vader. And why am I so tired just from sitting on my bum? I ought to be really good at that by now. If there was a Sitting on your Arse Olympics, I'm very confident that I'd be up for the gold.

At one point I ambled to the buffet car, swaying drunkenly with the motion of the train and cannoning off other passengers with each lurch of the carriage. One coffee, a Snickers and second-degree burns later I was back in my seat, having first to squeeze past BO Man and contort my body to fit around his bags. I munched away and hoped I'd made the right decision. My usual manner of coping with feeling this miserable is to go on a mega shopping spree and burn the plastic to melting point, but oddly this no longer holds any appeal, probably because I'm going to really need to watch the pennies from now on. I've also had a couple of really peculiar letters from James in which he asks me to contribute to various bills and even the mortgage.

Well, he can stick that up his bottom. Why should I? I don't even live with him any more, and besides, he earns quadruple what I do. Let Alice bloody Saville sort it out.

I look out of the window. Acres of gently rolling countryside whiz past in a green blur. It's really very pretty. Odd as it may sound, I've never ventured further west than Devon before, so the train journey is something of an adventure. I'm boldly going where I've never been before and I'm amazed by the stunning scenery that is unfurling before my eyes like something from *Wish You Were Here*. The rippling ploughed earth is the most amazing brick red, bright against dark woods and the duck-egg-blue sky. Crumpled cottages huddle next to thick copses like little islands floating in an ocean of corn and pasture. Hailing from Ealing, where no one feels safe unless they're a five-minute drive away from Sainsbury's, it is all refreshingly alien. Perhaps I will be able to gain solace from the natural world around me like some great romantic heroine in literature? It's a pity Wordsworth cornered the market in romantic poetry about three hundred years ago, because I feel certain that some great lyrical ballad could spring forth from my present tormented state.

The best bit of the journey is when the train winds its way along a section of track that is so close to the sea I can practically dip my toes in. I feel like I'm on a trip to another land; the sparkling sea is nothing like the sluggish brown waters of the Thames, and neither do the slow, rich accents of the passengers who board and disembark have anything in common with the guttural tones of the kids I teach. The bobbing fishing boats and windsurfers with bright sails make me think of Ollie. If he was here he'd have his face pressed against the glass and would be busy explaining how they float and all the manoeuvres they can do. Ollie will talk about windsurfing all day, given half a chance.

Not that he's really talking to me at the moment. He could hardly drag himself to my leaving do and just about managed to grunt good luck.

Nina's charm and grace are rubbing off on him, it seems.

Just like I promised Jewell, I've taken a sabbatical from my job and am moving in with Maddy for a while to begin my new life as a romantic novelist. Maddy's desperate to show me the local talent, and of course I'm going to rewrite my novel in the new writing book Frankie bought me in Paperchase at Paddington.

'Now, darling,' he said as we located my platform, 'are you sure about this?'

Frankie has misgivings about my running away to stay with Mads. Exciting as he thinks a man in a frock is, he isn't keen on the sound of Richard. I daren't tell him that Mads hasn't even told Richard yet. We thought a fait accompli would be better. And after all, what can he possibly do to us when we do tell him? He's a vicar.

'I'm totally sure,' I replied. 'I can't bear to be around for a moment longer. James is driving me mental, and anyway, it's best I leave Ollie and Nina in peace.'

Frankie's smooth brow crinkled. 'I just can't get my head around the whole Nina thing. She's totally wrong for him, you know. Can't you stay here and convince him to dump her? I'm sure they'd let you have your job back if you asked the head really nicely.'

'I don't want my job back. That cancer scare was a real wake-up call. No matter how hard it is, I am moving on even if it bloody well kills me.'

'I guess you're doing the right thing,' Frankie said, helping me on to the train. 'Jewell's right, you'll feel so much better by taking positive action to get over James instead of sitting on your arse feeling sorry for yourself. That wouldn't have got Hamlet very far, would it?'

'Hamlet went mad and died,' I pointed out.

'Really?' Frankie was amazed. 'I never did see it to the end; far too tantalising for me having to look at all those beautiful boys in tights for four hours and not being allowed anywhere near. I just had to go for a drink to calm myself down.' He pulled himself out of this most absorbing memory with some effort and turned his attention back to the far less exciting me. 'You do remember what I said about Gabriel Winters?'

'If I see him I'm to ring you straight away,' I chanted dutifully.

'Exactly!' Frankie clapped his hands. 'Now I have your number and I'll be down to visit very soon.'

And off he went to check Pinchy in with the guard, leaving me dangerously close to tears. In spite of his affectations, I'm really fond of Frankie. Carrie from *Sex and the City* is so right – every girl should have a gay best friend.

Heterosexual ones, though, are another matter entirely . . .

'You said Liskeard,' says the lady sitting opposite me.

'Better get a move on, my lover! You've got a lot to carry.'

She's not wrong. I've got more luggage than Louis Vuitton, not to mention Pinchy, who is stowed in the guard's van, floating lazily in a plastic tub. Once more I've picked up my life and moved it on.

As the train pulls into the station, I gather up my bags and dangle out of the window in a feeble attempt to open the door. I end up falling out of the train and scattering my belongings everywhere.

Bloody marvellous.

So here I am on the station platform with all my things at my feet while disembarking passengers flow past me. Everything is really different. The light seems brighter somehow and the air is sharp and fresh. I draw great greedy gulps of it into my poor polluted city lungs.

'This yours, m'bird?' the portly stationmaster asks, wheeling a blue plastic tub containing Pinchy towards me.

I nod. Pinchy shoots me a knowing look from his boot-button eyes.

'I had that Rick Stein on my platform once,' says the stationmaster. 'He didn't bring a lobster with him, though. Dinner, is it?'

Pinchy looks most offended. 'It's a long story. He's more of a pet really. I'm taking him to the sea to release him.'

The stationmaster rolls his eyes.

'Blooming emmets! A pet lobster? Whatever next? It'd be 'andsome with a drop of that Mary Rose sauce. Still, up to you. Do you want a hand carrying your things?'

'Please.' My arms feel so stretched from lugging my cases I'm amazed they're not dragging along the floor gorilla-style.

I follow him along the platform through the throng of weary commuters and jaunty holidaymakers, up a steep flight of steps, over a footbridge and up another set of steps to the road. By the time I put my bags down I'm puffing more than Dot Cotton on a Bensons and Hedges. I really must get fit, yet another addition to my rapidly growing list of things to do.

'Shall I call you a taxi, maid?' asks the stationmaster. 'Only I lock the station up at six and the call box is out of order.'

'I'm fine, thanks. I'm getting a lift.' I peer up and down the road for Maddy, but as yet there's no sign of her. I'm not perturbed by this, though, because Mads is habitually late wherever she goes. She was even an hour late to her own wedding. 'I'm staying with my friend in Tregowan.'

'Pretty place, Tregowan,' he says, putting Pinchy's box down. 'I wouldn't live there, though. Me and the missus like to park outside our house, see.'

As he returns to the platform I'm left mystified. What sort of place is Tregowan if you can't park cars there? In my mind's eye I picture narrow cobbled streets and smugglers rolling barrels of brandy into caves.

'Isn't it exciting?' I say to Pinchy, but he turns his back on me and starts to clean his antennae. Ungrateful creature. Next time I'll let Ollie cook him.

Only there won't be a next time, will there? My eyes sting and I blink furiously. This is my fresh start, the beginning of my exciting new life. I'm not going to cry. It's time to move on.

'Onwards and upwards,' I tell myself sternly.

The trouble is, there's a bit of a problem with the onwards part because Mads still hasn't arrived to pick me up. At first I'm pretty relaxed with this. The setting sun is warm on my face and the soft breeze is heavy with the tang of wild garlic. Apart from the distant rumble of a tractor and the trembling baa of sheep, everything is still. Only a couple of cars have driven past, which I take to be the Cornish equivalent of rush hour. I settle down with my belongings and wait.

Forty minutes later I'm still waiting and starting to panic. The setting sun's dipping behind the hill, and although it casts the most amazing pink blush over the countryside, the warmth is slipping away. It's still only April and in my gypsy top and floaty skirt I start to feel chilly.

I fish my mobile out of my bag but the screen tells me that there's limited service. Fan-bloody-tastic. I shove it back in and wait for a bit longer. By the time the sun is little more than a golden fingernail against a scarlet sky, I'm contemplating abandoning my post and walking to town. Wherever that might be. I look down at my legs, which are stretched out in front of me, and mourn the fact that I will surely ruin my lovely suede Shelley's boots. It might be spring in Cornwall but the road looks like a mud pit.

I am going to kill Maddy Lomax when I see her.

I'm at the point of despair when the most enormous black BMW 4x4 drives by, its sidelights sweeping over me as it passes. I hear a crunch of gears, then it reverses rapidly and comes to a halt right next to me. The driver kills the engine and one tinted window lowers.

Maddy? Surely not in a BMW unless the Church of England's just given vicars a significant pay rise I don't know about?

I crane my neck in an attempt to see who the driver is, but the setting sun glances off the shiny paintwork and dazzles me so all I can make out is one toned arm resting at the bottom of the window. One toned *male* arm.

Definitely not Maddy then.

Just my luck. The only kerb-crawler in Cornwall and he has to find me. I prepare myself for a slimy git and rack my brains for a stinging put-down.

Then the driver peeks his head out of the window, smiles at me and I almost pass out with shock.

Oh God. The stress of the last few weeks must have taken more of a toll on me than I realised.

'Pinch me, Pinchy,' I say to the lobster. 'I'm hallucinating.'

I must be, because otherwise I would swear that the driver, who's smiling at me, his teeth so white that I need shades, is none other than Gabriel Winters himself. I look away, count to five and look back.

Christ on a bike! It is! It really is!

'Hey there!' says Gabriel Winters, in the gravelly, sexy voice that the nation has so recently heard persuading Jane Eyre into bed. 'You look a bit lost.'

'I'm waiting for a lift.' I'm aiming for a sexy purr but sound instead like Orville the duck. 'My friend hasn't turned up. I'm meant to be going to Tregowan.'

He pulls off his shades and bright sapphire eyes twinkle at me. 'Well, by happy coincidence I'm going there too. Why don't we put your things in the boot and I'll drive you? I can't leave a beautiful woman stranded by the side of the road.'

I look around just in case Angelina Jolie is also stuck here.

No, just one small ginger Katy Carter.

Oh. My. God. Mr Rochester thinks I'm beautiful!

Mind you, he was blinded in the final episode.

I ought to say no to this lift; after all, I've seen all the stranger-danger videos going, but this is Gabriel Winters, possibly the hottest actor in Britain, not some old perv in a mac. He's not going to do anything unspeakable to me.

I should be so lucky.

'Are you sure?' I ask, totally transfixed by the long denim legs emerging from the BMW. The muscles ripple beneath and strain at the fabric. I also glimpse a tantalising strip of taut, tanned stomach as his white T-shirt rides up. Oh my God! He's a virtual-reality Mills and Boon alpha male!

'Of course I'm sure.' Gabriel lifts my suitcases into the boot as easily as though they were made of polystyrene. 'Besides, I'm going there anyway. Didn't you read in the papers that I've bought a house in Tregowan?'

'No,' I say.

'Oh.' He looks really disappointed, and it's as though the sun has gone in.

'But I'm sure it's all over the papers,' I say quickly. 'I haven't read any for ages.'

Gabriel looks slightly happier.

'I'm filming down in Tregowan so I thought I might as well buy myself somewhere there,' he continues, helping me climb into the passenger seat. I take his hand as I spring up and hope my bum doesn't look too ginormous in my skirt. 'Property in Cornwall's an excellent investment, isn't it?'

'Absolutely!' I nod manically, although I can't even afford a doll's house.

Gabriel puts the car into gear and I find I can't tear my eyes away from his strong brown hand upon the gear stick, the very same hand that brought Jane Eyre to ecstasy. 'The house is called Smuggler's Rest. It's the most amazing place, with stunning views. Needs a bit of work, though, so I thought I might invite Sarah Beeny down to have a look.'

'Really?' I try very hard not to sound too impressed. Sarah Beeny! Wow!

Gabriel guides the car down a steep hill and into a densely wooded lane. Purple and lilac shadows pool across the road. The sky is smeared with turquoise and a slice of moon beams down at us like a smile in the sky. I feel as though I'm in a very weird dream.

'Tregowan's amazing,' Gabriel says. 'It's like a model village. You'll love it . . . um . . .'

'Katy,' I say. 'Katy Carter. I'm staying with Maddy Lomax, the vicar's wife? She's not been here long.'

But Gabriel doesn't want to talk about Maddy.

'Did you enjoy *Jane*?' he asks, swinging the car around a hairpin bend and up a very steep hill.

I think about telling him that I think the post-feminist representation of Jane is a mistake and that I found his portrayal of Rochester to be distinctly misogynistic, but something about the expectant look on his face stops me in my tracks.

'It was great!' I fib. 'I loved the wet-trousers scene.'

Gabriel nods, his golden ringlets bobbing.

'Colin Firth was really put out about that,' he grins. 'Helen says she's going to use it in her next book.'

'Helen?' The only famous Helen I can think of was in *Big Brother* donkey's years ago. I'd be amazed if she could write her name, never mind a book.

'Fielding.' He changes down a gear and we crawl up a hill. 'She wrote *Bridget Jones*? My agent's going to get me an option on the part of Rochester, Bridget's new lover. Renée is up for it. And Hugh.'

My head's swimming. It's like being in a real-life copy of *OK!* magazine. Posh and Becks will pop out from under the back seats in a minute.

'But enough about me!' laughs Gabriel, and his laugh is deep and gravelly. 'What about you?'

How do I compete with that?

'I'm writing a novel,' I say, because this sounds better than unemployed and dumped. 'Mads is letting me stay with her for a bit to work on it. She says Cornwall's inspirational.' I decide to leave out the bit about all the fit men and finding myself a romantic hero. It would sound ridiculous, seeing as I'm sitting next to the personification of one.

Gabriel turns his head and shoots me a really cute smile, and I like the quirky way that his mouth is higher one side than the other. I wish I could get my notebook and jot down some ideas. Millandra could do with another suitor to give Jake a run for his money.

'It certainly inspires me,' he drawls. 'There are eight pubs in Tregowan, and sometimes you find cute girls at the side of the road!'

Cute *girls*? The kids at school think I'm practically dead! Wayne Lobb once asked me what life was like in the war, cheeky little bastard.

Gabriel's got more cheese than the cheddar factory, but I'm absurdly flattered that he's making the effort to chat me up. We pass the twenty-minute journey to the village chatting, mostly about Gabriel, and flirting mildly. By the time the 4x4 descends down an almost vertical hill, I know everything about his career, from his toothpaste commercial to the latest pirate movie. And if Gabriel knows little more than my name, it's hardly surprising; he is after all a television star and I'm just an unemployed English teacher.

'Welcome to Tregowan,' he says.

I'm holding my breath, because the view that dips away beneath us is dizzyingly beautiful. It's early evening and the twilight seeps in from a darkening sky, but I can still see the lichen-crusted rooftops of crumpled cottages where seagulls huddle against chimneypots. Other gulls are wheeling crazily above the village, swooping towards distant trawlers whose green and scarlet lights herald their return. Down against the harbour wall, boats rise and dip with the swell of the tide, and from the windows of a pub fairy lights glitter and spill dancing patterns into the water.

Lewisham it isn't.

'It's stunning,' I breathe.

'That's my house,' Gabriel tells me, gesturing to a large white building perched precariously on the side of the valley. 'The Lomaxes live over there, in the pink cottage just above the fish market.'

I lean forward and squint at the rectory. Either all the years of marking have wrecked my eyesight or there is no road anywhere near it.

'That's right,' nods Gabriel when I mention this. 'There's a path up to the rectory from behind the fish market. The vicar can help you with your bags.'

That will really make Richard's day.

'I'll have to drop you here,' Gabriel says, pulling up by a paved seating area. 'We can't get the car any nearer.'

'This is fine,' I say, unbuckling my seat belt. 'Thanks. I owe you one.'

'Buy me a drink then.' Gabriel retrieves my luggage, leaving me to carry Pinchy. 'If you want?'

I can hardly believe my ears. Gabriel Winters is asking

me to go for a drink with him! James who? Mads was right; this move to the country *is* a good idea.

'It's the least I can do,' I say calmly, as though rich and famous actors ask me out for drinks on a daily basis.

So I follow him down a very narrow street past higgledy-piggledy cottages and gift shops whose windows are crammed full of piskies and fudge. We stroll past the fish market, where a crowd of holidaymakers watch oilskin-clad fishermen weighing their catch. The smell of fish is strong and I wrinkle my nose, but Pinchy waves his antennae with great enthusiasm, as though to tell me that he's nearly home.

'We'll go to the Mermaid,' Gabriel says. 'It's a great pub. You'll love it.'

We climb some steep steps cut into dark rock, which lead up to the fairy light-dappled building I spotted from the car. Gabriel dodges a crowd of smokers huddled beneath a feeble patio heater and pushes open a sturdy wooden door, ducking his head as he does so. I follow him, catching the whispers of 'Is it really him?' that spread out in his wake like wash behind a boat, and wish that I'd had time to drag a brush through my curls. My one and only sort of date with a celebrity and I look like I'm wearing Ronald McDonald's hair.

Just my luck.

Inside the pub it's very dark and very hot. People jostle elbow to elbow at the bar and vie impatiently with each other to attract the barmaid's attention. In the window seat, tourists dressed in walking boots pore over guide-books and play dominoes. The locals, who seem to be crammed into a dim corner at the far end of the bar, chat amongst themselves. By the fireplace a man in a big hat plays the guitar and sings enthusiastically while his girlfriend tries to persuade the drinkers to put on silly hats and join in the fun. Before long I'm wearing a sombrero and singing along while Gabriel, ridiculously attractive in a tricorn hat, signs autographs good-naturedly. Several people admire Pinchy in his blue crate but nobody seems to think it at all weird that I've brought a lobster in for a pint.

'Here.' Gabriel thrusts a fifty-pound note into my hands; at least I assume that's what it is because I've never seen one before. 'Get the beers in! I'll find a seat.'

Feeling like a ginger dwarf in a land of giants, I dodge elbows and pint glasses and worm my way to the bar. I narrowly miss having my eye put out by a flailing cigarette and clamber up on to a foot rail. That's better. I'm at least four inches taller now, and I enjoy surveying the world from my newly acquired vantage point. Even so, I'm just one small hand waving a note amongst a crowd worthy of a Madonna concert.

I catch the barmaid's eye and she smiles apologetically as she serves the most enormous round to a fisherman with a very loud voice who's happily telling all and sundry why the Common Fisheries Policy is a bad idea. Eventually he pays up and it's my turn. While the barmaid pulls me two pints of very potent-looking scrumpy, she keeps looking first at me and then at Gabriel. I like the way her nose stud twinkles in the candlelight. Maybe it's time for a piercing. I can do whatever I like now I don't have James bossing me around.

It's a heady thought. Perhaps I'll get a tattoo as well, one of those ones on the small of the back that he always said were common. I could ask for *Up yours James* in Sanskrit or something. That could be fun.

'Katy! Over here, darling!' hollers Gabriel. He really

doesn't need to tell me where he is, though; the throng of holidaymakers clustered around clamouring for autographs kind of gives it away. I take a sip of cider from the brim of each pint glass so as not to spill it before negotiating a path through the throng, which is easier said than done. This tiny Cornish pub is so packed it makes the Piccadilly Line in rush hour seem roomy.

'Thanks, sweetheart!' Gabriel takes his drink and guides me through the press of people, and I'm struck by how bizarre life can be. I mean, this time last night I was still in London, terrified that James would pop up again with half of Kew Gardens, and this evening I'm in a Cornish pub drinking with Gabriel Winters! Nobody at home will believe me.

I hardly believe me.

Gabriel and I sit down in a window seat and admire the view. By that I mean he looks at the rolling sea and the boats straining against their moorings and I sneak sideways looks at him. How can anyone be so physically perfect? Even the sprinkling of golden stubble that shades his jaw is designer. What's really strange, though, is that although I can admire him from a purely aesthetic point of view, I don't feel remotely attracted to him.

I'm probably still in shock from breaking up with James.

'Excuse me.' A woman dressed in the tourist uniform of fleece and jeans approaches our table. 'Aren't you Gabriel Winters?'

Gabriel swells visibly. 'I certainly am.'

'Could I possibly take your picture?' She waves her digital camera at him. 'I'm a huge fan. I taped every episode of *Jane*.'

'My pleasure.' Gabriel smiles. 'I'm always happy to oblige my fans. You guys have put me where I am today.'

The camera flashes. I can't help but feel a little queasy. Beautiful he might be, but Gabriel could rival the Jolly Green Giant when it comes to corniness.

'Sorry,' he says, looking anything but. 'This happens to me a lot.'

'I think she'll be disappointed.' My eyes are still dazzled from the flash. 'I'm sure I was in the shot.'

'She can edit you out,' he replies, totally without irony.

Charming! Still, he's probably right. Lots of people seem to be editing me out lately.

As we drink, Gabriel tells me all about his pirate movie, which is still in the planning stages, his latest romance with a soap star and the renovations to his new house. Pinchy and I listen attentively for at least thirty minutes, during which Gabriel scarcely draws breath. I try to tell him about *Heart of the Highwayman* but his eyes keep sliding sideways and I soon realise that he's checking his hair in the shiny horse brasses.

Blimey, even James wasn't that vain.

Mind you, if I was as beautiful as Gabriel Winters I'd most likely be glued to a mirror too. I check my own reflection and wince. With my frizzy ginger hair and cheeks flushed from the heat, I look even more like Ronald McDonald. Not a good look.

'Well, I'm here because—' I begin, and then stop because he's blatantly not listening. In fact he's looking at his watch. I think it's a Rolex but I can't be sure. Humble English teachers seldom get to see such things.

'Christ!' Gabriel exclaims loudly, attracting admiring glances from the female population of the pub. 'Is that the time? I'm due at Rick Stein's at eight to meet my director. Drink up, darling. I'd better make tracks.'

I'm obediently finishing my pint when the door of the pub flies open and a tall figure strides in.

'Has anyone seen my wife?' he asks, scanning the pub like the Terminator.

'She hasn't been here all day,' the barmaid says quickly. She has her back to me and I notice her fingers are crossed.

'Well if you do,' the man barks, 'please remind her that she was supposed to be chairing the mother and baby group this afternoon. And,' he adds tetchily, 'that music's far too loud. I can hear it in my study. Unless someone sorts it out I'll be putting a complaint in to the local council.'

And with this parting shot he spins around in a whirl of black clothing and stomps out of the building.

'Maybe his missus is having an affair,' says the pub singer, pulling a face. 'That's the third time this month he's come in here looking for her.'

'Can't say I blame her if she is,' says the loud fisherman. 'He's a miserable bastard.'

I sink down into my seat and pull the sombrero over my eyes as the cross husband stamps past the window and down the steps. I feel like turning tail and running back to London as fast as my feet can carry me.

I have a very bad feeling about this, because the annoyed husband in question is none other than the Reverend Richard Lomax.

Chapter Thirteen

By the time I've plucked up the courage to venture to the rectory, twilight has fallen in and the lights of Tregowan twinkle below like hundreds of stars. Thanks to the steep climb up, I'm panting as though about to give birth.

'Who needs a gym?' I ask Pinchy as I collapse on the doorstep. After a few weeks of living here I'll be the size of Nina. Just as well I built my strength up with a couple more pints of scrumpy.

I've been skulking about the fish market, pretending to be engrossed in the evening's catch but really waiting to see if Richard is still about. I know that he's a man of the cloth, but quite frankly I don't want to enrage him any more. I haven't the foggiest what's been going on, but I know Maddy, and I have a horrible feeling it's nothing Richard will like. If she is having an affair, though, I'll be staggered, because I've always thought she really loves him. Can't quite see the attraction myself, although I suppose he's OK in a tall and aesthetic kind of way. He's allegedly got a fit body beneath that cassock too, if Mads is to be believed.

I tug on the rope by the front door and somewhere in the rectory a bell tolls ominously. I peek through the window into a cosy kitchen, and sure enough there's an Aga in the chimney breast and piles of clutter spread across all available surfaces. Mads is the queen of clutter. She makes Steptoe and Son look neat and tidy.

Then the front door swings opens and Mads appears, her dark hair up in curlers and a layer of green goo spread over her face.

'Shit,' she gasps. 'Katy! Bollocks!'

'Nice to see you too,' I say. 'Thanks for abandoning me at the station.'

'I'm so sorry!' She cries, ushering me inside. 'I can't believe I forgot you were coming. It just went out of my head.'

'Luckily for you, I got a lift,' I tell her, putting Pinchy's crate down and rubbing my aching back. 'But I've had to leave my stuff at the pub.'

'We'll get it later,' says Mads airily. She peers into the crate. 'This must be the famous Pinchy.'

'Infamous more like,' I say darkly. 'Single-clawedly responsible for ruining my relationship with James.'

'Good boy!' Maddy grins. 'Well done for seeing off that tosser.'

I open my mouth to point out that she's hardly one to preach about being in a relationship with a total dickhead, but close it again. After all, I'm going to have to be a well-behaved guest for a while.

'Let's sort you out,' Mads says to Pinchy, carrying the crate up a very narrow staircase. 'Then Mummy and I will have a nice cup of tea.'

'I'm not its bloody mummy,' I mutter. Honestly! If I had a quid for every time I've wished I'd let Ollie cook the sodding thing, I could give the Beckhams a run for their money. It seems to me that I can trace all my problems back to the moment Ollie entered my flat with the crafty crustacean.

The rectory is even tinier on the inside, like the Tardis in reverse. It's very sweet, all wooden floors, bright rag rugs and low beams, but even I have to duck my head going up the stairs. The bathroom is more of a cupboard, and while Mads runs the bath I have to stand on the landing because there's no way we can both fit in. I notice that there are two rooms leading off from this area and another vertical flight of stairs to the attic space.

'Pop up and check your room,' Maddy suggests. 'I cleaned it especially.'

Mads is to cleaning what I am to nuclear physics, so I'm pleasantly surprised to find a really cosy little room in the eaves waiting for me. There's a double bed covered with a pretty quilt and blue gingham curtains at the tiny window. Mads has even put some flowers on the sill and piled up some books on the bedside table. I don't relish the thought of negotiating the stairs after a night in the Mermaid, but apart from that it's perfect. I kneel on the window seat and look down over Tregowan. Sure enough the view is all that Maddy promised, rolling waves and twinkling lights. I can just picture myself curled up here writing the next instalment of Jake and Millandra's story, and for the first time in ages my skin prickles with excitement. I *know* I can write here, I'll have loads of fun with Maddy, and already I've met a romantic hero who's totally inspired my next chapter. Everything is going to be great. I just know it.

For the first time in ages the nasty twisty sensation of unease in my tummy vanishes and I feel . . . I feel . . .

I feel like *me* again.

My God! I really do. Not Chubster, or Miss Carter, or Ollie's mate, but *me*, Katy Carter. How brilliant is that?

Jewell was right. Coming here is exactly what I needed to do. My life in London had been out of balance for so long that I'd just accepted it. James and I weren't equal partners towards the end – maybe we never had been – and for far too long I'd been stuck in a rut thinking I needed him both emotionally and financially. It wouldn't have mattered how long or how hard I tried to make the relationship work, it never would have been healthy because we were just too different. And maybe I was too reliant on poor Ollie as well?

It's about time I stood on my own two feet and made some changes.

Like Jewell said, it's time for me to find out what I want.

'Tea!' calls Mads, interrupting my deep and meaningfuls, and from downstairs I hear the chink of cups.

'Coming!' I cross the room swiftly, but on my way I notice that the corner of a box is sticking out from under the bed. I won't want to bash my shin on that in the middle of the night. Giving the box a shove back underneath, I'd have thought no more of it except that it starts to make a noise.

Buzz! Buzz! Buzz! goes the box.

My poor heart nearly bursts out of my chest.

Buzz! Buzz!

I look around guiltily. What have I done? What have I broken? It's bound to be something expensive that belongs to Richard, another blot in my exceedingly smudged copybook. What to do?

I totally understand where Pandora was coming from when she opened her box, because my little fingers are itching to unfasten this one. I can't just leave it buzzing, can I? I'll actually be doing Richard a favour if I turn it off and save the batteries. I'm not being nosy. I'm being helpful.

Before I can stop myself, I'm dragging the box out. The buzzing gets even louder. Knowing my luck, it's a giant hornet.

I pull off the lid.

Oh. My. God.

It's giant all right.

But it's not a wasp.

I only wish it was.

Buzzing away with a life all of its own is the most enormous vibrator I've ever seen in my life. Not that I've seen that many. And not just the one, either. This box is packed full of vibrators of every shade and variety known to man, or rather woman. Some have the most realistic network of veins (why?), others are bright candy pink, and one terrifying specimen is ten inches of black plastic complete with what look like revolving spikes. I stare at it in fascinated horror.

I'm a twenty-first-century chick, I'm pretty liberated and I've been known to wander into Ann Summers. OK, so I left my hood up. Can you imagine what my life at school would have been like if Wayne Lobb and Co. had seen their English teacher testing chocolate body paint or playing with love beads? It's OK for those *Sex and the City* girls to act out their fantasies all over New York; they don't have to work with a bunch of teenagers with hormones so rampant you can practically see them. There's nothing like teaching to put you off sex for life – the thought of ending up with your own teen is too hideous for words.

So I do know all about vibrators; I've just never actually met one before, although this is less of a vibrator and more like a weapon of mass destruction. My eyes are watering just thinking about it.

Why has Mads got a box of sex toys under the bed? She's always telling me how she and Richard have an amazing sex life. I'd rather pull my nails out with pliers than shag the Rev, but Mads has always insisted that beneath the cassock Richard is a love god. I've always assumed that's why she married him.

Certainly wasn't for his sense of humour.

Then I have a horrible thought. What if the sex aids are Richard's? What if Maddy doesn't know? That must be it. Maddy was trying to tell me something on the telephone the other day but had to stop because Richard came into the kitchen. She's worried that he's having an affair. And he's pretending to be annoyed about her whereabouts in order to create a smokescreen.

The absolute bastard!

I'm a genius at solving mysteries. Hercule Poirot has nothing on me.

I reach into the box and switch the vibrator off.

'Gross.' I shudder.

'You don't like the Throbbing Theo?' I almost have a cardiac arrest when Mads leans over me and plucks the spiky monster from the box. 'Perhaps the rabbit is more to your taste?' She waves a girlie pink creation under my nose. 'It has revolving pearls for total clitoral stimulation.'

It does? And I thought rabbits had cute twitchy noses and cotton-ball tails. I've clearly been with James too long. His idea of exciting sex was a midweek shag.

'Don't look so shocked,' laughs Mads, throwing herself on to the bed and waving the Throbbing Theo around like Obi-Wan Kenobi's light sabre. 'It's supposed to be fun. Don't be a prude.'

'You know about these?' I just want to be sure. I feel

like I'm in a kinky parallel universe. Gone is the rectory and I'm in some Soho sex shop.

'Course I do! They're mine. Well, not exactly mine, but they're the demo models. The ones we play with.'

'Whatever you and Richard choose to do is your affair,' I say primly. 'I'm sorry I was nosy but the box was buzzing.'

'Me and Richard?' snorts Mads, laughing so hard green goo slides down her chin and plops on to the duvet. 'You must be kidding. Can you imagine Richard with this lot?'

Er . . . best not repeat my earlier thoughts.

'Richard would kill me,' Mads says. 'It is so not his scene. But . . .' she pauses and fixes me with a Paddington Bear stare, 'it is a lot of people's scene. Apparently two out of three women have a vibrator. And they have to buy them from somewhere, especially here in the sticks where we can't just pop into town. Honestly, Katy, it's brilliant! I've cornered the market. You would never believe how many unfortunate frustrated women there are out there.'

Wouldn't I?

Maddy boings off the bed and pulls six more boxes out. 'So here I am to put a smile on their faces. Nipple drops. Edible knickers. Chocolate willies. No more boring sex.'

She's finally flipped. I *knew* we smoked too much dope at uni.

My stunned expression evidently isn't what Mads was hoping for as she piles the bed high with packages like a kinky Christmas. 'Don't you think it's brilliant? I'm going to make a fortune.'

'Let's get this straight,' I say. 'You're selling this stuff?'

'Of course I'm selling it. You didn't think it was all for my consumption, did you? You did!' shrieks Maddy. 'You are hilarious! Of course it isn't all mine. You silly moo! I'm an Anna Spring party girl!'

'This is your job?' I'm still trying to get my head round it. 'You're an Anna Spring rep?'

'Don't sound so surprised,' Maddy says, looking offended. 'I might be married, but I'm not dead from the waist down, you know.'

'You're married to the *vicar*,' I point out. My eyes are drawn like magnets to the vibrators. 'What does Richard think about your *job*?'

Mads doesn't say anything. I feel a sense of doom akin to descending very fast in a lift.

'He doesn't know, does he?'

'Would *you* tell him? Can you imagine what he'd say?'

We're both quiet for a moment while we contemplate the ghastly thought.

'I don't think it would do his career much good if he did know,' sighs Mads. 'It's better to marry than to burn, remember? But only just. The bishop would probably have a heart attack. Wives submit to your husbands and all that bollocks. Richard would rather I dedicated myself to the Sunday school and the WI.'

'They posed naked,' I remind her.

'They didn't sell sex toys, though,' says Mads.

It's a fair point.

'Anyway,' she continues, dabbing away face pack with the sleeve of her bathrobe, 'Richard must never find out. It would be the end of our marriage if he did.'

'So why do this job if you know Richard would hate it? What's the point?'

Mad's eyes fill with tears. 'Where shall I begin? I think I need a glass of wine first.'

Back in the kitchen she pours me a class of icy Blossom

Hill and I curl up in the window seat with the inky sea churning below. Mads leans against the Aga and swirls her wine thoughtfully. 'I think Richard's having an affair.'

'What!'

'I said I think Richard's having an affair. He's been acting so strangely lately. He's out most evenings and when he comes back he doesn't seem to want to talk to me. As soon as he's in he jumps in the shower and then he says he's too tired to have sex.'

I think of James. Isn't this all par for the course?

'That's what happens in a relationship,' I tell her wisely.

'Bollocks is it,' scoffs Mads. 'Richard and I always had a fantastic sex life but lately he just doesn't want to know. He's so preoccupied. I keep trying to tell him that there's more to do in bed than sleep but he looks at me as though I'm insane. And . . .' she pauses dramatically, 'he's always washing his clothes.'

'Perhaps he just wants to be clean and smell nice?'

Mads looks sad. 'Or he doesn't fancy me any more.'

Mads is gorgeous. Five feet ten, slim as a reed and with tumbling ebony curls, she makes supermodels look fat and ugly.

'I'm sure you're wrong,' I say and tell her about the earlier incident in the pub. 'He looked like he thought *you* were having an affair!'

Mad's pales when I recount how the barmaid was interrogated.

'She didn't say anything, did she?'

I shake my head.

'Phew!' Mads breathes. 'Jo knows everything. Can't believe I forgot the mums and toddlers, though. I had to go to Plymouth to pick up more stock.'

'There's more?'

Mads grins. 'Course there's more! Don't keep it in the house, though. I keep it in the church minibus. In boxes marked "NIV Bible". Ingenious, huh?'

'As long as nobody wants a Bible,' I say. 'Babe, you've flipped. Why set yourself up for all this stress? Can't you just get a normal job?'

Maddy crosses the kitchen and starts to rummage through a drawer. She unearths string, old corks, tea towels and a sock before laying hands on a pile of brochures.

She hands them to me. 'This is why.'

' "Sandals," ' I read, ' "the ultimate in Caribbean romance." Let me get this straight. You're selling vibrators so you can go to Sandals?'

'Just look at it!' cries Maddy, almost shoving the brochure up my nose. Pictures of tanned couples frolicking in the azure sea blur before my gaze. 'If I can save up enough for Richard and me to go to St Lucia, I just know that we can put the romance back into our marriage. All we need is a little bit of time together. You went there once with James, didn't you?'

'Yes,' I say reluctantly.

'And wasn't it the most romantic place in the world?'

It might have been, I suppose, except that James whinged non-stop about the heat and spent most of his time tapping away on his laptop, frantic to check the Dow or the FTSE while I watched loved-up couples sipping cocktails and my pallid skin fried.

'Katy! Hello!' Mads snaps her fingers at me. 'It must have been amazing. You were miles away.'

'Very romantic,' I agree dutifully.

'When I've saved six grand I swear I'll give Anna Spring up. But for the moment it's the best-paid work I can get.

The wages down here are so unbelievably low. I work two days in Piskies and Pickles for minimum wage and I can earn double that in a night selling Throbbing Theo and his pals.'

I don't say a word. I've known Maddy long enough to not bother attempting to change her mind.

'It's great you're staying. If Richard finds any evidence or takes a phone call we can say it's your job.'

Professional scapegoat? Excuse me if I don't jump for joy. The prospect of Richard thinking that I host sex-toy parties is not a pleasant one. He'll go ballistic and probably throw holy water at me or something.

'Not that that's why I asked you to come and stay,' adds my friend hastily.

Yeah, right. Mads could knock Machiavelli into cotton socks.

'And you wouldn't need to do anything. Just pretend it's all your idea if Richard asks.'

I have a bad feeling about this. 'It's only a matter of time before he finds out.'

'Whatever!' Mads says airily. As far as she's concerned, the matter is taken care of. I've gone from teacher of English to purveyor of sex aids in less time than it takes to drink a glass of wine. Even Harry Potter would struggle to transform so quickly.

Mads tops up my glass. 'You'll soon see what it's all about. I'm doing a party tonight in Fowey.'

I groan. 'I'm shattered. Can't it wait?'

To be honest, I was really looking forward to curling up with Jake and Millandra. There's another character lurking in the back of my consciousness. He looks a bit like Gabriel and I can't wait to put him on to paper. A room full of shrieking women trying on nurses' outfits and basques is the last place I want to be. Can't I just be left alone to brood?

'Certainly not,' says Mads firmly when I propose this idea. 'This is the start of your new life, Katy. Remember the new you who is going to write bestsellers and bag herself the ultimate romantic hero? The new you who works out and eats healthily? What's happened to her?'

I have a feeling I'm going to be sick of the new me very, very soon.

'Besides, there are loads of gorgeous men here, all gagging to meet a single chick like you.'

'I'm not going to meet them at an Anna Spring party,' I point out.

'No,' Mads agrees. 'But you can order all the kit you need to pull, starting with sexy new undies, something red and black, maybe.'

'I'm looking for my Mr Darcy. Not auditioning for the Moulin Rouge.'

'A cute thong? Peekaboo bra?' Mads doesn't give up easily. I bet she's a brilliant saleswoman. 'Something to make you feel really feminine? And we need to sort your hair out too.' She ruffles my curls and shakes her head. 'And your clothes. You'll never survive Tregowan in those silly boots. You need a makeover.'

Mads makes Trinny and Susannah look sensitive, but I'm too tired to argue. Besides, maybe she's right. The old Katy Carter hasn't had much success with men.

'You'll never guess who's moved to Tregowan!' Mads starts to brush her hair, one eye firmly on the clock. 'I thought of you at once because he's perfect. Only Gabriel Winters Mr Rochester!'

'I know. He gave me a lift from the station when you abandoned me,' I say nonchalantly.

'You kept that quiet, you sneaky cow. He's gorgeous! And he picked you up? Oh my God! That's fantastic!'

'He gave me a lift, Mads,' I laugh. 'He didn't propose.'

'But he rescued you in your hour of need. That is so romantic. Katy Carter! You've only been here a few hours and you've pulled Tregowan's most eligible bachelor. Didn't I tell you it was crawling with gorgeous men here? Aren't you glad you came?' Mads dances across the kitchen in excitement and I can hear her brain ticking. She's all but married us off already.

'Calm down,' I say. 'It was only a lift and a drink in the pub.'

'He took you for a drink!' Mads is beside herself with delight. 'Gabriel Winters took you for a drink? Do you know what that means?'

'That he was thirsty?'

'Jesus, Katy!' Maddy looks at me in despair. 'How do you expect to write romantic novels when you haven't got the first idea about romance? It means he likes you, you muppet!'

It does? Can't say I got those vibes. Can't say I got any vibes at all, actually. Gabriel may be the most beautiful man I've ever seen in my life, but there's something rather sexless about him. But hey, what do I know?

'Does it?'

'Duh! Of course!' Mad's eyes have a manic glint to them. 'Get yourself changed, girlfriend! You are going to come to my party and buy yourself some sexy knickers. I have a good feeling about this.'

As Mads bounds up the stairs, all glossy bouncing curls and endless energy, I drag myself along in her wake. I seem to have left my enthusiasm for life in general somewhere far behind.

If I can't dredge up the slightest drop of enthusiasm for Gabriel Winters, a man that the majority of the female population of Britain is drooling over at the moment, I must really be in trouble.

★

I wake the next morning not to the cry of gulls as I'd expected, but to the soft throaty call of a cuckoo. For a moment I lie still, enjoying the feeling of the sun on my face as it falls in ribbons through the gap in the curtains.

I'm in bed on a weekday morning and I don't have to get up or go anywhere if I don't want to. It's weird to be without my usual sense of panic (Shit! Forgot to mark Year 8's books!) or heavy sensation of impending doom (Arse! Year 11 last lesson!). I ought to feel guilty that I'm lying here in bed while my poor ex-colleagues cram themselves on to the tube before embarking on a long day nagging stroppy adolescents about taking off their trainers and doing up their ties. But do you know what? I don't feel guilty at all.

I feel free!

I push off the duvet, pad across the wooden floor to the window and swish the curtains apart. Instantly the room is drenched with buttery light and outside the sea is a deep glittery blue. Boats rock merrily in the harbour and seagulls bob idly on the waves.

'Cuckoo! Cuckoo!' I hear again, and now I'm sufficiently awake, I realise that it's actually the text alert on my mobile phone. The seagulls are calling outside and one very persistent individual is busy attacking a fish head on the quayside. I rub my eyes and yawn, retrieve my phone and take it back to bed with me.

Maddy's party in Fowey was actually really good fun. A

group of fishermen's wives, their purses bulging with the fruits of their husbands' latest catch, were merrily pissed and desperate to spend as much money as possible. Before long, basques, suspenders and leather corsets were doing the rounds and Throbbing Theo and his cronies were buzzing and wiggling like a lively boy band. I won a willy-shaped soap in the rude-word bingo, and I also have a hazy memory of ordering some ridiculously frilly underwear. Mads reckoned she took a record amount of orders.

I hope so. The sooner she pays for this holiday, the sooner I'll be able to breathe easy. Thinking of Richard driving around in a minibus stuffed full of sex aids that I'll be blamed for isn't conducive to a good night's sleep. At least I managed to write another chapter of *Heart of the Highwayman* during the night, and, if I say so myself, it's pretty steamy stuff! Perhaps all this Anna Spring business will have an odd effect on me and I'll end up writing sizzling erotica. My parents would be so proud of such evidence of my sexual liberation!

I ignore the mobile and pull my notebook out from beneath my pillow. No way am I going to risk this copy falling into enemy hands. Besides, if Richard finds it, his opinion of me will be even lower, and since it's already at earthworm level, this is a risk I do not want to take.

'Oh Jake,' Millandra breathed, 'I can resist you no longer. Please take me now.'

Jake groaned. She was heartbreakingly lovely as she stood there before him in her gossamer-thin nightdress. Through the fabric he could distinguish the curve of her bosom, her concave belly and the dark triangle at the top of her thighs. She was so pure and fragile that surely the nature of a man's passion would crush her?

Millandra lay back on the four-poster bed, her hair a golden halo around her head. She saw Jake above her, and then he was kissing her neck and gently stroking her breast. Desire rippled through her maiden body. She felt as though she was melting.

Sadly all the product of my fevered imagination, but a girl can dream, can't she? One day I'm sure my body will melt too, although I can't imagine any man having to worry that his passion will crush me. Still, I'll soon show Mads there's more to romance than those rabbits she's sold to half of Cornwall.

The message tone sounds again. It's certainly persistent. I scroll to my inbox and discover I have four messages waiting, one from James, two from Frankie and one missed call from Ollie. At least they haven't forgotten me.

James's message is short and to the point.

We need to discuss money.

Whatever happened to I miss you and I want you back? 'Bastard,' I say, erasing the message.

What is it with James and money? You'd think he was destitute from the way he carries on. I thought investment bankers earned a fortune? Well, he's got no hope of squeezing cash from me at the minute, if ever. Jewell may have paid off my credit cards, but I too may be reduced to flogging vibrators if I don't find a job in the next week or so. I'll ask Mads to take me to the job centre after breakfast.

The other texts are from Frankie. I open the first message, which was sent yesterday, and laugh aloud because Frankie texts just as he talks, all exclamations and hyperbole.

O my god!!! U won't believe it! The most exciting thing ever has happened!!! Paramour Records have signed us!!! will b famous!!! Prada and Versace here I come! xxxxx

Fantastic! I'm delighted for Frankie. Even if I think the Screaming Queens sound like they're being hung, drawn and quartered, somebody somewhere must like them. I open the next message expecting more of the same, but drop the phone as though it is red hot when I read:

Have u pulled? Am jealous!

I stare at the phone. What is going on?

I text back:

What r u talking about?

It's only a matter of seconds before the phone cuckoos again and Frankie replies.

Suggest u buy a copy of the sun!!!

What?

I stare at the text until the letters blur and start to dance. What is going on? Why should I buy the *Sun*? It might be Frankie's rag of choice, but I'm an English teacher and honour-bound to pretend to read the *Guardian*.

But I must admit I'm curious.

Hopping out of bed, I pull on a T-shirt and some tatty jogging bottoms that were Ollie's in the very distant past and patter down the stairs and into the kitchen.

'I've just has the weirdest text,' I gasp, waving the phone. 'You'll never guess, but—'

'There's a lobster in the bath?' says Richard from the kitchen table, where he's munching dry toast and drinking tea. 'You've come to stay indefinitely?'

Ten bums in a row. Shouldn't he be at a prayer meeting or something? I'm suddenly conscious that my Little Miss T-shirt is a size too small and the word *Naughty* is stretched across my boobs in a highly inappropriate manner. Richard has a strange effect on me. Whenever I'm around him I'm either compelled by a perverse desire to be as obnoxious and outrageous as I can or to confess all my

215

sins and see what he does about it, which, let's be honest, could take some time.

I'm sure I was a Catholic in a past life.

'Hello, Katy.' Richard rises and kisses me on the cheek, which feels awkward, a bit like being kissed by your headmaster. 'Mads tells me you're staying for a while.'

'If that's OK with you,' I say quickly. 'It was a sudden decision.'

That we've been planning for weeks.

'Indeed?' Richard raises an eyebrow.

Yes in-bloody-deed.

'Do you want some tea? The kettle's just boiled.'

'Thanks.' I fish a mug out of the sink and give it a rinse. 'Where's Mads?'

'Exactly what I was wondering yesterday,' says Richard, fixing me with a penetrating look.

Fuck. He saw me in the pub.

'If you want to go incognito, I should try dying the ginger hair,' he suggests, biting viciously into his toast. 'I suppose she went to collect you? And you popped into the Mermaid for a drink?'

'Er, something like that,' I say and wait for a thunderbolt to strike me dead. 'And then we went to a party.' That's not a lie, is it?

Richard sighs wearily. 'Katy, you need to realise that Madeleine isn't like you. She's a married woman with all the responsibilities that her state entails.'

Her state? What is she, the bloody Queen?

'If you're going to stay with us,' continues Rich, 'you'll need to abide by the standards of this household. And that means not encouraging Maddy to lie to her husband.'

I'm struck dumb by the unfairness of this. I seem to

recall *I* was the one who pointed out to Mads that deceiving Richard was not a good idea.

'Maddy is a vicar's wife,' Rich says solemnly, folding his hands together and fixing me with a stern look. 'She has responsibilities towards the people of this parish, a duty of care to them, and a duty to lead an edifying life. She isn't free to take off when she feels like it, and she knows that. If you are to stay here then I need you to understand this.'

Hello! Have I gone back to the Middle Ages without noticing? But then for Richard, feminism is just something that happened to other people, so he ploughs on regardless of, or maybe because of, my incredulous expression.

'Wives must submit to their husbands, Katy. It's a Biblical truth. The husband is the head of the household, and there's a reason for that. It makes for a stable and happy marriage,' he finishes sanctimoniously.

It does? Sounds like a recipe for disaster to me.

Especially when the husband's an idiot.

'Thanks for telling me.' I know I'm being flip but I can't help it. 'I'll make sure I remember all that when I next go on a date.'

'Just remember it while you're here,' Richard says, popping open the washing machine and shoving in some clothes from a carrier. The smell of white spirit wrestles with Comfort. Slamming the door shut, he straightens up and fixes me with a beady look. 'Get that lobster back in the sea, do a bit of brass cleaning and I'm sure we'll all get on famously.'

I'm glad you're sure, I think as I splosh hot water on to a tea bag, because I'm starting to feel freaked out.

'Mads has gone to fetch milk and papers.' Sermon safely delivered, Richard gets around to answering my earlier question. 'There she is, look!' He points down towards the village, where sure enough, Maddy's curly head is bobbing along through the streets. Then she rounds a corner and approaches the quay at a run, scattering seagulls and tourists in equal measures.

'Does she always run?' I ask, bemused. The Mads I know makes snails seem speedy.

Richard frowns. 'Never. Something must be wrong.'

'Katy!' pants Mads, tearing in through the side door. 'You've got to see the papers!'

Not her as well.

'I'm making tea.' I fetch milk from the fridge, very calmly, even though inside my heart is pounding. 'You want one?'

'Tea!' cries Mads, flinging a wad of red-top papers on to the kitchen table and shoving Richard's breakfast out of the way. 'I think you'll need something stronger than tea when you've read this lot, babes!'

I put the mug on the table and let Maddy sit me down and push a copy of the *Sun* towards me.

What I see makes me gasp.

ROCHESTER DUMPS JANE FOR MYSTERY REDHEAD! screams the headline, and below it is a blurry picture of Gabriel Winters looking divine in his white T-shirt and jeans with his laughing blue eyes and perfectly tousled hair. Nothing unusual there, except that next to him, looking dishevelled and pink-cheeked, is a woman leaning forward and displaying a rather Jordanesque cleavage and quite a bit of thigh, actually. Of course, it's me. All that red hair, as dear Richard has already pointed out, is a dead giveaway. I could try ringing the *Sun* and saying it's actually Chris Evans in drag, but I don't think they'd fall for it. This hair of mine is such a pain. All my life I've never been able to get away with anything.

'It must have been that bloody woman with the digital camera!' I peer closer. No cellulite. Thank you, God, for dimly lit pubs. But how come I never noticed how low-cut that gypsy top is? And has Gabriel got his arm around my waist? I wasn't so pissed I wouldn't have noticed that.

Has the photo been tampered with?

Oh my God. All these years I've taught Media Studies and the mysteries of Photoshop and I never once thought of that.

'Just remind me,' I say, and my voice is shaky, 'isn't there a hideous conflict in Iraq? Aren't people being persecuted in Zimbabwe? Why is this . . . this crap on the front page?'

'Because people love Gabriel,' Mads tells me, twirling her hair up into a knot and securing it with a chopstick. 'And they love gossip even more.' She looks at me through narrowed eyes. 'Are you sure there's nothing going on? You guys look pretty cosy.'

'I only met him yesterday!'

'But he's got his arm round you,' Mads says. 'What happened exactly?'

'You were there,' says Richard. 'Weren't you?'

Bum. Bum. Bum. No time to get our stories straight.

I try frantically to catch her eye.

'I was? I mean, I was!' says Mads hastily. 'But this is something else. I must have, um, been in the loo.'

'This is a disaster.' Richard has his head in his hands. 'The press will be here in droves. I'll never get any work done.'

'What will Gabriel say?' I wonder.

'Don't worry about him,' says Mads airily. 'He'll love it.

No such thing as bad publicity, remember?' She flips through the rest of the paper. 'You're mentioned in Richard Kaye's column in the *Mail*, and the *Dagger* has an exclusive interview with Gabriel's now ex-girlfriend, who apparently wants to kill you. The *Sport*'s running a competition to guess the size of your boobs.'

Richard groans.

'Page three in the *Express*, nothing in the broadsheets, except a tiny piece in the celebrity section of *The Times*,' Mads finishes. 'Enjoy your fifteen minutes of fame.'

'I don't want to be famous,' I wail.

'Then don't go out drinking with celebrities,' snaps Richard. 'I'm sorry, Katy, but you'll have to go home.'

'What!' chorus Mads and I.

'This is the last thing I need,' Richard tells his wife. 'Bishop Bill will be seriously unimpressed. Having a seedy tabloid affair taking place under my roof won't do my career any favours.'

'I'm not having a seedy tabloid affair,' I protest. 'I only had a drink with him in the pub.'

'Trouble is,' says Mads, 'it doesn't look like that.'

I examine the picture again. She has a point. That low top doesn't exactly scream 'innocent drink!'.

'I was leaning forwards to get out of the shot.'

'Sure you were.' Maddy pats my shoulder. 'But to Joe Public it looks like you were saying "come and get it".'

Oh Lordy. No wonder Frankie sent me that text. It really looks as though not even twenty-four hours after I left for Cornwall, I'm bonking Gabriel Winters' brains out.

Actually, I don't think that would take too long.

'You'll have to leave before we get doorstepped by the press,' Richard tells me.

'Don't be daft,' Mads says firmly. 'This'll blow over. There's no way you're going back, Katy. You've got a hero to find and a novel to finish. Gabriel's just the first man you've come across. I promise there are lots more.'

'This is a rectory, not a knocking shop,' bursts out Richard.

Richard, if you only knew what lives under my bed, you wouldn't be so sure!

'Besides,' he carries on, 'what about Katy's teaching job?'

'Don't worry about that,' says Mads cheerfully. 'She's resigned.'

'What?' Richard's mouth is a little 'o' of horror. 'Can't they take her back?'

'Hello? I am in the room, people!' I point out.

'What's she going to do?' Richard is really agitated now and starts to fiddle with the edge of the *Sun*, tearing at it and scrunching it up with equal ferocity. I watch in fascination. 'What's she going to do to earn money? Go fishing? Bake pasties? We're not exactly crying out for unemployed teachers in Tregowan.'

'I'm going to write a book,' I say helpfully.

'You gave up your teaching career to write a book?' Richard buries his face in his hands. 'Dear Lord, give me strength.'

'It's a romance,' I tell him. 'It's about a highwayman who—'

'Spare me the details. Save them for the press, who I'm sure will love it.'

'Darling,' Mads adopts a soothing tone of voice, 'you're overreacting. This will all blow over, the press will push off and Katy and I will have a lovely summer together. There

221

are loads of things she can do. We're off to the job centre this morning.'

'But what about the bishop? He won't be impressed by all this press attention. It detracts from what we're really here for.'

'He's an open-minded man,' argues Maddy. 'In the world but not of it, remember, darling? Katy needs our support right now. She's had a terrible time lately, with her broken engagement and then the cancer scare. She needs her friends about her at such a difficult time. Show some compassion, Richard. What would Jesus do?'

Whoa! She's good! I'm almost in tears myself.

'He'd love and care for her, wouldn't He?'

Richard's torn between booting me out and behaving in a charitable and Christian manner. 'I suppose so. Yes, of course He would. All right, Katy. You can stay.'

'Oh, thank you, darling!' Mads flings her arms around Richard and plants a kiss on the top of his head, winking at me over it. 'Katy will be an asset to us. She'll clean the brass, do the toddlers and sort the flowers.'

Sell the sex toys?

I nod manically. 'And the first thing I'll do is put Pinchy back in the sea.'

'Katy's lobster,' explains Maddy swiftly. 'Besides, you must admit that her rent will come in handy.'

Richard's ears prick up. Mammon is so tempting.

'I'll pay lots,' I tell him. 'And I'll clean and cook.'

'Don't overegg the pudding,' he says drily. 'I've already said yes. Just try and stay away from TV stars, please.'

'Oh, totally! No more of those!'

Let's just hope Frankie doesn't choose to turn up unannounced on the hunt for his crush. Good old Rich would burst a blood vessel.

Richard disentangles himself from his wife and mutters something about going to Truro. Once the front door slams, Mads and I heave a sigh of relief.

'Fuck me,' she says. 'That was a close shave. Next time let me know what fibs you've told my husband.'

'Next time let me know when you're going to show your husband sordid tabloid stories about me,' I retort.

I put the kettle back on, although to be honest I could do with something stronger. Mads rummages through the papers again, but I can't bear to look. Ollie, James and most of Britain think I'm Gabriel Winters' latest bit of crumpet.

What a mess.

A mess? Who am I kidding? I've made a Ground Zero of nearly all the relationships in my life. My family only still talk to me because I hardly ever see them.

While I think these gloomy thoughts, the house phone rings. Maddy answers, tucking the receiver beneath her chin while she pours boiling water into a blue china teapot.

'Tregowan Rectory. Oh! Hi! Yes! Fine!'

What's happened to her voice? She sounds like Marilyn Monroe with asthma.

'Katy? Yes. She's right here.'

Maddy puts her hand over the speaker's end of the receiver. Her eyes are fever bright.

'Are you sure you've told me everything, Katy Carter?' she asks, wagging her finger at me. 'You are in so much trouble otherwise.'

'Course,' I say. 'Why?'

Mads holds the phone out.

'Because, you lucky, lucky cow, Gabriel Winters is on the phone, and he says he can't wait to see you again. Katy! You've pulled!'

Chapter Fourteen

' "Waitress required for the Piskie's Kitchen. No previous experience required. Minimum wage",' I read. 'What do you think?'

We're standing outside the job centre with our noses pressed against the glass. There are several boards covered in cards that have handwritten details of a vast array of jobs. I could apply to be a pasty cook, a care assistant or a barmaid. Any of those will do as far as I'm concerned, but Mads has other ideas.

'No, no and no,' she says firmly. 'The whole point of this exercise is to find you that romantic hero you said you needed.'

And there was I thinking we were job-hunting.

'And you won't find one of those in a care home,' Maddy adds when I express an interest in the next advert. 'Maybe a rich one, like Anna Nicole Smith did, but not a young, fit love god.'

'Give it a rest. I'm not interested in love gods! In fact I'm thinking about donating my sexual organs to charity since I'll probably never use them again.'

'Bollocks! Of course you will! You couldn't get down here quick enough when I told you all about the talent.'

'I needed to get away from London,' I remind her.

'And we need to find you a hero, for your novel

224

obviously,' carries on Maddy, busily jotting down job details and phone numbers. 'Although you already seem to have done that without my help, you crafty moo. Mr Winters was gagging to talk to you. What's going on?'

Our eyes meet in the reflection in the window and I laugh because Mads is waggling her eyebrows suggestively. 'You've been really quiet since he phoned. What did he say? Did he ask you out? Tell me everything! Has he proposed to save your honour? Has *OK!* got an exclusive?'

'Who's the romantic novelist here?' I laugh. 'Listen to yourself! He's just asked me up to Smuggler's Rest for dinner to discuss the situation and how we can best handle it.' I glance at my reflection in the mirror. Big shades and a baseball cap might work wonders for Victoria Beckham, but they do nothing for me. I'm desperately hoping Gabriel's means of avoiding the press are more sophisticated than Maddy's. Still, at least we've managed to lose the lone reporter from the *Cornish Times* who was doorstepping us.

'Arrgh!' shrieks Mads, so loudly that several passing tourists turn and stare at us. 'I can't believe you kept that to yourself all morning. No one else I know in the village has been invited up to Smuggler's Rest. Gabriel's been really funny about his privacy. Wear your new knickers. I reckon you're in there, babe.'

'It isn't like that,' I insist. 'He's just being kind.'

'Bollocks is he,' grins Mads. 'Men are only ever helpful when they want something.'

'Believe what you like. He's not interested. I can tell.'

Take our earlier telephone conversation, for example. It wasn't exactly melting the phone wires with sizzling passion.

'Hi.' I'd turned my back on Mads, who was making

kissing faces. 'I'm really sorry about the misunderstanding in the papers.'

Gabriel had laughed his dark, velvety laugh. 'Don't worry about that. It's all par for the course in my business. I'm just phoning to make sure that you're OK. I hope your boyfriend isn't too pissed off.'

'I haven't got a boyfriend. So you needn't worry about that.'

'Oh,' said Gabriel slowly.

'If you were worried,' I said hastily.

'I wasn't worried.' Gabriel paused, presumably for dramatic emphasis. 'I was just wondering what the matter is with all the men in London. Still, at least I don't have to worry about an irate partner charging over to challenge me to a duel.'

I laughed. 'No, you have absolutely no worries on that score.'

'Well, the press is likely to be a pain in the rear end for a day or two,' he said. 'Don't be surprised if some of them turn up. We need to get together to work out a story.'

'Can't I just deny it all?' Call me naive, but I thought if I kept my head down all this would go away. Ostrich tactics have never failed me before.

'I'd prefer it if you didn't,' said Gabriel carefully. 'That might just make them even more persistent. We'll be doorstepped until they can find a story, and if they can't find one they'll make something up, or dig about for anything unsavoury. You haven't got any skeletons in your cupboard, have you?'

I thought about the vibrators under my bed. Snooping reporters were the last thing we needed. A vicar's wife with a double life as a purveyor of sex aids would make a fantastic story.

Richard would go mental.

And even worse, I'd be homeless.

'Of course not,' I said. 'Have you?'

Gabriel was silent.

Oh shit, I thought, and my hands began to sweat. He's into something awful.

'Not exactly.' He sounded awkward. 'But there is something I need to discuss with you.'

My mind wasn't so much boggling as performing Olympic-standard gymnastics. What did he have to hide? 'Well, you're the expert on this fame stuff. What do you suggest?' I asked.

'I'm out most of the day.' I could hear him flipping the pages of a diary. 'Why don't you come up to Smuggler's Rest this evening for dinner? About seven?'

I didn't answer. Did I want to have dinner with Gabriel?

'We can decide how to handle the situation then. I'll ask my manager for advice,' he continued. 'Don't worry, Katy, we'll sort this out. And I'm a good cook. My coq au vin is legendary.'

It was a surreal situation. One of the most gorgeous men on the planet was asking me over to his place for dinner. Most of the female population in Britain would give anything to be in my shoes, so why wasn't I more excited? Wasn't this exactly what I'd decided to do? Move on? Wasn't that why I came to Cornwall?

'Sounds lovely,' I heard myself agreeing. 'Tomorrow at seven it is then.'

Gabriel gave me instructions how to find his house, which apparently involved a hike up the hillside, and rang off, leaving me to pace the kitchen until Maddy frogmarched me upstairs to get dressed. A morning's job-hunting was exactly what I needed to take my mind off my Andy Warhol fifteen minutes, if only she would let me.

Now that I've repeated the details of this phone conversation, I doubt we'll ever talk about anything else again. You'd think I'd won the lottery or something, not just been invited up to the house of a celebrity. Gabriel might be on the telly but I'm sure he burps and farts like the rest of us.

'Go, girl,' Mads whoops. 'A date with Gabriel Winters! Bet you're glad you bought those sexy knickers now.'

'It's not a date,' I say firmly. 'It's damage limitation.'

'An intimate dinner for two in a secluded house,' Mads squeals. 'Come on! Even you aren't that naive.'

I shake my head. Mads can think whatever she likes but I'm sure Gabriel's motives aren't sexual. I mean, he is fantastically good-looking and he has all the talent and charisma that an actor could ever require, but I'm positive he isn't interested in me. Sure, we laughed and chatted and even flirted a little, but there was nothing there, no frisson of sexual excitement.

'Aha!' Mads is distracted from Gabriel and is looking at a job advert with interest. 'This one's more like it. How's your riding?'

I drag my attention away from thoughts of Gabriel and back to Maddy. 'My what?'

'Your riding?'

'Horse riding?'

'Of course horse riding! What kind of riding did you think I meant, you rude girl?'

It's official. Mads has flipped. All this Anna Spring stuff has blown her mind.

'I haven't ridden since I was about fifteen.' I think back

to when I had nothing more pressing to worry about than getting my horse on the right leg in canter and was passionately in love with a pony called Toffee. It was certainly a whole lot simpler than being an adult.

'But it's like a bicycle, right? You never forget?'

'I suppose so,' I say doubtfully.

'Excellent! Then we may have found you a part-time job. Tristan Mitchell needs a stable girl for the Tregowan trekking centre. Must be able to exercise horses and lead rides, it says. How hard can that be?'

'I'm very out of practice.' I'm doubtful of my expertise in the saddle. 'I don't really think—'

'Tristan Mitchell is gorgeous!' Maddy is fizzing with excitement. 'You have to see him, Katy. He's pure testosterone. He'd be perfect for taking your mind off James.'

'I really don't think it's me,' I protest, but Mads isn't listening, she's too busy dialling on her mobile and arranging for me to have an interview. I sigh and resign myself to having to go along with yet another of her crazy ideas. I'm starting to see a pattern developing.

'Fantastic,' she crows, snapping the phone shut. 'Tristan says he'll be around tomorrow and he'll see you then. You'll love him, Katy. His thighs are like a vice; horses tremble when he wraps his legs around them.' Her eyes grow dreamy. 'Lucky old horses.'

I'm alarmed. Whatever's going on between Maddy and Richard, it doesn't bode well if she's starting to fantasise about other men. And all this horse stuff is far too Jilly Cooper for my liking. The sooner she saves that six grand and drags Richard off to Sandals the better.

'And here's another.' Mads is on a roll. 'This is perfect for you. "Part-time childminder required five nights a week to collect two children from Tregowan Primary

School and look after them from three thirty to six thirty. Please contact Jason Howard." You'd love Jason, Katy.'

'Don't tell me,' I say wearily. 'He's lush.'

'He is! He so is! How did you know? You haven't met him as well, have you?' Mads says suspiciously, not wanting to be denied her role as matchmaker.

'No.'

'He's got the art gallery on the quay, Arty Fawty?' Mads is scribbling down this number too. 'His wife left him about a year ago and abandoned the children. Poor motherless darlings! Just think, Katy. You could be like Maria in *The Sound of Music*.'

I have a hideous vision of me with a severe lesbian crop running through fields of buttercups dressed as a nun. Being a teacher has never seemed so appealing, and I think of my litter-strewn classroom with a pang.

'If it doesn't work out with Tristan,' decides Maddy, 'we'll give Jason a call. He's ever so sweet, all long hair and hippy clothes. You'll love him.'

'What I'd really love,' I tell her, spying a tea shop, 'is some lunch.'

'You have no soul.' Maddy puts the notebook away and links her arm through mine. 'I'm working really hard here to find your Mr Right and all you can think about is food. Still,' she continues, leading me across the street to the cosy tea shop, 'we'll sail better on a full stomach, I suppose.'

'Sail?' I echo. 'What do you mean, sail?'

Mads looks shifty. 'Didn't I mention that we're going out to sea this afternoon, to release Pinchy?'

'No, you conveniently forgot to mention that.' Suddenly all the plump buns and pasties piled high in the steamy window don't look at all appealing as I envisage them reappearing over the side of a boat.

'Oh! Silly me!' Mads taps her head. 'We're going out on *Dancing Girl* at two. I've had to do some serious grovelling as well, so you and Pinchy boy owe me one. Fishermen don't like taking women on board. They think it's unlucky.'

'I agree.' I have a hideous sense of foreboding. Boats and I are not a fortuitous combination. 'I think it's *really* unlucky. Give me a break, Mads. You know I'm a rubbish sailor. Remember the university booze cruise to Cherbourg?'

Mads has the grace to look abashed.

'We hadn't even left port and I was throwing up,' I remind her. 'I spent the entire time lying on a bench outside the hypermarket while you guys got pissed.'

There was also the Sir Bob's staff boat trip up the Thames when I seem to remember Ollie had his work cut out scraping me off the deck and back on to dry land. But I don't mention this to Mads. I really can't talk about Ollie right now. The more I think about what a great friend I've lost, the more I feel like sticking my head in the oven.

'Don't be such a wuss!' scoffs Mads. 'It's the least you can do for Pinchy. He needs you there to support him.'

'We're tipping him into the sea,' I say. 'Not going to his graduation.'

We wander away from the tea shop and towards Boots. 'Get in there and buy some Kwells,' orders Mads. 'I'm not having you chucking up in front of the skipper. That won't impress him.'

'I thought we were releasing Pinchy, not man-hunting.' My legs feel weak. From where I stand I can just about see some trawlers bobbing up and down on the tide. Is it my imagination, or do I feel sick already?

'We're women,' says Mads. 'Multitasking is our speciality. Besides, when you see Guy Tregarten you'll be too busy drooling to feel ill. He's got the most amazing body under those oilskins. Think George Clooney in *The Perfect Storm* and you'll get the picture.'

'*The Perfect Storm*? Didn't they all drown?'

'For pity's sake!' She propels me into the shop. 'The sun is out and the sea's flat calm. What can possibly go wrong? Think of poor little Pinchy.'

'Pinchy's fine in the bath.'

'Well he won't be if Richard comes home and finds him still there. It'll be Thermidor quicker than you can say Rick Stein.' Mads pops some tablets and a pair of bright orange wristbands alleged to ward off sickness into her basket. 'Look on the bright side,' she adds. 'Any press who turn up will never find you ten miles out to sea. Am I not a genius? Don't worry about thanking me. It's what friends are for.'

'Bring on my enemies,' I mutter.

This is not what I had in mind when I decided to spend the summer in Cornwall. So much for long lazy days writing my novel and strolling along the cliffs; I think I'd rather be back battling to get Wayne Lobb's homework in. Even dealing with Cordelia and her endless criticism would be a breeze compared to Maddy Lomax on a mission.

'Don't look so worried,' Mads says, paying for the Kwells. 'It'll be fine. We'll find you a hero or die in the attempt.'

'That,' I say through gritted teeth, 'is what I am afraid of.'

Have you ever tried climbing over the decks of two fishing boats in order to reach the third, which happens to be tied just beyond? No? Well, lucky you is all I can say, because you need the agility of Spiderman and the balance of a trapeze artist to do it with any degree of success.

The decks are speckled with seagull poop, a yellow slime that seems to coat pretty much everything in Tregowan, and my feet in their flip-flops slither and slide until several times I end up in a most undignified heap. By the time I scrape myself up from fish guts and gull crap for the third time, I'm starting to lose my sense of humour, unlike Guy bloody Tregarten, whom I instantly recognise as the loud fisherman from the pub, and who is finding the whole spectacle of the landlubber townie in inappropriate shoes going arse over tit absolutely hysterical.

'What kind of fucking silly shoes are those?' he hoots as I pick myself up again and attempt to clamber on to *Dancing Girl,* which isn't as easy as it sounds when you're wearing a little skirt that threatens to give the world a view of your knickers.

I look down at my feet, and feel insulted. My pink flip-flops with the yellow flowers are gorgeous. Frankie is totally jealous of them.

'Katy's from London,' explains Mads.

Guy nods, as though this explains it all, and watches me from his vantage point on the deck of his boat, arms crossed over his oilskins and a mocking smile playing on his lips. He makes no attempt to help, but seems happy enough to watch and laugh.

I hate him.

'You might help,' I snap, belly-flopping across the side of the boat and finally slithering on to *Dancing Girl*.

'Why?' asks Guy, expertly balancing along the edge of the deck like a tightrope walker. 'You're perfectly capable of getting on board. No limbs missing? Thought not. Isn't my fault if you insist on wearing silly clothes, is it?'

He bounds across the decks of the moored boats and zips up a ladder up on to the quay.

'Nice arse,' breathes Mads, watching the muscular denim-clad posterior.

'Total arse, more like.' I shoot a glare at Guy's retreating back. 'Next time you have a brilliant idea, please let me know and I'll make sure that I have something else less agonising planned, like open-heart surgery without anaesthetic, maybe.'

'Don't be like that.' Mads brushes bits of seaweed and seagull crap off my clothes while I stand and sulk. 'You must admit, he is attractive.'

I shield my eyes against the glare of the sun. Guy is silhouetted on the quayside, legs braced as he lifts Pinchy's crate. His biceps swell. With his dark hair, cut so short that it looks like a mole's pelt, skin tanned from the wind and white teeth, he is a dead ringer for a younger, less lived-in George Clooney.

Shame he has the manners of George's dead pet pig.

'OK,' I agree. 'I can see where you're coming from, but he is no way a romantic hero.'

'Only trying to help,' says Mads sulkily. 'Take your mind off James and help you finish the book, you said. That's what I'm trying to do.'

'I know, but could you be a little less full on.'

'What the fuck is this?' interrupts Guy, thrusting Pinchy under my nose.

'It's a lobster,' I say calmly. 'They live in the sea.'

'I know it's a bloody lobster,' says Guy. 'What I want to know is why I'm taking it out to sea. Let me explain how fishing works. I get stuff out of the sea and sell it. Fucking simple, I'd have thought.'

Gordon Ramsay's monopoly on the F word is under serious threat.

'We're going to release him back into the wild,' I tell Guy. Pinchy looks a little nervous, which is understandable, since Guy's probably massacred scores of his relatives and must feature regularly on *Lobster Crimewatch*. 'He's a rescue lobster.'

'You want to tip that into the sea?' Guy's incredulous. 'It's a beauty. I'll save us all the hassle and give you a tenner for it. I could sell it on the fish stall ten times over.'

'You will not!' I cry. 'I'm not giving up now. If you had any idea of how much hassle this lobster has caused, you'd never dream of suggesting that. Take us out to sea, buster!'

'Bloody emmets,' Guy says, but his eyes are twinkling, no doubt at the thought of the fat fee he'll charge and the mileage he'll get out of retelling this story in the pub. 'Still, you're paying.'

'Certainly am,' I mutter under my breath. Don't know quite what I'm paying for exactly, but it must have been something pretty awful. I don't think I'll be going for past life regression any time soon. The thought of what I could discover is too horrific. Besides, I'm not doing a fantastic job of running this one, am I?

The Kwells must be working because once we've cast off from the quay and rounded the headland I find that I'm actually enjoying the gentle rolling motion of the boat as she bounces over the waves. The water glistens and sparkles in the sunshine and I tip my face back and enjoy its warmth on my cheeks. The wash spreads out behind us like white lace and Tregowan diminishes beyond, more like a model village than ever. Up on the cliff path tiny matchstick figures are strolling along or sitting admiring the view. One waves to us and I wave back, before we round a headland and leave them far behind.

Suddenly I feel a bit more hopeful.

Mads is sitting at the stern, one hand tightly clutching the gantry, the other holding her tangled hair back from her face. Guy is nowhere near as idle as his passengers. Setting the boat on autopilot (and alarming me terribly before I check), he scoots about the deck coiling the ropes that trail serpent-like around our feet, stacking bright yellow boxes and heaving debris into the ocean. Now that he's in his element and his mouth is firmly closed, I can appreciate what Mads was trying to point out. There's something earthy and essentially masculine about him. Whether it's the knowledge that he risks his life on a daily basis or simply because his work is so physically demanding, he has a confidence that borders on arrogance. Add that to a well-muscled body, a large kissable mouth and a set of cheekbones that most women would pay a fortune for, and the combination is pretty devastating.

He's attractive, I can see that. But I don't fancy him at all. First Gabriel and now Guy. What's wrong with me? Frankie would think he'd died and gone to heaven with all these gorgeous men on tap.

I feel a bit miffed. It's like going to Cadbury World and suddenly developing an aversion to chocolate.

I watch Guy move around the boat, admiring the way his body adjusts to the motion of the sea. In my mind's eye I have him dressed in tight white breeches and a billowing linen shirt, with a cutlass at his waist and a diamond glittering dangerously in his ear. The rusting metal skeleton of the trawler vanishes too and instead she becomes a stately galleon with acres of white sails and rigging that stretches high above my head.

Hey! Maybe Mads is right about this crazy action-hero idea. I wish I had my writing book with me.

Millandra's hands were bound tightly and the harsh rope chafed against the soft skin of her wrists. The ship heaved and thrust beneath her feet, leaping over the brine with a power that would have felled her were she not tied to the mast.

The mast? Maybe that's overdoing it a tad. I look up and am surprised to see Guy dressed in cat-sick yellow oilskins rather than his pirate gear. He's doing some daredevil stuff up on the roof of the wheelhouse, and I notice, purely from the point of view of research for my novel, that he's shed the T-shirt and is working bare-chested. All that lugging nets about in the sun must pay off, because his torso is bronzed, taut with muscle and corded with sinew.

Peter Andre would die of jealousy.

'All right?' Guy catches me looking at his body and gives me a wink.

Shit! He thinks I'm checking him out! Face flaming, I look hastily away. How absolutely excruciatingly embarrassing.

'Absolutely fine, thank you,' I say primly.

'Absolutely!' mimics Guy, grinning. 'Get you! Sounds like I've got the bloody Queen on board.' And he jumps lithely down on to the deck and vanishes into the wheelhouse. Seconds later the engine is cut and all is blissfully quiet, except for the slap of the waves against the boat and the screech of the gulls which appear from thin air and circle above us.

'Right,' Guy says. 'Chuck it in then and we can go back.'

I look out to sea. Tregowan is little more than a cluster of dots amongst a smudge of green. All else is acres and acres of deep blue water. I feel like the Ancient Mariner, only in funkier shoes.

'What are all those little flags?' I ask.

'Markers for lobster pots, that's what,' Maddy says. 'Nice try, Guy.'

Grumbling about quotas and federal Europe and struggling to survive, Guy manoeuvres the boat another hundred yards or so.

'And that's it,' he says, fixing me and Mads with a steely gaze. 'I'm not wasting any more fuel on a fucking lobster. Throw it in, for Christ's sake.'

I look at Pinchy and Pinchy looks at me, and I know it's ridiculous but I feel quite emotional.

'Hurry up.' Guy crosses his arms. 'You don't need to kiss it.'

'Bye, Pinchy,' I whisper, lifting his box on to the side of the boat. 'Thanks for seeing off James. Guess I owe you one.'

Pinchy looks alarmed, probably wondering where his jacuzzi bath and expensive koi carp food have gone. He doesn't seem overly keen to be liberated from captivity. It must be like returning to shopping in Asda when you're more used to the Harrods Food Hall.

'Watch out for lobster pots,' advises Mads.

'Unless they're mine,' Guy grins.

I close my eyes, tip the box and splosh! Pinchy has gone.

'Thank Christ for that,' says Guy, returning to the wheelhouse and starting the engine. Moments later we're steaming back towards the harbour, with only a few ripples marking the spot where Pinchy dived down to his freedom.

Mads puts her arm around me. 'Don't be sad. We can always get you a hamster or something.'

I press my fingers into the corners of my eyes. I'm not going to cry over Pinchy. It's just that in some ridiculous way that lobster was the only link to my old life, the life where even if I wasn't always happy, at least we all knew where we stood. I was engaged, James was an arse and Ollie was my friend. Now it's all changed and I don't know how to make it right. I don't belong anywhere and I don't know where my life is going. It feels like I haven't just dropped Pinchy into the sea but also everything I used to know and hope for.

So much for embracing change and being grateful for my second chance. I seem to lurch from excited to terrified on an hourly basis.

Jewell would be ashamed. I really must try harder.

As the trawler rolls her way back to harbour, I stare out to the horizon and try to feel optimistic about new beginnings.

'Look!' exclaims Mads. 'What's happening on the quay?'

Dancing Girl has rounded the headland and Guy slows her down for the final approach through the narrow harbour entrance. The high stone wall of the quay looms above and a large crowd has gathered to watch our approach.

'They're waving!' Mads waves back excitedly. 'Hello! Hello!' She turns back to me, her cheeks pink with excitement. 'Isn't this romantic? Coming into an ancient fishing village by boat? The tourists love it. Look at them all waving.'

239

I shield my eyes against the bright sunshine. Sure enough there's a throng of bodies crowded on the harbour, jostling for pole position, cameras flashing and camcorders held out to capture the trawler's arrival. Even above the throb of the engine I can hear the rise and fall of excited voices.

You know, crazy as this is, I would swear they're calling my name, but that's impossible, surely?

'Katy! Katy! Is it true you're seeing Gabriel Winters? Has he really dumped Stacey Dean for you?'

I have a hideous sinking feeling, comparable to the time I taught my GCSE group the wrong book and only realised when they trooped into the exam hall, that something is very, very wrong. This bunch doesn't look anything like tourists. There's not a pasty or ice cream in sight, which in my limited experience tends to give it away. In fact the crowd, who now all but dangle from the quay, cameras extended at arm's length, look horribly like journalists.

'Maddy!' I gasp. 'I think the press have found me.'

There's an explosion of light as umpteen cameras flash. I throw my hands over my face.

'I haven't got any make-up on!'

'Never mind the make-up!' Mads drags me across the deck and shoves me into the wheelhouse. 'How are we going to get away from them?'

'Sod that! They're in my way.' Guy sounds the boat horn loudly. 'Fuck off! Out the way!'

'They're not going to listen,' I say as a camera is lowered towards the window, ingeniously strapped to a plank.

'Oh really? You think?' Guy shakes his head. 'Jesus! I should have just gone netting.' He storms on to the deck and starts hurling slimy ropes up at the journalists. 'I can't moor with you twats there!'

'How can I get off?' I'm starting to panic. Not only does it look as if I'll have to scale a ladder to reach the quay, but I'm also going to have to fight my way through the paparazzi. They look like they're ready to rip my limbs off and squabble over the soggy bits.

I glance at the water in the harbour and wonder if my swimming is up to me making a break for the other side. Surely all Ollie's training must pay off sometime? But the turgid water is oily and a fish head bobs past, fixing me with a disapproving glare. I don't really fancy a dip. I'll probably catch typhoid.

Guy rams a sou'wester on to my head and hands me an oilskin jacket. 'Put that on. They'll never see you underneath it.'

I screw up my nose and shove my arms into the cold plastic. To say that the jacket reeks of fish is an understatement. It's probably capable of walking by itself. Still, it's a disguise of some sort, I suppose.

'How did they know you were out at sea?' wonders Mads. 'I thought at least we'd be safe out there. I swore Guy to secrecy.'

Guy looks sheepish. 'I may have forgotten about that when I was talking to the old lady in the pub.'

'You total moron,' says Mads, giving him a look that in a fair world should have laid him out on the floor. 'I said to tell no one you were meeting us, and anyway, what old lady?'

'Just an old dear I met in the Mermaid who said she was looking for Katy. She had some poof with her too,' says Guy. 'Barking mad she was. Drank gin like it was water and played cards like a pro. Fucking round cleaned me out.

There she is now!' He points to the end of the quay, where a small figure dressed in green and sporting what looks like a turban with a feather in it is elbowing her way through the crowd and jabbing at anyone who gets too close with a purple parasol.

'Yoo-hoo!' she warbles. 'Katy darling! Is that you? Take off that ghastly hat. Yellow is so not your colour. Terrible with red hair. Come and say hello. Look! I've found all these darling people who can't wait to meet you. Everyone is so friendly here. Nothing like beastly London.'

I bury my face in my hands. I think we can safely say that the mystery of how the press has managed to find me has been solved.

'That's my godmother,' I say.

Jewell teeters on the edge of the quay. 'What are you doing hiding away, darling? Come up at once! There're lots of people simply dying to talk to you. It's too thrilling for words.'

Jewell couldn't have attracted more attention if she'd painted her body purple and danced naked on the fish-market roof. Being slightly deaf, she also assumes that the rest of the world is hard of hearing too and her speech volume is on a par with Concorde taking off. Consequently the few journalists who are still enjoying the real ale in the pub now stagger out, clutching cameras and notepads in their sticky paws.

'Come on.' The feathers on her hat bob furiously. 'There's a lovely man here from the *Sun* who can't wait to speak to you about that divine Gabriel. Although,' she leans dangerously far forward and sways a little before being snatched back from the brink by one of the hacks, 'I'm very hurt that you didn't tell me first.'

'There's nothing to tell,' I say, or at least I try to, but the minute I stick my head out of the wheelhouse door, cameras flash and my name is called by about twenty different people. I duck back inside quickly.

'Fuck,' breathes Maddy.

'Fuck indeed.' My heart feels like it's having a go on a pogo stick. Why would anyone want to be famous? This is hideous. I will never, ever apply to go on *The X Factor*. No matter how crappy teaching can be, at least I can normally make the little sods do what I tell them.

'I can't hear you, darling!' hollers Jewell. 'Come up here! We've travelled all this way to see you, don't hide.'

We? The pogo stick accelerates. Has she got Ollie with her? If Ollie's in Tregowan then somehow everything will be sorted. Ol practically has a PhD in sorting out my mess. What a relief.

'I'm coming!' I say, clambering over the piled fish boxes and coiled ropes. I trip a bit, OK a lot, in my flip-flops, and no doubt somebody somewhere gets a cellulite shot that will grace the pages of *Heat*, but I don't care. If Ollie is here to sort it all out, everything will be fine.

'Careful, darling,' calls Jewell, watching me struggle up the ladder, dazzled by migraine-inducing flashes. 'Mind your nails.'

My nails are the least of my concerns; in fact, as I slither and slip on the rungs I begin to fear for my life. The deck of *Dancing Girl* is suddenly a very long way below and not looking like a soft landing. God, I hate heights! Even sitting on the top of the 207 bus makes my legs go all wobbly. I start to feel sick and actually very hard done by. All I want to do is have a quiet break and write my novel in peace. And now I'll end up as a splat on the manky deck of a boat belonging to a man with all the social graces of a bout of diarrhoea.

Maybe in a parallel universe another Katy Carter has been rescued by a multimillionaire in a yacht rather than sewer-mouthed Guy in his stinky trawler.

My right hand slips on some fresh seagull shit and the crowd gasp as I wobble and slide. I scream and plunge several rungs before managing to scrabble a hold. One lovely flip-flop plops into the harbour and I feel stupidly close to tears.

Just my luck I inhabit the crappy parallel universe.

'For fuck's sake,' Guy says despairingly. Moments later he's climbed up behind me and placed his strong arms either side of the ladder. 'Look up and climb, you silly cow. I won't let you fall.'

Charming! He is so *not* going to be the inspiration for my romantic hero. Jake would never call Millandra a silly cow! Maddy has a serious taste-in-men problem if Richard Lomax and Guy Tregarten are her idea of heroes.

Still, I'm not going to argue with Guy. I look upwards and try to ignore the fact that an enormous lens is pointed at my chest. Several rungs later I sprawl across the quay, hands raw from gripping the ladder and legs jellified from the effort.

I'm alive!

It's all I can do not to kiss the ground like the Pope.

I am *never* setting foot on Guy's boat again.

Jewell pokes me with the parasol. 'Get up, Katy! We can see your underwear.'

Cameras flash. As apparently so do I. I leap up hastily and pull my skirt down.

'Where's Ollie?' I look round hopefully, but there are only strange faces and lenses. That curly mop of bright hair and familiar crinkled grin can't be far away.

Jewell's brow wrinkles so deeply that she looks like

Yoda dressed in Chanel. 'Isn't he the lovely boy with the pants who came to my birthday party?'

Togas and Romans was Jewell's last theme, and Ol and I had a great time ripping up bed sheets, unlike James, who insisted upon hiring a fancy Caesar outfit and trying to discuss high finance with a very plastered Jewell. Ollie was a major hit, especially when his toga fell off to reveal Batman underpants.

'Yes, yes!' I say impatiently. 'Where is he?' I crane my neck just in case Ollie is hiding behind a length of orange trawl or is sitting in a net bin.

'Whatever makes you think he's here?' Jewell puts her arm around me and beams for the cameras. 'The other side's my better side, angel!'

My poor heart's had more ups and downs than a ride at Alton Towers today. It's now plummeting like a crazy bungee jumper. No Ollie? I'm ridiculously devastated.

'I came with that lovely Frankie,' Auntie Jewell tells me, adjusting her turban and baring her dentures for the photographers. 'He called me when he saw the papers. He was adamant that you'd need our support. Bless him! What a sweetheart! He couldn't drive down quick enough.'

I bet he bloody couldn't. I make a mental note to murder Frankie horribly when I next see him.

'Didn't Ollie want to come?'

'Ollie?' Again the powdery old face furrows. 'I don't think he was even there, darling. Out with his girlfriend, Frankie thought. Why?' She fixes me with one of her piercing looks. 'Did you expect him to come?'

'Of course not,' I say quickly. 'I just wondered.' Then another thought occurs. 'Where *is* Frankie?'

Jewell laughs. 'I have simply no idea. We had a drink, or

maybe two, and then he vanished. I expect he's gone for a walk, the dear boy.'

I groan. This is all I need.

Jewell links her arm through mine. 'We want to know exactly what's been going on. Don't we?' The reporters nod and shout their agreement. As they press closer, I start to panic, because there's nowhere to escape to. On one side of the wall is murky harbour water and on the other are crashing waves, neither of which holds much appeal. Backing away as the reporters surge forward, I find that I'm trapped against a net bin. Bits of rotting fish and tangles of gut press against my cheek.

'Darlings, move back! Let us through!' Jewell demands.

'Not until we have a comment.' A thin-faced girl in a silver bomber jacket shoves a microphone under my nose. 'Angela Andrews, *Daily Dagger*. Did you steal Gabriel from Stacey Dean?'

'Is he good in bed?' demands another.

'Is he?' asks Jewell, agog.

'I don't know!' I snap. 'I hardly know the man!'

'Is it true that he's bought a house here?'

'Are you an actress? What are you in?'

'A mess, that's what I'm in,' I groan.

Jewell and I are pushed back again as more reporters press forward. Any further back and we'll be *in* the net bin. Jewell brandishes her parasol at them but the reporters are made of sterner stuff.

'Hit me with that and I'll do you for assault,' jeers Angela Andrews.

'Who says I'm going to *hit* you with it?' Jewell retorts, poking the reporter's bony rear. Angela backs off nervously. I can't say I blame her. Jewell looks like she means business.

'Out of the way, Grandma!' A burly photographer shoves through towards us. 'All we need's a quote from Katy.'

'That's enough!' A spray of water rises from the boat below, showering the journalists, who scatter shrieking and trying to shield their cameras. 'She said no fucking comment!'

Guy is wielding the boat's deck wash like Arnie wields an Uzi. All he needs to do is shout 'Hasta la vista, baby!' and the image will be complete. Icy-cold sea water drenches the reporters as he swings the hosepipe from left to right.

'How jolly!' trills Jewell, watching the reporters scurrying for shelter like disturbed ants. 'Will we be on the news?'

'Get back on to the boat,' yells Guy. 'Down the ladder!'

I'm just about to point out that I'm with an octogenarian who can't possibly be expected to shimmy down ladders when Jewell pushes past and starts the descent, calling, 'Hurry up, Katy! Don't be afraid!'

'Thank you, darling,' she coos when Guy lifts her on to the deck. 'Bless you for helping a frail old lady.'

Frail old lady? I've met frailer Sherman tanks.

Jewell, swooning in Guy's arms, winks up at me. 'This lovely young man will help you. He's ever so strong.'

'I'd rather die than let him help me,' I say as I inch my way back down towards the deck.

'Get your arse down here now!' Guy roars. 'Or we're going without you.'

I don't need asking twice, because Angela Andrews, sopping wet now, and shrieking blue bloody murder about her Prada bomber jacket being ruined, is back on the quay.

I'm down that ladder and on to the boat quicker than I'm out of school when the bell sounds.

And that's pretty bloody quick.

The boat engine roars into life, plumes of blue smoke cough out of the exhaust pipe and Guy tears about pulling in ropes and old tyres.

'Cast off!' he yells to Mads and me. 'As I go astern, push away from the wall.'

We do as he says, even though the wall is rough and slimy and we haven't the foggiest what astern means. Mind you, I'll do pretty much anything, to be honest, if it means getting away from Prada Bomber Jacket. She's almost on the boat now, one narrow foot stretching out towards *Dancing Girl* and the other anchored on the ladder. She's looking seriously pissed off, and I can't say that I fancy my chances if she gets her hands on me. Being a teacher, I'm more likely to go to the moon than I am to go to Prada, but I can imagine how much that jacket cost.

Luckily for me, while she's straddling the air between boat and ladder, Guy engages the engine and *Dancing Girl* shoots backwards with a jolt. Several alarmed seagulls caw in annoyance and rise into the air, crapping cheerfully on the reconvening journalists.

Jewell claps her hands. 'Marvellous!'

And what's even more marvellous is the loud splash Angela Andrews makes as she falls into the harbour.

'Whoops!' says Guy from the wheelhouse. 'Did someone fall in?'

Angela Andrews floats in the harbour, her face a picture of rage. The silver coat puffs around her like a trendy brand of life jacket and a gloopy mass of seaweed sits jauntily on the top of her head. High on the quay her colleagues cackle delightedly and take pictures.

'I hope Richard doesn't hear about this,' worries Mads. 'He'll go mental.'

It's on the tip of my tongue to ask her how she'll tell, but I stop myself just in time. Given the ugly expression on Angela's face, the thwarted crowd of reporters and the Ollie-shaped gap in my life, I'm going to need all the friends I can get. It's a sad sign of the times that I'm adding Richard to my rapidly dwindling list.

Guy emerges from the wheelhouse. 'Change of plan. We're going to Fowey. I know a good pub. You can wait there until it gets dark and then come the back way into Tregowan.'

'Good idea,' agrees Mads. 'If we walk down the cliff path we can avoid the press easily.'

'We can black our faces!' cries Jewell. 'And use leaves for camouflage!'

I sit on an empty fish box and bury my face in my hands.

'I need a drink,' I say.

Actually, make that several drinks.

And they can be doubles.

I'm starting to wish I'd stayed in London.

★

It's getting dark by the time the cab drops us all off at the top of Tregowan Hill. The light bleeds away from the sky, just like Jewell's scarlet lipstick has from her lips, and the lights of the village twinkle below. We've been deposited next to a rather overgrown footpath that doesn't look like it's been used since the days of smuggling, and left to pick our way down through the tangled brambles.

Not that anyone's perturbed by this. They're all far too pissed to care. Guy's wearing Jewell's turban and smoking a joint, Mads keeps lying down to gaze at the sky and

Jewell is singing 'Show Me the Way to Go Home' at the top of her voice. Every now and then somebody hisses, 'Ssh!' before erupting into cackles of laughter.

Oops! Think that's me!

'Katy!' Maddy grabs my arm and sways. 'Look!'

'What?'

'There aren't any lights on in the rectory. Where's Richard?'

We sway together and the twinkling village dips and rolls nauseatingly.

'He's out,' she declares. 'He's with some other woman.'

I think this highly unlikely. It's a cause of major amazement to me that Rich has found one woman who wants to shag him. The possibility of two seems to be pushing it rather.

'I'm going to find him,' Mads says, lurching off into the darkness. 'And then I'm going to chop his balls off.'

'Ouch,' Guy winces.

'I'll help you,' Jewell offers, stumbling in her wake.

'Where do you think you're off to?' Guy catches my sleeve when I try to follow. 'You're supposed to be meeting Gabriel Winters. Dinner at Mr Lover Lover's, remember? He lives over there.' And he stabs his finger wildly in the direction of some very distant lights.

I know I'm slightly pissed, but surely that house is about a mile away and at the end of some very thick woods? I glance down at my feet, now encased in a spare pair of Guy's wellies and slopping about madly. I look like I've got flippers for feet.

'I'll never make it,' I say. The path looks very dark and shadowy. I'm sure I can see a vampire lurking. 'Can't you come with me?'

'Bollocks to that! It's miles!' Guy gives me a shove. 'You don't need me. Whatever happened to girl power?'

I don't think I ever had any, to be honest, but I'm not telling him that.

It's only a woodland path. I'll show him.

Not that he'll leave me anyway.

'Fine.' I square my shoulders. 'I'll go on my own. Bye then.'

'Bye,' says Guy cheerfully and vanishes into the dusk.

What! That wasn't supposed to happen!

I'm all alone in the middle of the woods in the dark. And I've never seen dark like it. Where's the orange glow?

I wish I'd never watched *The Blair Witch Project*.

Or *Scream*.

Or any horror film at all basically.

Deep breaths, Katy. You can do this. I shuffle forward and stretch out my hands. It's only a walk in the woods, after all. Even if the woods are very dark and the path is getting steeper. I could cheerfully murder the sadistic bastard who thought building a house halfway through the woods was a good idea. Honestly! And I'm sure the air is getting thinner the higher I climb. If Gabriel wants guests to come to dinner then he really ought to provide an oxygen tank or something; at the very least a cable car.

Bloody inconsiderate I call it.

I pause for a moment to get my breath. It doesn't help that the fine weather has vanished, to be replaced by a depressing mizzling rain that is drifting in from the sea. My hair is starting to frizz and my nose is dripping, not a sexy look. Not that I want to look sexy for Gabriel, but a girl has her pride. And it's not every day that I get to have dinner with an A-list celebrity.

Pausing for breath, I lean against a tree and look at the

village falling away below. The mist is thicker now, wrapping itself around the ancient buildings. The beach vanishes. The houses that perch dizzyingly high above the sea are obscured, smothered and blanketed and the lights in their windows blinded. I have the horrible sensation that the world is slowly but surely being erased.

I pick up pace and scurry along the path. I seem to be suddenly possessed with ears on elastic. My hearing is superhuman. I can hear every twig that snaps and every bush that rustles for miles around. Someone is in these woods with me. I just know it. I can hear their breathing. In fact it's getting heavier by the second.

OK, Katy. Don't panic.

Crack! A twig snaps right behind me and that's it. I'm panicking. Stumbling in the huge boots, tripping over the roots of gnarled trees and ripping through bracken, I hurtle along the path.

Why didn't I get fit sooner? Why have I left it too late to become the new me? And it is too late, I know it is. I've seen this movie, I know what will happen. The small ginger girl gets caught by the psycho in the mask. I'll be wearing my entrails as a necklace and hanging from a tree quicker than you can say *slasher movie*.

I'm nearly at the house. Just a little way to go. I'm nearly there. I burst out of the woods like a cork from a bottle and hammer on the door with my fists.

'Gabriel!' I holler. 'Let me in!'

But there's no answer. The lights are on but no one's in, which would be funny in a metaphorical kind of way if I wasn't convinced that Freddy Krueger is after me. I bang on the door again, so hard this time that it swings open and I stumble in at exactly the same time that my mystery attacker hurls himself on top of me.

And starts to lick my face.

Wait a minute, that's not right. Shouldn't that be 'and pulls out a knife and guts me like a fish'? Have I got my genres mixed?

Peeling open an eye, I bravely face my assailant.

It's a toy poodle.

I know I've been drinking, but even I couldn't imagine this. I really am lying in the hallway of Gabriel Winters' country retreat being licked to death by a fluffy white poodle.

'Hello, Katy.' Gabriel descends the stairs, dressed in a bathrobe. Golden ringlets still wet from the shower bounce around his cheeks like springs. 'I see you've met Mufty.'

'Mufty?'

'My dog,' explains Gabriel. 'He was outside and wouldn't come in. Would you like a drink?'

Have I banged my head and am lying unconscious in the woods?

'Katy?' Gabriel says. 'A drink?'

'Oh! Me?'

'Of course you. How many dogs do you know that drink champagne?'

None, although I do know one that loves Guinness, not that I'm thinking about Ollie and Sasha. I'm alone with Gabriel Winters and he's stark naked under his skimpy bathrobe. Surely this is the stuff dreams are made of? Come on, Katy! Look at those golden legs and muscular calves. Think about the wet-trousers scene. Peel off that robe and run your hands over his rippling torso. Where's your libido gone?

Off on its holidays indefinitely, by the look of things.

Typical.

I follow Gabriel into his kitchen. Although he claims to be renovating the house, everything looks shiny and new. The scrubbed pine table is neatly set and candles flicker romantically.

'You're a bit early.' Gabriel puts Mufty down and rummages around in a cupboard. 'I'm not quite ready.'

'I'm not early,' I say in surprise. 'You said seven. Besides, it's been a crazy day.' And I tell him all about the journalists and my hasty retreat from Tregowan. As I gabble away, Gabriel pours me a glass of wine and stirs a bubbling pan of stew. He doesn't look very concerned, but I guess it's all in a day's work when you're famous. It's only when I mention Prada Bomber Jacket that he seems perturbed.

'Angela Andrews?' He raises a perfectly plucked eyebrow. How long is it since mine had some TLC? I touch one. Gross! They must look like ginger caterpillars.

'She writes for the *Daily Dagger*?'

'I know who she is.' Gabriel looks worried. 'She's a really nasty piece of work. They call her the Fleet Street Rottweiler. Once she gets a whiff of a story there's no way she'll let go.'

'Well, it's just as well there's no story, then.' I can't really see a problem. I mean, I've only gone to these lengths because I don't need to upset Richard any more than is necessary. 'We'll just tell them it's a misunderstanding. When she finds there's no scandal to be had, she'll get bored.'

'She may already be on to something. The lovely Miss Andrews has been trailing me for weeks. I was hoping you might be able to do me a favour, something that would be mutually beneficial.'

'Oh?'

'We could make it a job,' Gabriel says. 'I'd pay you really well.'

'I do need a job,' I say, thinking about the fifteen hundred pounds I owe Ollie, never mind the hideous amount Jewell loaned me. 'What is it? Cleaning? Dog-walking?' I reckon I can even bear walking a dog called Mufty if it saves me from Mads, the sex aids and her alarmingly long list of eligible men.

'Not exactly.' Gabriel lights a cigarette, inhales and then blows the smoke out of his nose. 'I was wondering if you'd like to be my official girlfriend.'

'What?' I *am* unconscious in the woods. A white rabbit will run past in a minute and ask me the time.

'Not for real, obviously,' says Gabriel, a bit too hastily. 'I'd like to hire you to play the part of my girlfriend, just to pretend to the press and keep them off my back. You have no idea what a pain in the butt it is always being quizzed about my love life, always having to have some brainless bimbo on my arm just to keep my manager happy. If we could say you were my long-term girlfriend living in Cornwall, it would be perfect.'

I stare at him.

'You could even live here!' cries Gabriel, warming to his theme. 'Rent free! Just name your price, Katy. You could write your novel in peace and not have to worry about doing some shitty job. All you'd need to do is be seen out with me now and again, maybe give a few interviews from time to time, but that would be it. You said you don't have a boyfriend, so nobody would care about you pretending to be with me.'

'But why do you need someone to pretend?' I'm confused and not half as flattered as he thinks I should be.

255

'You could date anyone. *Heat* magazine had you as Torso of the Week in the last edition.'

Gabriel sighs heavily.

'Can I trust you to keep a secret?'

'Of course,' I say.

His blue eyes narrow. 'It's a major secret and one that can't go any further than us. Ever.'

I'm all agog. 'What is it?'

Gabriel pets Mufty's fluffy head. 'Can't you guess?'

'You've got a secret lover? She's married? Famous *and* married?'

'Not even close.'

I rack my brains. I haven't a clue why a man as beautiful and successful as Gabriel Winters would need to pretend he has a girlfriend. From my weekly secret perusal of celebrity magazines – secret because English teachers are *supposed* to read edifying material like the *Times Literary Supplement* – I've been under the impression there's a queue of stunning women desperate for the job.

Why would he need to pretend?

I gaze around the kitchen in case a clue whizzes past and wallops me on the nose. There's a dirty plate and glass by the Belfast sink and a pair of pink cowboy boots by the door, but otherwise nothing. I smile. Frankie drove us mad until he managed to find himself a pair just like those. Perhaps I won't mention to Gabriel that he has the same taste in shoes as the lead singer of a gay rock band. That wouldn't do his image any good.

Hold on a moment. I think I'm on to something.

There's no way a man so gorgeous he makes Brad Pitt look ugly needs to *pretend* he has a girlfriend unless he really doesn't want one for real.

Unless . . . unless . . .

Unless he really doesn't want a *girlfriend*.

I point at the boots. 'I've seen those before.'

Gabriel says nothing.

'There's someone here, isn't there?' I ask slowly. 'Someone you don't want anyone to find out about? That's why you weren't expecting me, that's why the dog got out and you didn't notice.' I look around the kitchen wildly, as though a random member of Girls Aloud might be hiding under the sink. 'Is that why you need me? To take the heat off?'

'Not exactly, although there may be somebody.' Gabriel looks cagey. 'It's early days and very complicated. Do I need to spell it out?'

I look from the crazy boots back to the pink-faced actor. 'No, I don't think you do. I know whose boots those are.'

Those boots belong to Frankie, the very same Frankie who's creeping guiltily into the kitchen and has just made my life about a million times more complicated.

And I am going to kill him.

Chapter Fifteen

I wrap my hands around a thick ceramic mug and stare across the oak table at the two sheepish men opposite. 'Is somebody going to explain exactly what's been going on?'

Frankie and Gabriel exchange a look.

'You guys haven't just met, have you?'

'We met a couple of months ago at a backstage party,' admits Frankie. 'Gabe had a pass to the VIP suite and I managed to blag my way in because Nicky, my bass player, knew a member of the band. Gabe was there and he—'

'Offered you a canapé,' I recall. 'You've told that story a few hundred times actually.'

Gabriel blushes. 'Has he really?'

I nod. 'It's been told so often it's getting worn out.'

'We chatted for a bit and then I gave Gabriel my phone number,' Frankie recalls. 'I slipped it into his pocket and he promised he'd call.'

'But how did you know he'd be interested?' I ask. 'Seeing as Gabriel's kept this a secret?'

Frankie grins. 'My gaydar works better than yours, darling!'

'I lost his number,' says Gabriel. 'So I'd no way of getting in touch, otherwise I would have been seriously tempted.'

'Gabriel's manager wouldn't put any of my calls

through or give me contact details so I was getting desperate. I thought I'd blown it. Then I opened the papers this
morning and bingo! You'd found him for me.' Frankie
grins. 'I was frantic. I had no idea where you were staying,
Ollie had pushed off so I whizzed over to Hampstead to
ask Jewell. She was up for a jaunt and the rest is history.'

'But why didn't you say?' I ask. 'Instead of pretending it
was just a crush? I wouldn't have said anything.'

'I couldn't tell you.' Frankie swirls the tea around his
mug and gives me a rueful smile. 'I couldn't tell anyone.
Don't take it personally.'

'I don't get it,' I say to Gabriel. 'Surely no one's
bothered about people being gay these days? I thought
showbiz types were really open-minded?'

Gabriel laughs. 'Yeah, right. How many Hollywood
leading men can you name who are gay, or maybe I should
say openly gay?'

I think hard. 'Rupert Everett?'

'Rupert Everett and?' presses Gabriel, lifting Mufty on
to his lap and caressing the poodle thoughtfully. 'Anyone
else?'

Do you know, it's the weirdest thing but I can't think of
one. How bizarre is that?

'Exactly,' says Gabriel. 'There aren't any, are there? Can
you imagine Bruce Willis or Arnie being cast as action
heroes or Brad Pitt being a pin-up if everyone knew they
were gay?'

My jaw drops. 'Brad Pitt's gay?'

'No! Well I don't think so anyway, but that isn't the
point. Do you think they'd have the careers they do if they
were openly gay? Or do you think they'd be sidelined and
eventually forgotten? Think about it, Katy. How many
successful gay men do you see on television?'

I think hard. 'Paul O'Grady?' I venture. 'Graham Norton? The fat one in *Little Britain*?'

'Any actors?' presses Gabriel, his blue eyes burning with passion. 'Anyone in the same league as Sean Bean or David Tennant?'

'I can't think of anyone,' I say, totally amazed. If anyone had asked me before, I would have sworn blind there were hundreds of famous gay actors out there, but Gabriel's right. It's impossible to name more than a handful.

'And that's my problem,' he sighs. 'I'm an actor and a successful one too, and I want to have the pick of the roles on offer. I want to play action heroes and leading men; I want to fire guns and have sword fights. I even want to play James Bond and Hamlet!'

'Good for you,' I say. Makes my ambition to write romantic novels look a bit tame. Perhaps I should be aiming higher. Be the new Shakespeare or something.

'It's not going to happen if anyone finds out I'm gay. I'll be sidelined, typecast as the bitchy gay friend or something. No agent will touch me because I suddenly won't be half as lucrative, and before I know it my career will be over. I'll be washed up. A nobody.' He fixes me with an imploring gaze. One golden ringlet tumbles boyishly over his eyes and I can't help but think how attractive he is.

What a waste. No wonder I didn't get any vibes.

'Anyway,' he continues, a brave tremor in his voice, 'I tried dating lots of beautiful actresses to keep the press off the scent. I didn't want to be having my sexuality questioned at every turn.'

'The trouble is,' Frankie butts in, 'these girls that Gabe dates always expect more.'

'And that becomes an issue in itself.' Gabriel looks worried. 'It's only a matter of time before one of them goes to Max Clifford with a kiss-and-tell about what we *didn't* do. Clifford's no fool; he'll soon put a story to-gether. And if he doesn't there's that Angela Andrews sniffing around; she's on to something.'

Frankie looks down at the table and pretends to be fascinated by the smears of tomato ketchup. 'If that's the woman I think you mean then we could have a problem.'

'Prada bomber jacket?' I say.

'Yes! Divine thing!' Frankie's eyes light up. 'That's her. She called here earlier while Gabe was in the shower so I answered the door. She was ever so friendly. We had a super chat. Sorry,' he adds to Gabriel, who has buried his head in his hands. 'I thought she was a friend of yours. She knew so much about you.'

'Well that's it then,' Gabriel says. 'She knows.'

'She does not,' Frankie squeals in outrage. 'I never told her I was gay.'

Gabriel and I both look at him. Dressed in a flamboyant green silk shirt and his favourite purple leather trousers and sporting a generous coating of Yves Saint Laurent False Lash mascara, Frankie couldn't be more of a stereo-type if he dressed in PVC shorts and declared that he's the only gay in the village.

'She might have guessed,' says Gabriel gently. 'She's a clever woman.'

Frankie bit his lip. 'We'll just have to think of a reason why I was here. Shall I talk to her again? Say I'm the cleaner boy or something?'

'No!' Gabriel and I both say at once.

'See why I need you to consider my offer?' Gabriel turns to me. It's hard to tell who has bigger puppy-dog eyes, him or Mufty. 'It's perfect, Katy. You pose as my girl-friend, and because you're Frankie's friend he gets to come and go as he pleases. The press will soon get bored and push off and everyone's happy.'

'But it's lying,' I say.

Where did that come from? I've only been living in the rectory for twenty-four hours but somehow Richard has got right inside my head. And why is everyone asking me to lie lately?

'That's only a slight technicality.' Gabriel waves my concerns away with his beautifully manicured hand. 'You are a girl, and you are my friend.'

'I am?'

'Course you are!' cries Frankie. 'He adores you! Don't you, Gabe?'

Gabriel's nodding like that dog in the ads for Churchill Insurance. 'Absolutely!' he agrees.

I chew my lip. It's a tempting offer. Money for old rope, basically. All the perks of a relationship without the hassle of sex. I get to live in this fabulous house, write my novel in peace and everyone thinks that a gorgeous sexy actor is mad about me. One in the eye for all those men who've treated me like dirt over the years.

Not that there are that many.

Of course not.

But there are a few. James for one, and there's the added satisfaction of irritating Cordelia. Maybe part of the deal can be an account at Vera Wang and an agreement that Vera starts to make stuff in a size twelve.

Or maybe even a fourteen.

And bans Cordelia . . .

'What about Ollie?' I ask Frankie, who has leapt up from the table and taken a bottle of Cristal out of the fridge. 'What will he think?'

Frankie shakes the bottle like Lewis Hamilton after a Grand Prix. 'What's this got to do with Ollie?'

Gabriel's eyes narrow. 'You said you didn't have a boyfriend.'

'Ollie's not her boyfriend.' The cork pops and whizzes across the kitchen. Champagne fizzes from the bottle and the kitchen is filled with a delicious biscuity smell. Frankie has gone up in the world. We normally struggle to afford cava on payday.

'He's my cousin. He's going out with some hideous harridan with the worst boob job you've ever seen.'

'It's a boob job?' I ask. 'And it's still on with Nina?'

'As far as I know.' Champagne sloshes into three glasses. 'He was out a lot before I came down here and she's always ringing him. To be honest, I haven't seen as much of him since you moved in with Jewell. He's become a right miserable bastard. And yes, that's got to be a boob job. No one that thin has norks that big. Not even Victoria Beckham.'

'Never mind this Ollie,' says Gabriel impatiently, peering at me over the rim of his champagne flute. 'Will you take the job?'

'What have you got to lose?' adds Frankie. 'You're always on about finding a romantic hero; now you can have the real deal.'

'Name your price,' urges Gabriel.

I have a feeling I'm going to regret this. 'I'll think about it, OK? Give me a bit of time to get used to the idea. Besides, I don't look anything like an A-list actor's girlfriend.'

'We can change the way you look,' says Gabriel quickly. 'I'll get your hair done, buy you some clothes and teach you how to deal with the press. It'll be fun. Just like *My Fair Lady*.'

A new wardrobe! I'm seriously tempted. Get behind me Satan!

'And I'll get your teeth fixed.'

'My teeth? What's wrong with my teeth? I'm not exactly Austin Powers.'

'They could do with a whitening treatment or even veneers. And we'll find a gym so that you can shift a few pounds and tone up.' Gabriel strokes his golden-stubbled chin thoughtfully, enjoying his role as Professor Higgins to my Eliza Doolittle. 'We'll soon have you looking the part.'

'Get lost!' I say, insulted. It's all hideously close to Cordelia and her food fascism. I'm miserable as it is; being condemned to an indefinite period of eating rabbit food and doing sit-ups makes me want to cut my wrists, quite frankly.

'Not that I don't think you're great as you are,' says Gabriel quickly. 'It's just in case people get suspicious. I could have anyone, remember? People need to believe that I am really with you.'

I stare at him in amazement. He really is this conceited and tactless. He ought to get a prize.

'Go on,' says Frankie. 'You're supposed to be all for romance.'

'I'll think about it,' I say firmly. 'And that's my final word on the matter. I'll let you know tomorrow.'

And in the meantime I'll do my best to get another job, preferably one that doesn't involve Throbbing Theo and crotchless knickers.

But from the way Gabriel and Frankie are clinking

glasses and beaming at me, you'd think I'd just agreed to their crazy idea.

I have a very bad feeling about this.

★

When I let myself into the rectory I'm totally sober, in stark contrast to Frankie and Gabriel, who have worked their way through another bottle of champagne. I'm also absolutely exhausted. Stumbling down the dark woodland path with the Cornish drizzle beading my hair and the smell of damp sheep rising from the thick ethnic sweater that Jewell insisted on buying me in Fowey, I am very tempted to pack my bags and hotfoot it back to London. I came to Cornwall for some peace and quiet, time out to write and to recover from my cancer scare, and what happens? I'm embroiled in more deceptions than MI5.

The kitchen is dark apart from the soft glow of a table lamp and the red blush of heart-shaped fairy lights that Mads has strung above the window. I pick up the kettle, and as I fill it I look down over the village and the dark rolling waves. The window is ajar and I can hear the music from the Mermaid as it carries on the night breeze. The mist is thicker now, more like fog, and it billows in from the sea all quiet and ghostly.

I'm just planning a scene where Millandra runs away from the evil Lady Cordelia and gets lost in the mist when I hear a loud sniff from the corner of the room, then another. Turning my head, I see Mads curled up on the armchair in the corner, clutching half the Kleenex factory and sobbing her eyes out.

'Whatever's the matter?' I ask, flinging my arms around my friend and letting her sob for a good few minutes until my shoulder starts to feel decidedly soggy. Mads sniffs again and raises her head, wiping her eyes on the back of her hand and drawing a shuddering breath. Her eyes are so swollen she looks as though she's gone five rounds with Mike Tyson. She must have been crying for hours.

'Sorry,' she gasps, pushing damp fronds of hair back from her hot face.

I squeeze on to the seat next to her. 'What's happened?'

She takes a shuddering breath. 'Where do I start?'

'You were fine when I left you.' I remember her stumbling into the mist, ready to cut off Richard's bollocks. 'Where are the others?'

'Guy went to the pub and took Jewell with him, so I came back to look for Richard. But he wasn't here!' More tears well up and trickle down her wet cheeks. 'He's out and I don't know where he's gone.'

'Church stuff?' I guess wildly. 'Prayer meeting? Um . . . hymn practice?'

'There's nothing on tonight.' Mads dabs at her eyes with a disintegrating tissue, which is falling to pieces almost as fast as she is. 'And he's not in any of the pubs. I've checked.'

I'm stumped. 'Maybe he's at a friend's house? Or visiting a parishioner? It's bound to be innocent, Mads; this is Richard we're talking about.'

'I would have agreed with you once, but not any more.' She reaches into her pocket and pulls out an envelope. 'I found this when I was cleaning on top of the wardrobe.'

'You were cleaning the top of the wardrobe?' I'm alarmed. This isn't healthy. Things must be bad.

Mads looks guilty. 'I was looking for some cash. Rich keeps it there secretly sometimes.'

'Whatever happened to thou shalt not steal?'

'What about thou shalt not commit adultery?' She

thrusts the envelope at me. 'Go on, have a look in there and then tell me you think it's all innocent.'

I open the envelope cautiously, feeling as though I've got an unexploded bomb in my hands. Inside are five crisp ten-pound notes and a folded piece of paper. With trembling fingers I unfurl it and read:

Richard! You were fantastic! Thank you! Isabelle! xxx

'Who's Isabelle?'

'How the fuck should I know?' Mads starts to cry again. 'Some slag he's screwing, I suppose.'

'Let's not jump to conclusions,' I say, which is pretty ironic coming from me, the Queen of Conclusion Jumping. 'Perhaps she's just a grateful parishioner.'

'Why's she giving him money?'

'Maybe it's his?'

'Richard hasn't got fifty pence, never mind fifty quid. He's having an affair, I just know it. That's why he's never in, why he's gone mad on running and why he's pouring gallons of aftershave over himself every time he sets foot out the door.'

'We don't know that for sure,' I say soothingly. One thing I've learned from working with hysterical teenagers is speak with authority and they generally end up agreeing with you. That and show no fear; like animals, teenagers can sniff out any weakness at one hundred paces.

'Don't give me that teacher-tone-of-voice bollocks,' snaps Mads.

Oops. Forgot she's thirty not thirteen.

'No, he's having an affair with someone and we are going to find out who it is.' Mads heaves herself out of the chair and pads towards a cupboard, from which she plucks a bottle of brandy.

What's all this *we* stuff?

'I'm so glad you're here, Katy.' Sloshing Courvoisier into mugs, Mads gives me a watery smile. 'I don't know how I'd get through this without you.'

Maybe I should tell her I'm considering going back to London.

'There's something I need to tell you,' I start.

'Oh God.' Mads starts to cry again, tears plopping into the brandy. 'You're going to go home, aren't you? You're leaving? How can I bear it? First Richard and now you. I'm all alone. And if Richard leaves me I'll never have a baby!'

'A baby?'

'Richard and I always said we'd try for a baby once we had a church. And now we've got that, he never comes near me. We haven't had sex for months! How can I have a baby if my husband never wants to touch me? If he's shagging some slag called Isabelle? That's why I have to get him away from here, why we have to go to Sandals.'

I'm alarmed. I've known Mads for more than ten years and I've never seen her so distraught. When she mentions the word 'baby', her eyes takes on the gleam of the religious fanatic. It's a look that I've seen in the expressions of countless colleagues and friends shortly before they get pregnant and shuffle off, never to be seen again, into a wilderness of Pampers and cracked nipples.

'Children are overrated,' I say, thinking about Wayne Lobb and Co. 'Trust me, I'm a teacher.'

'You don't understand. When you want a baby, you want a baby. I can't explain it, Katy, it's a powerful urge.'

'So I see.'

'And,' she continues, 'when you find the right man it's the most natural feeling in the world. You'll find that too, Katy, when you find The One.'

I think I can be forgiven for not holding my breath. I'm more likely to win *Britain's Next Top Model* than I am to find The One.

'You still love Richard?' I ask. 'Even though you think he's cheating?'

'Of course I do.' Maddy looks at me as though *I'm* the crazy one. 'When you love someone, you work at it. I haven't always been perfect either.'

So much for cutting off his bollocks with blunt scissors. Chaucer was right: love really is blind.

'We need to follow Richard and find out what he's up to,' Mads decides. 'You'll help me, won't you?'

'Of course I'll help,' I hear myself say.

What! Where did that come from?

Mads throws her arms around me and gives me such a bear hug that my ribs are in terror for their lives. 'I love you! You're the best friend anyone could have! I don't deserve you!'

I hug her back. Escaping back home will have to wait. Or at least until I can find out what Richard is up to. And I swear to God, if he really is cheating on Maddy, he's going to be sorry.

Bollock-chopping will be a walk in the park in comparison to what I'll want to do to him.

★

The most annoying thing about the country is that everywhere looks exactly like everywhere else. All the lanes are approximately one car wide and edged by hedges of such height and width that it's possible Sleeping Beauty's castle lies somewhere behind, and as for signposts, I don't think they've been put back since they were removed during the war.

Basically, I'm lost and I haven't got a clue where I am.

I check my watch. It's eleven twenty-five. I'm due to meet Tristan Mitchell at half past and I haven't got a flipping clue where I am. I could actually be anywhere in south-east Cornwall. Someone may well find me in fifty years' time, a skeleton behind the wheel of the church minibus, wearing an ancient pair of jodhpurs and with dozens of sex aids in Bible boxes.

'Bollocks squared,' I mutter to myself, turning Maddy's scribbled map upside down just in case it makes more sense that way. It doesn't. 'Where am I?'

Today hasn't got off to a flying start, not least because I have a thudding headache thanks to all the late-night brandy drinking and endless discussion of whether or not Richard is having an affair. We talked it round in ever-decreasing circles until we convinced ourselves that Isabelle was probably an old granny in the Eventide Home who'd given Richard money for the collection. Then Mads wondered what exactly had been *fantastic* and we were off again, until we'd devised so many scenarios that Richard made Casanova look like the Virgin Mary. I didn't feel I could slope off to bed and hide under the duvet because in the past Mads has spent hours listening to me bang on about James, so helping her dissect Richard's behaviour was the least I could do.

God, I think as I grind the gears on the minibus, what a waste of emotion. I'm so over James! I'd like to travel back in time and give the me of several months ago a good hard kick up the arse. I would so do things differently.

I check my watch again. I'm running late. Maybe I need to reverse back up to the crossroads and try another direction. Trouble is, I can't remember which way I came from.

I rub my throbbing temples. Today is not getting any better.

By the time Auntie Jewell staggered back to the rectory, Richard had come home and was having a blazing row with Mads in the hall.

'Don't mind me, darlings,' hiccuped Jewell, tottering past them. 'Much healthier to let it all out.'

Richard paused in amazement, mid-row, as Auntie started to climb the stairs, swaying like she was still on *Dancing Girl*.

'Who's that?' he demanded, lips white with rage.

'Katy's Auntie Jewell,' Mads yelled. 'Who the fuck's Isabelle?'

Richard winced. 'You know I don't condone that kind of language.'

'And I don't condone you shagging other women,' shrieked his wife, and off they went again, hammer and tongs, until the small hours. This was all right for Jewell, who passed out the second her head touched the pillow, but not so funny for me, who tossed and turned until dawn, sleep kept safely at bay by Mads and Richard's yelling and Jewell's snoring.

Anyway, this morning Jewell went to sea with Guy, the two of them seeming to have formed a bizarre friendship, and I decided that I was going to seek alternative employment and tell Gabriel to shove his job up his bottom. Richard went out running at the crack of dawn, slamming the front door so hard that the rectory almost slid down the hill, and Maddy attacked the vodka while she ate her cornflakes.

Things are not looking good.

I may well be lost in deepest Cornwall but I'm grateful

to be out of Tregowan. Next time I want a peaceful life I'll go somewhere quieter, like the fast lane of the M25.

I let up the clutch and the minibus goes shooting backwards. I try to stamp on the brake but my short legs are waving in the air because the pillow I shoved in my back has slipped. It's been a few years since I was let loose on the Sir Bob's minibus, chiefly because the last time I was behind the wheel I took out four bins and a skip, but they say you never lose the knack.

Although you have to have it in the first place, I suppose.

In any case the minibus shoots backwards and ends up in a hedge, where it sits, wheels spinning, while I bash my head against the wheel in frustration. My parents must have forgotten to invite the bad fairy to my christening or something, because this run of bad luck is beyond a joke. Then I remember that they're pagans and didn't bother with christenings. Well, my aura's dented or something. The minibus is *definitely* dented. Richard will freak.

There's a tap at the window and I nearly jump out of my skin when a dark head pokes in through the window. 'Are you OK?'

'I think so,' I say. 'But I'm very lost. I'm supposed to be at Tregowan Stables.'

The young man grins at me. He's got a mop of dark curls and his front tooth is chipped. There's a dusting of freckles across the bridge of his bumpy nose and the beginnings of dark stubble across his cheeks. He's not conventionally good-looking but he's got a cute smile.

'You're not as lost as you think you are,' he says. 'You've just backed into the south paddock.' He sticks his hand in through the window and shakes mine. 'I'm Tristan Mitchell. You must be Katy Carter.'

'Afraid so,' I say glumly. This is not the way to impress a potential new boss.

Tristan opens the door. 'The yard's only a few minutes up the road. I'll rescue this while you get sorted. Gran can't stand people who are late.'

'Thanks.' I hop out gratefully. Once out of the minibus I can see that he's wearing tight cream breeches that show off his long, lean thighs. Mads is right. Tristan is gorgeous. What she failed to mention, however, is that he's about eighteen years old. Seriously! He looks like he ought to be sitting in my A-level group discussing iambic pentameter or something. I'm starting to think all this country air is getting to Maddy.

To cut a long and very painful story short, I'm back at the minibus in less than twenty minutes. If Tristan is pure Jilly Cooper, then his grandmother is like something out of Stephen King.

In other words, she's a horror.

'Katy Carter?' she barks when I tear into the yard. 'You're late!'

'Yes, sorry!' I gasp. 'But—'

'Never mind but, girl! Time is time! I'm Mrs M. I own this place. You can ride, I take it?'

'Well, I have—'

'Yes or no?' she snaps. 'Come on! Look lively! I haven't got all day.'

'Yes,' I say uncertainly. And then, almost before I know what's happening, I've got a crash hat rammed on my head and have been zipped into some kind of body armour that is pushing my poor boobs practically through my spine. I must look as though I'm about to be shot out of a cannon.

'Right!' bellows Mrs M, leading the most enormous

grey horse out of a stable. 'This is Spooky. Up you get! Let's see what you can do.'

This is the point in the proceedings where I really ought to tell her thanks but no thanks and toddle off with my pride intact. But there's something about Mrs M that doesn't brook arguing with. She's wearing those old-fashioned breeches from the 1950s, all puffed out at the sides, which makes her a dead ringer for an SS commander. All she needs is a swastika. And I don't like the way she's tapping her whip against her boots either.

'Chop chop!' snarls Mrs M, heaving me up so violently that I almost fly over the other side of the horse. 'Leg on!'

And it's downhill from then on. I don't think I even last five seconds because Spooky puts in an enormous buck and I go sailing through the air and land on my backside. Mrs M tuts loudly and legs me up again, and once more I'm launched into orbit.

'I give up!' I puff, after I've been deposited for the third time.

'Give up?' bellows Mrs M in disgust. 'What's the matter with you young people? I was taught by a member of the Household Cavalry, my girl, and there was no giving up in my day. It takes seven falls to make a horse-woman! Up you get!'

Seven falls? I'll be dead. My bum is dislocated as it is.

'Sorry,' I say. 'I don't think this is going to work out.'

And I'm out of there like last week, leaving Mrs M muttering about young people and our lack of commitment. Well, she is so wrong. I *am* committed – to keeping my neck in one piece.

When I get back to the minibus I'm relieved to see that Tristan has extricated it from the hedge and managed to turn it around. But there's no sign of him.

Strange.

I open the driver's door and ease myself in. My bones are screaming and I've got aches in places that I didn't know could ache. I suppose that it's a sad fact of life that when you hit thirty you don't bounce.

'Oh!' I gasp, when I glance in the rear-view mirror and glimpse Tristan. 'I didn't see you there.'

Tristan's looking in amazement at Maddy's kinky cargo, which has spilt out of the boxes when they toppled with the collision. He's got Throbbing Theo in one hand and an edible G-string in the other.

'What sort of church do you go to?' he asks. 'I feel the need to get religion.'

'Put those away!' I hiss. 'They're not mine.'

'Keep your hair on!' He stuffs the goods back into the boxes. 'That was a quick interview. Did you get the job?'

'No.'

'Pity.' Tristan winks at me. 'We could have had some fun.'

Am I being chatted up by a fit eighteen-year-old?

He jumps out of the bus and slams the door. 'Any time you want a ride, you know where I am. See you!'

And off down the road he saunters, firm young bottom wiggling jauntily. I'm blushing from head to toe but also feeling something close to pride. I may not have Nina's boobs, or the perfect teeth and perfect body that Gabriel requires for his pretend girlfriend, but I've just had an eighteen-year-old flirt with positively geriatric me. I haven't lost it!

I put the minibus in gear and lift the clutch. Every bone in my body aches but I'm still smiling even when I get back to the village. I may not have a job yet but I'm feeling more cheerful than I have for ages. And I've got the number for Jason Howard in my bag. Maybe I'll pop down to Arty Fawty and have a chat with him. After all, how hard can it be to look after two small children? Unlike my encounter with Spooky, it's hardly likely to kill me, is it? After all, I'm a secondary school teacher. I'm made of sterner stuff.

★

How wrong can a girl be? It's only quarter past six but already I'm drooping with exhaustion and longing for Jason Howard to come in from work. My head is pounding and my throat's hoarse from screeching at the two imps of Satan so cleverly disguised as sweet-looking children. Ever since I've picked them up from school I've needed eyes in my backside.

Note to self: never, ever have kids.

No wonder Jason Howard pays so well. This is danger money.

After leaving the stables I'd parked the minibus, cunningly lining the scraped side alongside the wall so that hopefully Richard won't notice the new dents, and wandered into Tregowan. It was a glorious afternoon, primroses clustering the gardens and cow parsley frothing the hedgerows. Seagulls wheeled and plunged above and the village throbbed with holidaymakers, who crowded the narrow streets and clustered round the harbour. Munching on a pasty, I meandered with the tourists, peeping into the gift shops and admiring the views until I eventually arrived at the quayside.

There was no missing the Arty Fawty shop. It was painted in vivid primary colours with the name picked out in the most violent shade of pink I'd ever seen. The place looked like a migraine with a roof. Throwing my pasty crust to the gulls I wandered through the open door and was almost blinded by the bright pictures jostling for pole position on every surface. Bright blobby boats in rainbow hues competed with splashy cottages and splats of vermilion and crimson screamed for attention. It was bold and bright and unbelievably funky, even if it did all look a bit as though a gang of six-year-olds had been let loose.

'Can I help you?' A bit like the shopkeeper in *Mr Benn*, a man appeared as if by magic. He was wearing paint-splattered combat trousers and a faded blue fisherman's smock speckled with the same lary colours that filled the shop. His wavy hair was caught up with an elastic band and there was a smudge of paint across his nose, Adam Ant-style.

I was a bit disappointed. I'd been expecting a tragic Captain von Trapp type. Jason was attractive in a trendy hippy kind of way, with long skinny limbs and a funky headscarf, but he wasn't my type at all.

For a start, he was ginger.

I know! I know! I'm the last person in the world to be gingerist. But I can't help it. If we got it together we'd look like two ginger peas in a ginger pod. And imagine the poor kids, cursed with two sets of pale and freckly genes. I just couldn't go there.

I'd have to have words with Mads. She has no idea what constitutes a romantic hero. I may need to force her to read my entire Mills and Boon collection.

'Jason? I'm Katy Carter.' I held out my hand. 'I've come about the childminding job.'

'Thank God!' Jason Howard grabbed my hand and clutched it tightly. 'It's yours!'

277

I was taken aback. 'Don't you want to see my references or something?'

'I'm sure they're great,' Jason said. 'Besides, you're staying with the vicar. I trust you.'

I opened my mouth to point out that I could be anyone, but then shut it again. After all, I wanted this job. Anything had to be better than posing as Gabriel's girlfriend. And though in my usual experience most parents would rather cut their hair with a Flymo than hand over their precious children to any old body, I wasn't instantly suspicious. After all, my parents had always been more than happy to dump Holly and me on just about anyone who'd have us. And with his hippy-style long hair and dreamy expression there was something about Jason that reminded me of them.

'I'm a qualified teacher,' I told him. 'I've taught in inner London for the past seven years.'

'Aren't the kids really tough there?' asked Jason.

People *always* ask me that, like the children are a pack of flesh-eating monsters who would tear a teacher limb from limb as soon as look at them. In reality all it takes to tame them is a loud shout, big shoes and a funky pencil case. Still, who am I to shatter the illusion?

I nodded. 'Like wild animals.'

'Excellent!' cried Jason.

Excuse me?

'I mean, excellent you're a teacher,' he amended quickly. 'You're hired.'

Well that was easy, I thought, as I left the shop. Jason had promised to call the head teacher at Tregowan Primary to let her know that I was coming at home time to collect Luke and Leia.

Luke and Leia! I chortled to myself as I climbed the hill

on top of which some thoughtless sod had built the primary school; they shouldn't be hard to identify. Just spot the boy with the light sabre and the girl with the Chelsea buns on the side of her head.

Nearly three very long hours later I'm laughing on the other side of my face. Luke and Leia? Satan and Lucifer would be more appropriate names.

'Katy Carter?' A harassed-looking primary teacher elbowed her way through the throng of waiting mums, dragging a small boy and girl in her wake.

'That's me!' I said, all Mary Poppins brightness. 'And you,' I added, crouching down to beam at a carrot-haired little boy, 'must be Luke.'

Luke looked at me with bright eyes.

'No shit, Sherlock,' he drawled, and his sister shrieked with laughter.

I was momentarily gobsmacked. Maybe I'd heard wrong? I took a deep breath and smiled at the little blonde angel, who was shaking with mirth.

'And you're Leia?'

'No, dumbass, I'm Luke,' she shrieked, and dissolved into more gales of laughter. In the meantime her brother had tripped up another boy and was busy kicking his school bag around the playground.

'Come and get it, shithead!' he screeched.

My jaw was practically on the floor. Never in seven years at Sir Bob's had kids spoken in front of me like that. I looked at the teacher, who just shrugged her plump shoulders in resignation.

With a growing sense of doom I watched Luke and Leia terrorise the other kids. By the time I'd dragged them back down the hill and into the village my nerves were starting to fray. I lost Luke in between the post office and

Arty Fawty, only to discover him in the sweetshop cramming pick 'n' mix into his rucksack. Dragging him out by his collar, to screams of 'I'll get Childline on you, bitch!', I then discovered Leia busily untying rowing boats and chortling to herself as they floated out to sea. Once I got the pair of them safely inside Jason's flat, surely I was home and dry?

No such luck. I opened the door and was almost flattened when Luke and Leia stampeded past me en route to the fridge.

'Fucking hell!' roared Luke, flinging it open and finding little more than a pint of milk and some mouldy cheese. 'That stupid bastard has forgotten to shop again.'

'Wanker!' screeched his sister, hurling herself on to the sofa and starting to bounce like a thing possessed. 'Wanker! Wanker! Wanker!'

I looked at my watch. Quarter to four. I had no idea how I was going to last until six thirty.

Luke slammed the fridge door shut and was delving in the vegetable basket with a look of intense concentration on his evil little face. After a bit of a struggle with some carrots he plucked out a bottle of vodka.

'Yes!' he yelled. 'Found it!'

'Cool!' Leia bounded into the kitchen. 'Pour us a drink.'

Luke started rummaging in a cupboard for glasses. I'd been frozen in stunned horror, but this galvanised me into action. There was no way I was letting an eight-year-old and a six-year-old drink vodka while I was in charge. I flew across the kitchen and snatched the bottle.

Luke glared at me. 'Give that back.'

I breathed in slowly and out slowly. I'd watched that *Supernanny* programme. Calm and controlled works best, apparently.

'This is grown-up juice,' I told him. 'I'll get you some milk.'

Luke's top lip curled like I'd just offered to pour him a cup of vomit. 'What the fuck do we want milk for?'

'It's good for you.' I clutched the vodka to my chest.

'Bugger good,' said Luke.

'Look what I've got, Katy.' Leia tapped me on the shoulder. 'Sammy says hello.'

I looked down. Wrapped around her neck was the most enormous snake I'd ever seen.

Crash! The bottle slid from my fingers and shattered. Vodka spilt everywhere.

'He's friendly.' Leia waggled the snake in my general direction. 'He loves babysitters. For tea!'

I hate snakes.

And right now I hated children.

'He ate the last one,' Luke said. 'What was she called?'

'Stupid cow!' Leia cried. 'That's what I called her.'

'Put the snake away,' I ordered. 'Or I'll have to get your daddy.'

'Oooh!' Luke grinned. 'Like, we're so scared.'

'Dad doesn't mind what we do,' Leia told me, planting a kiss on the snake's head. 'He has to be nice to us because we haven't got a mum.'

'He lets us do what we want,' Luke added. 'He believes we should be able to express ourselves.'

And they went on to express themselves too. Leia poured paint all over the carpet, Luke threw his homework down the toilet, and they both spat out the window at the tourists. I cowered in the lounge, one eye on the snake and one on the clock.

These two monsters made my bottom set Year 11s, the hardest kids at Sir Bob's, look like pussycats.

★

Jason is half an hour late. Can't say I blame him – if these two were mine, I'd be buying a one-way ticket to Mars – but I'm not sure how much longer I can carry on here. I've tried every technique I know, from threats ('Yeah, like we're so scared!') to the naughty corner ('You're even uglier than Supernanny!') and nothing works. Short of a bullet, I can't think what would.

Still, if Mads is still broody when I get home, I think I've found a brilliant way to cure her. I'm going to make an appointment to get my tubes tied asap.

Jason finally skulks in at seven, which would be understandable apart from the fact that he works downstairs. There's a distinct whiff of alcohol about him too. Never mind Dutch courage, I think, as I grab my bag and prepare to run. I'd need nerves of steel to come back here again.

'So.' He runs a hand through his hair and glances nervously at the children, who are sitting angelically on the sofa and pretending to be engrossed in *Emmerdale*. 'Everything OK?'

He can't believe I'm still alive.

'Fine,' I say, backing towards the door. 'Must go.'

'Same time tomorrow?' asks Jason hopefully.

I look at Luke and Leia and I swear they're licking their lips.

How to put this tactfully? Your children are the spawn of Satan and there's not enough money in the world to persuade me to come within two miles of them?

Hmm. Maybe not.

'I've just been offered another job.' Technically that isn't a lie. 'I'm afraid I won't have time for Luke and Leia.'

Jason Howard deflates before my eyes. 'That's a shame. It looks as though you all got on like a house on fire.'

'Oh yes.' I recall how I had to wrestle a lighter from Luke when he tried to set his sister's hair alight. 'We certainly did.'

And then I'm scuttling out of Arty Fawty as quickly as I can, heading straight for the Mermaid. I think I deserve a drink or six after the day I've had.

★

It's quiet in the pub, a strange in-between time when the afternoon drinkers have staggered home and the fishing boats are yet to come in. There's one crazy mumbling woman at the locals' end of the bar, and two men who look suspiciously like journalists drinking real ale by the fire. I buy a glass of wine and settle into the window seat, and watch the red and green lights of the trawlers as they roll slowly homewards. I pull my notebook out of my bag and stare at it for a moment before putting it back in. I'm too tired to write a word. My backside aches from the morning's exertions and my nerves are shredded thanks to my afternoon with Satan's children.

I hate to admit it, but Gabriel's job offer is looking more attractive by the minute. Should I take it?

Of course I should. Anything's got to be better than babysitting Beavis and Butthead.

So what's stopping me?

I take a gulp of my drink. The only thing that is holding me back is Ollie. I know it's stupid, I know he's with Nina, but I don't want him to think I'm with somebody else so soon after James. It makes me look really shallow, doesn't it?

I'm being ridiculous! This is Ollie I'm talking about

here. Ollie who is my friend, my mate, the person who knows me better than anyone, not some distant fantasy figure. Surely he's the one person I should be able to tell about Gabriel's bizarre proposal?

Taking another swig of my wine, I make a bold decision.

I'm going to phone Ollie and tell him that I miss him. I'll swallow my pride, lay it on the line and basically mix metaphors left, right and centre if it means we can sort out this ridiculous mess and be mates again. No more playing silly buggers. If there's one thing I've learned from the whole hideous cancer scare, it's that time isn't elastic.

Carpe diem and all that!

My fingers leap over the keypad and dial Ollie as though they have a mind of their own. The phone rings and rings and I cut it off impatiently and try his mobile number instead. After several rings I hear a click as it's answered.

'Ol!' I cry, and those flipping butterflies are back in my stomach, only this time they've brought all their mates along too. 'It's Katy! How are you?'

'Hello, Katy.'

Nina's clipped tone sounds less than enthralled to hear from me. I almost drop my mobile in horror.

'Oh, hi.' I hope I keep the disappointment from my voice. 'Is Ollie there?'

'He's busy, actually. Can I take a message?'

'Not really. I need to talk to him.'

'It's not very convenient right now,' says Nina, as though I'm a nuisance caller who's phoned right in the middle of dinner. 'Actually,' she lowers her voice, 'we're late-night shopping.'

'Shopping?' I couldn't be more taken aback if she'd said

they were walking naked through Ealing Broadway. Ollie *hates* shopping. I always used to leave him in the pub with a Guinness while I indulged in a spot of retail therapy. 'Ollie doesn't like shopping.'

Nina says smugly, 'He loves shopping with *me*. And I'll let you into a secret. I've been to the jeweller's, looking at rings. I've seen a beautiful white gold solitaire and Ollie's obviously going to go back for it. And you know what that means, don't you, Katy?'

Sure do. That Ollie has seriously lost the plot.

'You're getting engaged?'

She laughs. 'You said it.'

I think I'm going to throw up. How can Ollie have gone from saying that he and Nina *might* be back on to getting engaged to her in little more than six weeks?

'Congratulations.' How I say this without choking I'll never know. 'Could you give Ollie a message from me?'

'He's here now,' says Nina. 'Shall I pass you over?'

'No!' Shit, no! What on earth would I say? Actually, could I say anything, when the thought of lovely, funny Ollie marrying Vile Nina makes me want to howl? 'Just say hi and, er . . . congratulations from me.'

'Of course,' says Nina, prepared to be generous in the face of her victory. 'But you really need to stop harassing him, Katy. Move on with your life.'

'Oh, I have!' I give a false, squeaky little laugh. Ol would know straight away I'm lying but Nina hasn't a clue. 'Haven't you seen the papers? I'm seeing Gabriel Winters. Mr Rochester? We're together. That's all I called to say. I wanted Ollie to hear it from me just in case the press start to hassle him. You will tell him, won't you? I'd love to chat but I'd better go. Gabriel's taking me out for dinner.'

And I ring off, having the satisfaction of leaving her speechless for once.

My heart is thudding. I need a drink. In fact, if Ollie's getting engaged to Nina, I'll need a lot of drinks.

I go to the bar and notice that the pub's absolutely silent. The fire crackles and the loo flushes upstairs but otherwise all is still. I'm suddenly aware just how loud my telephone conversation has been. Everyone in the Mermaid, from Jo the barmaid to the dotty old woman propping up the bar, has heard every word and is staring at me. The two journalists sitting by the fire are practically drooling, and one is already on his mobile dictating copy to his editor.

Oh bollocks.

It looks as though I'm going to be taking Gabriel up on his offer after all.

Chapter Sixteen

You know the old adage *Be careful what you wish for because you may just get it*? Take it from me, it's bloody well true. When I was a poverty-stricken teacher I used to splurge what little money I had on glossy celebrity magazines and turn green at the smug photoshoots and luxury mansions. While writing reports or shoehorned on to the tube with my nose rammed into a stranger's armpit, I'd imagine how fabulous it would be to live that celebrity lifestyle, with money and fame and fans galore.

But the reality's very different.

It's only been three days since I made my Faustian pact with Gabriel, but already my world's turned upside down. Everywhere I go someone's pointing a camera in my direction or trying to entice me to talk about my so-called relationship. Two days ago, while minding my own business posting an engagement card to Ollie, I was hassled by Angela Andrews offering to buy my story for an amount of money so high I needed an oxygen tank to even consider it. Although the constant attention's driving me crazy, Maddy says that every B & B in Tregowan is crammed full with press, which apparently makes me very popular with the locals.

It's just a shame the same isn't true of my hosts.

'This can't go on any longer!' Richard exclaims, drawing

the curtains across the sitting room window to shut out the press. 'I can't think and I certainly can't work. You'll have to move out, Katy.'

'Don't worry,' says Gabriel from the sofa where he's perusing the morning papers; Iraq, Afghanistan and Zimbabwe pass him by as he trawls the gossip columns. 'This will calm down in a few weeks.'

'A few weeks!' Richard pales. 'There's no way I can live in the media spotlight for that long.'

'Me neither,' cries Maddy, no doubt imagining her double life being exposed in the *Dagger*.

'You won't have to,' says Seb, Gabriel's manager, looking up from his BlackBerry. 'Katy's going to move up to Smuggler's Rest this afternoon. It makes more sense for her to live there, seeing as she's his girlfriend.'

'I can't condone unmarried people living together,' says Richard sanctimoniously.

'Don't worry, we won't have sex until we're married,' I say glibly.

Richard glares at me.

'I'll find it really hard to keep my hands off her though,' Gabriel adds hastily, abandoning the papers to drop a kiss on my cheek. 'I'll be permanently taking cold showers.'

Mads and I exchange looks. Of course I've told Maddy about Gabriel and Frankie; how could I keep something like that from my best friend? She's sworn to secrecy, and I've no concerns about her keeping quiet. Maddy is very good at keeping secrets lately.

'Your mobile's ringing now.' Richard scowls at yet another distraction. 'Can you turn it off?'

I glance down at the screen where *Ollie Mob* flashes in neon green. He's probably ringing to thank me for the

288

twenty quid I bunged in with the card as an engagement present. I switch the phone off and shove it into the Chloe bag Gabriel gave me. I've enough stress right now without having to deal with Ollie and Vile Nina.

'I've arranged for all Katy's things to be moved this afternoon,' says Seb, 'and Alice Temperley is sending some samples over by courier. There's also a personal trainer booked for five thirty and a hairdresser due at nine tomorrow.'

'Great,' I say faintly because I'm rather nervous around Seb. He's so razor sharp it's a miracle he doesn't cut himself and the rest of us too. Terrified I'll give the game away, I force myself to relax against Gabriel's muscular chest and paste a smile across my face. To be honest I'd be more at ease strolling across hot coals. Gabe's playing the part of devoted lover to perfection, but I'm more wooden than Guy's boat.

Gabriel squeezes my shoulder. 'You'll be giving Victoria Beckham a run for her money in no time.'

'Katy looks great as she is,' says Maddy loyally.

'Of course she does,' he agrees. 'I can't wait to go out for lunch and show off my beautiful girlfriend.'

'The restaurant's booked for twelve thirty.' Seb consults the itinerary. 'Maybe you ought to make your way there now. I've briefed the press that you'll let them take some shots as you walk into the village.'

'Let me just check your outfits.' Lisa, Gabriel's stylist and make-up artist, bounds forward to tweak his blond curls carefully and adjust the collar of the faded denim shirt chosen to set off his periwinkle eyes. Then she powders his perfect nose and adds a sweep of mascara to his thick lashes.

'Perfect,' she declares.

I glance at Gabriel, who does indeed look perfect. With his golden curls caught back with a simple strip of leather, he could have walked straight out of an Armani ad. I can hardly believe that here I am, plain old Katy Carter, about to be photographed with one of the most eligible bachelors in Britain.

What a shame it's all a farce.

'Never mind about Gabriel,' Mads says. 'It's Katy they want to see.'

I swallow nervously. This is my first official outing as Gabriel's consort, and the whole thing's been planned meticulously. We're having lunch in Trawlers, a sweet little seafood restaurant on the quayside, and the short walk downhill from the rectory should be just long enough for the photographers to bag some good shots. After that, Seb assures me, they'll lose interest and move on to another victim . . . I mean celebrity.

'Do I look all right?' I'm not convinced that teaming sky-high heels with skinny jeans is a good idea for me, and don't the big sunglasses make me look a bit like an insect?

'You look great,' smiles Lisa, giving me a squirt of Coco. 'Go out and enjoy it.'

'And leave us in peace,' mutters Richard from behind the *Church Times*.

Somehow I resist socking him in the teeth and follow Gabriel along the hallway. My stomach feels as though someone's doing macramé with my guts. No wonder celebrities are so skinny if they feel like this all the time.

The door swings open and instantly cameras flash and people call my name. Thank goodness I wore the shades. Blinking like a mole in the sunshine and smiling manically

I clutch Gabriel's manicured hand for all I'm worth and trot down the garden path after him.

'Look happy,' he whispers, pulling me close and almost asphyxiating me with Paco Rabanne. 'Put your hand in my back trouser pocket and lean your head against my shoulder.'

I do what he says and my neck clicks. Ouch! Still, at least I look loved up even if it hurts like hell. Gabriel can always add a chiropractor to his entourage, can't he?

'How did you guys meet?' shouts a reporter.

'Is it true you do it six times a night?' cries another.

'Ignore them and just look happy,' Gabriel advises. 'Give them a good picture and then they'll leave us alone. It's only when they can't get a shot that they go crazy.'

'Right,' I say, as though it's every day I get doorstepped by the paps. 'Look happy. Got it.'

We pause outside Trawlers. It's a mild spring day and the eggshell-blue sky is stitched with white cloud. The fishing boats are long gone and the tide's followed them, leaving a slice of beach glistening in the sun. A dog races across the wet sand like a flame, plumy tail held aloft as it barks at the gulls.

A red setter, all fluid grace and sawdust brains, just like Sasha.

'Look at the cameras,' hisses Gabriel. 'Or at me.'

I rip my gaze away from the dog and back to the handsome man at my side. There must be millions of red setters in Britain and of course they all look and behave exactly like Sasha, but even so . . .

As Gabriel chats with the press I smile vacantly and let my gaze slide back to the beach. The dog's owner throws a stick, and something about the way he moves makes me take a third look. I'm being ridiculous. There must be hundreds of thirty-something guys who wear Timberlands and faded jeans. It isn't Ollie. It can't be. He's hundreds of miles away, being tormented by bottom-set Year 9.

'Stop staring at that guy on the beach,' Gabriel orders, holding the restaurant door for me. 'We're supposed to be together, remember?'

'I was looking at the dog,' I start to say, but Gabriel's too busy admiring his reflection in the glass door to listen. All he needs is a millet spray and a bell and we could add him to Jewell's menagerie.

As the proprietor shows us to our table, almost prostrate with delight at the thought of all the free publicity, I start to wonder whether I've made a mistake agreeing to this job. If Gabriel's driving me crackers after three days, how will I stand a whole summer? I'd be better off taking my chances with Luke and Leia.

'What do you think of the restaurant?' Gabriel asks, as we're seated at a table set in the bay window and so close to the sea we could almost paddle. 'Isn't it the most beautiful setting?'

'It's lovely,' I agree, and if I was writing a novel it would be the perfect scene for a romantic meal. Anyone who reads the gossip columns or celebrity magazines will be overcome with envy when they see the pictures of us looking all romantic and in love.

Who ever said the camera doesn't lie never dated Gabriel Winters.

Gabriel scans the menu while a waiter pours champagne. 'How do you like your fish?'

I open my mouth to say smothered in batter and hanging out with a huge pile of chips but think better of it. Where's Captain Birdseye when I need him?

'Rare tuna for us both,' Gabriel tells the waiter before I've even drawn breath, 'with the dill salad and go easy on the dressing. No bread either.'

'No bread?' I stare at him aghast. The crusty rolls are the only things I feel brave enough to eat.

'Carbs are a no-no, Katy. You're watching your figure.'

I'm just on the brink of telling Gabriel exactly where he can stick the bread rolls when he clutches my hand so hard I squeak.

'Don't make it obvious you've noticed, but Angela Andrews is at the table in the corner,' he whispers.

I turn my head slowly, and sure enough there's Bomber Jacket dissecting an unfortunate fish with the precision of a brain surgeon. Ouch. I don't fancy my chances if she decides to exact her revenge for that ruined Prada number.

Gabriel's grasp on my fingers tightens. 'How did she manage to sneak in here? I knew she was on to something.'

'Can't you ask the owners to throw her out?'

'What for? She's only eating.' His eyes are blue circles of dismay. 'She knows there's a story and she'll never let it go unless . . .'

Gabriel leaps to his feet, and before I can protest I'm swept into a sink-plunger kiss, while his arms tighten like a vice and his tongue does an impression of a washing machine on spin cycle. If he carries on much longer he'll dislocate my mouth.

'Sorry,' he murmurs when he eventually comes up for air. 'I had to give her something to think about.'

'You've done that all right. I thought you said you were g—'

'It's called acting.' He tosses his golden curls. 'I'm pretty good at it.'

'I'd rather you left your *acting* for the film set,' I say, resisting the urge to wipe my lips on the back of my hand.

'It worked though. She's looking.' His eyes light up like gas flames. 'I knew this was a good idea. Let's give her something to *really* write about!'

And before I have a second to argue he's clamped his mouth over mine again, staring intensely into my eyes and winding his hands through my hair. Bloody hell, that designer stubble is agony, I wish he'd stop. I'm as up for a good snog as the next girl but this is ridiculous and not half as good as he evidently thinks it is.

I'm going to have to lay down some very firm ground rules with Gabriel.

Kissing over, we eat our meal slowly, feeding each other slivers of fish and chinking our champagne flutes together. Angela Andrews' eyes are out on stalks and if she taps away on her BlackBerry for much longer she'll have RSI in her thumb. By the time we finish, all heads in the restaurant have turned, and probably quite a few stomachs too.

'Did you enjoy your meal?' asks the proprietor when Gabriel calls for the bill.

'Wonderful.' Gabriel fixes him with a dazzling smile. 'We've had a fantastic time, haven't we, Katy?'

'Fantastic,' I parrot, although the tuna looked to me like something out of *Casualty*. Still, what do I know?

The proprietor beams at us. 'I'm delighted to hear that. And can I say what a joy it is to see a couple so much in love?'

I feel my dinner, or what little I ate of it, come bouncing back up.

'That's why I didn't want to disturb you when that man insisted on seeing you,' he continues. 'It must be difficult enough getting privacy without people trying to hound you over lunch.'

'My fans are certainly persistent, but they put me where I am today,' shrugs Gabriel. 'Did he leave something for me to sign?'

'He was looking for Miss Carter, actually,' says the proprietor, looking embarrassed.

'Someone was looking for me?' I'm surprised. 'Who?'

'A young man in his early thirties. He had a big dog with him so there was no way we'd let him come inside – we've got public health to think about. Whoever he was, he was pretty insistent on coming in for a chat, until you two lovebirds started kissing. I'm not surprised you didn't see him; you only had eyes for each other.'

'Too right,' says Gabriel. 'We adore one another.'

'Katy's friend could see that, and he said he'd leave you guys to be alone, that it was obvious how you felt.'

That tuna is starting to swim laps in my stomach. I can't believe I've missed Ollie. Why didn't I trust my instincts and go down to the beach? I knew it was him.

'Don't look so worried, Katy,' says Gabriel as we walk back to the rectory. The press have melted away, just as he predicted, which is just as well because the expression on my face is hardly that of someone who's blissfully loved up. 'If he's the good mate you say he is then he'll be back.'

But I'm not so sure. Seeing me with Gabriel has really upset Ollie for some reason and he's obviously stormed off in a rage. The question is, of course, why he's so annoyed that I've moved on from James. It's not as though they were ever friends, and I never said I'd be a nun.

Although that is starting to seem quite an attractive proposition.

But the bigger question, the question I'm too scared to even start trying to answer, is why am I so totally and utterly devastated to have missed Ollie and why it bothers me so much that he thinks I'm with someone else.

What on earth is going on here?

Chapter Seventeen

I used to love reading *Hello!* and *OK!*. Sitting on the 207 bus I'd flick through the glossy pages and look at the toothy celebrities lounging around their impossibly glamorous houses in designer gear with 'envy me' smiles pasted to their tanned faces, and imagine how perfect their lives must be. I'd look like that too, I used to tell myself, if I had hot and cold running personal trainers at my beck and call and nothing more pressing to worry about than my latest beauty treatment. I was perfectly justified looking scruffy and having split ends because I was just so darn busy working! Not like the ladies of leisure on the shiny pages. Then I'd shove the magazines into my bag and get on with the daily grind of being an English teacher, with not a Juicy Couture tracksuit or a telephoto lens in sight.

Oh God! Those were the days.

Jordan and Posh, I take it all back. It *isn't* easy at all looking that good.

In fact it's blooming hard work.

'That's lovely, darlin',' a photographer says, measuring the light around me with a piece of equipment that looks like it belongs on the *Starship Enterprise*. 'Just lie back a little! Yeah! Like that!'

I'm in the newly renovated drawing room in Gabriel's house, reclining like some twenty-first-century Caesar on a plush white sofa and, to my shame, wearing a lime-green velour tracksuit. Not that I actually have much say in what I wear lately – Gabriel Winters' girlfriend has to look the part – but I seriously object to the tracksuits. Hideously expensive, they're like romper suits for the rich and famous to wear in their playpens.

Did I say playpens? What I meant to say was houses.

'Head to the left a little, Katy.' The photographer prods me and I oblige.

'So tell me, Katy,' begins a horsy-looking blonde at his side, twiddling a pencil in her beautifully manicured hands, although I have to admit that my hands are also pretty well manicured these days, 'the readers of *Hiya!* are dying to know how you and Gabriel spend your time in your beautiful Cornish retreat.'

Can you believe these people? They even speak like glossy magazines.

'Well,' I say, sinking back into the plump cushions, 'I sell sex toys and write while Gabriel spends all his time draped over my gay friend.'

Actually, I don't say that at all, but I'd really like to. I take my hat off to all these serial adulterers. Full-time fibbing is really complicated, a bit like holding all the plot lines from *EastEnders, Corrie* and *Emmerdale* in your head without getting them confused.

'We entertain.' I'm practically word-perfect by now; two months into my job as Gabriel's consort, I'm an old hand at interviews. I've spoken to the *Mail* about being in love with a famous man, had my cellulite unflatteringly displayed in *Heat*, and now Gabriel and I are going to feature in the autumn edition of *Hiya!*.

'We certainly do.' Gabriel treats the reporter to his one-hundred-watt smile and she swoons. He looks stunning in faded jeans and the softest cashmere sweater the exact hyacinth shade of his eyes. The long corn-coloured curls frame his smooth tanned forehead and brush the sharp planes of his face, the same face that the nation will soon see as a gallant pirate captain. He takes my hand and kisses it. 'Katy's an amazing cook.'

Pass the sick bag.

'She's also a very gifted writer,' gushes Gabriel. 'She's just completed her first novel.'

'Writes novels,' repeats the journalist. 'Lovely.'

I glance over at the coffee table where my two note-books nestle between bowls overflowing with fruit and I feel a little gush of pride. In spite of everything – James ripping up the first draft and me having to spend an enormous chunk of my time talking trivia or selling sex toys with Mads – I have actually managed to finish *Heart of the Highwayman*. Inside those books are thousands of words brimming with so much smouldering passion I'm surprised the manuscript doesn't burst into flames. Just thinking about the final scene when Jake makes love to Millandra on the clifftop makes me go all tingly.

Sadly, it's the nearest I've got to sex for a long time.

'I'll have to edit it and find an agent,' I say, but Gabriel's moved on from my novel and on to a far more absorbing subject: himself. With a sigh I check my watch, some hideously expensive thing Gabriel insists I wear for show, and discover it's not even dinnertime.

Time wears concrete boots when you're a lady of leisure, that's for sure. It used to race by at Sir Bob's. Ollie and I used to go for hours without sitting down or even pausing for a coffee, only stopping when we collapsed into the pub at half four.

I catch a glimpse of myself in the enormous mirror that

Laurence Llewelyn-Bowen insisted went over the mantel-piece and experience amazement that the woman looking back is really me. Walking up and down all the sodding hills in this village has knocked pounds off me. I shake my head and the sleek-haired girl in the mirror looks sadly back. I'm so miserable. If only I could turn the clock back to the lunch date in Trawlers . . .

After Ollie left the restaurant I rang him, howling in frustration when his mobile was switched off. When he finally answered he wasn't in the mood to talk, and every time I tried to explain as best I could about Gabriel he changed the subject.

'Listen, Katy,' he said eventually, 'you really don't need to explain. I was there after all. You guys looked really happy together. I'm glad for you. I really am.'

'But it isn't what you think!'

'Of course it is. Gabriel Winters is the perfect romantic hero. He's exactly what you've been searching for.'

'No he isn't.'

'It's OK,' Ollie said gently. 'The minute I saw you and Gabriel together, a lot of things fell into place. He's perfect for you, he can give you exactly what you need.'

'He can't! He really can't!'

'He can, Katy. He can give you everything you've ever dreamed of and I'm really happy for you. You deserve it. You're perfect together and I'm glad you've found him.'

'If that's true, why were you in Tregowan? Was it because—'

But Ollie wasn't prepared to let me finish. 'Nina and I are really happy too. It's great, isn't it, how everything's worked out for us both?'

'But I really need to explain. Gabriel and I are just friends.'

There was a long exhalation of breath. 'Katy, I've got eyes in my head, you don't need to try and spare my feelings. Look. I've got to go. Nina's just pulled up outside. I'd better not keep her waiting. Talk soon.'

'Please don't go!' I begged. 'Look, I can't tell you what's going on, even though I really want to, but please believe me when I say that there really isn't anything between me and Gabriel. Honestly!'

'Katy,' he said in a tight voice that I hardly recognised, 'please don't treat me like an idiot. Just concentrate on Gabriel like I'm going to concentrate on Nina and move on. In fact, don't call for a bit. I think you and I need some space, don't you?'

'No, Ollie, I don't. What the hell for?'

'Because it's for the best, Katy. We need to deal with the choices that have been made, stick with them and move on, which means maybe not seeing each other for a while because it makes things easier.'

'Easier?' I echoed incredulously. 'Not for me it doesn't. It makes everything worse. Why would you even suggest such a bloody stupid idea?'

'It's called tough love,' he said, and I heard a wry smile in his voice. Then the phone went dead, leaving me shaky with misery. I'd let the best friendship of my life slip though my fingers. What was the matter with him? How the hell had it come to this?

I went back to Maddy's and spent the rest of the afternoon bawling my eyes out and working my way through a family pack of digestives and a bottle of Richard's whisky. Nothing made any sense and the more I drank the more muddled I felt. I couldn't believe Ollie would call time on our friendship just because I was seeing

Gabriel Winters. He'd never made this kind of fuss about James.

Why had he overreacted in such spectacular fashion? And why was I so upset? If I cried any harder I'd flood the rectory. I blew my nose hard on a bit of kitchen roll and attacked my ninth biscuit. God! I hadn't been this devastated on the day James threw me out, and *we'd* been engaged and living together.

Ollie was only a pal, whereas I'd loved James.

Hadn't I?

And then it hit me, with all the force of a sledgehammer falling out of the sky and landing on my head.

I was in love with Ollie.

What?

How did that happen?

Ollie wasn't my type.

Ollie was *not* a romantic hero.

But amazingly it seemed this didn't matter. Abandoning the sodden kitchen roll, I wiped my eyes on my sleeve and contemplated the awful truth. I'd made the stupid mistake of falling in love with my best friend and my timing was crap because he was now engaged to Vile Nina and as far as Ollie and the rest of the world was concerned I was with Gabriel Winters.

I tried to call Ollie back but his phone was switched off, and the following day my romantic tryst with Gabriel was plastered all over the papers. The next time I called, his mobile number was unavailable, and after that it was always Nina who answered the landline and I was pretty sure she never passed on my messages. I even wrote to him, telling him exactly how I felt and how there really wasn't anything going on with Gabriel.

'If you don't believe me then ask Frankie,' I pleaded in

my letter. 'He won't like it but he'll explain everything. But I miss you, Ol, and I need you to know that my feelings for you have changed beyond friendship. If you feel the same then please call me.'

But he never replied and all my emails and texts went unanswered too. Ollie, as he'd promised, had decided to concentrate all his energy on his fiancée and leave me to my romantic hero. I contemplated driving up to London and confronting him, but what would be the point? He'd made his choice and he'd chosen Nina. It was hardly dignified behaviour to start stalking him, was it? Besides, I'd moved to Cornwall to make a new start and to say goodbye to the sappy, passive Katy who only saw herself in terms of the man she was dating. Well, I was through with that version of me.

I would just have to accept Ollie's decision and move on with my own life.

So, with this thought firmly in mind, I threw myself into the charade with Gabriel, which paid well, enabling me to finish my novel and send Ollie a cheque to pay back what he'd spent on my medical bills. By the end of the summer I had money in the bank, a manuscript to sell and the most coveted wardrobe in south-east Cornwall. But did these things make me happy?

Did they heck.

I sigh. At least my hair looks good. It's amazing what expensive products can do to a girl. Several appointments at Nicky Clarke and a pair of ghds later and it's goodbye ginger curls and hello new sleek hair, the same colour and silky texture as Sasha's coat.

My eyes still well up when I think about Sasha. Why does everything always come back to Ollie? Frankie says he hardly sees his cousin now, which is hardly surprising because since the Screaming Queens were signed, Frankie's feet have hardly touched the floor. It's been one promotion after another, and there's great excitement this week because his first single has just been released. I still think the Queens sound like they're having their entrails ripped out with cocktail sticks, but hey, what do I know? Everyone else seems to love them.

'Everything OK, Katy?' Gabriel's manager, Seb, materialises at my side.

'Fine,' I say. 'How much longer will this take?'

Seb raises an eyebrow. 'Not enjoying it?'

This is possibly the understatement of the year. I feel cocooned in misery but at least I've had the time and space to finish my book and reassess my life. And I've made a few decisions too.

But before I mention any of this to anyone, I need to sort out Mads, who's convinced Richard is betraying her with some harlot called Isabelle, and who is still selling vibrators the length and breadth of Cornwall. I can't leave her to self-destruct.

'I'm going out soon with Maddy,' I tell Seb. 'I need to get going.'

'Celebrating finishing your book?' He jerks his head towards the notebooks.

'Something like that,' I hedge. Actually Mads is taking Throbbing Theo et al. to a hen night over in Bodmin and I'm going to lend moral support. That and boost sales when one of the guests invariably recognises me and wants to buy the same knickers as Gabriel Winters' girlfriend. Mads's profits are really up since I became his official consort and she'll soon be Caribbean-bound.

And I'll be Prozac-bound if the strain of lying to

Richard, the press and the world in general carries on much longer.

'Katy!' coos the reporter. 'Could you join Gabriel on the terrace? We need to have a sunset shot of the two of you gazing into each other's eyes. To go with you telling the readers how you found your very own romantic hero.'

Do you know, I'm totally off romantic heroes. They all have something wrong with them anyway. Take Gabriel, for instance: he's so self-absorbed that if you wrung him out he'd just re-form, like that policeman in *The Terminator*. Then there's gorgeous Guy with his sewer mouth, and even Jake has a propensity for barmaids with heaving bosoms. They're all a total let-down if you ask me.

I think I'll write my next novel in a different genre altogether; perhaps a farce, which is what my life resembles lately.

★

'You're late!' accuses Mads, when I eventually make it to the rectory. 'I was about to give up on you.'

'Sorry,' I call, bounding up the stairs and heading into the minuscule bathroom. '*Hiya!* was doing a photoshoot. Let me get this crap off and I'll give you a hand with the boxes.'

I squirt a generous dollop of cleanser into my palm and then smear it over my face. After several minutes of scrubbing furiously, Clinique's finest surrenders and I look like me again, albeit a little pinker. I'm just fluffing up my hair when I hear raised voices from downstairs. Sounds like Richard and Mads are rowing again.

'Don't deny it's yours!' Mads is screeching.

'OK.' Richard sounds calmer, but experience tells me

that it's the calm before the storm. 'It's mine. Do you have a problem with that?'

'What do you think?' Mads cries. 'I know what this means! You're seeing that slag, aren't you?'

I'm halfway down the stairs at this point and I freeze. There's no way I'm going to interrupt this mother of all rows.

'Not this again,' says Richard wearily. 'I've told you, there's no one else.'

'So what do you need this for then?'

I'm holding my breath. What on earth has she found?

'What do you think?' There's the sound of movement. 'I haven't got the time or the inclination to go through this again, Madeleine. I've got to out.'

'Out! Out! Always out!' she yells. 'Where to now?'

'A prayer meeting,' Richard says. 'Where are you going?'

'A friend's house, you got a problem with that?'

'Of course not, it's just that you seem to be spending an awful lot of time lately at *friends'* houses.' He pauses. 'Are you sure it's not you having the affair?'

This is horrible. I feel like a child perched on the stairs listening to her parents rowing. Not that I've ever heard my parents rowing – they're normally far too stoned and anti-conflict – but I've seen enough clichéd TV dramas to get the picture.

'That's right. Turn it round on me! I know you're seeing some slag, so don't even try to pretend you're not. It's always one *prayer* meeting after another, isn't it?'

'I'm a vicar. Of course I go to prayer meetings.'

I shuffle down a few more stairs until I can peek into the kitchen. Mads is standing by the sink with her hands on her hips, cheeks flushed and snaky curls bouncing in outrage. Richard, tall and considerably more muscular lately, has his back to me. I'm almost asphyxiated by the overwhelming waft of Aramis.

'So why do you need that?' Mads jabs her finger at the ghetto blaster in Richard's arms. It's made from a hideous yellow plastic and looks like the remainder of the Beatles' submarine after decommissioning. Until I came to the rectory I'd never seen anything like it. It'd probably fetch a fortune on some 1980s' *Antiques Roadshow* special.

'The Bishop and I thought we'd play some hymns while we pray.' Rich grabs his jacket from the chair and shrugs himself into it. 'If that's OK with you?'

Mads says nothing, but her mouth is pursed tighter than a crab's bottom.

'I'll take that as a yes. Don't wait up. I'll be late. Enjoy whatever you're up to.' Spinning on his heel, Richard almost knocks me flying. I flatten myself against the wall as he charges past like a human tornado.

All is not well in the house of love.

'Bastard!' shrieks Maddy when Richard slams the door. 'Cheating bastard!'

'Calm down!' I beg, not liking the way her knuckles glow chalky white through the flesh or the way her eyes are fever bright. 'You can't carry on like this.'

'Too right I bloody can't,' snarls Mads. 'What kind of idiot does he take me for? I swear to God, Katy, I'm going to leave him. I've got nearly five grand saved, that will be a start.'

'You can't! What about loving him? What about Sandals?'

'Forget Sandals. I'm not going there with a lying, cheating bastard.'

'You don't know he's cheating.' Goodness knows why I'm sticking up for Richard. The man drives me round the twist. But I have the strongest conviction that he isn't cheating on Maddy.

'Yes I do.' Mads holds out a box. 'There's the proof.'

' "Grecian 2000, Real Natural Black",' I read aloud. ' "Shampoos in in just five minutes." ' I raise my eyes. 'I thought you'd found condoms or something. How is this proof that Richard's cheating?'

'Because,' explains Maddy in the tone of voice normally used with idiots or very small children, 'he's dying his hair. He wants to look good. For another woman, obviously, because I know he's going grey. He's even starting to get grey pubes.'

Too much information!

'I dye my hair,' I point out. 'So do you.'

'But we're girls! It's our job to be vain. This is Richard we're talking about, Katy, not your Gabriel.'

'He isn't *my* Gabriel,' I mutter. Mads know that anyway; she's the only person I have been allowed to tell apart from Jewell. Not that Jewell counts. The last I heard she was in booked into Champneys for a month's detox before getting ready for her birthday bash. Typical Jewell. Most people detox after hammering their livers but she likes to get hers prepared to take some serious abuse.

'Whatever.' Maddy flaps her hand dismissively. 'But Richard, of all people! Did you ever meet a man who was less bothered about worldly things than Richard?'

No, probably not. I think Rich was born middle-aged and wearing a cassock.

'And now,' wails Mads, 'he's got a mobile, and he's never in, or when he is he's in the bathroom washing away the evidence of whatever tart it is he's seeing!' Her voice rises and wobbles dangerously. 'And what about the money and the note I found on the wardrobe? It doesn't look innocent from where I am.'

'But sometimes you have to look a little more deeply to see what's beneath the surface,' I say, thinking about how my life appears lately.

Mads stares at me. 'Who do you think you are? Yoda? He's a cheating git and I'm going to prove it.'

'And how do you intend to do that?'

She shrugs. 'When I've thought of a way you'll be the first to know.'

From the way Maddy then proceeds to stomp around the rectory, grumbling under her breath and thumping the boxes of merchandise down the stairs, I sincerely hope I'm nowhere near if she does discover Richard is cheating, not that I believe he is for one minute. Granted, his behaviour is certainly fishier than Guy's boat, but I just can't believe he'd commit adultery. Apart from the fact that he's a vicar, I know he totally adores Maddy.

As I follow her down the cliff path, my arms full of brochures and boxes, I'm wrestling with this dilemma. None of it makes any sense.

Maddy rants and raves about Richard all the way to Bodmin. For twenty-three miles I listen to 'Bastard!' this and 'Wanker!' that, saying 'Mmm' or 'Tosser' when appropriate.

I look out of the window and try to enjoy the view; not easy when the human equivalent of Mount Etna is behind the wheel. It's a perfect summer's evening and I wind down the minibus window to breathe in the heady scent of warm earth and cut grass. Our route takes us through some woods, and I marvel at the emerald green of the trees and the white candles that nestle against the plump pillow leaves of the horse chestnut trees while rays of light trickle through the leafy canopy above us and break-dance across the tarmac. Even the hedges are foaming with cow parsley and splattered with pink campion, and the verges are starred with buttercups.

'Isn't it pretty?' I say, hoping to drag Mads out of her evil temper, but she is too busy grinding her teeth and trying to think of the most painful way to disembowel her husband to wax lyrical about nature.

'Bastard,' she mutters. 'Just you wait.'

Something tells me I'm in for a long night.

★

Bodmin is a small town that seems to pop suddenly out of nowhere. One minute we're driving through the country, with sheep bleating and the birds singing their heads off, and the next we're coming up to a massive roundabout and heading through an industrial estate.

'Is this right?' I wonder, glancing nervously at the concrete wasteland outside. It looks like the set of *A Clockwork Orange*.

'Trust me.' Mads turns right and we pass under a railway bridge. There's a school on my left; the grey walls and blinded windows remind me of Sir Bob's. Or maybe that's because all schools look like prisons. Not that it was all bad. Looking back, I feel quite nostalgic. I can't believe I actually miss school! Usually at this stage in the summer I'm frantically buying lottery tickets and sending random chapters of my novel off to agents in the desperate hope that on the first of September somebody will rescue me. And now here I am, saved from a life of chalk dust and leaky red biro, being paid to hang out with celebrities, and I find I'm longing to strut my stuff in front of a bunch of surly adolescents.

Life is so weird.

And, of course, I'd love to see Ollie. I'm sure that if we sneaked down to the boiler room for a fag or two we could sort out all our misunderstandings. Failing that, I could always force-feed Nina some school pasta, a strange gloopy concoction that has more in common with wallpaper paste than nutrition and should finish her off pretty quickly.

'Right!' Mads yanks up the handbrake so abruptly that I'm amazed it doesn't fly off. 'We're here.'

Here is a small estate composed of little doll's house-type dwellings in an assortment of sugared-almond shades. Baby-pink townhouses and butter-yellow terraces are gathered around a pretty green, complete with a duck pond in which they practically dip their toes.

'Number eleven.' Mads flings the minibus door open and leaps out. 'Grab some stuff and I'll go and let them know we're here.'

I open up the back doors of the minibus and start to lug boxes to the house. As I do so I have to squeeze between parked cars. Not that that's unusual, but my eye is caught by a small blue Fiesta that is parked neatly in front of number eleven. That's not unusual either, and neither is the fish sticker that decorates the rear window. It's just that Richard has a car exactly like that, right down to the dent in the wing where somebody allegedly got too close with the minibus.

Not that I know anything about that, though!

It's got to be a strange coincidence, because there's no way Richard's going to be at a hen party in Bodmin, and this car is full of paint pots and brushes rather than Bibles and vicary stuff. Chuckling to myself at the thought of Richard at a hen night, I put it from my mind and concentrate instead on setting the party up. While Mads guzzles wine and nibbles with the already plastered hens, I set up the rack of lingerie and sort out the cards for rude-word bingo, tutting at how Mads thinks you spell cunnilingus.

Once an English teacher, always an English teacher.

It's a good party. The hens are desperate to play the games and even more desperate to part with their cash, and pretty soon the orders are flooding in. The decorators are in apparently but have been moved to the dining room so the girls have total privacy to shriek over Throbbing Theo and pals, and Mads and I can hardly keep up with the paperwork. I'm keeping my fingers so tightly crossed that Mads will meet her target tonight that I'm in danger of cutting off the circulation. I know I'm boring, but I really can't handle the strain. All I want is a quiet life.

And Ollie.

Mads and I are sitting in the kitchen so that we can concentrate on our sums. I'm frantically trying not to pursue my cul-de-sac train of thought about Ol again and focus instead on scribbling down requests. Mads has her glasses on and is tapping away on a calculator, pink tongue poking out in concentration. We're almost through adding up the bills when there's a flurry of activity from the lounge and much excited squeaking.

'It's the stripper!' shrieks a hen. 'Get your kit off!'

Mads and I take no notice, totally absorbed by our sums. Strippers at hen nights are a perk – sorry, I mean a distraction – we can do without. Besides, I don't think Gabriel will be chuffed if his girlfriend's spotted joining in the general leering. As the music begins, predictably Tom Jones crooning about keeping hats on, I finish off my notes and steal a sneaky glance.

And nearly pass out.

The music is booming out from a daffodil-yellow ghetto blaster. Surely the odds are stacked against two of those existing in the UK, never mind this weeny corner of south-east Cornwall?

Oh. My. God. Surely not?

While the hens whoop and cheer, the stripper, fetchingly dressed as a policeman, is down to his G-string and whirling his handcuffs around his head. I can't see his face through the crowd of excited hens, but suddenly that revolting ghetto blaster, the Fiesta parked outside, the odd absences, the hair dye all start to make perfect sense.

Surely Richard isn't . . .

Wouldn't . . .

Couldn't . . .

I crane my neck, but as usual I'm too short to see over the taller folk. The evidence is pretty conclusive, though, and like a short ginger version of Hercule Poirot I'm sure I've solved the mystery.

I pluck at Maddy's sleeve. 'Come and look at this stripper.'

She frowns, resenting being distracted from her sums. 'I'm still a vicar's wife you know. Anyway,' she returns her attention to the account book, 'once you've seen one stripper you've seen them all.'

'Believe me, you've never seen a stripper like this one.'

'I'm trying to do my orders.'

'Seriously, Mads. You really need to see this stripper.'

'Fine.' Maddy slams her notepad on to the table. 'If it keeps you quiet, it's worth it.' And she puts down the calculator before pushing her way through right to the front of the crowd of cheering hens.

I close my eyes and begin to count. One, two, three . . .

'Very nice,' says Mads. 'Although I can't see what all

the fuss was about. You need to get out more if you're so easily excited. Mmm, now *he's* not bad!' she adds, peering into the kitchen where a man is bending over the sink rinsing paint brushes. 'Their decorator has a nice bum.'

'Never mind the flipping decorator! Can't you see who the stripper is?' I shriek, up on tiptoes as I try my hardest to see for myself. 'Mads! The stripper is Richard! Reverend Rich is a stripper!'

Right on cue the music stops and my comment shrills through the place. The hens turn round and stare at me. Then someone moves aside and I finally see the stripper, smeared in baby oil and lipstick kisses, standing in the midst of the hens with his handcuffs swinging limply from his hands.

And it isn't Richard.

Oops.

But the decorator, whose backside Mads was just admiring, turns round, and even though his face and hair are streaked with paint, there's no mistaking that disapproving gimlet glare or his horror at seeing his wife and lodger catching him in overalls.

'Richard?' gasps Maddy, looking totally confused. 'What's going on? Why on earth are you here? Please tell me you're not stripping?'

'Of course I'm not stripping!' he snaps. 'Katy, what do you think you're doing casting aspersions like that? How dare you say I'm a stripper? Have you finally lost your mind?'

'But the ghetto blaster!' I squeak. 'The showers! The constant washing! The hair dye!'

'I'm decorating to earn extra money and I like listening to music while I work. This young man borrowed my

314

ghetto blaster because his was broken,' Richard explains, a note of irritation creeping into his voice. 'I need to shower to get the paint off when I get home. The only stripping I do is wallpaper. For heavens' sake, Katy! I'm a vicar.'

'You're decorating?' Mads echoes.

'But what about the hair dye?' I pipe up, because this is really bugging me.

Richard rolls his eyes. 'I'm going grey, Katy! I'd rather you didn't broadcast that fact to your friends in the tabloid press, though.' He blushes. 'It's bad enough that my wife now knows how vain I am.'

'I knew already,' says Maddy. 'But what do you need extra money for?'

'Grey hair! That explains everything,' I interrupt. Can I run now before Richard rips my head off and wallops me with the soggy end?

'Not quite,' says Richard. 'What have you two been up to? Are you at the party?'

'Er, not exactly.' Mads pulls a face. 'Let's just say you're not the only one who wants to earn some extra cash.'

Richard looks across the room to the rails of frilly lingerie, merrily gyrating rabbits and edible G-strings and blanches. 'Oh dear Lord! Surely not?'

'I think we have some serious explaining to do, darling, seeing as both of us have been less than truthful,' says Mads hastily as Rich clocks Throbbing Theo and a vein starts to pulse in his temple. 'Maybe we should discuss everything somewhere a little more private.'

'Good idea,' I say quickly. Anywhere I'm not in the firing line sounds great to me. How about the moon?

While Mads and Richard beat a hasty retreat to the minibus, I pack away in record time, leaving the hens to go clubbing. To say I'm confused is the biggest understatement of all time. Richard Lomax, a secret decorator? I can't say I ever saw that one coming.

But thank God he wasn't stripping. I'd need therapy to get over that sight.

The hens conga out of the front door, squeals of girlish glee splitting the air, as I lug my final box of 'Bibles' back to the minibus. There's no more putting it off. I'm going to have to bang on the window and start loading the boxes in. The Lomaxes have had about twenty minutes to either kill each other or sort it out. At least I can't see any splats of blood on the windows.

Fingers crossed.

'Katy!' cries Mads, all pink flushed cheeks and sparkling eyes as she opens the door. 'Sorry I didn't help with clearing up, but . . .' Her voice tails off and her glance slides towards Richard in his paint-spattered clothes, 'I had a few things to clear up with Richard.'

'So I see!' I say brightly, jumping inside and trying to ignore the fizzing atmosphere. 'What's going on? Or maybe I shouldn't ask.'

'Oh, Katy!' gushes Mads, beaming more widely than a Halloween pumpkin. 'It's just so sweet. Richard found my Sandals brochures and he wanted to be able to earn some extra money to whisk me away for a romantic break. We both had the same idea! Doesn't that tell you how much we love each other?'

'I knew Maddy wasn't happy,' continues Richard, 'but I didn't know what to do about it. Then I saw an advert for a painting job and figured if I worked really hard I could earn enough cash to whiz her away to St Lucia and make up for being such a useless husband. I was only doing it for a few months until I'd saved enough. I wanted it to be a surprise, that's why I didn't tell anyone.'

'You're not useless,' cries Mads, taking his hand and pressing it to her cheek. 'I love you, you idiot! I thought you didn't want me any more and that you were having an affair. I only wanted to go on holiday to try and get you to fancy me again.'

'But I do fancy you!' protests Richard. 'I fancy you like crazy! I just didn't think I was good enough for you any more, and the longer I said nothing the worse it became. You seemed so unhappy and there were so many secrets that I didn't know where to start.'

'Like the money on the wardrobe,' I recall. 'And the steamy note from Isabelle.'

'You've been looking on top of the wardrobe?' Rich groans. 'Is nowhere safe? And that note wasn't steamy except in your vivid imagination. It was given to me after the first job I ever did. Isabelle's sixty and her daughters paid me to paint her bedroom for her birthday. She gave me a fifty-pound tip and got me a couple of jobs working for her friends. I owe her a lot.'

Mads kisses the tip of his nose. 'I'm so relieved you're not having an affair. And I don't know why you thought you weren't good enough for me. Your body's great!'

'I think all the extra physical work has got me fitter,' explains Richard, pulling his wife on to his lap. 'I must admit I actually feel quite good about myself lately. But it's time for me to stop. Seeing you two tonight was quite a shock. Imagine if it had been the Bishop?' He goes a bit grey at the thought. 'I'd probably be excommunicated if he knew I was moonlighting and my wife and her friend were selling sex aids. I know the money's good doing the parties but it's far too risqué for a vicar's wife.'

'I agree!' I say quickly. 'And for the record, I was just helping.'

'I'm hardly in a position to have a go, am I?' says Richard ruefully. 'Seeing as I've been less than truthful myself. But it's got to stop before it lands us in hot water or one of your tabloid pals runs an exposé.'

'They're not my friends!' I protest. 'It's hardly my fault everyone's obsessed with Gabriel.'

Richard raises an eyebrow at this and I brace myself for another lecture. Then he sighs.

'Actually, Katy, this is one mess I can't blame you for. But,' he adds to his wife, 'we need to talk to each other, Maddy, rather than just guessing how the other feels.'

From the way Maddy's gazing at him I would say that talking is the last thing on her mind. She's got a minibus-load of sex toys and the newly toned Richard in her arms and I think it's time for me to beat a hasty retreat. The looks that are passing between them are enough to set the bus alight.

I've had enough green and hairy moments recently to know when I'm not wanted.

'I'll take the car back,' I suggest, grabbing the keys and backing out. 'Then you guys can, um, catch up.'

But Mads and Richard are too busy kissing to answer. Somehow I don't think I'll be getting any sense out of them for a while. Feeling like some prudish maiden aunt, I scuttle out of the bus and head for the car.

★

Driving back to Tregowan, I mull over the events of the evening. Wouldn't life have been a lot easier lately if Mads had just told Richard how she was feeling? Then he could have told her how unhappy he was and *voilà*! No rowing, no tears and certainly no moonlighting with other jobs. Now they can jet off to Sandals, come back all loved up and everybody lives happily ever after, especially my good self, who no longer has to live in fear of Richard finding out about his wife's secret life.

Parking the car and trudging up the path to the rectory I can't help but think that my life would also be a lot easier if I'd only been a little more truthful in my own relationships. If I had taken a really long hard look at how things were with James I could have saved years of wasted emotion. And if I'd had the guts to tell Ollie how I really felt about him then who only knows? I certainly wouldn't be pretending to be Gabriel Winters' girlfriend and basically lying to everyone.

It doesn't feel good.

In fact it's feeling more and more bloody awful as the days go on.

I've got to do something about it.

Once inside the rectory I pour a huge glass of wine and take it outside into the garden, or rather the patch of grass that passes as one. Maddy isn't much of a gardener. The ground is tangled with bindweed and brambles and the only flowers are the wild dog roses and rampant nasturtiums that hurl themselves over the dry-stone wall. Sitting on the doorstep I breathe in the salt tang mixed with the acrid aroma of barbecue smoke and watch the reflections of the lights in the water. A couple wander out of the Mermaid, arms entwined around each other, and stand for a while gazing out over the harbour. They look closer than words.

I think of Maddy and Richard all loved up in the mini-bus and of Gabriel and Frankie cuddled up at Smuggler's Rest and feel desperately lonely.

I knock back my wine and fish into my pocket for my mobile phone. Sod it. I'm going to call Ollie. After all, what have I got to lose? It's not as though he's talking to me anyway.

I dial his land line and brace myself for the usual endless ringing or curt answerphone message. When he actually answers I'm momentarily thrown.

'Ollie?' I say quickly. 'It's me. Please don't hang up. I really need to talk to you.'

'Katy?' Ol sounds taken aback to hear from me and not overly thrilled. 'Have you any idea what time it is?'

'It's Friday night,' I say. 'I thought you'd still be up.'

'It's one a.m.,' Ol says, with a sigh. 'I was asleep. Honestly, it's really inconsiderate. I don't hear from you for weeks, except through the tabloids, and then you call in the middle of the night.' I hear the creaking of bedsprings as he sits up. 'What do you want?'

'I have called you. And I've written.' I feel very wronged. If only he knew just how many times I've dialled his number and spoken to Vile Nina, or left messages on the answerphone. And of course my letters. Just thinking about how I poured my heart out in those makes me feel all hot with shame. 'You're never there and your mobile's always switched off.'

'I lost my mobile months ago,' Ol says. 'God knows what happened to it. I haven't bothered to replace it because I quite enjoy the peace.' He yawns loudly and I can picture exactly how he looks, hair sticking up at crazy angles and pink tongue poking out between slightly crooked teeth.

Isn't it strange how Ollie's wonky front teeth are so much cuter than Gabriel's pearly gnashers?

'Well?' Ollie snaps impatiently when I don't say

anything. 'What's the matter? It must be urgent, seeing as you've woken us up. Or are you pissed?'

Us? That must be him and Nina then. My vision of Ol, all rumpled in his T-shirt and boxers, is instantaneously replaced by a vision of Nina, all silken negligée and toned flesh, coiled around him like a designer python.

'Sorry,' I whisper. 'It's just . . . it's just . . .'

My throat grows tight and my eyes sting. I grip my phone so tightly that I hear the pink plastic crack.

'I miss you.' There, I've said it.

'Really?' Ollie isn't exactly jumping for joy. 'I'm surprised you've had the time to miss any of us, what with your new celebrity lifestyle and everything.'

'That's not all it seems. I told you to ask Frankie.'

'As if I ever see Frankie now he's joined the celebrity circus. But you've really moved onwards and upwards, Katy. Sir Bob's must seem like a different world.'

'I miss Sir Bob's too,' I choke.

'Bloody hell. You *have* been drinking if you're missing school. I can't wait to leave.'

'You're leaving?'

'I quit teaching at the end of the summer term,' Ol reveals, and even though I can't see him I know that he's smiling at the thought. 'We're going to go travelling. I've bought a camper van and I've put the house on the market. It looks like things are going through. You're not the only one who's changed their life.'

I'm not quite sure what to say to this. Congratulations sounds like I want to get rid of him, but if I tell him that my heart's sinking faster than a pair of concrete wellies I'll sound petty. I experience a hideous sense of panic. Ollie's leaving Sir Bob's, selling his house and basically moving on with his life. I have a sudden image of him and Nina sipping cocktails against a glorious magenta sunset, before wandering off along a beach of powdery white sand.

That sodding Sandals brochure has even got to me.

'I have you to thank really,' adds Ollie. 'I'd never have done it otherwise.'

'Me?'

'Absolutely. I saw how you picked yourself up and moved on with your life without so much as a backwards glance and it made me think, why shouldn't I do the same? I want to be pragmatic and emotionless. Just like you.'

I'm staggered. 'Pragmatic and emotionless? Me?'

This seems unfair in the extreme. If Ol only knew the buckets of tears I've shed over him. I mean, it might *look* as though I'm all loved up with Gabriel, but I'm not the one who went and got engaged, am I? And I'm not the one who's broken off our friendship and ignored all contact.

'That's bloody rich coming from you!' I splutter. 'You never once got in touch.'

'Me? Come on, I've left countless messages with your *management*.' Ollie almost spits the word. 'Would it really have hurt you to just make one call? I thought we were friends, Katy. Whatever happened to that?'

I can hardly believe what I'm hearing. 'You've tried to contact me?'

'Come on, you must know I have. I've probably made a total idiot of myself. God knows what that guy Seb must think. He probably has me down as some kind of stalker.'

'I never got any messages, Ollie. I swear to God. Seb's Gabriel's manager. He must have screened them all.'

'Fuck,' says Ollie.

'But what about *my* messages? I must have left hundreds on your answerphone! And my letters? Didn't you get them?'

Ollie's silent for a minute. Then he sighs heavily. 'I think I can guess what happened to those. Bloody hell, what a mess.'

I start to laugh but it turns into a sob. 'So you weren't ignoring me?'

'Of course I wasn't! But Katy, you're with Gabriel now and I can understand exactly what his manager was thinking. I'm sorted too. Maybe it was for the best.'

'Of course it wasn't!' I wail. 'We've got so much to catch up on. There are things I really need to talk to you about.'

Ollie sighs. 'I'm sure there are, but I'm canoeing at six tomorrow and I really need some sleep.'

I can take a hint. I'm being dismissed. But I just don't want to put the phone down. What I really want to do is howl that I'm sorry, that I know I've cocked things up and that actually, Ol, I really think I'm in love with you, but I don't think this is what he wants to hear since his life's so sorted and flipping peachy without me.

So much for telling the truth.

'Fine,' I say quickly, swallowing back the lump in my throat. 'We can catch up another time. Are you coming to Jewell's birthday party next week? I know she sent you an invite.'

This week random people the length and breadth of Britain have had Jewell's rainbow-coloured invites plopping on to their doormats. This year the theme is 'Come as your favourite celeb', which may or may not be Jewell's idea of a joke. In any case, the house on Hampstead Heath will be festooned with fairy lights and filled until the small hours with drunken revellers. Jewell's determined that this year will be the best party yet. The announcement of her birthday has already gone out in *The Times*.

'I did get an invite,' Ollie confirms. 'But I didn't know whether to come. I wasn't sure it was a good idea.'

'You must come!' I'm horrified how desperate I am to see him. 'You and Nina, obviously.'

'Nina?' asks Ol, sounding as bemused as though I'd suggested he bring Liz Hurley.

'Of course!' I so will get treasure in heaven. Still, I reckon I can even bear Nina if it means I get to spend a few minutes with Ollie. I know the girl hates me, but how much damage can she do at a party? Stab me to death with her hip bones? 'Please come, Ol. Jewell will be devastated if you don't show.'

'Just Jewell?' asks Ollie softly.

Those butterflies are back in my stomach, only this time they're clog-dancing. I take a deep, shaking breath and dredge up the scattered remnants of my courage. Honesty, remember?

'Not just Jewell,' I whisper. 'I'll be devastated too. Please come, Ollie. I really miss you.'

Over the miles between us something crackles in the ether. I'm holding my breath. Then Ollie exhales slowly, as though he's let go of something he's been gripping tightly.

'I miss you too,' he says, so softly that I'm not even sure I hear him say it. 'I'll be there, Katy. I'll be there.'

Then there's a click as he puts the receiver down and all is still. My phone slithers to the floor and I realise that the pounding in my ears isn't the sea but my galloping heartbeat.

I sit on the steps and hug my knees to my chest. I know I'm being ludicrous but I feel hugely, ridiculously happy.

Ollie misses me.

I grin madly into the darkness. I feel like dancing and

singing; I feel so light-hearted that I swear I could launch myself from the hillside and glide like a gull over the village, somersaulting and diving in pure joy.

OK. He only said that he misses me.

But it's a start.

★

The next morning I'm up with the lark, or rather, in the case of Tregowan, the gulls, and as I make breakfast I can't stop yawning. I've hardly slept a wink, firstly because I'm so angry about my calls from Ollie being screened and secondly because the endless squeaking from Mads and Richard's bed is pretty hard to ignore. I almost wish I'd gone back to Gabriel's, but I'm so mad at Seb I don't think I can trust myself not to rip his head off.

Besides, I've got so much to do. I hardly know where to start. I rest my bottom on the Aga and munch some toast, but I feel too wound up to eat and drop it back on the plate practically untouched. Blimey! I've lost my appetite. Maybe I am like Millandra after all.

And talking of Millandra, I really ought to grab my manuscript and do something with it. It won't get very far sitting on the coffee table up at Smuggler's Rest. And I'm going to have to hope that somebody wants to buy it, because I've made another decision in the silent watches of the night, based on my new honesty-is-best policy.

I'm going to finish this whole ridiculous business with Gabriel.

He's had a few hassle-free months out of me. Any longer and *Hiya!*, *Hello!* et al. will start speculating about engagements and before I know it I'll be dressed in leopardskin, draped across a sofa and showing off a ring the size of an ostrich egg so ostentatious that even

325

Liberace would heave. Seriously, I wouldn't put anything past Gabriel. He's obsessed with his career. Still, I'm sure Seb can orchestrate us a fairly dramatic split. I'll even go on the record and say what a fantastic lover Gabriel is if it makes him feel any better.

'Can you please keep it down?' groans Mads, stumbling into the kitchen and blindly shoving the kettle under the tap. 'Some of us are seriously shattered this morning.'

'If you must stay up all night shagging, what do you expect?'

Mads laughs and pushes her tangled hair back from her face. 'I feel like I'm on honeymoon all over again. I love him so much.'

'That's fantastic, babes!' I say, giving her a hug. Ollie misses me and he's coming to the party to see me, so all is well in my world too and I feel generous to just about everyone. Except maybe bloody Seb. 'I'm really pleased for you.'

'We've talked and talked!' carries on Maddy, throwing open the window and inviting in a fresh salt breeze. 'And we're going to go away, just like we planned, and we're going to try for a baby. Everything is coming together at last.'

I open my mouth to tell her my news but she is too excited and I shut it again. This is her time to be happy. Hopefully mine will come later. Perhaps I should go to Truro and buy a killer frock just to guarantee it? Mind you, if Ol sees me in a killer frock he'll probably die laughing. Maybe I'll just stick to the old faithful velvet flares.

'Morning!' Bob the postie sticks his head through the kitchen window, holding out a sheaf of letters. 'Lovely day!'

'Oh yes,' agrees Mads. 'It's amazing!'

'Where's the Rev?' asks Bob, looking hopefully at the kettle. 'Got Saturday off?'

'Something like that.' Mads closes her eyes and raises her face to the sun. 'Richard is spending the day in bed.'

'Not well? Poor bugger,' sympathises Bob. 'Just as well I told the Bishop not to bother coming up. I said I heard someone yowling like they were in pain.'

'I was singing!' I say indignantly.

'The Bishop?' Mads is momentarily plucked from her fluffy land of shagged-out bliss. 'What did he want?'

'Nothing important,' Bob tells her. 'He said he didn't want to disturb you on your day off, but he wanted you to know that he was borrowing the minibus because his car's in the garage and that it hasn't been nicked. He said to tell you he'll unpack all the boxes of Bibles when he gets to the cathedral. They're a bit short apparently.'

'Fuck!' Mads drains of colour and flies out of the front door, clad only in her slippers and dressing gown.

'What did I say?' asks Bob, helping himself to my leftover toast.

I'm laughing too much to even try to explain, so Bob gives up and wanders away, muttering about mad incomers as he munches his second-hand breakfast.

I sort the post out, mainly bills for Richard and a letter to Mads from Anna Spring, and one neatly typed envelope for me. I rip it open and almost fall down with shock.

It's from James.

Katy,

Since you refuse to answer my messages or contact me in any way I am faced with no choice but to write to you.

Our financial affairs need addressing. I assume that since your circumstances have changed you are now in a position to offer me a respectable settlement.

I look forward to seeing you on the occasion of your god-mother's seventieth birthday.

Yours in anticipation,

James

I screw up the letter and lob it into the bin. What is it with James and money? Why he thinks I, or to be more accurate Gabriel, should give him any is beyond me. And aren't I the one without the house and assets? Shouldn't he be paying me? Surely his credit can't be that crunchy?

I'm filled with a sick feeling at the thought of seeing James again. I don't have a clue who Damocles is but I'm getting very tired of always having his sword dangling above my head. I wish Jewell would ask me before she invites random men in my life to her birthday parties. Why can't she get her kicks out of knitting and Werther's Originals like all the other old people?

My phone may be cracked but it still works. I think I know somebody who can shed some light on all this. Without hesitating I speed-dial Millward Saville and ask to be put through to Ed.

'Hello? Edward Grenville speaking.'

'Hello, Ed,' I say, feeling surprisingly pleased to hear his hee-haw tones. I never had anything against Ed. It was always Sophie and James who did their best to make me feel as comfortable as Kate Moss in a chocolate factory. 'It's Katy, Katy Carter.'

'Katy Carter! Good God!' Ed couldn't sound more surprised. 'How the devil are you? You and your new actor chappie? Sophie showed everyone that spread you did in *Hiya!*. Told all her chums that she knows you.'

'Actually, Ed, this isn't really a social call. I'm ringing up because I'm a bit concerned about James. I'm getting the oddest letters from him. He keeps asking for money.'

There's a deathly silence at the end of the line, apart from a faint grinding, which is possibly the sound of the cogs in Ed's brain turning. 'Ah,' he says at last. 'There's a bit of a story there, old girl. The thing is . . . gosh, Katy, this is dashed awkward. James doesn't work here any more.'

I experience a sudden stab of guilt. 'Is that because of the dinner party?' If it is, no wonder James feels entitled to my money.

'Dinner party?'

'You must remember?' I can't believe I have to remind him; it's seared on my memory for life. 'Lobsters? Cactus? Red setter in the office?'

'Oh yes!' Ed chortles. 'Tremendous fun! Julius still laughs about it.'

I'm glad somebody does.

'But no, it's nothing to do with the dinner party.' Ed lowers his voice so that it's slightly less booming. People in Australia will have to strain their ears now to hear. 'The problem is that James got involved in some stuff.'

'Stuff? What, drugs, you mean?' And I thought I was the one with a Nurofen addiction.

'No!' Ed says quickly, almost as quickly as Mads is running along the quay after the minibus. 'It's nothing like that. It's financial stuff. He was a bit of an idiot, got involved in some insider business.' I can practically see him tapping his nose. 'He had some tips from an insider source about a takeover and took some pretty heavy losses. You know how it is.'

Erm. No, I don't actually. All I know about the world of

high finance comes from watching *Wall Street* in the Eighties. Red braces, Greed is Good and Lunch is for Wimps is about the extent of my knowledge.

'Is that bad?'

'About as bad as it gets,' Ed says. 'It's illegal, Katy. And it wasn't a recent thing either. James had got himself into a right state. He owes hundreds of thousands, and that's a conservative estimate, I'm afraid. The speculations go back years.'

My mouth is dry. 'How many years?'

'It's hard to say, but at least four I should think. It got worse about the time you two got together, actually. He said you had a rich aunt who was on her last legs. She was going to bung you guys some cash as a wedding present?'

I know I don't love James any more, maybe never did if I'm painfully honest, but it's never nice to have your worst suspicions confirmed, is it? Nobody likes to be used.

What an idiot. He must have seen me coming. And I was a pushover; no, I was worse than a pushover, because I was grateful, pathetically grateful, that someone so successful and who was the antithesis of all that my crazy parents stood for was actually interested in me.

It had seemed too good to be true and it was.

Ollie was right. James must have thought all his birthdays and Christmases has come at once. No wonder he couldn't wait to get that ring on my finger.

'Thanks, Ed,' I say. 'I think I've heard enough.'

'Sorry, old bean.' Ed coughs awkwardly. 'Unpleasant business, I know. Julius had to let him go, less negative publicity for the firm and all that. Malcolm Saville was furious and of course Alice dropped him like a hot brick. I think poor old James is pretty desperate. Rumour has it that he hasn't got long to settle his debts.'

We say goodbye and I sit for a moment nursing the phone and chewing my bottom lip. There's a feeling in the pit of my stomach like a pack of hyenas are having a good old gnaw. You don't live with someone for several years without learning something about them, and one thing I know about James is that he can be pretty ruthless when pushed. I think Jake and Millandra can safely vouch for that.

Maybe now is a good time to take up nail-biting again? It's either that or get Richard to shove a few prayers into the ether, but judging from the speed Mads is now haring up the path, I think he may need all the prayers for himself.

I think it's time to make myself scarce and head off to Smuggler's Rest. Hopefully by the time I've hiked up there I won't be feeling quite so savage towards Seb and Gabriel.

Otherwise they may need more than prayers to help them.

★

The walk up to Smuggler's Rest is far from soothing, and with every stride my blood boils and my head pounds. By the time I push the front door open I'm seething so much it's a miracle I don't combust there and then and leave a smoking pair of wellies on the Delabole slate floor. How dare Seb and Gabriel decide who I can and can't speak to? That was never in our agreement!

The thought of sneaky Seb manipulating me by screening my calls makes me wild, and I know this had to have been his idea because quite frankly Gabriel doesn't have the intelligence to think up such a nasty little scheme. He might be beautiful, but when God gave out brains Gabe was far too busy preening in a mirror to turn up and collect his share. But this doesn't mean he's off the hook. No way! From now on he can fend for himself, because as far as I'm concerned my summer job's well and truly over. I'd rather babysit Luke and Leia for the next six months than spend another second pretending to be Gabriel's girlfriend.

Maybe Richard has a point, I admit grudgingly, as I slam the front door so hard that one of Gabe's BAFTAs falls off the dresser. There's a lot to be said for honesty in relationships and it certainly makes life easier. Maybe it's time I sent Richard to have a chat with his famous neighbour and Seb.

A lecture from Richard is the *least* they deserve.

Luckily for Gabriel he's in the shower when I arrive, and Seb's cloistered in the office deep in conversation on his mobile, which gives me a few moments to get my breath back and simmer down a little. It probably won't help matters if they both end up wearing their bollocks as earrings, even if it makes me feel better. I need to be calm and in control, don't I? I'm shored up by justifiable anger and icy fury because I'm in the right, for heaven's sake!

Or at least as much in the right as a girl who's lied to most of Britain for three months can be.

While I wait for Gabriel to appear – which may take some time if past experience is anything to go by, because he could teach Marie Antoinette a thing or two about doing her toilette – I stomp around the kitchen oblivious to the beautiful views and the golden sunshine bouncing off the solid oak surfaces. The place is a pit: plates are piled in the butler's sink, a week's worth of grease festers in the grill pan and the surfaces are speckled with coffee granules. Gabriel might look divine but he lives like a pig, and good luck to Frankie if they ever move in together. Even though cleaning up after him isn't part of my official role as his girlfriend, I vent my bad temper on the mess, crashing plates into the dishwasher and slamming pans into cupboards while poor Mufty cowers in his basket and wonders what's got into the madwoman in the kitchen.

'Fury, that's what!' I tell him, flinging a bin bag out of the kitchen door and almost taking out a seagull. 'How dare Gabriel and Seb think they can run my life? Who the hell do they think they are?'

It's strange that only a few months ago James totally ran my life and, feeble and apathetic as it was, I let him. So maybe I did believe he knew best and that he was only guiding me for my own good. That turned out to be total rubbish at best and emotional abuse at worst.

Thank God I got out when I did.

'If Gabriel *dares* to try and pull the same stunt he'll be wearing one of these pans,' I tell the worried-looking Mufty as I heave another one out of the sink. 'No more Mrs Nice Katy!'

I catch a glimpse of myself in the stainless-steel fridge; it isn't just the sleek hair and slimmer frame that are different, but the steely glint in my eyes and the determined set to my chin.

Chubster has left the building. If only Jewell was here to watch!

'If you sit in the passenger seat too long, you forget how to drive,' I point out to the bemused poodle. 'And I'm a great driver, no matter what James said. I was a legend in Ollie's Beetle. No one else I've ever met could paint their nails and get round the Hanger Lane Gyratory System at the same time.'

'Who are you talking to?' Snapping his mobile shut, Seb strolls into the kitchen and flicks the switch on the kettle. He's grown a goatee since he was last down and it makes his already thin face even more weasel-like.

'Interesting you should ask,' I say, glaring at him. 'Who would you like me to be talking to? Or maybe I should rephrase that and ask who you'd rather I *didn't* talk to.'

Seb eyes me suspiciously. 'Have you been drinking? It's only nine a.m.' He sighs heavily. 'Please don't go all Kerry Katona on me. I can do without having to fight to book you into the Priory when I know for a fact they're full.'

Seb's lucky that the kitchen island, more of a continent actually, separates us, otherwise he'd have been booking *himself* in to the local A&E.

I take a deep breath. Calm and cool, remember?

'Would you like to explain why you've been screening my calls?'

'Ah.' His gaze slides from mine like butter from warm crumpets. 'That.'

'Yes, that.' I advance around the island, passing the Sabatier knives on my way. As I pause by their wooden block Seb looks distinctly uneasy, and so he should, because cool and collected doesn't actually seem to be my forte.

I knew there was a reason I have red hair.

'What gave you the right to decide who I'm allowed to talk to?' I snarl.

He shrugs. 'I'm your manager. It's part of my job.'

'It's part of your job to screen calls from my friends? That was never in the arrangement I made with Gabriel. Besides, you're not *my* manager.'

'I have Gabriel's image to consider. As do you, seeing as he pays you enough for this whole charade. You were risking everything by allowing male *friends* to call and turn up unannounced. One of us had to think logically.'

334

'Don't you dare try to blame me! I agreed to be Gabe's official girlfriend, not to live in a police state!'

'I presume we're talking about your persistent mate Ollie?' Seb sighs. 'OK, I'm not going to deny it. I may have put him off a few times.'

'A few? More like every time he called!'

'So it's my fault he's a telephone stalker? How was I to know you wanted to speak to him? If he was so keen he could have called your mobile or the rectory.'

'He'd lost his phone so he didn't have my mobile number. And why would he ring the rectory when you'd given him the impression I didn't want to talk to him?' My shrill voice echoes and bounces off the shiny surfaces. When I quit my role as Gabriel's girlfriend I can probably be employed straight away as a fishwife.

'Look,' says Seb, sidling away, one eye fixed nervously on the knives, 'my job is to manage Gabriel and his image, and we both know exactly what makes that so difficult. The last thing I needed was a lovesick friend of yours turning up and wrecking all the hard work. It made sense to keep him off the scene.'

'Maybe I didn't want him off the scene?'

He fixes me with his beady ferret's eyes. 'That was *exactly* what I was afraid of. The last thing Gabriel needs is his so-called girlfriend leaving him for another man. Just imagine the headlines if that had happened; it would have been a disaster. Call it damage limitation if you like, Katy, but it really wasn't personal. I was just doing my job.'

'Damage limitation?' I echo. Is this guy for real or did someone amputate his emotions at birth? 'Have you any idea just how unhappy I've been? You were playing with people's lives, Seb, and it isn't on. I love Ollie and you've

335

led him to think I didn't want to know him. You've probably ruined everything. How could you?'

'Calm down!' Seb raises his hands and starts to back away from me. I'm just congratulating myself on not losing my teacherly ability to terrify people when I realise I've plucked the biggest, meanest knife from the block and am brandishing it in time with my words. Blimey. I put it down quickly; tempting as it is to make Seb into a doily, he isn't worth doing time for. Perhaps I should revisit my anger management training.

'Look, I'm sorry!' Seb insists, backing into the corner by the fridge. 'Calm down and we can talk about it, OK?'

'I'm not feeling very calm. In fact I'm feeling quite the opposite. So sod this stupid job. Find someone else to manipulate. I quit!'

Seb turns the exact hue of the snowy-white robe that Gabe is wearing as he saunters into the kitchen.

'You can't quit now. Not with the launch of *Pirate Passion*. It'll ruin everything.'

I glower at him. 'And I'm supposed to be bothered?'

'You should be. You agreed to all this.'

I fold my arms across my chest. 'I never agreed to my entire life being controlled. I'm not the one who's moved the goalposts, Seb.'

'Hey, what are you guys rowing about? I'm trying to meditate and you've totally broken my concentration,' complains Gabriel, sloshing orange juice into a glass. He would be scowling but he's just had Botox and looks rather like a startled hard-boiled egg.

'I know about Ollie's calls and how they were screened,' I say, so coldly that I'm amazed a few penguins don't waddle past in an arctic blast. 'I'm through with people controlling my life, Gabriel. Find yourself another pretend

336

girlfriend. I'd rather do supply at Tregowan Comp than put up with this farce a second longer.'

'What's she on about?' Gabriel asks his manager. 'What calls have been screened? What the hell's been going on?'

He seems so genuinely perplexed that I realise he hasn't a clue what Seb's been up to. Gabe's not that good an actor, especially with a frozen face.

'I may have not passed on some messages from her friend Ollie,' Seb mutters sulkily.

'He ignored them all,' I spit. 'He let Ollie think I didn't want to speak to him.'

'And now she's quitting,' Seb continues. 'Just when you need her most for the TV awards and the launch of the new movie, she's decided to leave you in the lurch and declare her love for another man. Angela Andrews will have a field day and the game will be well and truly up.'

'You can't!' Gabe's hands fly to his mouth in horror. 'This week's crucial. It could be the start of my Hollywood career. If everything comes out now, I'm finished. Seb, tell her she can't. Katy, please, you can't do this.'

I glare at them both. 'I bloody well can. Watch me!'

'I was wrong to lie to your friend,' says Seb swiftly. 'I can see that now, Katy. I should never have done it. It was stupid. And wrong. I'll call him myself and tell him what I did, if it will help. But please don't quit now. Gabriel needs you.'

Gabe nods his golden head and his sapphire eyes sparkle with tears. 'If the truth comes out, nobody will take the new movie seriously and the studio will lose millions. I'll probably never work again.' He reaches out and clutches my hands. 'Please, Katy, I'm begging you. Don't walk out on me now. I'll double your wages, I'll pay anything!'

'It's not about money, Gabe. It's because I can't lie any more.'

'You don't need to,' says Seb swiftly. 'Just give me a week to put a story together and see if I can find a soap star to attend the premiere with Gabriel, then you can go. I'll call Ollie and explain everything, I promise, but please give us a week.'

I shake my head. 'I need to see Ollie now. I can't wait a whole week.'

'We're going to London tomorrow for the TV awards. Can you give me two days?' Seb is tapping frantically at his BlackBerry. 'Sienna owes me a favour, so maybe she'll do the premiere, but we have to have *you* at the awards tomorrow. The *Dagger* journalists are all over that like flies on crap, and if you don't show they'll never leave Gabriel alone. They'll dig up something.'

'It's true,' wails Gabriel. 'Please, Katy, just a few days? You can invite Ollie over if you really must, but don't leave me and Frankie in the lurch. You know your being there is the only way we can be together without worrying. Please, just this one last weekend? So Frankie and I can have some time?'

It's a masterstroke mentioning Frankie. I know just how much it's meant to him having me around so that he has the freedom to be with Gabe. Frankie's my gay best pal, or so the gossip rags think, and this gives him total freedom to come and go from whatever smart venue Gabriel and I happen to be staying in. I also know Frankie has been touring solidly for three weeks and is desperate to see Gabe. He'll be broken-hearted if he can't.

Oh crap. I may be the strong new Katy Carter, but I think I still have some work to do on the old guilt thing.

'Please?' Seeing me weakening, Gabriel fixes me with

huge tear-filled eyes. 'If not for me, then for Frankie? Just this one last weekend?'

'And after that you can do whatever you like,' chips in Seb. 'Go and be with this Ollie if you must. I'll see to the press and make a statement about your split. There'll be nothing to stop you. Come on, what's one weekend in the general scheme of things?'

I bite my lip. I've already arranged to see Ollie at Jewell's party, where hopefully we can salvage our friend-ship, so I suppose one last weekend as Gabriel's girlfriend can't hurt. It'll be something to tell the grandchildren – if I ever get round to having any, which at this point in time seems pretty unlikely.

'One weekend,' I say firmly, 'and then that really is it.'

'You angel!' Gabriel smiles so widely that I'm almost blinded by his veneers, while Seb visibly heaves a sigh of relief. 'You won't regret this, I promise!'

'I hope not,' I say, because already I'm wondering if I should have just walked out and left them to it. But then what about poor Frankie? He'd have been devastated if he hadn't been able to see Gabriel.

So one last weekend it is.

Surely that can't hurt?

Chapter Eighteen

As an avid reader of such literary tomes as *Heat* and *OK!*, I've always thought I had a pretty good knowledge of such important world events as the National Television Awards and Soap Personality of the Year. I've even been known to fill in the voting slip in *TV Quick*. But compared to Gabriel I'm an ignoramus. If he was to appear on *Mastermind*, his specialist subject would probably be 'Obscure Awards for Television Personalities', and I have no doubt he'd score full marks. The only subject dearer to Gabriel's vain little heart is that of himself. He holds a PhD in that one.

Since I decided to hand my notice in from this increasingly bizarre job, my desire to quit is increasing with every passing second. All this fibbing is starting to make me feel dizzy, and I hate having to look over my shoulder all the time just in case Angela Andrews and her mates are lurking in the undergrowth or a diehard fan is hiding behind the dustbins. I'm even starting to look forward to earning an honest crust supply-teaching at Tregowan Comp, and seeing as teenagers give supply teachers a similar reception to the one the lions in the Colosseum gave the Christians, you can gather how desperate I am. Life as a celebrity's partner sucks.

'As soon as Jewell's party's over, I'm quitting,' I tell

Maddy from my comfortable nest of pillows on the enormous bed in Gabriel's suite at Claridges. My head is hanging over the edge and I enjoy the rush of blood to my brain. In all honesty, it's the most excitement my brain's had in ages. 'That's going to be our last official outing as a couple. I've promised Gabe I'll stick it out until then so he can spend some time with Frankie. Frankie's going to do his best to persuade Gabe to come out; he says he can't stand the deceit any more either.'

'Any chance of that happening?'

'About as much chance as I have of flying to the moon but I don't want to disillusion Frankie. He's so miserable about being Gabe's guilty secret. Honestly, you should see him. He's lost all his bounce and sparkle.'

'So have you,' Mads points out.

'That's because I can't stand another minute of having to grin vacuously at the cameras and pretend I don't want to thump Gabriel. Besides, all these awards ceremonies are doing my head in.'

'Poor you. Which one is it tonight?'

'National Television Drama Awards,' I say, feeling the familiar surge of boredom. 'Gabriel's having a full body wax right now.'

Mads splutters. 'Too much information already. Treatments aside, though, how's the trip to London? What's Claridges like? Have you met Gordon Ramsay? Is he sex on a stick?'

I laugh. 'Where do you want me to start? The trip is tedious and if Gabriel has any more plucking and exfoliation he'll be a totally new man, which actually may be a good thing. Claridges is . . .' I glance around the sumptuous hotel room, all white Egyptian cotton and gold fittings, 'nice.'

'Nice? Hark at you, Mrs Blasé! I'll probably go to the moon before I go to Claridges, you bitch. Information, now! What's Gordon like?'

'Cool. He told Gabe to fuck off when he asked for a low-carb main course.'

Mads laughs. 'I'd have liked to see that. What's your suite like?'

'Enormous. Your entire house could fit in the bedroom.'

She whistles. 'Tell me more.'

Dutifully I flick the speakerphone switch and wander around the suite, describing the thickness of the carpet, the piles of towels softer and whiter than snowdrifts, and the contents of our not-so-mini bar. I even pull back the heavy curtains and open the windows so she can hear the growl of the London traffic. As Mads oohs and aahs I feel such a fraud. I've written a novel, moved on with my life and here I am in this amazing hotel, and I have never felt so unhappy. What's the point of being in these fantastic surroundings on my own? All I've done since I arrived is watch satellite telly and miss Ollie. I've even called him at the house and left him a message telling him I'm in town if he wants to catch up. I've left the hotel name and number, but so far so silent. I just hope he keeps his promise and comes to Jewell's party.

I decide against telling Mads I've rung Ollie. She won't be impressed to know I've called six times just because hearing his voice on the answerphone makes me feel all tingly and warm. I don't want my best friend thinking I'm a psycho stalking bitch from hell.

Because I'm not. I'm just taking Fate into my own hands, aren't I?

'Katy!' There's a tinny but indignant shout from the

speakerphone. 'Stop ignoring me! What are you wearing tonight? What shoes have you got? Tell me!'

Obediently I pad across the carpet to the enormous wardrobe – in which I fully expect to find fauns and lions – fling open the doors and look at the beautiful green Alice Temperley dress, all beading and embroidery and by far the most gorgeous frock I've ever seen. Below is the pair of strappy Jimmy Choos I'll wear as I trip, hopefully not literally, up the red carpet. It's a bitter irony that once I would have died of joy to possess such wonderful things, but now I have them I feel as flat as week-old Coke.

I look in the full-length mirror at the new gym-toned and straight-haired Katy Carter and suddenly miss the old curvy, boingy-haired version so much it's a physical pain.

I collapse on to the bed. 'I'm so sick of lying to everyone!'

'It's only for a few more days,' soothes Mads from her Cornish kitchen. 'Anyway, think of your writing. It must have been fantastic research material hanging out with Mr Rochester.'

'I don't remember the bit when Mr Rochester had manicures.' Call me a hypocrite, but there's something just wrong about a man hanging out in the bathroom for longer than I do.

'But the point is,' says Mads with the patience of one explaining particle physics to a single-cell amoeba, 'that women the length and breadth of Britain *do* find Gabriel sexy, and that's just the type of material you need. That was the entire point of your hero hunt.'

I murmur agreement and try to ignore the small voice telling me that Ollie in his holey fisherman's sweater, faded Levis and tanned bare feet is a million times sexier than the achingly beautiful Gabriel.

'Katy! Is there something you're not telling me?'

Don't you just hate it when your friends can read your mind?

'Surely you're over James by now?'

I think I'll demote Maddy from her position as best friend. She asks way too many personal questions. I've explained that I'm quitting because of what Seb did, but I have't told her *why* I'm so angry and upset. Mads knows something's up, but luckily I'm saved from damning myself with even more lies because there's a sharp rap at the door, followed by copious nervous throat-clearing as the hotel manager pops his head around it.

'Pardon me, madam, but there's a gentleman at reception demanding to see you. He's being most insistent. Shall I send him away?'

Oh my God! My heart starts to head-bang under my rib cage and I feel faint. It's Ollie! He's picked up my messages and he's come all this way to see me! My blood poings all over my body and someone has tipped half the Sahara in my mouth. I can't speak, so I nod dementedly.

'I've got to go. Call you later,' I tell Mads, cutting her off and dashing around the room like a loony, biting my lips and pinching my cheeks like a Jane Austen heroine before standing sideways in front of the mirror and hoping my DVB jeans really do make my bum as peachy and my tummy as flat as the shop assistants swore they would. Will Ollie like the new me?

There's a sharp knock at the door. As I fling it open, my heart swells like a helium balloon, only to pop when I see who the visitor is.

'Hello, Chubs,' purrs James, elbowing past me into the suite. He looks around, feasting his eyes on every sumptuous detail. 'My, my. Haven't you gone up in the world?'

I don't return the compliment. James looks like a grubbier version of himself. His skin has a grey tinge and his eyes are threaded with tiny red veins. Even his suit is crumpled, the collar of his shirt grimy around the neck.

I shut the door and fold my arms across my chest. 'What do you want? And how did you find out where I am?'

James taps his nose with a forefinger. 'I have my sources.' He smiles, but it isn't a nice smile; it's the kind of smile that a crocodile might have prior to gobbling you up. My scalp prickles with unease.

'Get out, James, before I call security.'

'I wouldn't if I was you. What would your boyfriend say,' James wonders, perching on the edge of the bed and bouncing thoughtfully, 'if he knew you'd invited your ex-fiancé into his private suite?'

'I didn't *invite* you,' I point out. 'You barged in.'

'A mere technicality.' He shrugs, and I notice that his suit looks loose on his shoulders. 'All the hotel staff will know by now that Gabriel Winters' girlfriend is all alone with another man. What will they think?'

'James, Mick Jagger keeps a suite here. Do you really think they'll give a toss if an ex-merchant banker pays a total nonentity a visit?'

'But you're not a nonentity; you're the girlfriend of Britain's most handsome man. Everyone's talking about you and wondering how on earth you managed to pull him.'

Charming as ever, he meanders around the room, helping himself to some grapes from the fruit bowl and checking out the enormous bathroom.

'Where's Gabriel anyway?'

'Press stuff,' I say.

James wanders back into the bedroom, two pots of Jo Malone shower gel in his hands. 'Won't he be upset when he opens the Sunday papers and reads all about how his girlfriend cheated on him while he was out working? Our afternoon of passion isn't going to make very comfortable reading for him.'

'James,' I say through clenched teeth. 'I don't know how I can make this much clearer. It's over, you and me, we're finished. We're not going to get back together. I'm not going to sleep with you. Ever.'

James rolls his eyes. 'You always were so fucking slow, Chubster. Have you any idea how annoying that was? I've got no intention of screwing you now. Christ! It was enough of a chore when I had no choice.'

I stare at him.

'No,' he continues, moving to the window and looking down at the scuttling pedestrians. 'I'm through with all that shit, thank Christ. I tried being nice. I tried sending flowers. I tried being reasonable. And where exactly did that get me? Absolutely fucking nowhere. So you haven't left me a choice. I was prepared to wait until the old bag kicked the bucket, I was even prepared to marry you, but that wasn't good enough, was it?'

He turns and gives me a chilly stare. Flecks of spittle are collecting in the corners of his mouth.

'So now I've got to play it the nasty way. When I describe this suite in perfect detail to,' he plucks a card out of his breast pocket and looks at it thoughtfully, 'a certain Ms Angela Andrews of the *Daily Dagger*, and bung the hotel lackey fifty quid to back me up, it's not going to look very good for you, is it? Just imagine the whole of

346

Britain waking up to read about how Gabriel Winters' girlfriend has been shagging about. It's not going to do his image much good.'

'You can't do that!'

'I think you'll find I can,' smirks James. 'What a shame, you'll be chucked yet again. Won't lover boy be upset?'

Yes, but not for the reasons he thinks. Image is everything to Gabriel. I look at James's cold face, the eyes as chilly as sea-washed glass, and wonder what I ever saw in him. My self-esteem must have been lower than the worms.

Jewell will be proud. I really have changed.

'So,' ploughs on James, 'unless you want this little romance of yours to end, we need to come to an arrangement. One hundred thousand should cover it. In cash.'

My chin practically hits the carpet. All the pressure of losing his job has blown his brain. 'I don't have that sort of money! You know I don't!'

He shrugs. 'Gabriel does. Ask him for a new dress or something.'

'He's an actor, James, not Bill bloody Gates.'

'I'm sure you'll think of something, darling. And if you don't . . .' he pauses and smiles, 'it will all be over. Poor old Gabriel. Won't he be devastated?'

I hate him. If I hated him before for what he said about Jewell, I *really* hate him now, because he doesn't know I'm not head over heels in love with Gabriel. He doesn't care either. He'd ruin everything for me without a moment's thought.

'This is blackmail,' I whisper.

'What a nasty word. I'd rather call it a business arrangement.'

'Like our whole relationship was,' I say bitterly. 'I know

about the money, James. I know about the problems with the bank. But what I don't understand is why, if you needed money so badly, you ended it with me.'

James helps himself to some whisky, holding the glass up to the light and admiring the generous amber measure.

'Ed's been blabbing, I suppose. He never could keep quiet about anything, never had the nerve to take the risks I have.'

I say nothing. Like a *Scooby-Doo* villain, James can't wait to spill the beans.

'So what if I made some speculations that didn't quite work out, lost some money and speculated more and lost some money again? I thought that old godmother of yours was bound to die sooner rather than later, but the silly old bag just didn't oblige. She got increasingly funny about lending me money too. Then the bloody recession started and the screws were really on.' He takes a swig of his drink and wipes his mouth on the back of his hand. 'When I met Alice, I thought my luck was in. No more waiting for some old dear to snuff it; her father was worth millions. So, my darling, when you fucked up the dinner party in such spectacular style, it was the perfect excuse to end our engagement. Who in their right mind could have blamed me?'

'Nobody,' I murmur. 'Even I didn't blame you.'

'How touching,' says James, polishing off another whisky and starting on a third. 'Since you care so much, you'd better sort out getting some cash to me, hadn't you? Otherwise off Gabriel Winters will go like a shot. One hundred thousand in cash. You can give it to me tomorrow evening at your godmother's party.'

'You expect me to raise that sort of money overnight?'

He drains the drink. 'You'd better, or otherwise Angela

Andrews will have the scoop of the year. I'm sure she'll pay me well for that. Have I made myself clear?'

'Perfectly,' I say faintly.

'Good. Then I'll see you tomorrow.' Business completed, James bangs the glass down and saunters out of the room, leaving me alone and trembling.

All his horrible words are like poison darts in my ears, and I keep hearing them over and over again until I think I'm going to go insane. How could I have loved such a horrible person? How could I have been so stupid?

I mustn't be stupid any longer. James has given me the push I need to make things right, right with Ollie, right with Gabriel and right with myself.

James would be furious if he only knew that his stirring has actually done some good. Tonight's the last time I'll put on my make-up, straighten my hair and play the part of Gabriel's girlfriend. Tomorrow, after the party, I'll end it. I'll tell Gabriel the truth and let James run his story. Who knows, it may even do Gabriel some good. At least nobody will be on to the truth.

Dashing the back of my hand against my eyes, I swallow my tears. I can't turn up at the awards ceremony with a red nose and puffy eyes; that wouldn't look good in the papers. And I certainly don't want to turn up to Jewell's party looking like a goblin. Jewell deserves to have a fun night.

And even if Ollie is in love with Nina, I want to look as good as I can.

A girl can dream, can't she?

Chapter Nineteen

'What do you think?' Maddy does a twirl and her black robes spin out around her. She leans forwards, smooths her red wig down and tucks the wriggling Mufty under her arm. 'Can you tell who I am yet?'

'Richard's a bit of a giveaway,' I point out, as Richard, done up as Ozzy Osbourne in a straggly black wig and purple shades, gives me a cheerful V sign. I'm impressed actually that Richard's favourite celebrities *are* Ozzy and Sharon. Although like Mads said, who was I expecting them to be? Cliff Richard and Thora Hird?

I guess I should have learned by now that nobody is ever exactly what they seem. Still, there's the benefit now of both Richard and Mads having to be extremely nice to me since the Bishop found Throbbing Theo hiding in the Bible boxes. I took the rap for that, of course, and suffered a long lecture from the Bishop about my moral fibre – which apparently isn't something Kellogg's makes – but the upshot is that I'm getting lots of free drinks in the Mermaid and Richard has given up nagging me about lack of honesty in relationships.

Well, pots and kettles spring to mind, don't they?

'I wonder if I need more eye shadow?' Mads peers at her reflection through narrowed eyes. 'Have you finished with that green yet?'

'Almost.' I cake another layer on and bat my false eyelashes experimentally. 'Done, I think.'

There's a whole crowd of us shoehorned into Jewell's dressing room, frantically putting the last-minute touches to our fancy dress. 'Come as your favourite celebrity' turned out not to be a joke, and the Hampstead house is awash with Kylies and Robbies and even a Darth Vader, although I'm not sure he actually counts as a celebrity. My parents are wafting around in their habitual cloud of cannabis smoke, loosely dressed up as Lily and Herman Munster, although this hasn't required much work on Mum's part, and even my sister Holly has come as a very butch-looking Lauren Bacall.

I haven't seen Jewell yet, but I'm sure she'll have really pushed the boat out. Her parties are always spectacular, but this year's is something else and I can't imagine how she'll top it next time. There's a stunning marquee set out in the garden all festooned with white and pink fairy lights and crammed with waxy lilies and fat pink roses. A string quartet is playing on a dais and there's an ocean of champagne being carried around by black-suited waiters, each gliding along with an elegant arm held behind his back. Rumour also has it that the Screaming Queens, currently number one, will be doing a turn later and lots of the guests seem really excited about this. Certainly Frankie, who is busy strutting around in full Freddie Mercury garb, appears to be having the time of his life. Everywhere I look I see celebrities chatting and drinking. Chris Evans is talking to Posh Spice and Henry the Eighth is dancing with Cher.

And I haven't even started drinking yet.

I fluff up my blonde wig and suck my index finger

suggestively as I squat in front of the mirror. 'What do you think?'

I'm pretty impressed with this get-up, because it hasn't taken too much effort. A pair of hot pants, a low-cut vest top and Wonderbra, and white high-heeled boots teamed with fake tan and drag-queen make-up, and ta da! I'm Jordan. Or at least I hope I am.

Call me a sad cow, but didn't Ollie once mention a fantasy about Jordan and a trampoline? And if I'm not mistaken, Jewell has hired a bouncy castle, which is practically the same thing.

I just hope Ollie comes, even if Vile Nina is with him. I keep peeking out the window but there's no sign of him yet.

'Scary,' says Mads, eyeing me up and down. 'You look just like Pamela Anderson. Let's hope nobody comes as Tommy Lee.'

'I'm Jordan!' I protest, but Mads isn't listening; she's far too busy sticking her tongue down Ozzie's throat. Honestly! The pair of them are worse than teenagers lately; they can hardly keep their hands off each other. Just as well I can escape up to Smuggler's Rest to leave them to it.

Giving up on Mads and Richard, who may be some time if past experience is anything to go by, I give myself one more practice pout and amble on to the landing. Pausing for a split second at the top of the curved stairway, I look down at the busy scene below. There's no sign of James yet, thank heavens, but I'm sure that it's only a matter of time. Can't think who he'll come as, though; I don't think BBC News 24 is that big on celebrities.

Spotting some familiar faces, I make my way through the throng, accepting a glass of champagne on the way, and join Gabriel and Guy, both of whom look absolutely normal.

'Who are you?' I ask Guy, who's swigging Stella from a can and sporting his usual yellow bib-and-braces attire. I'm amazed he came. He must really rate Jewell to allow himself to be dragged to London, a place on a par with Sodom and Gomorrah for decadence as far as he's concerned. He also has to be the only person I've ever met who has never been to a Pizza Hut. It was hell last night trying to prise him away from the Ice Cream Factory.

'Can't you tell?' Guy does a twirl. 'I'm George Clooney in *The Perfect Storm*!'

I clap my hands. 'Great outfit, Guy! And who are you?' I ask Gabriel, who's looking perfectly normal in a plain DJ and bow tie, golden curls caught up in a ponytail.

'I've come as myself,' replies Gabriel, totally without irony. 'I couldn't think of anyone else I'd rather be.'

'Of course you couldn't,' I say, patting his arm. Gabriel is the most conceited person on the planet, it's official. When *Cosmo* phoned the other day and asked me what his favourite position was, and I replied 'In front of the mirror', they had no idea how honest I was being. Frankie literally has to peel Gabe away from the looking glass before they can go anywhere. 'You look great.'

'Thanks.' Gabriel looks me up and down. 'Why did you come as Lily Savage?'

I give up.

'Just felt like it,' I say.

'Smile!' A camera flashes and for a moment I see stars. Blinking rapidly, I eventually distinguish Angela Andrews, cunningly disguised as Cruella de Vil, with her photographer decked out as a Dalmatian.

'Hello.' Angela smiles, or at least I think she does; it's a bit like being beamed at by a piranha. 'Marvellous party. We'll chat later. I'm sure you have loads to tell me.'

'Who invited her?' asks Frankie, sidling up to Gabriel and looking nervous.

I frown. 'She's probably gatecrashed. Just be on your best behaviour, you guys. No snogging, OK?'

'I should be so lucky,' sighs Frankie. He looks so genuinely miserable that my heart goes out to him. It's just a shame that Gabriel won't come out for him. Surely life would be so much easier?

'She's got to be on to something,' worries Gabriel. 'The Rottweiler, remember? Katy, you'll have to stick next to me like glue. Hold my hand or something.'

But I have absolutely no intention of holding his hand. In fact I hardly hear a word that he is saying because my attention has been totally diverted. Walking across the hallway, dressed in a billowing white lawn shirt, tight cream breeches and knee boots, with his long curly hair caught back at the nape of his neck in a velvet bow, is none other than Ollie. A three-cornered hat swings from his hand.

I am totally and utterly lost for words.

He's come as Johnny Depp in full *Pirates of the Caribbean* mode.

And he looks absolutely gorgeous.

My legs morph into overcooked spaghetti and my heart really does start to pound when I catch his eye across the room. And when he gives me that wry little dimpled smile, I'm lost. Honestly! All these years of churning out romantic clichés, and now I'm actually experiencing them for real. All this over Ollie, the man I dismissed out of hand as ever being hero material. Ollie, who leaves the loo seat up and has a passion for garlicky olives, who smokes sneaky cigarettes and has terrible taste in daytime television.

That Ollie. The one I've thought of every single day since I left London.

'Ollie!' screeches Frankie, 'Oh! My! God!' And then he does what I'm far too shy to do but am actually desperate to: he flies across the hall and launches himself at Ol, flinging his arms around his neck and hugging him. 'Darling! You look absolutely gorge! I could eat you up!'

Gabriel scowls. Funny how his pretty-boy looks appear a bit petulant sometimes.

'Who's that?' he hisses.

'That's Ollie,' I say, and there's a lovely glowy feeling spreading through me. 'Frankie's cousin.'

'Get off me, you old bender!' says Ollie, and they wrestle for a minute before joining us. Ollie's hair has come loose and I notice how much longer it's grown, presumably because I haven't been around to hack off the ends for him with the kitchen scissors. His face is thinner too, and very tanned from the wind and the sun. Freckles dust the bridge of his tilted nose and I'm overwhelmed by the urge to kiss each one.

In a desperate attempt to distract myself I take an enormous mouthful of champagne and practically choke. It takes Ollie and Frankie several minutes of slapping me on the back before I gain sufficient control of my lungs again.

Not a good start.

'Are you all right?' asks Ollie.

I nod desperately. My wig is a bit skewwhiff and I think I've lost an eyelash, but I'll live to fight another day.

'You've come as Jordan?' Ol asks. 'Thought you

couldn't stand her? When I put her calendar up in the loo you said she was a vacuous bimbo.'

Oh yeah. I forgot that. Still, honesty and all that gubbins. Taking a deep breath, I look him in the eye and, no doubt turning a fetching shade of beetroot, remind him of his trampoline fantasy.

Ollie throws back his head and laughs. I can't help but notice how the muscles ripple in his throat. Kiss me! they say.

'That was a joke,' he chuckles. 'I can't stand her. I was just winding you up.'

'You were?' He was? I stare at him aghast. Ten bums in a row. There goes my seduction plan; unsophisticated as it was, at least it was a plan of some kind. Now I'm dressed in a revealing chilly outfit that's as sexy as control knickers. If only I'd come as someone beautiful and glamorous, like that girl over there who's exquisitely dressed as Marilyn Monroe, all chiffon skirts and bouncing peroxide curls. If I was dressed like that I'd be home and dry.

Marilyn heads our way, gore-red lips parted in a smile.

'Hello,' she says, linking her arm through Ollie's. 'Lovely to see you again, Katy. And even lovelier to see *you*!' she adds, batting her eyelashes so manically at Gabriel that I half expect Charlie from *Casualty* to come rushing in and start to apply first aid to her eyelids. 'I'm Nina.'

Plop. There goes my heart into my patent-white tart boots, even quicker than you can say broken dreams. Sure enough, under the Marilyn outfit is Nina. And from the way her bony hand grips Ol's bicep, they're still very much an item.

I'm such an idiot. Why don't I just invite everyone to drive a steamroller over my emotions?

'Everyone,' I say, injecting maximum false cheer into my voice. 'This is Nina, Ollie's fiancée.'

'Fiancée!' squawks Frankie, looking at me and then at Ollie. 'Fiancée?'

'Katy,' says Ollie, 'I think—'

But what Ollie thinks we don't get to find out, because at that very moment Jewell makes her entrance, to much cheering and a loud blast on the electric guitar from Ricky, the candyfloss-maned bass player in the Queens. She pauses theatrically at the top of the stairs and waves at the speechless guests.

We're speechless because it's not every day you see a seventy-year-old woman (and that's discounting that fact that Jewell's been seventy for at least the last ten years) dressed as Madonna. And I'm not talking Madonna in her Ray of Light hippy phase.

If only.

No, Auntie Jewell has plumped for the full Vogue era, complete with Jean Paul Gaultier pointy-coned basque and blonde wig. She looks as though she's about to burst into a rendition of 'Hanky Panky' at any moment. I wouldn't put it past her.

'Darlings,' cries Jewell, flinging her arms wide and sending the feathers on her hat bobbing. 'Thank you so much for coming tonight to celebrate my birthday! It's not every day that a girl reaches seventy.'

No, just every year.

'I'm delighted to see you all here,' Jewell beams. 'There's booze and nibbles, and darling Frankie's kindly lent me his band for the evening too. But before you all get carried away, I need you to indulge a little old lady and play a game for me.'

Little old lady my bottom. Beneath the wrinkles Jewell

is pure steel. I dread to think what she's cooked up tonight. All Jewell's party games tend to end up with me making a prat of myself in one way or another.

I expect that surprises you, doesn't it?

'I've got the names of famous lovers from film and literature and history,' announces Jewell as she descends the staircase. 'I'm going to attach the names to your backs. But the game is that you won't know what your name is, so you'll have to ask all sorts of questions to find out!'

She claps her hands, and at once two waiters scurry forward with baskets of name badges.

'And when you do eventually find your partner,' she adds, busily pinning the name *Becks* on to Guy's plastic back, 'you have to stay with them for one drink. So have fun! Get chatting, and meet lots of lovely new people.'

'Watch her,' warns my sister Holly, passing by with the name *Posh* pinned to her suit. 'She's up to something.'

Of course she is. Still, at least it buys me some breathing space from Ollie and Nina. I move away, helping myself to another glass of champagne, and begin to ask questions. I circle the room endlessly. I know I'm from literature, I know that I've been in a film, but I've drawn a blank. Frankie has teamed up with Marilyn, good luck to him, and Guy and Holly are whispering in each other's ears.

People are pairing off left, right and centre and I'm starting to panic. This is like being back at the school disco when the slow dances begin, pressing my back against the wall and praying either to vanish into the floor or for somebody not too ugly to ask me to dance. Being short and ginger, I was invariably left until last.

Not a happy memory.

Ollie sidles up to me, twisting round. 'Who am I?'

'That's cheating!' I say sternly, trying to ignore the way

the very sight of him turns my insides to ice cream. 'You're meant to ask me questions.'

'Sod questions,' Ollie says. 'Yours says Elizabeth. What's mine?'

'Darcy,' I read. Nice one, Jewell.

'Hello, Miss Bennet.' Ollie reaches out and takes my hand. 'Do you want a drink?'

No, what I want is for you to love me and not Nina.

'A drink would be lovely,' I say graciously. Well, may as well get into Lizzie Bennet mode, even if I'm dressed more like a hooker. A girl can dream, can't she? I try to slow my tattered breathing. Any more oxygen and I'll pass out.

Ollie returns with two brimming glasses.

'Are you all right?' he asks. 'You look a bit odd.'

'It's very hot in here,' I improvise wildly. How I can be hot dressed in hot pants and a bra is one of life's great mysteries.

Ollie raises his eyebrows; the same thought has obviously just occurred to him too. He puts both glasses into one hand and steers me towards the garden.

Once through the French doors and into the darkness of the terrace, the noise of the party starts to recede, chatter just a distant ebb and flow like the tide as it sucks at the pebbles on Tregowan beach. The air is heavy with night-scented stock, the sky sprinkled with stars like glitter on a child's Christmas card.

'Have a sit-down.' Ollie guides me towards a lichen-crusted stone bench and I sink on to it, wincing a little when the stone grates my thighs.

Ollie fixes me with a steady gaze. 'Katy, what's going on?'

This is it. Honesty time.

I take a gulp of cool night air. Thank goodness it's dark and he can't see my Edam face.

'Why are you marrying Nina?' The words bolt out at about one hundred miles an hour.

'I'm not marrying Nina.'

'I mean, I know that she has great tits and can cook and all that—' Whoa. Brakes. 'What did you say?'

'I said,' Ollie repeats slowly, like he's talking to bottom-set Year 7, 'I'm not engaged to Nina. I don't know why you think I am. Your imagination again, I suppose.'

'No!' I'm most indignant. My poor old imagination is often to blame, but not this time. 'She told me. When you went shopping and went to the jeweller's. You looked at rings?'

Ollie's face registers nothing but disbelief. 'Is that why you sent me an engagement card?'

'Of course it was! Nina practically told me you'd bought the ring.'

'Nina looked at rings. I went to Millets.'

I stare at him. 'But I assumed you'd bought her a ring. Of course that was why I posted you a card!'

He shakes his head. 'I thought it was your way of telling me to leave you in peace and make a go of it with her. When exactly did she tell you this?'

I think back. 'About three months ago.'

'About the same time you started seeing Gabriel Winters?'

'Try the same day, actually. After all, what did I have to lose? I left you loads of texts and voicemails on your mobile. And I was always asking Nina to pass on messages to you. You never got back to me, Ollie. And every time I called I had to listen to her going on and on about how absolutely flipping fantastic everything was between you.

360

How you were only being kind to me because you felt sorry for me. How . . . how . . .' My voice breaks at this point and I'm horrified to find that tears are trickling down my face, and they won't be elegant little diamond-like tears either, because when I cry, I blub. Just my luck that snot and froggy eyes aren't sexy. 'How you were pissed off with me for taking up so much of your time with the breast cancer stuff. How you wanted to be with her and I was wasting your time by dragging you to the hospital.'

Ollie looks shocked. 'That's the biggest load of old bollocks. Surely you know me better than that? Why on earth did you listen to her? And more to the point, why believe it?'

I exhale slowly. Three months on I don't believe it, but that's because I'm no longer the insecure mess who didn't think she was worth taking seriously. James's toxic effect has worn off and I'm proud of what I've achieved in Tregowan. I have a job (of sorts), friends who like and value me; I've finished my book and I've paid off a big chunk of my debts. Uncertain how to express all this in a way that actually makes sense, I just shrug. 'It made sense at the time, I guess.'

He reaches out and takes my hand, enclosing it in his and stroking my palm with his forefinger. 'It crucified me thinking that you might be sick. I wanted to be there for you. Of course I didn't resent it. Please don't cry, Katy.'

I try my hardest not to sniff. To be honest, that tiny motion of his finger against my palm is doing a beautiful job of taking my mind off crying.

'Why didn't you get in touch?' I say, because I'm not going to let him get away with this. 'I wrote as well as phoned and you didn't reply, not even a short letter to tell me to push off. That was really cruel.'

'My mobile went missing three months ago,' says Ollie slowly. 'I think we know who took it, don't we? And we already know Gabriel's agent wouldn't put my calls through to you. Nina must have scooped up any letters. She still had her key.'

'But why would she do that? She practically lives with you. It wouldn't have hurt her to let me chat to you.'

'She doesn't practically live with me!' protests Ollie. 'Bloody hell. She must have really hated me for finishing it.'

'You finished with her?'

'Months ago. Try the morning that I read in the papers you were with Gabriel Winters. I binned the paper, called Nina and told her it was over and drove like a maniac down to Cornwall. The rest I think you already know.'

'So who's the *we* you said were off travelling?'

'Me and Sasha of course, you wally! Not Nina, that's for sure.'

'You're not engaged?' I say slowly, because I really have to get this fact straight.

'Of course we're not bloody engaged! Honestly, I finished with her the day I saw you plastered all over the papers with Mr Lover Man.' Ollie shakes his head. 'Christ, I was beside myself. Nina went ballistic when I told her it was over. I thought she was going to boil Sasha alive or something.'

Personally I wouldn't put it past her. Sasha was very lucky not to have become a bowl of setter soup.

'But if it's over, why is she here tonight?'

'Because you asked me to bring her!' says Ollie, sounding exasperated. 'We're not together; we haven't been together for months. OK, maybe I might have had a relapse for that one night when you told me we were better off as friends, but apart from that I've hardly seen the girl. Which has taken some effort, I can tell you. She's like human Velcro.'

'I thought you wanted to be with her!' I'm glad I'm sitting down, because I'm in serious shock here. 'I thought you'd only come tonight if you were with her!'

We look at each other and start to laugh.

'I thought you were pushing us together.' Ollie shakes his head. 'I didn't understand it. And then when you started seeing Gabriel Winters, well, I won't lie, I was really pissed off with you. It seemed less painful just to let you think we were still a couple, because you were so happy with him.'

I squeeze his hand. 'My relationship with Gabriel isn't quite what it seems.'

'I don't care about that,' says Ollie. 'How long have you known me?'

'For ever,' I hiccup.

'So why did you prefer to listen to Nina? Didn't you know in your heart I'd never say those things?'

I have the answer to this one. It's all I can do not to shoot my hand right up into the air and shout 'I know, sir!'

'Nina's everything you look for in a girlfriend,' I remind him. 'She's blonde, thin and successful. Basically, the opposite of me. All your girlfriends are like Nina, Ol. It wasn't rocket science.'

'Just as well you teach English and not science then,' says Ollie. 'You total muppet, Katy! Why do you think I never stayed with any of them?'

Can I ask the audience?

'Because, you idiot,' Ollie's hand moves to cup my

cheek, 'I've been biding my time and waiting for someone else, somebody really special. Somebody who loves bacon sandwiches as much as I do, who rescues lobsters and keeps them in the bath, somebody who sneaks off for a fag at break time.' His hand caresses my cheek. 'Do you know anyone like that, Katy Carter?'

I can hardly breathe. 'I think so.'

'Well,' murmurs Ollie, 'I do. And this time I'm not being fobbed off with excuses about being mates, because to hell with being mates, Katy. I don't want to be your mate any more.'

I pretend to be very absorbed in the false eyelash. 'What do you want to be?'

But Ollie is done with speaking. Instead he pulls me closer and his lips brush against mine. It's amazing! Little ripples of desire fizz and pop through my bloodstream like champagne, and I feel all light-headed. Then he puts his arms around me and is kissing me softly, his tongue gently caressing mine and probing the inside of my lip. I coil my hand around his neck and at last I know what it feels like to bury my fingers in those soft curls at the nape.

It feels like heaven.

I could kiss him for ever.

'Christ!' Ollie pulls away first, his eyes dark with emotion and his hands trembling. 'You have no idea how long I've wanted to do that.'

Actually I think I have; about as long as I have probably. Why did I pretend for so long that Ollie was nothing more than a mate? Who was I trying to kid? I trace his full, sexy mouth with my finger and smile. How could I have thought he was nothing like a romantic hero? When I think of the motley crew I've met over the past few months, I want to punch myself for being such an idiot.

The perfect romantic hero was there all the time, right under my nose. Romantic heroes can wear beanie hats and make a mess in the kitchen when they cook. They can leave the loo seat up sometimes and forget to hoover. They can even play Xbox for hours on end. Sitting on a cold stone bench in Jewell's garden, I have a revelation a bit like that guy in the Bible who had fishes' scales fall from his eyes, only less messy. Being a romantic hero isn't about fitting some formula, because, let's be honest, Gabriel and Guy look perfect on paper but are both as about romantic as cold custard. Being *my* romantic hero is actually really simple.

It's about being Ollie.

There's a sigh of wind and the magnolia trees whisper softly. The fairy lights looped between them shiver and cast silvered beams on to us. Ollie lifts my chin and drops a kiss on my lips. It's as soft as the breeze but my stomach flips just like it did when Jewell forced me to go on Oblivion at Alton Towers.

Luckily this time I don't puke, though.

I suddenly feel really shy, which is mad, because I'm with Ollie. I can't be shy with him. He's seen me cut open and has seen me throw up on numerous nights out. He's seen me dribble after having a tooth out.

'This is wrong,' Ollie says suddenly. 'You're with somebody else.'

'It's over with him,' I say hastily. 'In fact it never really started.'

'He's a movie star. Mr Rochester. He's what you've always wanted. He can give you everything.'

Yeah. Apart from that one vital thing.

I'm going to have to tell him. 'There's something you need to know about Gabriel—'

Ollie places his finger on my lips. 'I don't want to talk about Gabriel or Nina any more. I know that I haven't got a lot to offer you. I've got a yellow camper van, a red setter and about three hundred quid to my name. I know that if you stay with Gabriel Winters you'll have a lifestyle that most people can only dream about and there's no way I can compete with him.'

I try to speak but Ollie's hand is in the way. He's known me long enough to realise that near suffocation is the only way to keep me quiet.

'But I love you. I love you a million times more than he ever could. I know that you make a mess, leave empty milk cartons in the fridge and eat all my biscuits.'

I do not! I never eat his biscuits.

Well, only sometimes.

'You don't clean the bath, you hide your credit-card bills under the sink and you have terrible taste in music,' carries on Ollie, working his way through what is starting to sound like a rather alarming list. 'But I wouldn't have you any other way. Gabriel Winters could *never* love you like I love you.'

Ollie, you don't know how right you are!

'Come away with me,' Ollie says, squeezing my hand. 'Tonight. The van's outside; all we need to do is get in it and drive. I'll sort things out with Nina – if I've mislead her then I must put that right – and you can sort things out with Gabriel. We'll travel together. Just you, me and Sasha.'

'Really?' There's a big bubble of happiness rising inside me, pushing aside all the scum of months of misery. 'You really mean it?'

'Of course I do!' laughs Ollie, and kisses me so fiercely that our noses bash together.

'Ouch!' I giggle, as I surface for air.

'Sorry,' he grins. 'I'm acting like a sixteen-year-old. But I really don't care. Life's too short for messing about; if I've learned anything over the past few months then that's it.'

Ollie and I sit for what feels like ages, not wanting to burst the bubble of our happiness, and we talk and kiss and laugh as the party goes on around us. The fairy lights twinkle, and from inside I hear Jewell's laughter. I can't wait to tell her about us, although I have a feeling she already knows. She's working her magic tonight.

'So,' says Ollie eventually, threading his fingers through mine, 'meet me in about thirty minutes, outside the house? That gives you some time to tell Jewell and sort things out with Gabriel. It also . . .' he pauses and looks at me long and hard, his eyes behind the lenses so full of mingled hope and uncertainty that I feel weak, 'gives you some time to think things over and, if you want to, change your mind.'

'I won't change my mind.'

'It's a big decision,' Ollie says firmly. 'I want you to think it through. I've had months of thinking about nothing else but I've sprung this on you. You need to think about Gabriel.'

Gabriel? It's like hearing a name from another lifetime, another world. How could I have been such an idiot as to embroil myself in all those fibs? Never mind tangled web, this is more like being stuck in one of Guy's trawls. I know that I've sworn to say nothing, but . . .

I *have* to tell Ollie the truth about Gabriel.

Honesty is my new policy, remember.

I take a deep breath, open my mouth and—

'There you are!' screeches Frankie, flinging open the

367

French windows and staggering into the garden. 'We were getting worried about you!'

Why does Frankie always have to interrupt us at a critical moment? He's starting to make a habit of it.

Seconds later Marilyn Monroe falls into the garden behind him, her high heels trip-trapping over the terrace and her full breasts threatening to escape any moment from the halterneck. In spite of myself I'm mesmerised. I've never seen a real false pair, so to speak, before. I can't really blame Ollie for being fascinated. I know that he's fantastic and all that, but at the end of the day he is but a bloke.

'We were paired together,' explains Frankie, pulling a desperate face that Nina misses; rolling his eyes, drawing a finger across his throat and twirling round, he points to his badge, which reads *Homer*. Nina looks less than thrilled to have *Marge* pinned to her back. 'I don't think it was me that Nina was hoping for, so we thought we'd come and find you guys.'

'Thanks,' says Ollie, but irony was never Frankie's strong point.

'No problem!' He plops himself in between us. 'Ooh! Tight squeeze! Shove up. You're a bit cosy, aren't you?' He peers closer. 'Hey! Are you holding hands? Oh!' Frankie looks from Ollie to me as slowly it's not so much the penny that drops as his entire and rapidly increasing bank balance. He claps a hand over his mouth. 'Oh shit! Sorry!'

'Oliver,' snaps Nina, her chest rising like twin hot-air balloons. 'I've been looking everywhere for you.'

'I've been talking to Katy,' says Ollie coldly.

Nina's eyes sweep over me.

'I thought *Cosmo* said you'd lost weight?'

Whatever charm school she went to owes her parents one whopping refund.

'Thanks for passing on all my messages to Ollie,' I say.

Nina doesn't even have the good grace to look embarrassed.

'I only did that because I hate to see Ollie used.'

'I've never used Ollie,' I cry. 'We're friends.'

'Really?' Nina looks amused. 'And you tell each other everything, I suppose?'

This is the part where I really ought to cross my fingers. I *will* tell Ollie everything just as soon as I get the chance.

'Of course we do,' says Ollie.

Nina looks sceptical. 'That isn't what James just told me.'

'James?' Ollie looks confused.

'Merchant banker? Very charming?' Nina smirks at me as she reels off this list. 'Used to live with Katy, who I believe now lives with Gabriel Winters?' She wags a crimson talon at me. 'All these men, Katy. How do you do it? I'm seeing you in a whole new light.'

She makes it sound as though it's a red one.

'Ollie,' I say quickly, because put like this even I think I sound like a right old slapper. 'I can explain it all. Especially about Gabriel.'

'No you can't,' squeals Frankie.

'But can you explain James?' Nina places her hands on her hips and I practically hear the bones grating. If I never ate again I still couldn't be that thin. 'Can you explain why he spent yesterday afternoon in your hotel room?'

'Is James here?' I look nervously over my shoulder, half expecting to see him lurking in the shadows, scattering trouble like a malevolent pinstriped Puck.

'Of course he's here,' Nina giggles. 'You invited him.'

'Did you?' Ollie turns to look at me, baffled.

'No, but I knew he was coming. Sort of.'

'Sort of?' says Ol.

'Just be honest,' Nina snaps. 'You're getting back together, aren't you? You're going to dump poor Gabriel and go running back to James.'

'No!' I splutter. 'I'd rather chew my legs off!'

'That's not what James says.' Nina's enjoying this. God only knows what rubbish James has been feeding her. I should imagine he's taken another look at Jewell's lovely house and is seeing pound signs again. 'He says you guys are on the phone non-stop.'

Ollie looks at me. Bewilderment is etched across his face.

'Hardly non-stop,' I say quickly. 'Just a few texts now and then. And he popped over to see me yesterday.'

'You never mentioned that,' Ol says quietly.

'That's because there's nothing to mention. Anything else I'll have to explain later. Alone.'

Nina places one claw on Ollie's arm. 'We really need to talk, but not out here. Let's go inside where it's warmer.'

'Five minutes,' says Ollie, his mouth set in a grim line. 'Five minutes and that's all.'

I feel queasy with nerves. What is James cooking up now?

'Half an hour, remember,' Ol says, looking back at me over his shoulder. The fairy lights bring out the golden streaks in his hair. 'Thirty minutes – unless you change your mind.'

'I won't,' I promise. 'No way.'

The door opens; chatter and music drift into the garden and are truncated swiftly when the door clicks shut.

Ollie doesn't glance back. In spite of the tender kisses of

only moments ago, I can feel the foundations of my happiness turn to quicksand.

Goose bumps pimple my arms. 'What's James been telling her?'

'Some old bollocks,' says Frankie airily. 'I shouldn't worry about that. Ollie loves you, girlfriend.'

'You reckon?' Now Ollie's gone, it's like the minutes before were a dream; certainties roll away like mercury.

Frankie nods. 'Oh yeah, I reckon. I could have told you that months ago. Everyone knows he's mad about you.'

They do? How come nobody ever thought to mention it to me? Thanks a bundle everyone.

Frankie gives me a watery smile. 'You're lucky to have someone who loves you like that.'

'You've got Gabriel.'

Frankie's head droops. 'Have I?' He looks up, and I'm horrified to see that his eyes are bright with tears. 'Is that the Gabriel who pretends to be straight so that his precious career is safe and who is paying you to pretend to be his girlfriend?'

Um, yeah.

That Gabriel.

'It's pointless,' wails Frankie, shoulders slumped and face buried in his hands. 'What sort of future do we have if he won't even acknowledge me? Is that love, Katy? Is it?'

'But he can't!' I remind him. 'You knew that from the start. Gabriel's career is really important. You told me that yourself.'

'More important than me?' Frankie dashes the back of his hand across his eyes. 'He's never going to tell anyone, is he? I'll always be the guilty little secret that's hidden away. What's the point?'

'So what's the solution? Gabriel has to come out?'

'God, no!' Frankie looks horrified. 'That would crucify him. And he's adamant it'll ruin his future as an actor. Nobody must ever find out the truth.' He grips my arms. 'Promise you won't say anything? To anyone?'

'I've got to tell Ollie.'

'No!' Frankie cries. 'You can't tell anyone. If this gets out it will wreck everything for Gabriel. It'll destroy him!'

'Then you'd better think very carefully about any decisions you make from now on, Katy.'

Hey? That's not Frankie's voice. I must have over-indulged in the champagne and am actually snoring in a drunken heap somewhere, because unless Frankie can add ventriloquism to his list of talents, I would swear that it was James who just spoke.

There's a rustle from behind the lilac trees and a black shape materializes.

I *am* having a weird trip. Not only have I spent the evening kissing Ollie, but now Darth Vader has appeared in my godmother's garden. I'm bitterly disappointed. I'll wake up in a minute, Ollie will still be with Nina and I'll still be eating my heart out in Cornwall.

Bummer.

'Arrgh!' squeaks Frankie. 'Who's that?' and he jumps to his feet, tipping me off the bench and smack on to the gravel.

Ouch. I'll be picking it out of my knees for weeks.

Guess that means I am awake then.

'Do you know,' says Darth Vader, slowly peeling off his mask, 'I often find that you learn some very interesting things when you skulk in bushes. People tend to be very indiscreet. ' He shakes his head and a lock of dark hair falls over his eyes. 'Hello, Chubs,' says James, 'fancy seeing you here, and Frankie too.' He looks us up and down and raises an eyebrow. 'Very . . . *interesting*.'

I gulp. Just how much has he heard?

'You've got exactly five seconds to fuck off,' Frankie says, in a voice tight with emotion. 'Otherwise I'm going to give you such a pasting that you'll be shitting teeth for weeks.'

'What with?' sneers James. 'Your handbag?'

'He's not worth it,' I say. 'Calm down.'

'Calm down?' Frankie sounds like he's ready to show Vesuvius a thing or two about erupting. 'He spies on us and eavesdrops and you think I should leave him alone? After all he's done to you?'

He steps forward and James takes a hasty pace backwards, stumbling a little over his robes. Not very Dark Side of him.

'This isn't about Katy,' says James quickly. 'But I'm fascinated by *your* little romance. Who'd have thought Gabriel Winters is a faggot? Not quite the image he wants to create, is it?'

'Right,' snarls Frankie, 'that's it.' And suddenly James is sprawling in the grass, blood dribbling from his nose.

'Frankie!' I shriek. 'You've punched him!'

'Ow! That really hurt.' Frankie rubs his right hand in amazement. 'I hope my hand isn't broken.'

James is mopping his nose with his Darth Vader sleeve.

'You're going to wish you hadn't done that,' he sniffs. 'You've just put my price up significantly.'

I sigh. 'I've told you already, James, I haven't got the kind of money you need. I'm really sorry that you've got yourself in a mess, but I can't help you.'

'*You* might not have any money. But Gabriel Winters certainly has. And I reckon he'll be more than happy to pay me to keep quiet about him and his boyfriend, don't you?'

'You can't do that!' I'm aghast. How could we have been so careless as to discuss Gabriel's secret somewhere so public? Why, oh why, wasn't my tongue amputated at birth?

'Of course I can,' smirks James. 'Unless you have a better idea?'

I haven't actually. I stare at him in horror, this cold stranger whom I once believed myself to be in love with. How could my judgement have been so bloody awful?

Actually, let's not answer that.

'That's blackmail,' Frankie says bleakly.

James pulls a morose face. 'Sorry and all that. Tell you what, though, Chubs, why don't I give you a little while to think about it?' He glances at his wrist, or rather at the blank space where his Rolex used to be, which spoils the effect somewhat. 'How about thirty minutes? That should be enough time to go and tap good old Auntie for a loan. Half a million should cover it.'

'Half a million!' Frankie starts to laugh. 'You're insane. Jewell isn't worth that.'

'Oh, I think you'll find she is,' says James. 'I did my homework there. Did you know she has a dicky heart too? Amazing the documents people leave lying around. So careless.'

I'm speechless.

'So, half an hour then?' James smiles, or rather his thin lips twitch. 'You can let me know if I need to go to the papers, or whether Gabriel Winters and I need to have a little chat about his love life. And don't think that I won't say anything. There's a little blonde journalist here desperate for a story. I'm sure she'd pay me a fortune for the information you've just divulged.'

That oblivion sensation is back. How did this go from being one of the best evenings of my life to the worst?

'Frankie! Katy!' The French doors swing open and Jewell's face peeks out into the darkness, her eyes straining into the darkness. 'You naughty things! You've ruined the pairings. What is darling Ollie doing with that vulgar blonde?'

Nothing, I hope.

Jewell beckons at us. 'Hurry up. I've got an announcement to make.'

'She's not the only one,' warns James.

Frankie clutches my fingers so hard the bones groan.

Jewell claps her hands. 'Everybody in now! The fun is just beginning.'

'It certainly is,' says James. He catches my arm, pulling me towards him. 'I'm not messing about; I will have that money one way or another.'

He stalks in ahead of me, black robes swirling around him. I'm surprised I don't hear the doom-laden tones of the Imperial Death March and see a couple of stormtroopers just for good measure.

'Help me, Obi-Wan,' I mutter.

'Is he bullshitting?' asks Frankie, pale with worry.

'I wish. Apparently he's in serious financial trouble, something to do with insider trading. Ed Grenville says he owes a fortune and it's being called to account any day now.'

'Christ,' whistles Frankie. 'That's serious shit. He could go to prison.'

'So he's desperate,' I say. 'If we can't find the cash he'll go to the papers.'

375

'That can't happen!' Frankie cries. 'It'll destroy Gabe. He'll never forgive me if I ruin his career. Acting is his life.'

As we enter the hall, Frankie glances across at the stairway where Gabriel, unaware that his secret is only minutes from being blown out of the water, is smiling and chatting with his adoring public.

'No chance of telling the truth?' I ask.

'No way! He'd never agree to that. He'd rather end it with me. You can't let that happen, Katy.'

Catching sight of me, Gabriel breaks away from his admirers and strides through the crowd to pull me to his side. 'Everyone!' He raises his voice, only slightly, but instantly all attention is focused on him. 'You all know my very special girlfriend, Katy Carter.'

There are nods and murmurs of assent. James is standing slightly apart from the others with his arms folded and a mocking smile on his face.

'Katy's made me really happy,' boasts the unsuspecting Gabriel. 'I want to make her happy too. I've been thinking of a way to thank her for ages, and then one evening it came to me.' He pauses, and every eye in the place is trained on him. 'Katy writes, and she's very talented.'

What would Gabriel know about writing? The only thing he ever reads is the reviews about his own performances, and even then he only bothers with the good ones.

'She's just written a marvellous novel,' he gushes, making sure that all attention is riveted on him. 'It's called *Heart of the Highwayman*. My agent has seen it and we've passed it to a team of screenwriters, who are desperate to make it into a film.' Gabriel pulls me into his arms and drops a kiss at the corner of my mouth. 'I'm taking the starring role. Congratulations, darling! You've made it!'

A ripple of applause spreads around the hallway. I'm frozen with disbelief.

How dare he?

How dare Gabriel help himself to Jake and Millandra without asking me first? How dare he decide that he's going to be Jake? He's nothing like Jake. As if Jake would spend three hours in the hairdresser's or employ a stylist. I don't think so!

This is my fault for leaving the notebooks on the coffee table. No wonder Seb was nosing around. He's like a bloodhound when it comes to PR, and spins more than my washing machine.

'Yes!' Gabriel is laughing in response to a question. 'Of course she'll be paid. Very handsomely.'

Plop. Plop. Hear the brown smelly stuff hit the fan. He's talking to James.

James turns to me. 'That's great news. You'll have lots of money, Katy.'

I open my mouth but there are no words. I ought to be over the moon, delighted, dizzy with success. But it's all wrong. I feel like I've been bundled into a car and am being kidnapped. A glass of champagne is pressed into my hand and a throng of people are asking me how I feel and congratulating me.

'Well done,' James says softly, drifting past in a swirl of black robes. 'At least someone likes that pathetic drivel. Doesn't this solve all our problems?'

I guess if it gets James off my back I can sacrifice Jake and Millandra to Gabriel's ego. I might have wanted to write romantic novels, but maybe I can grit my teeth and tolerate a cheesy bodice-ripper, with Gabriel sauntering around in leggings.

I look around for Ollie. There he is, by the door. I wish

desperately that Gabriel didn't have a possessive arm draped around me.

'Are you thrilled?' asks Angela Andrews.

'Of course she is!' says Gabriel. 'It's what you've dreamed of, isn't it darling?'

'Yes,' I bleat. In my worst nightmares.

'And we've got so much to look forward to.' Gabriel is a tsunami and I'm totally flattened before his plans. I try to edge away towards the door but his hand holds my wrist like a vice. 'My new series begins next week.'

Angela Andrews looks less than riveted. 'Will the rumours about your sexuality affect the reception that gets?'

Gabriel throws back his head and laughs. I'm quite impressed, to be honest. I know that he's wetting himself, but to all and sundry he just looks amused.

'Not that old chestnut!' He shakes his golden head and pulls me close. 'I think that Katy can vouch for the fact that it's nothing more than gossip.'

I try to cross my toes, fingers, legs, anything. I am so going to hell. 'Absolutely!'

Angela's eyes narrow. 'There's no truth in any of the rumours?'

I shoot a sideways glance at James, who raises an eyebrow.

'Of course not!' Gabriel sweeps me into his arms in true Mills and Boon style. 'In fact, you can be the first to congratulate us. Katy has just done me the honour of agreeing to marry me. We're getting engaged!'

My mouth is hanging open now. You could drive the 207 bus in there and still have room for the rest of the depot.

Gabriel's lost the plot. And I am going to kill him.

'Congratulations!' People surge forward and my cheeks are kissed and my hand shaken. For a moment I'm dazed, then I'm so pissed off that I'm surprised I don't explode.

'Gabriel!' I hiss, shoving him away. 'Are you insane? How can we possibly be engaged? We're breaking up on Monday, remember?'

Gabriel tosses his golden mane, beaming toothily at a photographer. 'Sorry, but I'm sure Angela Andrews is on to something. She's been making peculiar comments all evening. I didn't think you'd mind. We might have to postpone the break-up.'

'Well I do mind. And there's no way we're carrying this farce on.' I try to shake his arm off my shoulder. 'Sod Monday. I'm ending this arrangement right now.'

'You can't!' Gabriel snarls, dragging me into a corner and pinning me under his arm, so that it appears to all and sundry that we're kissing. I can't see Ollie but I can feel his gaze burning into my back. 'You'll make me look a fool.'

'Do you know what?' I shoot a glance at Frankie, standing alone at the foot of the stairs, his pale face a perfect study in despair. 'I think you're making a pretty good job of that yourself.'

I crane my neck, and sure enough, Ollie's watching this unfolding scene in disbelief. He mouths, 'Congratulations,' before turning swiftly on his heel.

'Frankie knows the score,' says Gabriel. 'And so do you. You agreed to this. One more weekend, you said.'

'I never agreed to getting engaged. Get your hands off me!' I try to shove his arm away but it's clamped on to my shoulder like a vice. 'Our agreement's over.'

'It bloody well isn't.' Gabriel's fingers increase their grip. 'Not yet, anyway.'

Across the crowds in the hallway I watch Ollie's head as it bobs towards the door. I can't let him leave!

'Let go of my arm!' I raise my voice, but nobody can hear above the din of the Queens. 'Get off me! I mean it, Gabriel. Our arrangement's over.'

'I've paid you until the end of the weekend,' he snarls, 'so do your job and smile; that's *OK!* magazine's photographer over there.'

'Sod *OK!*. You can have every penny back. Get off me, Gabriel, I'm serious. I won't let you do this to Frankie or to me any more.' I twist and turn but I can't shake him off; for such a pretty boy he's got an amazingly strong grip. All those hours in the gym must have been good for something. 'I want to be with Ollie. He loves me and I love him and no money you can throw at me will change that. I'm leaving with him.'

'You're not! Not now, with Angela Andrews watching. I won't let you screw my career up just for some whim.'

'Ollie's not a whim!' I'm yelling now. 'I love him! I always have!'

Teaching for seven years has given me a shout that could compete decibel for decibel with the Space Shuttle taking off. Heads swivel and suddenly we're the subject of intense interest. Gabriel pales, but his grip doesn't slacken. 'I'm begging you, Katy. Just one more hour. Please!'

Frankie pushes through the guests. 'For God's sake, Gabriel, have you gone mad? What are you doing to her?'

Gabriel's eyes are the cold blue of Glacier Mints. 'She only wants to ruin everything by running off with your bloody cousin. She promised she'd give us this final weekend, and now she wants to go back on our agreement.'

'If I don't catch Ollie up he'll leave thinking I've chosen Gabriel,' I half sob to Frankie. 'I can't lose him again.'

'Let her go to him, Gabe,' says Frankie, trying to prise those pincer-like fingers from my bicep. 'They're meant for one another.'

'She'll ruin everything I've worked for,' Gabriel spits. 'I can't risk it.'

'Gabe, this isn't about you any more,' Frankie points out gently. 'Not everything is, you know.'

But Gabriel doesn't look convinced.

'Darlings!' Jewell rushes over, hand on her heart and face pale. 'Please don't fight! This is supposed to be a happy occasion.'

'Well it isn't!' I kick Gabriel on the shin and he winces because my tart boot has a very pointy toe. 'I love Ollie, Gabriel. I can't let him leave thinking I'm with you.'

The idea is unbearable. Ollie is somewhere outside in the darkness thinking . . . well, whatever he's thinking doesn't bear contemplating. Suffice it to say that I don't think I'll come out of it looking much like Mother Teresa.

More like a two-timing harpy.

'I've got to sit down!' gasps Jewell, staggering backwards and collapsing into a chair. 'I must have had too many champagne cocktails.'

'Let Katy go to Ollie,' Frankie orders Gabriel. 'You don't need to pretend any more. You can be a single man again because I'm leaving you. All this deception's turning you into a monster; you're not the person I thought you were. It's over.'

Gabriel releases me so abruptly that I stumble and cannon into Jewell's chair. Amazingly she appears to have fallen asleep right in the middle of all this kerfuffle, her chin resting on her chest and her feathers drooping. One knotted old hand hangs limply over the arm of the chair. A brindled terrier, one of Jewell's many dogs, trots over and paws at her lap. Over and over and over he claws at her leg, desperate for attention, until her head tips forward and the feathered headdress slithers on to the floor. Jewell, normally vain, doesn't even stir, not even with the cool air blowing against the thin tufts of hair on her scalp.

'Auntie?' I say, softly at first, and then a bit louder. 'Auntie?' I give her a little shake but there's no response.

The dog stops pawing Jewell and, abruptly throwing back its head, begins to howl; loud, heart-wrenching howls that rip through the champagne-fuelled chatter. It's the most chilling and primeval sound, speaking of distances, wide-open spaces and utter, utter unbearable loneliness.

Oh my God. What have Gabriel and I done?

Guy, trained in first aid, firefighting and goodness knows what other health and safety stuff, is quickly at Jewell's side. With a tenderness far removed from his usual brisk manner, he takes her frail wrist in his large hand and gently touches her neck. I don't need to see the way he shakes his head to know what has happened.

Ripples of mingled horror and morbid excitement spread around the room like a mill pond disturbed by a pebble. People gasp and murmur, and someone starts to wail.

My knees turn to water. I couldn't run after Ollie even if I tried. I'm frozen with disbelief and time seems to go into slow motion.

My mouth's so dry I can't speak.

Unfortunately James doesn't feel the same. He pauses by my side and looks at poor Jewell. Then he murmurs into my ear, so quietly that only I can hear, 'It looks as though your collateral has just gone seriously up.'

I stand trembling in a room that feels emptier by the second and stare in disbelief at Jewell lying in Guy's arms.

Outside in the street a car door slams and an elderly engine splutters. It roars into life, loud and throaty at first before growing fainter and fainter.

It's over. Ollie's driving away, into the distance and out of my life, because he thinks I've chosen Gabriel.

Jewell's house might be crowded, but I've never felt as alone in my life as I do right now.

Chapter Twenty

Normally I love autumn; it means snuggling up in front of huge fires, making vats of jam from hedgerow blackberries, new pencil cases for school and the relief of being able to hide my squidgy bits under baggy jumpers. I've always loved the smell of bonfires and the grey misty mornings and looked forward to stomping through heaps of russet leaves in my new winter boots. But not this year. It may only be early September but I can't help but feel that everything is tinged with melancholy. From the drifting leaves and blue wood smoke to the ploughed fields it all just seems so sad, season of mist and mellow fruitfulness and all that gloomy stuff.

It's late morning in Tregowan and I'm sitting outside the rectory, my hands wrapped around a chunky mug, watching the village below me. The sun is a blood orange in the pewter sky, the air has a nip in it that wasn't there before and the seagulls huddle together on the rooftops. It's a dismal day, which is fine by me because I'm in a dismal mood.

Jewell's funeral takes place at two o'clock. I don't think I could bear it if the weather was all sparkly and sunny – that wouldn't be right when it feels like all the glitter and fizz has been sucked out of my life. I want to be like King

Lear in his howling storm or like Catherine Earnshaw running into the rain and dying for love.

I want the whole world to mourn.

I take deep lungfuls of cold air and turn my face towards the pallid sun, watching clouds of my breath rise heavenwards. I wonder if they will eventually drift past Jewell. Will she recognise them if they do?

How weird death is. How can somebody be there one moment and then gone the next? Where does that vital part of a person, the bit that makes you *you*, go to? I'm trying to be logical about this but I'm finding it increasingly difficult. I mean, who do I listen to? Richard would have me believe Jewell's floating around with a harp somewhere, Mum's convinced that she's been reincarnated and Frankie says life is nothing but a simple chemical reaction. Who's right? Is there really a pattern to it all? Is it like a tapestry and I'm just confused because I'm looking at the back, with all the tangled threads and knots, rather than the overall pattern?

Trouble is, I'm crap at sewing.

I take a sip of coffee but it tastes of nothing. Just like the plates of food that Mads has forced me to eat. It's like all the colours and all the pleasures have bled away. I've lost the two people I love the most within moments of one another and my world is a dark and grey place without them.

It's six days on from Jewell's party and I'm still reeling with shock. Everything's a bit hazy and events have taken on a rather dreamlike quality. From the magical moments out in the garden with Ollie to James's threats and Gabriel's stupid proposal, everything seems unreal.

Except that James's threats are totally real. They keep popping up on my phone like evil mushrooms. He's convinced that Jewell's left me everything, and unless I pay quickly he's going straight to the press. Gabriel may not be my favourite person on the planet but I'm not inclined to wreck his career just yet. Some of that karma stuff that my parents are always on about has rubbed off on me by osmosis, which is a bit scary. When I start cooking lentil casseroles I'll know I'm in trouble.

I delve deep into the pocket of my patchwork coat and pluck out a tissue. It's all screwed up and in danger of disintegrating at any minute. A bit like me, in fact.

I dab my eyes and remind myself that Jewell wouldn't approve of tears. She mopped enough of mine up over the years, that's for sure, and I wish she was here now because I really need to talk to her. Ollie's vanished and there's no way of contacting him. I texted him until my finger was numb before I remembered that Nina has his mobile. He's somewhere far, far away, all alone and thinking that I chose money and success over his love for me. I can't bear it. Every time I go to bed and close my eyes, Jewell's party plays over and over again in my mind's eye like some hideous movie. I see myself running out into the street, minutes too late, where there's only a patch of oil and the faint smell of exhaust to prove Ollie's camper van was ever there. I feel again the tarmac under my knees and wake with tears running down my face. At this rate I'll have to buy shares in Kleenex.

Nobody knows where Ollie has gone, but I should imagine that it will be as far away from me as possible.

To the world I'm still Gabriel's girlfriend, but as soon as I've figured out what to do about James, I'll be sorting that one out. Actually, Gabriel has undergone something of a personality transformation these last few days. I guess he's blaming himself. He hasn't given any interviews and even cancelled his appearance on *Jonathan Ross*. He's spent a lot of time closeted with Seb too, so something must be up . . .

Frankie, bless him, has stuck by what he said to Gabriel. No more lies and no more pretending. He's ignoring Gabriel's calls, of which there are about ten an hour, and immersing himself in writing mournful songs.

At least I assume they're mournful. Listening to them certainly makes me miserable.

He's desperately unhappy and has spent the past six days in Maddy's spare bedroom, only coming out to shower or make a drink. All his camp inflections and bitchy comments have gone and instead he drifts around the cottage like a tear-stained shadow of his former self. He hasn't nicked my make-up for days. He must really love Gabriel.

I can't indulge my own broken heart when there's a funeral to sort out and Frankie to look after. Besides, poor Mads doesn't have an infinite amount of sympathy and Earl Grey, so I save my tears for late at night when everyone else is tucked up in bed. Then I can think about Ollie while the tears roll down my cheeks and on to the pillow. The sea licks the sand and whispers to the rocks and eventually lulls me into sleep, where I dream restless, uneasy dreams. I can't even turn to my writing for comfort because bloody Seb nicked my manuscript and I haven't the heart to write anything new.

I'm kind of off romance anyway, if I'm honest.

Once the guests left Jewell's party, Guy gathered her poor little body into his arms and carried her gently up to her bedroom. Telephone calls were made, the doctor visited and then an ambulance. The mechanics of death swung neatly into operation while I sat shivering in a

Lloyd Loom chair, holding a brandy in one hand and Jewell's cooling fingers, the skin papery thin and embroidered with blue veins, in the other.

In the peace of Jewell's room, all pretences were dropped. Guy smoked out of the window, Gabriel and Frankie huddled close together, their earlier row forgotten, and my parents skinned up. The other guests drifted home and from downstairs there was only the chink of plates being collected and scraped as the caterers packed away.

In the gloom of the bedroom a tasselled lamp soothed the bedside a little. The dogs came and lay outside the door, heads drooping sadly on their paws and eyes big with sorrow. Richard Lomax talked to undertakers and murmured prayers, which made me smile in spite of myself. Jewell would have adored to have prayers uttered for her by Ozzy Osbourne.

'This is my fault,' Gabriel said, his face white with shock. 'I upset her. I get so carried away, so obsessed . . .'

I said nothing, because at that moment I blamed Gabriel too.

'It's not your fault,' soothed Frankie. 'Don't blame yourself.'

'But it is.' Gabriel's periwinkle eyes sparkled with tears. 'All these lies, all the pretending. I'm to blame.'

'I wonder what Jewell was going to say?' mused Mads, who was curled up at my feet. 'She was desperate to make an announcement.'

I shrugged. 'I guess we'll never know now.'

Guy stood at the window. His shoulders were tense and his knuckles glowed chalky white through the flesh as he gripped the windowsill. He'd chain-smoked since Jewell's collapse, lighting one pungent roll-up from another. With a sigh he stubbed out his cigarette and flicked the butt over the ledge. Sparks fantailed into the darkness.

'I can tell you what she was going to say,' he said slowly. 'She'd told me already.'

I'd known that over the last few months Jewell and Guy had become friends. She'd enjoyed going out to sea on *Dancing Girl* and had adored drinking with Guy and his crew in the Mermaid, and knowing how special Jewell was, I hadn't found it odd that the abrasive Guy had been able to talk to her. Jewell always said age was just a label. She saw the person first; anything else was irrelevant.

'She had a problem with her artery, the artery in her neck.' Guy prodded his own with a chunky forefinger. 'It was blocked.'

'Carotid artery,' said Richard, who even at a time like this couldn't help but be a know-it-all.

'That's right.' Guy nodded. 'It was all furred up with stuff, blocking the oxygen to her brain. The doctors said they could operate but it was risky. It could have worked or it could have left her unconscious. Jewell spent some time in a clinic having tests but she decided against the operation in the end. She wanted to really enjoy the time she had left. Make the most of every second, was how she put it.'

My hand flew to my mouth. 'I thought she was at Champneys!'

'She could have died at any time,' Guy told us. 'There was no way she could have known when. It could have been months, it could have been years. But what she really wanted was to enjoy the time she did have.' His eyes grew misty. 'We talked a lot about it at sea. Being out there has a way of getting to you. It puts everything into context.'

'Is that what she was going to tell us?' I asked.

Guy spread his hands. 'Maybe not in so many words. But she spent a lot of time writing letters and planning her funeral. She wanted you to do it,' he said to Richard, 'in your church overlooking the sea. She wasn't afraid to die either. In fact, she was pretty peaceful about it all.'

We all looked at the small figure on the bed. Jewell looked like she was having a lovely snooze after slightly too much sherry.

'She wanted her ashes taken out to sea.' Guy's voice broke. 'She made me promise that I'd do that for her. And I did promise; I promised that everything would be done just as she wanted.'

Sitting on the terrace, warming my fingers on the mug, I think that Guy has been as good as his word. Jewell must have spent a lot of time thinking about how she wanted the funeral to be, and not one detail has been overlooked. The flowers are simple, the music is unusual to say the least and the coffin is a cardboard one from Totnes, covered in the most amazing paintings of Jewell's pets. The dogs bounce around the sides, cats curl up on the lid, Jo-Jo, Auntie's evil parrot, has pride of place in the centre with her wings outspread, and Cuddles the python winds his way around the pictures. It's stunning and just what she wanted.

'Katy!' Mads sticks her curly head through the kitchen window. 'You have got to come in here now. Gabriel's on the telly.'

I tighten my grip on the mug.

'I know,' I say bitterly. 'He can't make the funeral because he had to go on *This Morning*. It's nice that he's got his priorities right.'

'Seriously,' urges Mads. 'You have to come and watch this. He's behaving really strangely.'

Feeling resentful, since Gabriel's far from my number one favourite person at the moment, I follow Mads into the lounge, where sure enough Gabriel is chatting to Holly and Phil on the TV.

'Arse,' I mutter, watching him flick the blonde curls over his shoulders while Holly flutters her eyelashes.

Mads digs an elbow into my ribs. 'Listen!'

'So, Gabriel,' Phil leans forward conspiratorially, 'you've been hinting ever since you arrived at the studio that you have something really important to tell us, and we're just bursting to know what it is, aren't we, Holly?'

'Ooh yes!' giggles Holly. 'Although I think we can guess, can't we? It's to do with your love life, isn't it?'

'See!' says Mads. 'He's been dropping huge hints about being in love with somebody special ever since he parked that sexy bum on the sofa.'

Personally I find Gabriel's bum as sexy as Johnny Vegas naked.

Told you I'd gone off him.

'That's not unusual.' I'm grinding my teeth so hard I'm amazed they don't splinter. I swear that if he pulls any more stunts like he did at the party I'll save James a job and tell Angela Andrews the truth myself.

'You're getting engaged, aren't you?' says Phil, raising a silver eyebrow. 'We've heard rumours that you proposed to your girlfriend . . .'

'Katy,' supplies Holly helpfully as Phil struggles to remember my name.

'Yes, Katy,' continues Phil smoothly, 'at the weekend.'

Gabriel licks his lips. There's a nervous tic in his cheek, and his left foot, elegantly balanced on his right knee, is wagging with more enthusiasm than Lassie's tail.

He looks really scared.

He ought to be, if he's going to tell more lies about me.

'Come on!' laughs Holly, leaning over and stopping the twitching foot with a slender hand. 'There's romance in the air, isn't there?'

Gabriel inhales deeply.

'There is romance,' he says slowly. 'But not with Katy. There's never been anything romantic between Katy and me. She's just a good friend, that's all.'

'See!' says Mads. 'I told you!'

Holly and Phil are looking bemused. Their researchers must be quaking in their boots.

'I'm in love with someone else,' Gabriel tells them. 'I have been for ages. Something happened last weekend, something that has really made me realise what's important in life. And it isn't money, or fame, or even success. All that stuff is just a smokescreen. What really matters are the people you love. And in this case the one very special person that I'm totally and utterly head over heels in love with.'

Holly and Phil are positively drooling as they sense an exclusive coming their way. They're wondering what soap star or pop princess he's seeing now. I'm sitting right on the edge of the sofa and realise that I'm holding my breath.

'I absolutely agree!' Phil gives Gabriel a chummy grin, which Gabriel doesn't return because he's too busy chewing the inside of his cheek. 'Who is the lucky girl?'

'It's not a girl.' Gabriel looks directly at the camera so that his blue eyes, brimming with sincerity and emotion, are beamed at adoring housewives the length and breadth of Britain. 'He's Frankie Burrows, the lead singer of the Screaming Queens. I love you, Frankie. I'm really sorry I've been such an idiot. Please forgive me.'

Holly and Phil are doing amazed goldfish expressions, as presumably are all their viewers with the exception of me and Mads.

'I'm gay,' Gabriel tells Great Britain, just in case there's any doubt. 'And I always have been. If this means my acting career is finished, then so be it. But I love Frankie and I want everyone to know. I'm not ashamed. I'm proud.'

Mads and I clutch each other in amazement.

'He's come out!' she squeaks. 'Oh! My! God! He's come out on national television and told everyone that he loves Frankie!'

I can hardly believe it myself. Gabriel must really love Frankie to have done that.

On screen Holly and Phil are professional enough to recover swiftly and are busy asking Gabriel loads of questions. Mads flies upstairs to fetch Frankie – no more Victorian heroine-style decline for him – and I heave a massive sigh of relief. Somehow I don't think James will be pestering me again. Hearing the shrieks of amazement and joy from upstairs I can't help but smile.

At least one of us has had a happy ending.

★

As funerals go, Auntie Jewell's was bound to be a one-off. For one thing nobody is wearing black – bright colours are as obligatory for her in death as they were in life – and for another, the entire congregation is breathless after doing the Time Warp for the third time. The constant stream of expletives from Jo-Jo seems totally at odds with the peace of Richard's small church with its beautiful vaulted ceiling and glowing stained-glass windows.

'Please be seated,' pants Richard, mopping his shiny brow with a massive hankie.

We all obey as best we can, but the balloons and streamers that Auntie insisted upon tie themselves in knots around our ankles. I'm also really concerned that nobody except me has noticed that Cuddles, Auntie's beloved python, seems to have absented himself from his tank. I've never shared Jewell's conviction that dear little Cuddles is misunderstood. I'm of the school of thought that he actually enjoys scaring the shit out of people by entwining himself tightly around unsuspecting necks. It's never looked like the snake version of affection to me. I sweep my hand cautiously across the pew just in case, but thankfully Cuddles is off terrorising someone else.

Everyone in the church is here courtesy of small invitations written in lilac ink and on green paper. And a pretty eclectic mix it is too. Old lovers, television personalities and friends rub shoulders with window-cleaners, family and local shopkeepers. Even the pets are here.

I gaze across the nave and wish so much that I was able to sit with Ollie. But, of course, that's impossible. Ollie is long gone now. I may never see him again. Just thinking that is like slicing a blade through my heart.

Frankie pats my shoulder. Richard is rambling on about how Auntie was the pillar of the local community while Jo-Jo shouts 'Bollocks!' at surprisingly appropriate times. All I can think about is how much I'm going to miss Jewell.

While Richard drones on, I look up at the beautiful stained-glass window. It's weird, but just at the point when I really think that I'm in danger of breaking down, a ray of sunshine breaks through the gloom and warms my cheeks like kisses. Rainbow patterns skip over the worn flagstones and dust motes whirl and dance in the streaming light. The rosy hues tenderly blush the coffin.

If it wasn't for the fact that I've lost Ollie, I'd almost think Jewell was trying to tell me not to worry.

But it's hard not to worry when the man you love is miles away, convinced that you've chosen a vain and wealthy actor over him. I'd do anything to be snuggled up with Ol in his camper van right now, feeling his soft breath on my cheek and his strong, lean fingers stroking my body. We'd heat soup on a small stove, listen to the waves and make love under the stars . . .

I give myself a mental shake, or maybe not as mental as I think, because several members of the congregation look at me in alarm. I must be really shallow to be worrying about my love life at a time like this. But the last thing Jewell did for me was to ensure that Ollie and I spent some time alone together. She knew. I know she did.

She knew that I just don't work without Ollie.

★

'Are you coming?' Mads asks, once the committal is over. She nods her head in the direction of the pub. 'It should be a good party.'

Since Jewell has left the contents of her very considerable wine cellar to the good citizens of Tregowan, I don't doubt it for a minute.

'Give me a moment. I just need to get my head together first.'

Mads hugs me. 'Take your time, babes. We'll be waiting for you.'

Shoving my hands into the sleeves of my heavy coat, I wander slowly along the harbour, past the fish boxes stacked like children's building blocks and towards the sea. My nose wrinkles at the smell of fish and I pick my way carefully across the coils of rope and taut moorings that litter the quay, a solid arm of granite that stretches out into the sea. From the Mermaid I can hear the murmur of conversation as Jewell's wake gathers momentum. Guy, sprawled in the window seat, waves frantically at me and mouths something as he points towards the beach.

'I'll be along in a minute!' I call, turning away from his frenzied beckoning. I need a minute or two, a space to gather myself together, some mental elbow room before I go into the pub and listen to all the stories about Jewell, and the speculation about who's been left what in her will.

I don't want to know what Jewell has left me because that makes it all real. Listening to people dividing up her possessions, like scavengers picking over a carcass, means she really is dead rather than just popped to St-Tropez or New York for a spot of shopping. Knowing my luck I've probably been left the python. Fate doesn't so much smile on as French-kiss some people, but it has a nasty habit of flicking V signs at me.

Rain has started to fall now, that gentle, mizzling Cornish rain that gets you even wetter than the heavy, driving kind. My hair starts to frizz and beads of moisture sit on my thick coat. The air is thick with the smell of damp wool.

I scramble over some net bins and haul myself on to the top of the quay. Feeling very Meryl Streep in *The French Lieutenant's Woman*, I walk along the cobbled summit and raise my face to the rain. Below me the trawlers bump against the quay and above me the seagulls glide and plunge like a squadron of feathery bombers. On the small sliver of beach a red setter bounds across the sand, all fire and life against the grey of the afternoon. The dog barks and its owner, hood up against the rain, throws a stick. If I screw up my eyes I could almost believe that I'm watching Ollie and Sasha.

If only I was. I wouldn't stuff things up a second time.

OK, I wouldn't stuff things up a third time.

Once at the end of the quay I peer down into the water, an angry green colour today, and watch the waves boil and froth against the harbour gates. One seasick-looking gull bobs past and scummy foam gathers like an advert for Fairy Liquid.

I watch the water swirl and my thoughts swirl with it. So much has happened in such a short time. Breaking up with James, thinking I had cancer, leaving London, 'dating' Gabriel, Jewell dying, and losing Ollie. The list feels endless, and I'm tired, so tired, of trying to make sense of it all. Once upon a time I could have whipped out my notebook and written something cathartic, but lately my writing has left me too.

Well, I guess it's in good company.

I close my eyes and breathe in slowly. I am not going to cry. I'll probably never stop if I do.

'What a great view,' says a voice over my shoulder.

Grief does funny things to people, I know, but I could swear that's Ollie's voice. I sense somebody looking at me, their gaze so sizzling that it all but strips the flesh from my bones.

'It's a very pretty village,' I say.

'I'm not talking about the village.'

I spin round and cry out in joy. Ollie really is here, smiling that dear crooked smile, the dimples playing hide and seek and his eyes crinkling and sparkling. Sasha hurls herself against my legs, barking so loudly that the flock of seagulls trying to roost on the fish-market roof take flight, screeching in protest.

I'm not protesting, though, when Ollie pulls me into his arms.

Far from it.

'I'm sorry,' says Ollie. 'Katy, I'm so sorry.'

And he takes my face in his hands, kissing my forehead and my nose and even the tears that trickle from my eyes before he finds my mouth.

'It's OK now, Katy,' he whispers, in between kisses. 'It's all going to be fine.'

His mouth is as soft as an almond croissant and a thousand times more delicious. I kiss him back and hold him tightly, scared to let him go in case he vanishes, while Sasha bounces around us like a canine space hopper.

'I'm so sorry,' whispers Ol, over and over again, 'so sorry that I raced off like that. I had no idea Jewell had died. I acted like a total wanker because I was so jealous of Gabriel. Can you ever forgive me?'

'I'm sorry for not telling you Gabriel's gay,' I say. 'I wanted to but I never got the chance.'

'Whoa!' Ollie's eyes widen. 'Run that by me again! Did you just say that Gabriel Winters is gay? As in only-gay-in-the-village gay?'

'Not quite the only gay in the village. He's with Frankie, has been for ages. He paid me to pretend to be his girlfriend; it was a kind of summer job. Honestly. We were never a real couple.'

Ollie's mouth is literally hanging open. I shut it gently by putting my hand under his chin.

'You saw Gabriel on *This Morning*?' I say. 'When he told Phil and Holly? Didn't you?'

Ollie is looking completely blank.

'You didn't?'

'What sort of camper van do you think I have? I haven't got a telly. I'm lucky to have a stove.'

'If you didn't see it,' I say, looking up into his melting toffee eyes, 'if you didn't know . . . why are you here?'

Ollie strokes my cheek tenderly. 'I saw Jewell's obituary in *The Times* and I couldn't bear to think of you going through this alone. I know how much Jewell meant to you. Suddenly it didn't matter about Gabriel any more. Nothing mattered apart from seeing you again.'

He kisses me, then pulls away, shaking his head.

'Say something,' I whisper. 'Tell me what you're thinking.'

'I'm thinking that I can't believe Frankie managed to keep that secret to himself. He's got more mouth than Zippy,' whistles Ollie. 'Gabriel Winters is really gay and dating Frankie?'

I nod. 'They're like an old married couple. They've even got a poodle called Mufty. I know I was stupid to agree to Gabriel's plan, Ol, but I really thought you were getting engaged.' My throat goes all tight with misery just at the memory. 'I thought you hated me.' Bollocks. I'm crying again. At this rate I could give Tiny Tears a run for her money.

Not that I'm wetting my pants, though.

'Hey, don't cry,' Ollie murmurs, in between kisses. 'It's all going be fine.'

'I know,' I sniff. 'That's why I'm crying.'

'I can't have everyone seeing you with red eyes and a runny nose,' says Ollie, gently dabbing at my eyes with the sleeve of his coat. 'I don't want them to think I've made my future wife unhappy.'

I gape at him. 'Was that some kind of back-to-front proposal? If it was, it wasn't very romantic.'

'Sorry,' says Ollie, and his mouth curls into a shy smile. 'That came out all wrong.'

'Did you mean it?'

'Of course I did!' he replies, kissing me gently. 'We're both crap at dating, so why bother with all that? Besides, I already know all your annoying habits and I still love you.'

'I don't have any annoying habits!' I say indignantly. Then I think about it. 'Well, I may have one or two. But you have loads!'

'I don't doubt it for a minute,' he agrees. 'But that's the whole point, Katy. We already know each other inside out. Besides,' his hand strays to my breast and simultaneously raises my blood pressure, 'there's something even more important than the very obvious fact that I'm totally and utterly in love with you, and have been for years, lovely, sexy Katy.'

He loves me?

Lovely and sexy?

Me?

It's no good. I can't listen to this and have him doing that thing with his hand. Sorry, women everywhere. I must be the only one who can't multitask. I clamp my hand down over his, stopping the tummy-melting squishy feeling in its tracks.

'What could possibly be more important than love?'

'My dog likes you,' says Ollie simply. 'So it's a done deal.'

'Well, far be it for me to argue with Sasha. I've seen what she did to James's office.'

Then we're both laughing and crying.

And I'll probably get a bright red nose, but do you know what?

Am I bothered?

But what, I hear you ask, about the romantic champagne-and-roses proposal I've always dreamed of?

It's a strange thing, but as I kiss Ollie, lovely funny Ollie with his thick chestnut hair and sexy curling mouth, I find that I don't care about that any more. Nothing could be more romantic than being here with him on a drizzly autumnal afternoon.

And then I suddenly get it, like the final piece in the jigsaw. This is what romance really is. It's about being with the right person; all the rest is immaterial.

Bloody Mills and bloody Boon! Somebody should sue them for being so misleading. Tall, dark handsome heroes in breeches?

Highwaymen? Actors? Fishermen?

Why didn't I realise that my real hero was right under my nose all the time? Making me laugh, taking me to the hospital, putting up with me even when I kept his starter in the bath.

I think I've had my fill of romantic heroes.

'Is that a yes?' asks Ollie.

'It's a yes,' I tell him. 'But only on one condition.'

Ollie looks a bit concerned, no doubt worrying I'm going to demand a prenuptial agreement that includes my right to spend the housekeeping in Waterstone's or something.

'Which is?'

'That we don't have lobster Thermidor at our wedding reception,' I say firmly. 'I don't think I can go through that again.'

'Amen to that,' says Ollie fervently. 'I like to shower and keep my toes intact.'

And as we kiss and laugh and kiss some more, something very strange happens. I swear that below me, in the depths of the churning sea, a claw breaks the surface and waves at us before vanishing back into the depths.

I open my mouth to tell Ollie, but close it again.

After all, we know about the power of my imagination.

But as Ollie threads his fingers through mine and leads me back towards the Mermaid, where the fairy lights are twinkling and Mads, Guy and Frankie are hanging out of the window and cheering, I know that even in my wildest dreams, in my most purple Jake and Millandra prose, I could never have imagined how it feels to be this happy.

It's not a roller coaster.

Or like drowning in eyes like deep pools.

Or any of the other old clichés, actually.

Being loved by Ollie is about a billion times better than that.

It feels like coming home.

Epilogue

Six months later

'Quick,' squeals Mads. 'Stop snogging, you two, and come and sit down! It's starting!'

Ollie and I break apart guiltily. We're supposed to be putting the Pringles and dips into bowls, but he looked so cute as he bent over to reach into the fridge that I couldn't resist grabbing his bum. Honestly, love has done weird things to me. There used to be a time when I would have been more interested in grabbing the Pringles.

'Could you bring the pickled beetroot in too!' calls Mads. 'And some condensed milk!'

Ollie pulls a face. I must admit that pickled beetroot dipped in condensed milk isn't my first choice for a snack, but Mads can't get enough of either.

The joys of being pregnant.

'Thanks, babes,' Mads says, her eyes lighting up when Ollie puts the food in front of her. 'The weenie beanie can't get enough of this.' And she rubs her bump with one hand and fishes out a hunk of beetroot with the other.

'Shove up,' orders Richard, joining her on the sofa. 'I'm looking forward to this. Aren't you, Katy?'

'Sort of,' I say. Actually I'm really nervous. What if it's awful?

'It'll be great,' Ollie tells me, collapsing into a beanbag and pulling me on to his lap. 'Have some faith.'

Guy, entwined with my sister Holly on the armchair, raises a can of Stella to me. 'Watching the filming was excellent. Loved all the tits.'

Holly sloshes him with a copy of *New Scientist*. Her glasses slip down her nose and she pushes them back with her forefinger. 'Guy! You are awful!'

But she's laughing as she says it.

Life is certainly stranger than anything I could ever have written, and there must have been magic in the air that night at Jewell's party, because her pairings game has had some very peculiar results. I could never in a million years have imagined that my strait-laced sister would end up quitting academia and moving to Tregowan to be with Guy, but they seem blissfully happy. Guy goes to sea and props up the bar in the Mermaid while Holly lectures in Plymouth and sorts out his accounts.

Even stranger is the rumour that James and Nina also got it together that night. According to Ed, Nina made a fortune when she floated Domestic Divas on the stock market, and paid off all James's debts. But being Nina, she was clever enough to legally loan him the money and now she doesn't wear the trousers so much as the entire suit. What a lovely couple. I'm not sure who I feel sorrier for. Maybe Cordelia? Nina has a tongue like a Samurai sword and I can't imagine her being bossed around.

Oh to be a fly on the wall when those two lock horns.

'Here we go!' Ollie holds me close as the titles begin. The haunting tones of Enya drift from the television, and on the screen mist billows across a deserted-looking moor. Above the soundtrack we hear the rumble of wheels, the pounding of hooves and the jingle of harness as a carriage appears at the brow of a hill. The camera pans to the left where a lone rider waits, a handkerchief over his mouth and a blunderbuss in his hand.

Heart of the Highwayman, boasts the title, and a host of illustrious names follow, the first of which is Gabriel Winters.

'You've done it!' screams Maddy.

'Calm down,' warns Richard, placing a tender hand on her tummy. 'Your blood pressure.'

'Bugger my blood pressure!' Mads says. 'My best friend's a screenwriter! It's fucking fantastic.'

Richard winces.

'Sorry, darling.' Mads doesn't sound very sorry; in fact she winks at me. 'It must be my hormones.'

'Gabriel looks quite good in a dark wig,' Ollie says. 'And he worked very hard to get fit for the part. His swimming really improved.'

'He thought the riding lessons with Mrs M would kill him,' I recall. 'Frankie said he was in agony for weeks.'

We fall silent and watch the story unfold. It's a really weird experience seeing all these people who've lived and breathed and talked in my mind for all this time actually coming to life in front of me.

As Gabriel holds up the carriage, the tight breeches showing off his long, lean legs to perfection and those sapphire eyes brimming with passion for Millandra, I almost want to cry with relief. The scriptwriters and producers have done a really good job of turning my story into a gripping drama. Jake is handsome and dangerous and the young soap babe playing Millandra is porcelain-fragile.

'It's good!' I say, so thankful I feel dizzy.

'Of course it is.' Ollie smiles at me. 'Haven't I just spent the last six months telling you that?'

I think back to the weeks we spent travelling in our camper van, all the conversations we had late into the night, wrapped in each other's arms and watching shooting stars whiz across the sky. It was like when we were best friends, only better.

You probably don't need me to tell you why.

'Isn't it funny how Gabriel's even more popular since he came out?' says Mads, dunking a lump of beetroot. 'And he wasted all that time terrified that his career would be over.'

'Honesty is always the best policy,' states Richard sanctimoniously. It's interesting that he can't quite look me in the eye when he says this.

It is strange, though, just how popular Gabriel is since he outed himself on *This Morning*. The press certainly had a field day but Seb handled the whole situation so well that Gabriel emerged smelling of roses.

OK then, Paco Rabanne.

In any case, crying on Philip Schofield's shoulder didn't do him any harm, and the Screaming Queens are so popular that his street cred increased about tenfold once it was common knowledge that he was with Frankie. Now they have their own reality TV show, hang out with Elton and David, go shopping with Posh and Becks and next month are rumoured to be having the first televised civil partnership on *This Morning*. These days Frankie poses for *Hello!* and *OK!* in Gabriel's idyllic retreat and does a much better job of it than I ever did.

So maybe Richard does have a point after all about honesty.

'Ssh!' says Guy, leaning forward and practically joining Gabriel as he rescues Millandra from a runaway carriage. 'I'm watching this!'

So we watch the rest of the episode in silence, and I can't quite believe it's really happening. From being scrawled in Wayne Lobb's exercise book to being ripped up by James, the odds always seemed against me ever getting published. Maybe writing television drama is the way to go.

There's one problem, though.

I haven't written a word for months.

I'm scared I can't do it any more.

I'm scared that I'll fail.

★

Early the next morning I'm up with the fishermen, who shout, drop things and chug their noisy boats out to sea. Ollie sleeps through it all, goodness knows how, and when I slip out of bed he barely stirs. Dropping a kiss on his cheek, I slip out of bed and creep downstairs.

Auntie Jewell didn't leave me her millions – or Cuddles, thank God – but she did leave me enough to buy this tiny fisherman's cottage right by the water. So when Ollie and I get tired of travelling we have somewhere to put down roots. Or maybe when we have a baby . . .

There's no under-floor heating, no laminate floor and no Le Creuset. The furniture is battered and tatty, cushions, throws and painted glass clutter the place and Sasha has chewed a massive lump out of the sofa.

It's just the way I always wanted my house to be, and it's home.

I pad into the kitchen and throw open the top half of the stable door. Cool morning air rushes in and Sasha stirs in her basket but like her master can't be bothered to get up. I make a cup of coffee in a chunky ceramic mug, then sit down at the scrubbed pine table. In front of me are a notebook and a pen.

Can I?

Is it the right time?

I close my eyes and visualise Ollie, all bronzed and naked and tousle-haired in bed, his limbs strong and dark against the white sheets.

The perfect romantic hero.

Taking a deep breath, I pick up the pen and begin to write.